So Long At The Fair

Jess Foley was born in Wiltshire but moved to London to study at the Chelsea School of Art, then subsequently worked as a painter and actor before taking up writing. Now living in Blackheath, south-east London, Jess is currently working on a new novel *Too Close To The Sun*.

Praise for *So Long At The Fair*

'Jess has really captured the sense of a family united against great odds. The heroine, Abbie, is strong but flawed as all good heroines should be and as we follow her triumphs and trials we see her change from a girl to a woman in the most dramatic and satisfying of ways' Iris Gower

'A jolly good read ... Abbie is a great character, buffeted by fate but a powerful woman of her time' Susan Sallis

SO LONG AT THE FAIR

Jess Foley

ARROW

Published by Arrow Books in 2002

4 6 8 10 9 7 5 3

Copyright © Jess Foley 2001

First published in the United Kingdom in 2001 by Century

Arrow Books
The Random House Group Limited
20 Vauxhall Bridge Road, London SW1V 2SA

Random House Australia (Pty) Limited
20 Alfred Street, Milsons Point, Sydney,
New South Wales 2061, Australia

Random House New Zealand Limited
18 Poland Road, Glenfield
Auckland 10, New Zealand

Random House (Pty) Limited
Endulini, 5a Jubilee Road, Parktown 2193, South Africa

The Random House Group Limited Reg. No. 954009

www.randomhouse.co.uk

A CIP catalogue record for this book
is available from the British Library

The Random House Group Limited supports The Forest Stewardship Council
(FSC), the leading international forest certification organisation. All our titles
that are printed on Greenpeace approved FSC certified paper carry the FSC
logo. Our paper procurement policy can be found at
www.rbooks.co.uk/environment.

Mixed Sources

Product group from well-managed
forests and other controlled sources
www.fsc.org Cert no. TT-COC-2139
© 1996 Forest Stewardship Council

ISBN 0 09 9415763

Typeset by Deltatype Limited, Birkenhead, Merseyside
Printed in the UK by CPI Bookmarque, Croydon, CR0 4TD

For Victor

PART ONE

Chapter One

In the near darkness Abbie's foot struck an old tin tray that Lizzie had earlier leant against the table leg. It fell with a clatter. She froze, waiting.

'What are you doin' down 'ere?'

She turned at the sound of her brother Eddie's voice. She could just make him out in the shadows, sitting up in his bed on the far side of the room. 'I'm sorry,' she said. 'I didn't mean to wake you.' Her voice bore the broad accents of the West Country, though not so pronounced as his.

'Well, you did,' Eddie said. 'What're you doin' down 'ere, anyway?'

'Hush,' she said, 'you'll wake the little 'uns. I came down to get a drink of water.'

'Then for God's sake get it and leave me in peace. I got to work in the morning.'

Abbie drank from the china mug she held. 'Eddie,' she said, 'Mam's gone out.'

'Gone out? What d'you mean?'

'What I said. She's gone out – somewhere.'

Eddie struck a match, put the flame to the candle and looked at the clock. 'It's gettin' on for one,' he said.

Abbie gazed through the window. From behind her came the sounds of Eddie getting out of bed and pulling on his trousers. After a few moments he came towards her, the light from the candle making the shadows dance. She turned to him as he stopped by the table, the candle

3

flame lighting up his grave, earnest face and catching dull gold in his tousled hair. 'You didn't hear her leave?' Abbie asked. Her hair, much darker than her brother's, had for the night been fashioned into a single plait that hung down her back. She had turned twelve earlier that month of July 1862. Eddie would soon be fourteen.

'I didn't 'ear a thing,' Eddie answered. 'When did she leave, d'you know?'

'Ages ago. Soon after ten, I reckon.'

A pause, then he said, 'Go on back to bed. You'll catch cold sitting down 'ere.'

Glancing at the range, Abbie saw that the fire had almost completely burned out. 'Where can she have got to, Eddie?' she said.

'I dunno. But she'll be back soon, I don't doubt.'

Abbie studied him in the pale light. His lips were compressed, his grey eyes unreadable, shadowed pools. Moving forward, he set the candleholder on the small table beside the window and sat down next to her on the seat. In the short silence that followed, the church clock struck the hour of one.

'I couldn't sleep,' Abbie said. 'I heard her go down the stairs and waited for her to come back, but she didn't. When I went into her bedroom I saw that her bed's not been slept in.' She paused. 'It's not the first time. Did you know that?'

'No, I didn't.'

'She went out last week, too – while you were staying at the farm and Father was in Frome. She was quiet but I still heard the door. When I went to the window I saw her goin' up the lane. It was just gone ten.'

'Did you ask 'er where she went?'

'No fear. She'd only get mad.' She sighed. 'I wish Father was here.'

'Well, 'e won't be back till Sat'day.'

'I know that. I don't like it when he works away. I like him to be here.'

'Well, you'll be off yourself soon. So you'll 'ave to get used to bein' without 'im.'

Silence but for the ticking of the clock and the occasional creaks of the cottage's settling timbers. Eddie said, 'Well, there's no point in us sittin' 'ere. And she won't like it if she comes back and finds us up. Anyway, I'm sure she've got a good reason. She wouldn't go off just for nothin'.' He stood up. 'I'm goin' back to bed.'

Abbie didn't move. 'Leave the candle,' she said.

He moved away across the room and Abbie heard the sounds of him returning to his bed. Alone at the window, she gazed out. The scent of the geraniums in the pot on the ledge was fragrant in her nostrils. In the moonlight the roofs and chimneys of the cottages on the other side of the lane were dark silhouettes against the sky. Looking to the left, she could see the wooded hills, beyond which lay the town of Frome. Somewhere an owl hooted. The lane was deserted.

She thought again of her mother having gone out the previous week. The following morning Abbie had found her sitting on her bed, her face in her hands. Closing the door behind her, so as not to alert Lizzie and Iris, Abbie had gone to her. 'Mam – are you all right?' Abbie's voice had been uncertain, tentative, for often, and sometimes when least expected, her mother would react in irritation and anger. This time, though, she had only shaken her head. But then a muffled sob had escaped her and Abbie had realized that she was crying. 'Oh, Mam, what's the matter?'

'Nothing.'

Her mother had shaken her head, lowering her hands so that Abbie had seen the redness in her eyes, the tears

5

on her cheek. She was usually so pretty, but not now, not like this.

'I'm all right,' her mother had said, wiping her cheeks with her fingers. 'Go on back downstairs.'

Abbie had done as she was told, but now as the memory returned she realized that there had been anger as well as sorrow in her mother's tears.

Turning her head, she looked to the right and suddenly there was the figure of her mother coming along the lane. Quickly she rose, picked up the candle and crossed the room. She set it down on the chair next to Eddie's bed and blew out the flame. 'Mam's just coming,' she whispered – not knowing whether he was awake or asleep – and then, hurrying in the dark, started up the stairs.

She entered the bedroom quietly, closing the door behind her. There were two beds, separated one from the other by the rag rug she had made the year before. In one bed her two younger sisters, Iris and Lizzie, lay asleep. Getting into the other bed she pulled the blanket up to her chin and closed her eyes.

After a little while she heard the soft sound of footfalls on the stairs. Moments later the door opened.

'Abigail?' The voice came in a whisper.

Abbie said nothing, hoping her mother would think she was asleep.

The whispered voice came again. 'Abbie?' A pause. 'I know you're awake so you might as well answer me.'

After a moment Abbie sat up. 'Yes, Mam?'

'Come into my bedroom. I want to talk to you. And don't wake your sisters.'

As her mother turned away, Abbie pushed the blankets back, got out of bed and, in the dark, crept out onto the landing. The door opposite, that to her parents' room, was open. Abbie went in. Her mother had lit a candle and

6

was standing beside the bed. 'Close the door behind you,' she said.

Abbie did so.

'What were you doing up?' Her mother's voice held a note of barely contained suspicion and anger. 'And don't say you weren't. I saw you at the window.'

'I was waiting for you. I wondered where you were.'

'What were you doing – spying on me?'

'Oh, Mam, *no*. I – I heard you go out and you didn't come back. I began to get worried.' She noticed that her mother was wearing her best blouse beneath her coat. 'Mam, please,' she said, 'don't be angry with me.'

Her mother glared at her. She was a woman of middle height, with small, delicate features, still pretty for her thirty-eight years. Her cheeks, Abbie noticed, were unusually flushed, while her dark hair, usually neatly braided and pinned to her crown, hung loose about her shoulders. Her brown eyes were cold.

'Does anyone else know I've been out? Does Eddie know?'

Abbie nodded. 'Yes – I'm afraid I woke him up.'

'You would. What did he say?'

'Nothing. He wondered where you'd gone.'

Her mother sat down on the bed, rested her chin in her hand and sighed.

Abbie sat down beside her. 'Mam,' she said, 'what's happening?'

'What?' Her mother turned to her, dark eyes widening slightly as if coming out of a dream. 'What do you mean?'

'Something's happening. I don't know what it is.' In the light of the candle Abbie saw that her mother's mouth appeared a little reddened, as if her lips were slightly inflamed.

Her mother gave a melancholy little smile. 'You wouldn't understand.'

The thought went through Abbie's mind that so often lately her mother appeared unhappy. Not that she had ever been a woman who laughed a great deal, not like Jane's mother. Ever since Abbie had been old enough to be aware, she had sensed a certain reserve about her mother – as if for some reason she had kept around her some fine, invisible shield. Out of fear? Out of contempt?

Abbie said, 'If there's something worrying you, Mam, per'aps you ought to tell Father about it.'

Her mother raised an eyebrow. 'Tell your father? Oh, yes, you think your father can solve every problem, don't you? One day you'll learn.' With a faint snort of scorn she turned away. 'God, how I hate this place.'

'Oh, Mam, don't say that!' Abbie moved closer to her, putting her arms around her. Not that she expected the gesture to bring any closeness, and she was not surprised when her mother gently extricated herself from the embrace. She had never been at ease with displays of affection – which was odd, Abbie sometimes thought, considering her appetite for romantic novels.

'Do you really hate it?' Abbie asked. It had never occurred to her that life in Flaxdown could be loved or hated. It was the way it was, and that was that.

'Sometimes, yes,' her mother said.

'Do you miss London?'

'London . . .' Her mother said the word as if she were examining some unusual, prized object. 'Oh, London is the place. No question of that.'

In earlier years it had been a matter of some pride to Abbie that her mother had been born in London. At school it had given her a touch of specialness, as almost without exception the parents of the other children had been born in and around the village. That Abbie's mother had come from Highgate in London before her marriage and had a different accent from the rest of the village

8

women had set Abbie a little apart and made her – quite unwarrantedly, of course – something of an authority where London was concerned.

Abbie's mother – Elizabeth Porter as she then was – had come to Wiltshire in her employment as governess to the child of a wealthy family who owned a house in London's Kensington and a country home near Hallowford. While at the country retreat in the summer of 1843, she had met there Frank Morris, a handsome young bricklayer who had come to work on the building of an extension to the house. Elizabeth had been nineteen and Frank twenty-three. They had married the following April, and Beatrice, their first child, had been born eleven months later.

'Would you like to go back there,' Abbie asked, 'to London?'

'Go back?' her mother said. 'No, I shall stay here till I die, I don't doubt.' She was quiet for a while, then turned to Abbie sitting beside her. 'Go on to bed now.'

Abbie nodded, got up and silently on her bare feet moved to the door. As she reached it her mother's voice came from behind her: 'Don't say anything to your father when he gets back. About my going out, I mean. Nor Beatie when she comes on Sunday.'

'All right.'

A little silence, then her mother said, 'If you want to know where I was tonight, I went to see Mrs Marling.'

'Has she had her baby?'

'Not yet. It's due any day. I just . . . went to sit with her for a while. She needs somebody, and that husband of hers is as useless as a collander in a rainstorm.'

Abbie nodded, relieved. She had known all along that there would be a reasonable answer to the mystery of her mother's absence. Also, she welcomed the revelation as it showed a new side to her mother's character – a side

9

Abbie had not seen before. Usually her mother was not one to associate much with the other women in the village – at least not to the point where she could actually be said to be a friend of any of them. The other women were always popping in and out of each other's houses, breaking up their days with little gossips. Not Abbie's mother. She had always frowned upon such a practice and kept herself aloof from such needs.

'Still,' Mrs Morris was saying, 'there's no need for your father to know. He'd get mad to think of you all left alone. You were all right, though, weren't you?'

'Yes, of course.'

In the bedroom across the landing Abbie climbed into bed and closed her eyes. Although she now knew the reason for her mother's absence from the cottage a sense of unease still nagged at her. On the Sunday night before her father had left for Trowbridge she had heard her parents quarrelling again, the bitter sounds of her mother's voice coming from their bedroom, and then the more subdued tones of her father. She had not been able to distinguish their words, so she'd had no idea what they had been quarrelling about. Could it have been about her schooling ending and her going away into service? This had been a subject of altercation between them recently. Though it was not the only one. And anyway, quarrels were not a new phenomenon. Not like her mother's tears. And she saw her mother again as she had been tonight, sitting despondently with her red lips and her hair loose. And then her words: 'God, how I hate this place.' With an effort Abbie tried to thrust the thoughts from her mind. It didn't do to dwell on such things. Whatever it was, in time it would all come right.

Chapter Two

The next morning, Friday, Abbie spent helping her mother around the cottage. School had been over for almost a week now, and whereas Lizzie and Iris would be returning to their classes in September, Abbie had finished for good and would soon be out at work, earning her own living – a fact of which she was now reminded again.

'What time are you going to Eversleigh tomorrow?' her mother asked as she stood at the scrubbed pine table, peeling potatoes.

Abbie was sitting at the window, darning the elbow of one of Eddie's shirts. 'In the morning.' She paused. 'Jane and I are going together.'

'Jane.' Mrs Morris gave a little snort. 'I don't know why you have to live in each other's pockets. Still, at least she'll be company for you on the road, I suppose.'

'Well,' Abbie said, 'she's looking for a position too.'

'What's that got to do with anything? You can't *both* go there.'

'We might be able to. Jane's mother says she heard that Mrs Curren's looking for two girls to oblige.'

'I'd believe that when it happens. But if there's only one position going just remember that you heard about it first.' Mrs Morris finished peeling the last potato and dropped it into the pot. 'Here' – she tapped the pan holding the peelings – 'these can go out for the pig. Then call the girls to come and get their dinners.'

Abbie put her mending aside, took up the pan of peelings and went out into the backyard. In his sty the pig lay sleeping, but as soon as she tipped the scraps into the trough he awoke and came grunting and snuffling towards her. She idly scratched his back for a few moments as he ate, then set down the empty bowl on the old trestle table and went around the cottage to the front where in the little flower garden stocks and wallflowers and nasturtiums grew – planted and tended by her father, who also grew vegetables on the allotment nearby. He was, Abbie reflected, probably the only man in the village who grew flowers. Although the other cottages had little flower gardens, they were invariably the dominions of the women. Abbie's mother had never bothered, though; it was always her father who had done the work.

At the front gate she stood looking from left to right along the lane. The Wiltshire village of Flaxdown was situated in a valley between wide, rolling hills, midway between Frome to the west and Warminster to the east, two of the few towns Abbie had seen during her twelve years – and then only very infrequently, so they still retained some of the magic of mystery. There was no mystery about Flaxdown, however. She knew it like the back of her hand, from the newly opened post office to the old church of St Peter's. And in truth there was not much to get to know, for a walk in any direction would, after just a few minutes, bring her to its outskirts.

Now as she stood at the gate there came again the realization that in a very short time it would cease to be the place of her abode. It would still be her home, but she would be living elsewhere, and except for high days and holidays she would, in all likelihood, rarely return. She thought of all the other girls from the village who had left to go into service. They came back only infrequently –

particularly if they now lived any great distance away. In those circumstances their visits were generally just annual affairs when, dressed in as much finery as they could muster, they would come to spend their two weeks' summer holiday with their families. And would that, Abbie wondered, be the same with herself? Perhaps. Once she had found a situation there was no telling where she might travel.

'Abbie?'

At the sound of her mother's voice she started slightly and turned and saw her standing at the now open window. 'Yes?'

'Yes!' Mrs Morris said in an exasperated tone. 'And I'm wondering how long you're going to stand there. Call the girls. I want to get dinner over with.'

Lizzie and Iris were at the foot of the back garden, playing with their dolls. She called them and they came running. As she looked down at their bright, upturned faces she reflected how very different they were. Lizzie, at nine, was little more than a year older than Iris, but although they were so close in age they were very dissimilar in appearance. Lizzie's rich, dark hair and pretty, near-perfect features already gave a promise of beauty, unlike Iris with her fine, mouse-coloured hair and plain, freckled little face.

Back in the cottage Abbie resumed her mending of Eddie's shirt while her mother made tea and spread thick slices of bread with lard. As soon as the younger girls' plates and mugs were empty they got up from the table to go and play again.

Mrs Morris watched them go then said to Abbie, 'Have you got everything ready for tomorrow when you go over to Eversleigh?'

'Yes.'

'I don't know why you and Jane are set on going into service together.'

Abbie shrugged. 'She's my friend.' Then she added, 'When I told Father we were going to look for a place together he said it was a good idea.'

'Your father. Well, if *he* said it then it must be so, mustn't it?' Abbie said nothing to this. After a moment her mother went on: 'How do you think you'll like it – being in service, away from home?'

'I don't know. I'm sure there'll be a lot of work to do.'

'Yes, and *hard* work. For a start there won't be any staying in bed till seven.'

'Oh, I know that,' Abbie said. Her mother's words were disturbing; she was already uneasy at the thought of leaving home. 'Still,' she said, 'I'll get on all right. And perhaps we'll go away. Travel, I mean. Like Beatie, when she went with Mr and Mrs Callardine to France last year.'

'I wouldn't bank on it.'

'But *you* did, didn't you? When you were a governess you came down from London. *You* travelled.'

'Yes – and look where it got me. Well, just don't make the mistakes that I did. See a bit of life. Take your time before you think about marrying and settling down.'

'Mam,' Abbie said, 'I'm only twelve.'

'Only twelve. Don't worry, the time will soon pass.'

The next morning Abbie did her hair as neatly as she could and put on her best dress. Standing before the little glass that hung beside the range she made a final adjustment to her bonnet, then turned to her mother. It was just after ten o'clock. 'Oh, Mam, I'm going to be that nervous.'

'There's no reason you should be. Mrs Curren's no different from you – except that she's got money – which, I suppose, is all that matters in the end. Anyway – just be

14

polite. But if she asks you to bring your own caps and aprons tell her you can't. *She'll* have to provide them. We can't run to it.'

Abbie had no idea how she could be so forthright with a prospective employer, but she nodded and said, 'Yes, all right.'

Crossing to the door, she hovered there, moving from one foot to the other, suddenly uncertain about taking the first step into the outside world. Her mother looked at her for a moment, then said: 'Well, don't just stand there. At this rate you won't get there till tomorrow.'

'I'm going.' A pause. 'Father *will* be back later on today, won't he?'

'Of course he will; it's Saturday.'

Abbie nodded and went out.

Jane Carroll and her mother lived in a cottage in Tomkins Row on the west side of the village. As Abbie crossed the green she looked over to where Lizzie and Iris were playing with their friends. There were six of them, skipping with an old length of clothesline. Lizzie and another girl were twirling the rope while the others lined up, each waiting to take her turn, leaping into the arc of the looping rope and out on the other side to allow the next one to jump in. As they skipped they chanted an old skipping song.

Catching sight of Abbie passing by, Lizzie, still rhythmically twirling the rope, called out: 'Oh, look at Miss Fancy Drawers!'

'You shut up, our Lizzie,' Abbie called back.

'Where you goin', Abbie?' Iris yelled. 'To Eversleigh?'

'In a minute.'

'Can I come too?'

'You know you can't.'

'Can *I*?' Lizzie said.

'No, you can't.'

'I'm older than our Iris.'

'What's that got to do with it?'

'It's not fair.'

Abbie gave a superior smile, shrugged and went on.

Knocking at the door of the third of the greystone cottages in Tomkins Row, Abbie found it opened to her by Mrs Carroll, Jane's mother, a round-faced, jolly-looking little woman with fading red hair pulled back into a bun at the nape of her neck.

'Oh, thank God you're 'ere, Abbie,' she said with a little laugh. 'Come and take the girl away, will you? She'll just about have me down Devizes at the rate she's goin'.' Devizes, a nearby town, bore the dubious distinction of possessing the county's insane asylum.

Laughing sympathetically, Abbie entered the sunlit kitchen to find Jane sitting on a chair, fastening her right boot, her long, fair hair hanging down and obscuring her face. She wore a dark-blue cotton dress with a fine lace collar made by her mother. 'I thought you'd be ready,' Abbie said.

'Ready!' said Mrs Carroll. 'The girl was ready an hour ago, and would be again if she could make up her mind what she's going to wear!'

Jane said through the curtain of her hair: 'You make it sound like I've got no end of choice, when it's a matter of finding what I look the least dreadful in.' She finished fastening her boot and straightened, revealing a flushed face with a high forehead, short, straight nose, rather long, pointed chin and wide blue eyes. She spread her hands in a gesture of hopelessness. 'Look at me! This is the only thing that's half decent and it's too small. I can hardly move my arms!'

'For goodness' sake,' her mother said, 'you're a growing girl. You can't expect your clothes to fit you for ever!'

16

Jane groaned, having heard it all before, then turned to a looking-glass with a cheap gilt frame that hung on the wall. After fussing with her hair for a minute or two she began to tie it with a pale-blue ribbon.

'If you don't leave soon,' her mother said, 'there won't be any point in your goin'. Anyway, I heard as Mrs Curren was looking for a maid, not for a Queen of the May. You go there lookin' too vain and she won't think you're capable of scrubbin' a pot.'

A minute later Jane decided to wear her hair in braids and she sat down while Abbie stood behind her and wove her long hair into two neat plaits, which she then coiled around and pinned to the crown of her head.

While the girls were so engaged, Mrs Carroll got out a loaf of bread and a basin of lard. 'You better take summat to eat with you, Janie,' she said. 'It's a fair way to Eversleigh and you'll get 'ungry.' She looked at Abbie. 'You takin' some dinner with you, Abbie?'

Abbie had not thought of it; neither had her mother. 'No, I didn't think,' she said.

'Well, you better 'ave some too, then.'

Three minutes later the girls, each holding a little package containing a slice of bread and lard and another of bread and jam, were ready to leave.

Mrs Carroll followed them to the gate. 'Now you be careful,' she said, 'and remember to be polite to the lady.'

'Of course I'll be polite.' Jane sighed wearily and pulled a face at her mother across the gate. Abbie, watching, envied their closeness.

'And,' Mrs Carroll said, 'don't forget to wipe the dust off your shoes before you go in.'

A sigh. 'All right.'

'And don't go talking to no gypsies nor other vaga-bonds.'

Turning, assuming an expression of patience tried to its

limits, Jane said, 'Is there anything else I should remember?'

'Yes,' her mother said, grinning, 'remember not to lift up your arms.'

Jane gave a cry and dashed towards her, and with a little shrieking laugh her mother turned and ran back into the house.

The village of Eversleigh was seven miles to the northeast, between Trowbridge to the north and Westbury to the south, and as there was no convenient railway station – even supposing they had the money for their fares – the girls had no option but to walk.

The day was very warm, the sun shining from a clear blue sky, and as the time wore on the girls grew increasingly hot and uncomfortable. Eventually, however, there lay before them at the foot of a hill the cluster of buildings that was Eversleigh village. As they drew nearer they glimpsed the church tower with the hands of its clock pointing to ten to one.

'We'd better wait for a while,' Jane said. 'We mustn't call when the lady's having her dinner.'

They stopped in the shade of a small copse not far from the road, sat down on the trunk of a fallen tree, took off their bonnets and ate their sandwiches. Afterwards they found a little fast-running brook where, hitching up their skirts, they knelt down over the bank, dipped their cupped hands into the stream and quenched their thirsts and cooled and refreshed their faces.

'It'll be wonderful if we can get situations in the same house, won't it?' Jane said, sitting back in the grass.

Abbie nodded enthusiastically. 'Oh, it will.' She was silent for a moment, then she said, 'We'll be friends for ever, shan't we?'

'Yes, of course! Oh, Abbie, why ever shouldn't we?'

Abbie shrugged. 'My mam said friendships never last. She said one person ends up going one way and the other goes another. In the end, they always forget.'

'Well, I shan't forget,' Jane said emphatically. 'That won't be the case with me.'

'No.' Abbie shook her head. 'Not with me, either.'

'I wonder,' Jane said, 'what we'll do. Later on in our lives, I mean. When we're older. D'you think we'll get married and have babies?'

Abbie shrugged. 'I don't fancy getting married. I wouldn't mind havin' a baby, though. Just one. You could make nice clothes for her and dress her up and all that.'

'You'd want a girl, would you?'

'Oh, I think so. Boys are so rough.'

'Anyway,' Jane went on, 'if you want a baby you'd need to get yourself a husband first.'

'Why? Aggie Tarrant's got a baby and she doesn't have a husband. And Esther Strange, too. She hasn't got a husband and she's got two little 'uns.'

'*And* she's as big as a barn.'

Abbie laughed. 'Anyway, although a baby would be nice I don't think I'd want to do what's necessary in order to get one.'

Jane shook her head. 'Oh, no. Me neither.'

The previous summer the two girls, on walking to White's farm near Flaxdown to buy butter, had come to an enclosure where a stallion was about to mate with a mare. The farmer and some of his men were there, overseeing the process. Abbie's brother Eddie, who worked at the farm, had been in attendance too. Neither he nor the others had been aware of the girls' presence, and Abbie and Jane had stood watching, fascinated, as the stallion, hugely aroused, had mounted the mare and gripped her neck with his strong teeth. Being country

19

girls they had witnessed the mating of various animals, but that time with the horses had made a strong impression on their blossoming awareness. When the act was over – so quickly – the horses had been led away. It was then that Eddie had turned and seen the girls.

'What you doin' 'ere?' he had asked.

'We came to get some butter for Jane's mam,' Abbie replied, then, 'I hate it when they do that,' she added.

'What you on about?'

'The stallion and the mare. The way he treats her. Doing that and biting her like that. I'm surprised she stands there and puts up with it.'

Eddie reddened slightly. 'Well – she've got to, ain't she? If she wants a foal she don't 'ave no choice.'

And suddenly realization had come. Those other matings they had witnessed, they had been a part of the process of life, had been necessary for life to begin.

On the way back to the village she and Jane had discussed the matter. 'And people, too,' Jane had said, though not really believing it. 'Men and women do it. I suppose they've got to.'

'I s'pose so,' Abbie agreed. Then she had added, laughing, 'Though whoever done it to Esther Strange must have needed good strong teeth!'

They had shrieked with laughter all the way home.

Now, sitting beside the stream, Abbie took up the piece of newspaper that had wrapped her sandwiches and began to fashion from it a little boat, the way Eddie had taught her. Thinking of the meeting ahead with the prospective employer, she said, 'Oh, I wish we didn't have to go away.' Then she went on with a sigh, 'Course, if we were rich we wouldn't have to bother about working for other people.'

'If you want to be rich, then you must marry a rich man,' Jane said.

Having finished one paper boat, Abbie took up the sheet of newspaper that Jane had discarded and began to make a second. 'I told you, I'm not getting married at all.'

'You will when the time comes. All girls do if they get the chance. You'll probably get wed before I do.'

'I shan't.'

The second paper boat was finished, and Abbie plucked a buttercup from the grass and stuck its stem into a fold of the paper of one of them. Into the other boat she stuck the stem of the ragged robin.

'Here you are – here's yourn.' She handed the boat with the ragged robin to Jane. 'Come on – let's sail 'em in the water.'

On the bank of the brook they hoisted up their skirts once again, then reached out with the little paper boats. Jane turned her head, looking along the stream to where, some distance ahead, a weeping willow hung its branches over the water. 'Whoever's boat gets to that willow first will marry a rich man,' she said.

'No,' Abbie said, 'there's no rich men for the likes of us.'

'All right then . . .' Jane pondered briefly. 'The first one to get to the willow will be the first to get married – for richer or poorer.'

Abbie laughed. 'All right.'

They lowered the boats into the current, pointing the prows downstream.

'Ready . . . steady . . . go!'

With Abbie's final word they let go. At once the little vessels were taken by the current and the two girls watched as they sailed smoothly along, Abbie's on the right bearing the flag of the golden buttercup, Jane's with the little red flower of the ragged robin.

Taking up their bonnets, the girls moved along the bank, following the progress of the vessels. On the current of the stream the boats bobbed up and down, keeping more or less abreast, first one nosing slightly ahead and then the other. But then, slowly, the boat with the buttercup began to draw ahead.

'It's going to be you!' Jane said, then added, giving a little wail, 'Oh, look – my boat is losing her flag!'

The ragged robin in Jane's boat was now trailing its blossom in the water. As the girls watched, it fell free and began to drift along in the boat's wake. Hurrying to keep up, the girls found their way blocked by a mass of brambles that grew to the water's edge, forcing them to find a circuitous route around it. They returned to the bank close to where the willow stood. Nearby, the two boats had been halted, caught up in the reeds. Now neither bore its flower flag, for Abbie's buttercup also had gone. Further, one of the boats had fallen apart, the folds of its waterlogged paper collapsed. Even as they gazed it began to sink beneath the surface.

'Was that yourn or mine?' Jane asked. 'You can't tell without the flowers.'

'We'll never know.' Abbie shrugged. 'It doesn't matter, anyway – neither one of 'em got there.'

They turned and began to walk back through the copse towards the road. 'We'd better get a move on,' Jane said. 'At this rate Mrs Curren'll be having her supper before we get there.'

Chapter Three

Marylea House stood on the far side of the village, a large building on three floors, at the front a lawn with colourful herbaceous borders. Approaching by the side gate, Abbie and Jane entered a paved yard beside stables where a young man grooming a mare directed them to the rear door. They rang the bell and a minute later the door was opened to them by a young maid who at once went away to fetch her mistress.

Mrs Curren was a slightly built woman in her thirties with a thin face and prominent teeth. After dismissing the maid, she ushered Abbie and Jane into the kitchen.

'So,' she said, smiling, 'which of you is looking for a position?'

'Please, mum,' Jane said, 'both of us. We heard as you wanted *two* maids.'

The woman shook her head. 'Oh, no, there isn't the work to warrant two. There's only my husband and myself, and not all the rooms are used, and I do most of the cooking. No, dear, I only need the one.'

She then asked how old the girls were. Twelve, they replied in subdued chorus, and she nodded and began to outline the daily duties that would be required, the work starting at six in the morning and going on until nine at night. She would need her new maid to begin in two weeks, she said, adding that she would supply caps and aprons. To everything she said the two girls nodded and said, 'Yes, mum.'

'Now,' she said, 'that leaves us with a little problem, doesn't it? Which one of you should we have . . . ?' She gave her rather horsy, warm smile. 'As far as I can see you both seem like capable girls. I don't want to be the cause of any friction between you. Perhaps you'd like to decide which it will be.'

'Yes, mum,' they said in uncertain unison. Then there was silence. Mrs Curren looked from one to the other, then Abbie turned to Jane. 'You, Jane,' she said, in spite of her knowledge that her mother would be furious. 'You take it.'

'No, Abbie,' Jane said. 'You take it. You heard about the position first.'

'Perhaps', Mrs Curren suggested, 'we should toss a coin. Shall we do that?'

The girls nodded and waited, for they carried not a farthing between them. Mrs Curren went away and came back with a new halfpenny piece. 'Ready?' she said. 'Who's going to call?'

Silence.

'Which is the older of you?' Mrs Curren asked.

'Please, mum, I am,' Jane said. 'Six months.'

'Then you call. All right?'

Mrs Curren neatly flipped the coin into the air, caught it in her right palm and clapped it onto the back of her left hand. 'Heads or tails?' she said to Jane.

'Tails, please, mum.'

Mrs Curren lifted her right hand exposing the coin and Victoria's profile. 'Heads,' she said, raising her eyebrows to Jane in sympathy. 'Well.' She smiled at Abbie. 'I hope you'll be happy here.'

'Yes, mum. Thank you, mum.'

Mrs Curren turned back to Jane. 'I'm sure it won't be long before you find a place. Here . . .' Taking Jane's hand she put the coin into her palm. 'A little consolation for you.' Jane thanked her and dropped it into her pocket.

'Now,' said Mrs Curren, 'I'm sure you girls are hungry after your long walk, aren't you?' Without waiting for an answer she waved a hand towards the large, scrubbed table. 'Just you sit down there and we'll see if we can't find you a little refreshment before you start back.'

'Are you sure you don't mind too much?' Abbie asked as they walked back along the road towards Flaxdown. 'Me getting the position, I mean.'

Jane's failure had tempered Abbie's own satisfaction. She was well aware of how badly Jane and her mother needed the money. Since Jane's father had died she and her mother had lived little more than a hand-to-mouth existence, their only income being from the handmade lace that Mrs Carroll produced. Beautiful as it was, however, it was becoming more and more difficult to sell. Machine-made lace was available now, and only the wealthy and discerning chose to buy the exquisite, but relatively expensive, lace made by the likes of Mrs Carroll.

'No, of course not,' Jane said. 'She only wanted one maid so we couldn't both get the job. Besides, you heard about it first. And anyway, I'll find something soon.'

Rain began to fall soon after five o'clock, just as the village of Flaxdown came in sight, and they finished the last two hundred yards of the journey in a mad dash.

After saying goodbye to Jane, Abbie entered the cottage to find her mother preparing the evening meal, while Lizzie and Iris sat in a corner playing with their little rag dolls. 'Thank the Lord you're here,' her mother said. 'Eddie will be in from the farm soon and your father'll be back from Bath at any time.'

As Abbie changed her clothes in her bedroom her mother came and stood in the doorway. 'So, how did you get on?' she asked.

'There was only one place,' Abbie said. 'And we tossed for it.'

'And?'

'I got it.'

Her mother looked relieved. 'Good. When do you start?'

'In two weeks. She seems very nice – Mrs Curren. She gave us apple pie and tea. Tea with milk.'

'And what wages will you be getting?'

'A shilling a week and all found.'

'A shilling. Still, it's only a petty place. You won't need to stay more than a year, then you can find something better.'

'Mrs Curren said she hopes as I'll be very happy there and will want to stay on.'

'Well, she would, wouldn't she? But she knows well enough that no self-respecting girl stays in a petty place more than a year. It's not expected.'

Downstairs again, Abbie set the table for high tea and then, leaving her mother to finish preparing the meal, sat at the window and got on with the mending of some of her father's and brother's socks. The rain had stopped now. As she worked she kept an eye on the lane.

All at once she was putting her mending down on the window ledge, getting up and hurrying to the door.

'Oh, your father's back, is he?' her mother said. 'Must be. There's only one thing that makes you move that fast.'

Abbie did not hear these last words; she was already out and running from the cottage. She had seen her father's tall, lean, slightly stooped figure as he entered the lane. Now as she drew near him he bent to embrace her and she threw her arms round him and took his large, calloused hand in hers. 'Father,' she said, 'I got a place! I start in two weeks in Eversleigh. A doctor's house. Dr Curren his name is. I'm to get a shillin' a week and all found.' Looking up into his face she waited for his smile. 'Aren't you glad?'

He stopped and she came to a halt beside him. He was looking down at her with a quizzical expression on his lean, rugged face, his blue eyes shadowed now not only by fatigue but also by concern. He had a strong, curving nose and full-lipped mouth. As Abbie looked up at him he drew his lips back a little over his teeth and heaved a sigh. His coarse fair hair, Abbie noticed, had fine streaks of grey in it.

'Aren't you glad?' she asked again.

'Are *you* glad?' he said.

'Well,' she shrugged, 'I've got to get a place somewhere, haven't I? And Eversleigh's not so far away. Mam says it'll do for me for a year for my petty place.'

'It's not what I wanted for you,' he said after a moment.

She knew what he meant. In spite of the fact that most children of her generation left school at the age of ten, her father – and he had never made any secret of it – had hoped that she would remain on beyond twelve, at least for another two years or so. And she had hoped for it too. But it was not possible. She had already stayed on longer than Beatie and Eddie, and therefore it was only right, as her mother had said, that she should now go out into the world and start to earn her living.

'Anyway,' Abbie said, 'it's done now. And per'aps in time, after I've done my first year, I can study some more.'

He squeezed her hand. 'Perhaps so.'

Her father, she had learned not so many years before, had never had a day in school in his life. In the years he

27

had been a child, growing up as one of a large family, education was only for the privileged – the wealthy ones and the lucky ones. When the government had first donated public money for education in 1833 he had been thirteen and too old to take advantage of the new benefits. So, like most other children of his class and age, he had spent his childhood working.

Abbie, thinking herself fortunate in that she had attended school till the age of twelve, found it hard to envisage her father's early life. A childhood without schooling? She could hardly imagine it, though she knew that even now there were areas in the country where education was still not compulsory.

Her father, though, had miraculously risen above his peers for, in spite of everything, he had learned. And what learning he had acquired had begun when, at seventeen and doing manual work for a schoolmistress in Trowbridge, he had persuaded her to give him lessons in reading and arithmetic in exchange for his labours. He had gone on from there, studying in whatever spare time he could find.

Abbie's mother had had a more fortunate start. Taught by her own mother, who had also once been a governess, she had had schooling from an early age. Abbie – when the realization had come to her – had been not a little thrilled to learn that in having both a father and mother who could read and write she was, in Flaxdown, something of a novelty. Not that her mother made much use of her education. Neither did Mrs Morris set much store by its usefulness when it came to her daughters – or even her son for that matter. Abbie's father, though, was different. Not only did he love knowledge for its own sake, but he was always happy to use his learning for the benefit of others. Many was the time some illiterate neighbour would come to the cottage for the purpose of getting Frank Morris to write a letter or read one just received. At such times Abbie would have to vacate the kitchen so that the visitor might have privacy. Her mother, who usually remained in the room, regarded such visits with concealed disdain, frequently speaking of the visitors, after their departure, with contempt.

Now as Abbie and her father entered the cottage Abbie's mother called out to them, 'Make sure you don't bring mud indoors. I haven't long done the floor.'

Abbie and her father wiped their boots, then Frank Morris gave hugs to Lizzie and Iris, and kissed his wife on the cheek. Abbie noticed that her mother did not react to the gesture but carried on stirring the pot on the range.

'Sit down and rest,' Mrs Morris said. 'I'll heat some water for you to wash.' As he sank into his chair, she asked, 'How did you get back from Bath?'

'I got a ride as far as Road and walked from there. I would have been back sooner but I had to shelter from the rain.'

He sounded weary. Abbie bent, untied his bootlaces and pulled off his boots.

A few minutes later Eddie came in from White's farm, and when he and his father had washed they all sat down to eat.

Sunday tomorrow, Abbie thought as she got ready for bed that night. In their bed against the opposite wall Lizzie and Iris were sound asleep. In the faint light from the window Abbie pulled on her nightgown and climbed into bed. After a while she heard the sounds of her mother and father coming up the stairs. They never stayed very late downstairs, even on a Saturday, for they would have kept Eddie from his bed and he needed his sleep. There came the soft sound of the door to her parents' room closing and then all was silent again. Abbie thought her father had seemed especially tired this evening. And she had also seen the look of unhappiness in his face. The look was not new. And it was disturbing. He had always seemed so much in control, unaffected by the rigours of his routine, the shortness of money and the continuous grind to make ends meet. She had only ever been touched by her mother's discontent – which had lately seemed such a constant thing. With her father, though, there was something different.

As if in support of her realization, there came to her from across the landing the sound of her mother's voice – raised in angry exasperation – then her father's – quieter, controlled. Turning on her side, Abbie pulled up the bedcovers to shut out the noise. When she surfaced after a few minutes the voices were silent. Relieved, she settled again. Tomorrow afternoon, she reminded herself, Beatie would come visiting – and not alone. She would be accompanied by her young man, her Mr Thomas Greening, from Lullington. The Morrises knew about him from the letters Beatie wrote, but this would be the first time they would meet him face to face.

With Lizzie and Iris out playing on the green, Eddie visiting friends nearby and her father working on the allotment, Abbie spent the morning helping her mother make the kitchen as clean and neat as possible.

After midday dinner, with Eddie immediately off again to rejoin his friends and the two younger girls sent off to Sunday school, Abbie and her mother and father got ready for Beatie's arrival.

She appeared just before three o'clock, having journeyed from Lullington where she worked as nursemaid to the two small children of a mill owner and his wife, Mr and Mrs Callardine. Getting a free half-day every other week, she usually returned to Flaxdown about once a month, on which occasion she would spend a few precious hours on a Sunday afternoon with her family. Usually she walked the five-odd miles, or if she was lucky she would get a ride from some thoughtful cart- or carriage-driver. On this Sunday in late July she had walked from Lullington accompanied by her Mr Greening, a good-looking, tallish, dark-haired, dark-eyed young man.

After their arrival, Beatie and Tom sat in the kitchen drinking tea and eating the scones Mrs Morris had baked that morning. As usual, Beatie had brought little presents with her, and now she handed her mother three well-read paper-covered novels and – surreptitiously, so that no one should see – a shilling that she had saved from her wages. To her father she gave some copies of the *Penny Illustrated Paper*, which was taken regularly at Hillside House and which she had saved from being thrown away. Among other items, the papers carried several illustrations of events in the American Civil War, in which conflict Frank Morris was much interested.

Beatie, turned seventeen that past March, was small and slim like her mother. She had a flawless complexion the colour of cream and pink roses, and with her rich chestnut hair and wide, dark-lashed blue eyes she was, to Abbie's mind, one of the most strikingly beautiful young women she had ever seen. Her dress, recently given to her by her employer's wife, had the colour and sheen of a freshly picked damson. It was no wonder, Abbie thought, that young Mr Greening was so attentive to her and followed her so intently with his eyes.

Thomas Greening, eighteen years old, was the son of a Lullington inn owner, and he and Beatie had met that past spring when Beatie had been sent to the little shop at the rear of the inn to buy sweets for the Callardine children. It was Tom who came to serve her. Beatie had

31

previously glimpsed him in church at Sunday morning service – when he had also noticed her. He had admired her then, she later learned and, having met her at the inn, had determined to renew the acquaintance at the earliest opportunity. This he did by managing to be in the right place when Beatie left Hillside House to take her charges for a spin in the perambulator. In just a few weeks he was taking Sunday afternoon walks with her, while in the meantime they had also begun to exchange letters.

Beatie's tale, however, was not one of unalloyed joy. Tom's parents, having had dreams of their son making a marriage with a bride who had more assets than just a pretty face, frowned on his enthusiasm for the impoverished nursemaid and did what they could to discourage the assocation. He, however, was not so easily discouraged it seemed, and the relationship had continued and blossomed.

Abbie, on learning from Beatie of Tom's parents' antipathy, was indignant. Secretly she felt that far from it being the case that Beatie was not good enough for Tom Greening, *he* was perhaps not good enough for *her*.

Beatie, however, was completely enamoured of him, that much was clear. On the pretext of a matter concerning some clothing, she got Abbie to go upstairs with her and, as soon as the bedroom door was closed behind them, turned and whispered, all eagerness and anxiousness, 'Well, Abbie – what do you think? Isn't he fine? Isn't he good-looking?'

Abbie wrapped her arms round her sister's waist and hugged her to her. 'Oh, Beatie, yes. Yes, he certainly is.'

But even as Abbie spoke there were reservations in her mind. Notwithstanding that Tom Greening was a handsome young man with a fine figure, and with good prospects into the bargain, he appeared, for Abbie's tastes, a little too quiet and somewhat lacking in personality. With his slow smile and rather self-conscious manner, he seemed to her a little withdrawn and short on humour. Certainly he had about him nothing of Eddie's exuberance. Still, she reminded herself, she didn't really know him, and as Beatie herself was somewhat shy and retiring, they were probably well suited to one another. And anyway, what did it matter what she, Abbie, thought of him? It was no crime to be dull. It was only really important what Beatie felt, and Beatie was clearly very taken – just as Tom Greening appeared to be completely taken with her.

Later, as they all sat chatting downstairs, Lizzie and Iris burst in noisily, breathless from having run all the way home, and Abbie watched as her elder sister kissed and hugged them and gave them the little gifts she had brought.

Eventually the clock struck five and Beatie reluctantly rose, saying they had better be starting back. Abbie and the others followed her and Tom outside. There Tom shook hands with Beatie's parents and they kissed Beatie goodbye. A minute later, with Beatie calling back, 'I'll try to see you in a month or so,' the young couple started away.

At seven o'clock, soon after high tea, the Pattisons – Jack Pattison and his wife Agnes – came round for the evening.

Frank Morris and Jack Pattison played chess every three weeks, turn and turn about visiting one another's homes. They played from about seven until nine thirty. If a game was still in progress at the end of the evening they would write down the positions and resume it at their next meeting. These chess games had been going on for more than two years now, and were among the few things in Frank Morris's life in the way of a pleasurable pastime. When he was not out at work helping in the construction of some building, he was normally working on the allotment or the small cottage garden. And, whereas many men from the village went regularly to the pub, he went very infrequently. When he did go it would usually follow some disagreement at home; then he would take off for the Harp and Horses and sit with a few of the other villagers, making a couple of pints of ale last for two or three hours. So his chess and his books were the real sources of his relaxation, and with regard to the former he looked forward to his meetings with Jack Pattison. They might have had little in common outside of the game, but within it they were a good match and that was what counted.

Pattison and his wife, a childless couple, ran the post office on the far side of the village. Abbie found them an ill-matched pair – not only in physical attractiveness but also in their personalities. Mr Pattison was a tallish, handsome man of forty-five with thinning dark hair, a spare, wiry frame and a bright, ready laugh. His wife Agnes was a little wisp of a woman two years his senior, with spectacles and an out-of-date wardrobe, which Abbie's mother often said she wouldn't be seen dead in. To Abbie, Mrs Pattison always seemed to be weighed down by cares and tribulations which, with grave, ill-hidden relish, she described in low tones to Abbie's mother as they sat facing one another across the range, Mrs Pattison knitting, Mrs Morris mending. The subject of Mrs Pattison's weary tales was, as often as not, her aged mother who lived in Westbury and enjoyed very poor health, and had done so for many years.

Sometimes, if Mrs Pattison was a little off colour, or visiting her ailing mother, Jack Pattison came alone. He seemed more relaxed at such times. Usually, however, his wife was with him.

On the Pattisons' arrival Lizzie and Iris would be sent up to bed while Abbie put the kettle on for tea and then ran down to the Harp and Horses to get a jug of ale. In the meantime the two men would take their seats facing one another across the kitchen table on which Abbie's father had already set out the chess pieces, while the two women sat down to have a quiet chat – enjoyed by Mrs Pattison and suffered by Mrs Morris. When Abbie returned she would pour a mug of ale for each of the men and make tea for the women and herself. That done, she would sit at the other end of the table where she read or sewed and listened to the women's conversation while occasionally looking up as the men murmured to each other in the progress of their game. Eddie would keep well out of the way at such times.

'So I said to her,' came Mrs Pattison's hushèd, lugubrious voice to Abbie's half-attentive ears, ' "Mother," I said, "you got to remember that you ain't a young woman no more, and you can't do what a young woman does." '

'That's right,' said Abbie's mother, barely looking up from her mending.

'Right, indeed,' said Mrs Pattison, knitting needles clicking between her swiftly moving fingers. 'But she's a wilful woman and stubborn as a mule. "Leave the curtains," I says to 'er. "Leave 'em for now, and Jack'll come over next week and hang 'em for you." But no, she wants 'em up then and there, and if I won't 'elp 'er, she says, she'll get up on the chair and hang 'em herself. "Drat the curtains!" I says. I wish I'd never brought 'em over in the first place.'

'It must be difficult for you,' said Mrs Morris, while Abbie smiled inside herself – like her mother, giving nothing away.

'So, of course,' Mrs Pattison continued, 'I've got no choice but to climb up and hang the dratted things meself. Let Mother start trying to do it and she'd only 'ave a fall. And she ain't got over the last one yet. That was terrible that time. Did I tell you about that afternoon when she . . .'

Her voice went on.

Mrs Morris occasionally, if half-heartedly, complained about the Pattisons' visits – though more specifically of the visits of Pattison's wife. '*He's* not too bad,' she would say to her husband. 'And when it's just the two of you I can relax, concentrate on a bit of reading or something. But when *she* comes too, it's goodbye to any thoughts of relaxing, that's for sure.' Then she would sigh, as if relenting. 'Still, I suppose I can put up with it now and again. Just thank God it's not every week, that's all.'

As far as Abbie knew, Mrs Pattison was about the only person in the village who ever engaged her mother in conversation – if such it could be called – and even that was forced upon her. As for Mr Pattison, Abbie observed that her mother rarely exchanged more than a good evening and a good night with him.

Tonight the chess game finished just on ten past nine and as Abbie's father put the pieces away after his victory he asked Pattison and his wife if they'd like to stay for another cup of tea and another drop of ale. While Pattison gratefully accepted the offer of ale, his wife declined the tea, saying that as much as she'd like a drop more, it was inclined to give her insomnia, so if it was all the same she'd join her husband and have a little drop of ale too – which would help to settle her stomach.

What little ale was left Abbie, getting a nod from her father, shared between the visitors. For the next fifteen minutes or so they sat and chatted, the conversation coming mostly from the men. Abbie listened fascinated as her father spoke of a book that he had recently been reading, which had apparently caused considerable disturbance in the outside world. Written by a man named Darwin, she learned, it was called *On the Origin of Species by Means of Natural Selection* and all boiled down to the idea that there had never been any special time of creation; that there never had been that week in which God had created the world and everything in it – in fact, it appeared that God had not created the world at all, but that all the living things had somehow developed from other living things.

'Well, I never did!' said Mrs Pattison. 'Who ever heard of such a thing! That's blasphemy. And what about *us*, then? Where did *we* come from, I'd like to know?'

'Well,' said Abbie's father, 'according to Darwin we're like every other living creature – we developed from lower forms of life.'

'Lower forms of life?' Mrs Pattison said. 'What d'you mean by that?'

'Well – other animals.'

'Other *animals*, indeed!'

'That's what Darwin says,' Frank Morris went on. 'And going by what I read in the papers there's a lot that agrees with him.'

'Papers,' said Mrs Pattison contemptuously. 'People read too much in the papers, if you ask me. I never heard of such a thing. What kind of animals? Pigs and horses and such, I suppose.'

'What do you think, Mrs Morris?' asked Mr Pattison, turning to Abbie's mother. 'D'you think there could be anything in it?'

'I don't know, I'm sure,' she said shortly, barely glancing at him. 'Though looking at a few of the folks in this village I wouldn't be in the least surprised.'

The two men, and Abbie, too, laughed at this, laughter

in which Abbie's mother did not join – as neither did Mrs Pattison, who only clicked away with her needles, lips compressed.

And then it was nine thirty. The ale was finished. Mrs Pattison put away her knitting, and she and her husband got up to go.

'In three weeks, then, Frank, yes?' said Pattison to Abbie's father as they moved to the door. 'And your turn to come to us.' He chuckled. 'I'll have my revenge then, you'll see.' He turned to Abbie's mother. 'And you'll be along too, will you, Mrs Morris?' he asked, adding with a smile, 'Aggie's always glad of the chance of a chinwag.'

'Well,' Mrs Morris replied almost ungraciously, 'we'll see.'

When the visitors had gone she said, 'And there's another evening wasted.'

'Pleasure shouldn't always be seen as a waste of time,' protested her husband.

'Talk of pleasure's all very well,' she said. 'But you want to try sitting with that stupid woman for an evening. I don't think you'd call it pleasure.'

'Maybe not – but while they're here I think you might try to enter into it a little more. When Jack asked you round you barely answered the man.'

'He's *your* friend, Frank,' she said. 'And though I've nothing against him I've nothing much to say to him, either.' Turning, she caught sight of Abbie at the table, her open book before her. 'And you, Abigail,' she went on sharply, 'sitting there with your ears flapping like cabbage leaves – get on up to bed.'

Chapter Four

When Abbie got up the next morning her father had already left for Bath – which meant that she would not see him again until the weekend. Once she had finished her morning chores, she sat and wrote a letter to Mrs Curren in Eversleigh, confirming that she was pleased to accept her offer of the place and would be there on Saturday, 9 August. That done, she got her mother's permission to go and visit Jane for a while.

When she reached the Carrolls' cottage she found Jane mopping the floor while Mrs Carroll sat at the window, working on a piece of lace. Abbie stood to one side, talking to them as they worked.

'I'll bet your mam was pleased, wasn't she?' Jane said. 'About your getting the place at Marylea House?'

'Yes,' Abbie replied. 'She's pleased well enough.'

'And your father too? What did he say?'

'Oh, well – if he had his way I'd still be at school. Still, I told him that per'aps I can go back to my studies in a little while.'

'Pr'aps you can,' said Mrs Carroll. 'You're a clever enough girl. There's them that says girls haven't got the brains that boys have, but I don't hold with it meself. The trouble is though, Abbie, once you gets into something – like going into service – it's not always easy to stop, to break out. You've seen it yourself – girls go into service and they don't come out till they retires, or dies or, if they're lucky, gets married. Mind you, there's them that say women only swap one kind of service for another once they get wed – although most women wouldn't have it any other way.' She paused. 'I certainly wouldn't have.' Her eyes moved, resting on a photograph in a cheap tin frame on the mantelpiece. In sepia tones it showed her as a younger woman, sitting with Jane, a small child of four, on her knee. Her husband, solemn as his wife and wearing a uniform of the Infantry, stood stiffly at her side. He had been killed fighting against the Russians at Sebastopol. Abbie could still remember Mrs Carroll's grief.

'Oh, there's no doubt,' Mrs Carroll said, 'it's a hard life for the likes of poor people. But if you can share it with the right one it makes all the difference in the world.' She bent again over her lace. 'Anyway, you decide what you want out of life and try to get it. And if you want to study you must make up your mind to do it.'

As the days passed Abbie thought more and more of what Mrs Carroll had said. It was true, she would need to set her mind to it if she really intended to study and do something with her life. But going into service would be only a temporary thing, she was determined on that; she had no intention of spending years and years making beds and cooking and cleaning for other people, no matter that it was what so many other girls did. There had to be something better.

Frank Morris came back from Bath again at the weekend, and following midday dinner on Sunday afternoon he and Abbie walked together with Lizzie and Iris to Sunday school. After seeing them inside the little church hall they continued on, leaving the village behind and taking a footpath through the fields.

The afternoon was warm with a brilliant sun shining

out of a cloudless blue sky. They walked through a pasture where cattle grazed, and then beside a hedgerow where hazelnuts, blackberries and elderberries were ripening. On the other side of the hedge grew a field of wheat, its gold splashed here and there with the scarlet of poppies. Reaching the far side of the field they came to a little thicket and sat down in the shade of an oak. As they did so three white doves, momentarily alarmed, fluttered up on rattling wings and then descended to settle again on their perches. Out in the grass of the meadow a blackbird was feeding its young.

'So,' said Frank Morris, pulling at a blade of grass, 'next Saturday when I get back you won't be here.'

'No, I shan't.'

'How d'you feel about it – going away?'

She shrugged. 'A bit nervous – but I reckon that's only natural.'

'You'll let me know at once if things ain't right, won't you? If anybody mistreats you or anything like that, you let me know. I won't have you staying in a place where you're unhappy.' He sat with his arms resting on his knees, hands clasped low. His hands were broadened by years of manual work, the edges of his fingernails ingrained with the stains of soil and mortar that no amount of scrubbing on a Saturday would shift. 'It'll be strange without you,' he said. 'But there, you'll be back some weekends – and you'll come and spend your summer holiday back home, won't you?'

'Oh, ah, I'll do that. And when I come I'll try to bring you a nice present.'

'No, no,' he said, 'don't you go spending your money on me. My God, you'll have worked hard enough for it and you'll need it for yourself.'

She didn't say anything to this.

'You'll see,' he went on, 'your year at Eversleigh will

41

soon pass, and then you'll be able to move on to something better. Have a chance to work your way up.'

She looked at him. His words surprised her. Was he accepting the possibility that she would spend all her working life in service? 'Don't you think it's a good idea,' she asked 'what we talked about? About my studyin' to be a teacher?'

He was silent for a moment, then he said, 'I only want what's best for you, Abbie. But I suppose we've got to realize that what we want is not always to be had. If things could be different . . . ' He shook his head. 'But they're *not* different – no matter how much we might wish 'em to be.'

Abbie felt her spirits sink.

'But you'll be happy,' he said. 'I'm sure you'll make the best of whatever comes your way.'

She nodded, disappointment welling in her. Turning to face him again she could see the hurt in his eyes. 'Don't worry about me, Father,' she said. 'I shall be all right. And one day I'll make you proud of me.'

'I already am.'

Silence fell between them, broken only by the sound of birdsong. Abbie was suddenly aware of how much she loved him. Looking away over the green meadow she said, 'I'll miss you, Father.'

He did not respond at once, but then his left hand came round and clasped her shoulder. He held her close and the smell of him in her nostrils was the sweetest scent. 'I'll miss *you*, my girl,' he said.

She knew, without looking at him, that there were tears in his eyes.

Eddie returned late from work at the farm on Wednesday evening, telling his mother that both Mr White and his son were laid up with the flu, while Gresham, one of

White's right-hand men, had been confined to his bed following an accident in which he had injured his leg. An added complication was the fact that two of White's mares were about to foal at any time. As a result, Eddie had agreed to sleep over at the farm for the next few nights in order to be on hand when needed.

On Thursday, after midday dinner, Abbie concentrated on making sure that her things were ready for her move to Eversleigh. She did not have much to take in the way of clothes, but the little she owned had to be clean and mended and pressed. Her mother, it had been arranged, would accompany her to Eversleigh. Leaving Lizzie and Iris in the care of Jane and Mrs Carroll, Abbie and Mrs Morris would get a ride part of the way with Mr Taggart, the landlord of the Harp and Horses. Abbie knew that on a Saturday he usually drove to the market in Westbury, and on approaching him he readily agreed to take her and her mother in his cart. From Westbury the pair would walk the remaining two-and-a-half miles to Eversleigh.

When her box was packed, Abbie resumed her work in the cottage. Her mother seemed strangely preoccupied. Several times when Abbie spoke to her in the course of their work she gave no answer; she appeared not to hear, to be far away in some world of her own; then, when Abbie repeated her words, she would turn to her as if coming out of a dream. Once or twice Abbie was tempted to ask if there was something wrong, but each time she let the moment pass and put the question from her mind.

That night when she lay in bed her thoughts centred once again on her own concerns. After tonight there would be only one more day and one more night, then she would be leaving for Eversleigh.

From the other bed she could hear the soft, regular breathing of her younger sisters. They had been asleep for hours. As she should have been. Nervousness, excitement, however, all got in the way. Faintly, from the church, she heard the striking of the clock and counted the twelve strokes.

She was not sure whether her mother had come to bed. When Eddie slept at the farm Mrs Morris stayed later than usual in the kitchen. Tonight Abbie had been aware on two occasions of her mother climbing the stairs – it was impossible to use them without causing a few creaks – and then descending again. But that second time had been over an hour ago and since then she had heard nothing more.

From the church came the sound of the clock striking the hour of one. Abbie lay there for a few minutes longer and then, as quietly as she could, slipped from her bed and tiptoed out of the room.

In the faint light that crept past the thin curtains at the little landing window she saw that the door to her mother's room was closed. After hesitating for a moment she gingerly grasped the handle. It turned silently in her hand. Holding her breath, she gently eased open the door. The curtains at the window were still parted, and in the moonlight she saw that her mother's bed lay empty and undisturbed.

She turned back out onto the landing and went down the stairs. The kitchen too was empty.

Where had her mother gone? Not to Mrs Marling again, surely; Mrs Marling's baby, a boy, had been born two days ago.

Abbie stood, wondering what to do. Then she moved to the door, put on her pattens and slipped out into the night. At the gate she looked up and down the lane. There was no one in sight and not one single lighted window was in view. The whole village seemed to be asleep. After a minute she turned and went back indoors.

In the kitchen she took off her pattens and moved to the table. Taking a Lucifer match from its box she struck it and put the little flame to the wick of the half-burned candle. In the light of the flame she took Eddie's old winter coat from its hook behind the door and wrapped it round her shoulders. The fire in the grate had long since died and the room had grown cold. Moving to the window seat, she sat down and settled herself to wait.

She awoke with a start, stiff in her limbs, her bare feet cold in the early morning air. She stretched her arms and rubbed at her neck to ease the stiffness there. It was close on five o'clock and dawn was lighting the room. On the table the candle had burned out.

After raking the ashes from the grate she lit a fire. Then she washed her face and hands, and went upstairs. In the bedroom, moving quietly so as not to waken the girls, she got dressed and then crept again into her mother's room. Peering into the little wardrobe, she saw that her father's clothes hung there neatly, while most of her mother's things had gone.

Back downstairs she made some tea and sat slowly drinking it at the table. She had been sitting there for ten minutes when she noticed the envelope. Glancing over in the direction of the range, she saw it on the mantelpiece, propped up against a little china dog that Eddie had won at the last May fair. She reached up to take it down – and found that there were two others behind it. Each was inscribed in her mother's handwriting; the first was addressed simply: *Frank*; the second: *Edward*: the third: *Abigail*. All three envelopes were sealed.

At the table she laid the envelopes before her, then, carefully, she took up the one addressed to herself and tore it open. Inside, folded, was a single sheet of flimsy notepaper. Opening it up, she read the words that her mother had written.

My dear Abbie,

Please see that your father and Eddie get these letters as soon as possible. It's very important. Please be a good girl and look after your father and your brother and sisters. I'm very sorry about everything. Perhaps one day you'll understand. I'll try to write to you soon.

Your loving Mother

At seven o'clock Abbie went upstairs and woke Lizzie and Iris, and told them to get dressed. When they came downstairs she served them porridge, adding to it a little milk and honey. 'Where's Mam? Where's Mam?' they asked in plaintive, irritating tones, to which Abbie replied that their mother had gone out and would be back later.

When they had eaten – Abbie herself was unable to swallow more than a spoonful or two – she got them into their coats.

'Where are we going?' Lizzie asked, her question at once echoed by Iris.

'To White's farm,' Abbie said, 'to see Eddie.'

'What for?' Iris asked.

'Because we've got to.'

When they were all ready, Abbie set the guard before the fire, then took the three letters and put them into her pocket. With the girls at her side, she left the cottage.

It took about twenty minutes to reach the farmhouse and, on enquiring of the farmer's wife for her brother, Abbie was directed to the stable yard.

Eddie looked up in surprise as his sisters came towards him. 'What're you doin' 'ere?' he said, frowning.

Abbie came to a halt some ten yards away. 'Wait here,' she said to the girls. 'I want to talk to Eddie for a minute.'

46

'What for?' Lizzie asked.

'Just do as I tell you,' Abbie said sharply.

Leaving the girls standing side by side, she went to where Eddie stood.

His frown deepened as he saw the grave expression on her face. 'What's up?' he asked.

Abbie tried to frame words but none came, and suddenly her lip quivered and she burst into tears.

'Good God, girl!' Eddie said, all concern. 'What's the matter?'

'It's Mam,' she managed to get out at last. 'She went out again last night, but this time she didn't come back. And her clothes are gone from her room.' From her pocket she brought out the letters. 'Here . . .' She handed one to him. 'I got one as well, and there's another one here for Father.'

Eddie turned the envelope over in his dirty hands, then tore it open.

Abbie watched his face as he unfolded the letter and read it. She saw his mouth twist and the sudden shine of tears in his eyes. 'What does she say, Eddie?'

He hesitated and swallowed before replying, 'She've gone away. She've left us. She ain't comin' back no more.'

Abbie began to cry again, silently, the tears streaming down her cheeks. 'Tell me what she says. What does she say?'

'She says,' he said, looking back at the letter, 'that she've got to go away . . .' His voice trembling, he began to read aloud from it: ' "You've been a good son, Eddie, and from now on I want you to be a good brother to your sisters and look after them. It's no use me trying to explain now why I'm leaving, but perhaps one day I'll be able to, and you'll be able to understand. I'm very sorry." ' He paused. 'She signs it "Your loving Mother".'

Suddenly the tears were flowing unchecked from his

eyes and he sobbed out into the still morning air. He spun, took a few steps away, then turned back again. The tears were streaming down his face. In all her life, Abbie had never seen him weep like this. She watched as, in a fever of anguish, he tore at the letter, ripping it to pieces. 'Well, she can go!' he cried, letting the fragments of paper fall at his feet. 'Let 'er go! We'll manage without 'er. Let 'er go!'

A little later, after a brief conversation with Mr White, Eddie was given permission to saddle one of the mares and ride to Bath. He found his father working on site, mixing mortar. As Eddie approached, Frank Morris's eyes registered alarm at the sight of his son there, so far from home. In silence Eddie delivered to him the third letter.

His father read it and then turned away. 'I'll see the foreman. He'll let me off – though of course I'll lose the pay. It can't be helped. Tell Abbie I'll be back later on today.'

'Where's Mam gone, Father?' Eddie asked.

'She doesn't say. Though I've no doubt she's gone back to London.'

'But – but *why*? Why would she want to go off alone and leave us like that?'

'She hasn't gone alone,' his father said. 'She's gone with Jack Pattison. They've gone off together.'

That evening, after her father had returned, grave-faced, from Bath, Abbie went to tell Jane and Mrs Carroll what had happened. When they had sympathized and given her what comfort they could, Jane asked what she intended to do about her post at Marylea House. Abbie replied that she would have to write to Mrs Curren and tell her that she could not work for her after all, that from now on she would be needed at home. After some discussion it was decided that, if Mrs Curren would accept her, Jane would go in Abbie's place. So after Abbie had left, Mrs Carroll went to tell Mr Taggart that she and Jane would like to travel with him to Westbury the following day instead of the Morrises.

They approached Marylea House the next morning with some trepidation. They need not have worried, however. Mrs Curren was immediately agreeable – for, as she remarked, Jane had only lost out in the first place through the fall of a coin.

Later, after a rest over a cup of tea, Mrs Carroll and Jane went into the yard where they embraced and said their goodbyes. Then, with tears in her eyes, and watched by Jane from the gate, Mrs Carroll set off back on the dusty road to Flaxdown.

While Jane was learning her duties in Eversleigh, Abbie was trying to deal with the changes in her own life. At first she lived in hope that her mother would return, but the days dragged by and Mrs Morris did not come. How, Abbie wondered, could her mother leave them? It was understandable for a wife to want to escape from a husband who ill-used her and gave no thought to her happiness, but her father was a kind, considerate man. In any case, the relationship between husband and wife apart, how could a woman desert her children?

It was their father who broke the news to Lizzie and Iris. Their mother had had to go away, he told them, and might not be back for a time. They had wept till their eyes were red and swollen, always asking the same questions: Where did she go? When would she come back? Abbie and her father and brother had no answers for them.

Beatie heard the news from her father who wrote to her

that weekend. Abbie wrote a couple of days later. From her mother Beatie heard nothing. Much distressed, she tearfully confided in her mistress, who did what she could to comfort her and told her that she should go home to see her family. She could go in the trap on Saturday with the groom and he would call for her the following day.

Beatie arrived in Flaxdown early that Saturday afternoon, and was met outside by Lizzie and Iris. 'Mam's gone away,' Lizzie said dolefully, to which Beatie replied that she knew. Then, while the trap driver set off for the Harp and Horses, she followed the two girls indoors where Abbie was awaiting her arrival. A few minutes later, when the girls had gone out to play again, she and Abbie sat at the table drinking tea.

'What about the people in the village?' Beatie asked. 'Do they know about it?'

'They must do,' Abbie replied. 'And what they don't know for certain they'll get by putting two and two together. Everybody must know she's gone – and that Mr Pattison's gone too. It won't be hard for people to work it out.'

'Have you seen Mrs Pattison?'

'No – and I feel right sorry for her too. She's a funny, pathetic little woman, but well-meaning enough. Still, she must be managing. At least the post office is still open.'

Later their father arrived from Bath, then Eddie came in from the farm. Beatie and Abbie had prepared supper, and afterwards they spent the evening together, all six of them.

Abbie knew that her father was crushed by their mother's departure, while her brother, she quickly realized, nursed a bitterness towards her; she could see it in his set mouth and in his reluctance to speak of her. As he had never been one for staying about the house, but was usually off with his friends, Abbie had thought that he might be less affected by their mother's going. But she was wrong; he was clearly very affected by her desertion.

That night, Abbie and Beatie lay together in bed. In the other bed, Lizzie and Iris were already asleep.

'What about your Tom?' Abbie whispered into the dark. 'Does he know you've come here?'

'Yes, I sent him a note. I told him I had to come.'

'Did you say why?'

'No.' There was silence for a moment, then Beatie added, 'I'm afraid of what'll happen when he finds out about Mam. More particularly when his parents find out. What will they think?'

'What *can* they think? What are you talking about?'

Beatie sighed. 'Everything's been going so well lately with Tom and me. I know his folks don't think I'm good enough for him, but now that I've met them a couple of times things have been getting better. But now this has happened – our mam going off with some man from the village. They won't want him courting a girl whose mother's done that. They won't want scandal brought into the family.'

'Perhaps they won't find out about it.'

'Oh, they will. Scandal like that. They probably know about it already.'

'But they'll know it don't make any difference to what *you* are. It don't change *you*. Whatever our mam's done it don't make you into a different person.'

'Well, *I* know that and *you* know that – but I'm afraid they won't see it that way.'

'I'm sure they will. But what about Tom? He's a grown man. He's got some say in what happens to him.'

'Yes, of course, but . . . well, he'll only go against them

so far. Stands to reason. Oh, Abbie, I love him. I couldn't bear it if anything should go wrong.'

'Nothing's going to go wrong. And if Tom loves you as he says he does it won't make any difference.'

Beatie returned to her duties the following day and on the Wednesday Abbie received a letter from her. It was full of hope and happiness. She and Tom had talked, Beatie wrote, and everything was going to be all right. Although Tom had already learned about their mother's departure he did not appear to be unduly perturbed by the knowledge. And as for his parents, although they were unhappy about it he was sure that in time their doubts would pass.

Abbie sighed with relief on reading Beatie's letter. It had been a lingering concern in connection with her mother's leaving. But now it was over and Beatie, like the rest of them, could start to get on with her life again.

PART TWO

Chapter Five

'D'you realize what today is?' Abbie asked, looking up from the table where she sat writing a letter.

Eddie, standing at the mirror, gave a nod. 'It's Friday.'

'I don't mean the day. I mean the date.'

He turned, gazed at her blankly for a second then said, 'It's the seventh, is it?'

'Yes. Six years tonight since Mother went.'

They spoke of their mother only rarely and when they did it was as if they were speaking of some distant relative, or some acquaintance who had once touched their lives but was no longer a part of them. In all those six years they had heard not one single word from her beyond the three letters she had left behind on the night of her going.

And neither had they had much word *of* her. All they knew was that she was no longer with Jack Pattison. Not long after the two of them had left the village Pattison's wife had given up the post office and moved to Bath to live with her mother. A year or so later, Eddie came to Abbie with the news that Pattison had returned to his wife and that they were once again living together.

For a little while Eddie had considered going to Bath to find Pattison, to 'teach him a lesson', but after consideration he had decided against it. Perhaps, Abbie had thought, having never forgiven their mother for her action, he no longer cared that much about her.

Eddie, now showing no interest in the anniversary of

their mother's going, turned back to the glass. Abbie watched him as he smoothed a palm over his hair. Nearly twenty, he was a good-looking young man, straight, broad in the shoulders and already taller than their father. He looked very fit with his smooth skin bronzed by the sun, which had also bleached the crown of his fair hair a pale shade of yellow. Abbie studied him, taking in his wide-set grey eyes, his straight, perfectly shaped nose. Tonight he was wearing his best jacket, his new corduroy trousers and his best shirt. He stepped back for a final appraisal, then moved to the vase of flowers that stood in the centre of the table and selected a pink rose, its bud just half opened. Turning back to the glass, he tried the flower against his jacket, then, satisfied, cut the stem with his pocket knife and pinned it into his buttonhole.

'And very fetching indeed,' Abbie said approvingly. 'I'm sure Violet will be most taken with you.'

He shot a glance of suspicion at her, which she met with eyes of innocence. Smiling, she said, 'No, Eddie, it looks very nice. Truly.'

'Yeh?'

'Yes, really.'

Apart from his maturing he had not changed that much over the years, she thought. He was still the same warm-hearted, exuberant rough diamond. It was just that now some of his interests were different. Whereas in earlier days he had spent his leisure time in boisterous pursuits with his friends, he now preferred, when it was possible, to spend it with one Violet Neville, the third daughter in a family of eight who lived on the other side of the green. Violet, seventeen years old and very pretty, was away in service in Devizes for most of the year, so Eddie's meetings with her were few and far between. At present, however, she was back home in Flaxdown for her annual summer holiday, and she and Eddie met as often as they could.

Glancing at the clock, Abbie saw that it was ten minutes to eight. She was eager for her father to return, eager for his news.

Taking up his hat, Eddie moved to the door. 'I must go or I'll be late,' he said. In another moment he was gone.

Abbie sat motionless for a minute two, then got back to the task before her. She had just finished writing a letter to Lizzie and was now completing one to Iris. Her two younger sisters were also living away from home. Lizzie was fifteen and had been in service for two years. Having spent her first, petty, year in Trowbridge, she was now fairly happily settled as housemaid with a family in Radstock, some dozen miles away. Iris, fourteen, was still with her first employers, closer to home, in Frome. Both girls had only recently returned to their work after being at home for their annual summer holidays.

Abbie finished the letter – she had written to Iris much as she had written to Lizzie – and put it in an envelope. Now she prepared to begin one to Beatie.

Beatie had turned twenty-three that past March and, because of her wish to remain near Tom Greening, was still with the Callardines in Lullington.

The past six years of Beatie's relationship with Tom had not been all happiness and there had been a couple of occasions when she had feared that it would end. Now, though, any unhappiness she had known seemed to be in the past, for in June of this year, 1868, she and Tom had become engaged to be married. Whatever their past reservations, Tom's parents had either seen them as invalid, or had been won over by Beatie, for after Tom had agreed to wait for a time before marrying, his parents had at last given the couple their blessing. The wedding would take place late in October, Beatie remaining at her place in Lullington until a week or so before it, when she would return to Flaxdown to prepare for the big day and spend a last holiday with her family.

Taking up her pen, Abbie wrote:

Flaxdown
Friday, 7 August 1868

My dear Beatie,

Thank you for yours of the 5th. It's wonderful that everything is so well with you and Tom, and I'm not in the least surprised that Mr and Mrs Greening have been 'pleasantness itself' to you, as you put it – though I don't know what you've got to be nervous about, I'm sure. I know there have been times when you feared that things might not work out, but they have, and those doubtful times are now all in the past. You're both going to be very happy, I'm sure of it. I can believe you when you say that the time seems to be moving so slowly. But it will pass, and October will soon be here, and then all at once you'll find you've got a million things to do and not enough time to do them in.

It's well over a week now since Lizzie and Iris went back to their places. It was lovely to have them both home, and so nice that their holidays coincided so they could be together again for a while. The time they were here went by so fast; before we knew it they were both off again. Still, I hope it won't be long before they're back once more, at least on one or other of their free Sunday afternoons.

Father is in good health, you'll be glad to hear, and has got over his twinges. It's so nice when he can get work close by and is able to live at home all week. At present, working only a couple of miles away on the house in Corsley Heath, he's back home every evening well before half past six – and without being so awfully

58

tired from having to travel a long distance. He's able to spend a bit of time on the allotment too, making the most of his opportunities and the long evenings – though they won't last for much longer; autumn will soon be here. You'd be amazed at the amount of work he's managed to get done over the past few months; we certainly shouldn't be short of vegetables for a while yet, anyway . . .

She paused in her writing, tapping the end of the pen against her white, even teeth. Usually her father would have been out on the allotment in such fine weather as this. This evening, though, after he had finished his tea he had changed into his best clothes and set off for the vicarage to see the Revd Hilldew – to discuss with him the question of Abbie's future. He had left the house at seven fifteen. It was now almost half past eight.

Laying down her pen she got up, filled the kettle and put it on to boil. Moving to her right she stood before the mirror, took a couple of loose pins from her hair and fastened the heavy chestnut braids about the crown of her head more securely. She was eighteen years old now and her reflection was not unpleasing. She had a fine, straight nose; a wide, full-lipped mouth and arched brows. Her skin was soft and clear, and her dark eyes bright. Also – and to her relief – she had grown considerably during the past three years – so much so that on Jane's last visit to Flaxdown they had discovered that they were almost the same height.

As she turned from the glass she was aware of the quietness of the cottage; the only sound was the ticking of the clock. The appearance of the room had changed in the six years since her mother had left, it now reflecting only the lives and likes of those who were left. Nowadays there were nearly always flowers on the table. On the walls hung several prints – cheap but attractive – chosen by Abbie and framed for her by Eddie. Another frame held a drawing by Iris, who had a talent with her pencil; another an exquisitely wrought little sampler – 'Old Friends Are the Best Friends' – from Lizzie. There, too, were her father's books on the shelves he had built – books that he had previously kept upstairs. And beside them were Abbie's, the collection growing; books picked up at markets or given to her by various people.

Her books were a part of her work now, and she turned to them every day once her chores around the cottage were done. It had been her father's suggestion, made within a few weeks of their mother's going. 'It's your opportunity,' he had said. Now she could continue with her studies as he had wanted her to do; she could work at home and he would give her whatever help he could. Then later, he had said, when they felt she was ready and the time was right, they would apply for her to be interviewed by the Board of School Governors, with a view to being accepted as a teacher.

She had worked hard in preparation for such an eventuality, and not only as regards academic learning. She had been working, too, on her speech. She knew that were she to speak to the members of the Board in the vernacular and accents of the village she would be doomed before she had a chance to show what learning she had acquired. She had suffered a good deal of teasing from Eddie to begin with, but she was persevering. Now when she spoke there was not a dropped aitch to be heard.

And now, after all her work, she was of the opinion, as was her father, that she was ready to meet the Board – which was the reason for his visit to the Revd Hilldew, who was the Board's chairman.

Abbie moved to the window and looked along the lane.

There was no sign of her father. Turning back to the table she sat down, took up her pen again and continued with her letter to Beatie:

Eddie has just gone out for the evening – to see his Violet, of course. Though no *shrinking* violet she, as I know you also think. Still, he's very taken with her, so it's not for us to put in our two pennyworth. If he *is* making a mistake let's hope he finds it out before it goes on too long. He's a sensible enough chap, as we know, but how good his judgement is of females I'm not sure. Perhaps he thinks they're all as gracious and loving as his sisters! Ha ha!

This week I received a letter from Jane. She continues to do well. She seems very happy at Trowbridge so far, and is looking forward to going up to London in the autumn with her new employers, who have a house there. She tells me in her letter that she's coming to Flaxdown for her holidays in September before they all go off. Her mother, whom I saw yesterday, can hardly wait.

There's not a lot more to tell you right now and I shall have to stop as Father will soon be coming in. I am well, as ever, and getting on with my studies – but more of that another day. For now, goodbye from

Your loving sister
Abbie

She read the letter through, folded it, sealed it in an envelope and, along with those to Lizzie and Iris, put it on the mantelpiece. She was just about to put her writing materials away when her father entered.

'I'm just making tea,' she said as he took off his hat. 'I wondered where you'd got to.'

He hung up his jacket and sat down, and in silence

61

Abbie pulled off his boots and brought him his slippers. When she had poured and handed him his tea she sat facing him from the chair opposite. 'Well?' she asked.

He nodded. 'Well, I saw the vicar. And he was very sympathetic and understanding.' He took a swallow from his cup. 'But of course the fact that you left school at twelve doesn't exactly help your case.'

'Did you tell him I've been studying?'

'Of course. And I said you were doing extremely well, and that you're a very clever young woman.'

'What did he say to that?'

'Nothing much; it was what he'd expect me to say. Anyway, he says you must write him a formal letter of application. Then he'll consider speaking to the other members of the Board to see about them giving you an interview.'

'Oh, Father, that's wonderful! Did he say when the interview might be – if I get one, that is?'

'As soon as the Board meets, which will be next month, so he said.'

'Oh, it's a terrifying prospect – but all the same I wish I didn't have to wait.'

'It's all to the good,' he said. 'It means you'll have time to prepare.'

Sitting down at the table again, she wrote at once to the Revd Hilldew, making her application. When she had finished the letter she read it aloud to her father, who nodded his approval, and signed it. After sealing the letter in an envelope, she turned in her chair and regarded him in the soft glow of the lamp. She could almost feel his belief in her. She *would* do well; she was determined. And she knew that by doing so, by succeeding, she would be helping him to fulfil himself.

Since her mother's departure she had grown even

closer to her father – as, she realized, had her brother and sisters.

'Do you miss her, Father?' she asked after a moment.

He looked at her in surprise. 'Your mother,' he said; a statement.

Abbie nodded.

'What brought that question on?'

She shrugged. 'Sometimes I've wondered.'

A moment of hesitation, then: 'No, I don't.'

'Do – do you think about her?'

He frowned. 'Oh, Abbie, that's all in the past. Have we got to talk about such melancholy things?'

She said nothing. After a second or two he went on, 'Yes – I think about her now and then. But I don't miss her.'

'Neither do I,' Abbie said. 'And I wouldn't want her back. Not now.' She paused. 'But you loved her once.'

'Yes.' He nodded. 'Oh, she was a beautiful girl, your mother. And I thought she was so sophisticated – the way she dressed, the way she spoke. I was determined to have her if I possibly could.' He sighed. 'And I did. Though I'm afraid she married me as an escape.'

'An escape?'

'I came to realize it later. She hated her work. She was never cut out to be a governess – being patient with other people's children. And there I was – a young man with no ties. One of the few single men in the village who could read and write. I suppose she thought that together we – we'd amount to something.' He smiled, shaking his head. 'But it didn't happen like that. We had children. And as a result she felt trapped. Oh, I knew long before she went that she didn't love me. I'd got used to living with that idea.'

Into the silence that fell in the room Abbie said, 'Sometimes I almost hate her.'

'No,' he said, 'you don't mean that. Some women are just not cut out to be mothers. Motherhood comes naturally to most of them – but not to all.' He got up from his chair and put his empty cup on the table. Then, stepping to her side, he gently touched a hand to her hair. 'Don't be too quick to judge her, Abbie. It's like I said – I was probably equally to blame. And I was luckier – I didn't have to run away to find what I wanted. I had it here – in my children. I didn't need anything else.'

Chapter Six

Abbie stood back from the glass and looked at her reflection, while Jane, at her side, studied her equally judiciously. Jane had recently arrived back in Flaxdown for her annual summer leave. From now on it would be more difficult for her to visit, for once she returned to her post – she was now situated in Trowbridge – she would be accompanying her employers to London where they were to take up permanent residence. So she and Abbie were making the most of their time together, going off on jaunts to the market, taking leisurely walks, or on occasion, when the weather was fine enough, swimming in the river or the old clay pit. Swimming was one of their favourite means of relaxation on warm days, and whenever the rare opportunity arose they took it.

Today, however, was not a day for relaxation. Today was the day of Abbie's interview with the Board of School Governors, and Jane had come to give her moral support and help her get ready.

To her brown voile dress Abbie had attached a beautifully wrought lace collar lent to her by Jane's mother. It was a perfect foil for the plainness of her dress and she now looked almost elegant. Her hair, dressed by Jane, had been carefully fashioned into a chignon.

When she had put on her bonnet and cape – and gloves borrowed from Jane – she was ready to leave. Jane walked with her to the vicarage, wished her good luck and left her. Abbie watched until Jane had gone out of sight beyond the privet hedge, then walked up the drive to the front door and rang the bell. The door was opened by a maid who took her cape and showed her into the front parlour.

After a few minutes the Revd Hilldew came in. 'Ah, Miss Abigail.' He came towards her and she got to her feet and briefly took the soft handshake he offered. A short man in his late forties, he had a stocky build that gave no indication of frugality or self-denial. Abbie had always found him pleasant enough, however, notwithstanding that his sermons were overlong and inclined to ramble. 'The other members of the Board are here,' the vicar said. 'We have just one or two other matters of business to get through, then I'll call you in. We'll try not to keep you waiting too long.'

Twenty minutes later Abbie was ushered into the dining room where she found herself faced by the five members of the Board. They were seated around an oval dining table which was covered with a green velvet cloth. She sat down and the Revd Hilldew introduced her to the men, who in turn murmured brief, formal words of greeting. She knew all the faces there, including that of Mr Carstairs, the school inspector. He sat on the left, a short, thin man with spectacles. She could well remember from when she was at school the fear he had instilled into the hearts of students and teacher alike when he came into the classroom to carry out his annual inspections. Seeing him now, with his cold eyes and wide, unsmiling slit of a mouth, she felt that old fear reawaken.

Beside Mr Carstairs sat Mr Bradfield, the squire and local magistrate. A large man, in both girth and height, he dwarfed Carstairs, and the Revd Hilldew who sat on his other side. For all his physical stature and social elevation, however, Abbie had no fear of him. She had encountered him at a distance frequently over the years –

when she and Jane had watched him and his friends riding in the hunt, or when he had presided at fêtes in the grounds of the Manor House or visited village fairs and other social gatherings. He had always appeared to be genial and considerate, and as far as the gentry were held in any kind of affection by the villagers he could claim to be among that small, privileged number.

The man who sat on the immediate right of the Revd Hilldew was the obligatory representative of the non-conformist church, Mr Yates, the local Baptist minister. He was even thinner than Mr Carstairs and, with his pink, clean-shaven face and fine, delicate hands, looked untouched by life and experience. His expression was unreadable; whether he was well- or ill-disposed towards her, Abbie could not tell.

On the far right sat the fifth member of the Board, Dr Parrish. He, in his mid-thirties and easily the youngest, was a rather good-looking man of medium stature with dark, thinning hair. He was fairly new to the area, though Abbie had seen him from time to time going about the village on his calls.

'We have your letter here,' said the Reverend, glancing down at it. 'One difficulty, of course, as I told your father, is that your own schooling finished when you were only twelve years old and it isn't usual for the School Governors to employ schoolteachers who have had so little formal training. Our teachers are usually taken from among those young women who have remained on at school and served an apprenticeship by helping incumbent teachers.'

At this the school inspector opened his thin lips and murmured, 'Quite.'

'However,' went on the Reverend, 'you and your father tell us that you have been studying in your own time.

Would you like to tell us a little of what you've been doing in this respect?'

Abbie was so nervous that as she went to speak she found her mouth so dry that the inside of her upper lip adhered briefly to her gum. She wet her lip, swallowed, took a breath and said, 'I've been studying history, sir – and geography and English – and arithmetic.'

The five men looked at her, obviously waiting for her to amplify her answer. When she did not, the squire said, a faint smile lifting his red cheeks, 'And you obviously consider yourself qualified to teach, my dear.'

Abbie nodded. 'Yes, sir, I do.'

Mr Carstairs said – his smile taking nothing from the antipathy Abbie sensed – 'That's all very well, of course, but without your having some certificate of proficiency or acceptable references I'm afraid your opinion doesn't count for a great deal.'

'Well, now,' said the squire, 'I don't think we need to be too hard on the young lady.' He smiled encouragingly at her. 'I'm sure she finds this experience daunting enough as it is.' He glanced briefly at the other members of the panel, referred to a piece of paper before him, then added, 'If a man earns ten shillings and sixpence a week, for fifty-two weeks, minus three weeks due to sickness, how much would he earn altogether?'

The abrupt question took Abbie by surprise and for a moment she sat in panic, fingers touching at Mrs Carroll's lace collar. Then she answered: 'Twenty-five pounds, fourteen shillings and sixpence. Sir.'

The squire glanced down at his notes and smiled. 'Correct. Very good.'

As he spoke, Abbie saw Mr Carstairs flick a glance at Mr Yates, in his eyes a barely concealed contempt for the squire and his method of examination. In the eyes of Dr

Parrish, however, Abbie noticed a brief gleam of amusement.

The squire, blithely unaware of the reactions to his questioning, proceeded to give Abbie a series of arithmetical problems to solve, which she answered satisfactorily in each case. In the single instance her answer differed from that prepared by the squire, it was found that it was he who was wrong. When he jovially conceded the error Abbie began to feel a little more confident.

He had not finished, however. 'Now,' he said, adjusting another sheet of paper in front of him, 'the Battle of Hastings. Can you give us the date of that?'

Abbie was aware of further swift glances being exchanged between the school inspector and the Baptist minister. With a nod to the squire, she said, '1066, sir.'

'Correct,' said Mr Bradfield. 'What about . . . the Great Fire of London?'

'It was 1666, sir. I believe it destroyed about 13,000 houses and other buildings – including St Paul's Cathedral. Though few lives were lost. Seven or eight at most.'

'Excellent.' The squire gave a congratulatory nod. He opened his mouth to speak again, but the Baptist minister, Mr Yates, forestalled him.

'I wonder if you'd care to read something for us, Miss Morris. Allow us to have an idea of your reading ability.' As he spoke he pushed an open book across the table towards her.

She took it up and saw that it was Shakespeare's *The Merchant of Venice*, which she had recently been reading. 'Ah.' She nodded. 'Act Four, the Court of Justice.'

'Quite so,' said Mr Yates stiffly. 'Would you care to read a passage for us . . . ?'

Abbie looked down at the page, then up at the five pairs of eyes regarding her. She took a breath and began to read Portia's famous speech:

'The quality of mercy is not strain'd;
It droppeth as the gentle rain from heaven
Upon the place beneath: it is twice bless'd;
It blesseth him that gives and him that takes:
'Tis mightiest in the mightiest; it becomes
The throned monarch better than his crown . . .'

She continued to the end of the speech and came to a stop. Looking up, she saw Dr Parrish beaming at her.

'That was splendid, Miss Morris. If you don't teach perhaps you should consider becoming a Shakespearean actress and going on the stage.'

Mr Yates turned to him with a disapproving frown, then reached out and took the book back. 'Do you know anything of politics, Miss Morris?'

'Well,' Abbie replied with a shrug, 'I read the papers.'

'And what, for example, do you know of Mr Benjamin Disraeli?'

'Not a great deal, I'm afraid. I know that he was made Chancellor of the Exchequer in Lord Derby's Conservative administration at the beginning of July.'

Mr Yates nodded, then turned enquiringly to the Revd Hilldew.

Taking his cue, the Reverend said, 'Do you read for pleasure, Miss Morris?'

'When I have the time, sir.'

'And what have you been reading? Would you like to tell us?'

For a second Abbie's mind went blank, then she said, 'I've just been reading Thackeray's *History of Henry Esmond*. Before that I read *David Copperfield*. Also, I very much like Keats's poetry. Oh, yes, and I very recently read *Madame Bovary* by Gustave Flaubert.'

'*Madame Bovary*,' said Mr Yates, pursing his little pink mouth. 'I don't think that's the kind of book we'd want disseminated in a classroom. Where do you get your books from, Miss Morris?'

'Mostly from the lending library, sir.'

'What is this *Bovary* book, then?' asked the squire. 'I don't know of it, Mr Yates.'

'Then be content, Squire,' Mr Yates replied. 'I haven't read it myself and I've no intention of reading it. I've been told about it, though. It's a scandalous book: the story of a – a wanton Frenchwoman, a woman who reaches the kind of end she deserves. And not a moment too soon.'

'I read that,' the doctor said, 'when it came out a few years ago. In all fairness, Mr Yates, I don't think it's so bad.' While the minister gave a sniff, the doctor looked at Abbie. 'What did you think of it, Miss Morris?'

'I – I thought in a way it was an excellent book, sir.'

'Did you, now?' The doctor gave a little smile.

Mr Carstairs said, 'And what did you find so excellent about it, Miss Morris?'

'It – its truth.'

Mr Yates: 'Its *truth*?'

'Yes, sir.' Abbie nodded. 'It's a harrowing story – and, I agree, not a pleasant one. But I don't think it was meant to be.'

'What's it about?' said the squire.

Abbie hesitated briefly, then replied, 'It's . . . well, it's simply the story of a provincial housewife – a woman who is bored in her marriage and – and seeks distractions elsewhere. She longs for her life to be like the lives of the heroines she reads about in her novelettes – romantic and exciting.' As she spoke she had a sudden vision of her mother, sitting in the kitchen, reading. 'The woman's story ends in disaster,' she finished.

There was a little silence.

'Anyway,' said Mr Hilldew, 'I don't imagine for a

moment that Miss Morris would be teaching such a book to her students.'

'No, sir,' said Abbie, 'of course not.'

'Well,' muttered Mr Carstairs to the ceiling, 'that's something to be thankful for.'

Steepling his fingers and leaning forward slightly, Mr Hilldew said, 'Exactly what would you hope to teach your pupils, Miss Morris?'

'I think the most important thing,' Abbie said, 'would be to teach them to read. Once a person can read there are no boundaries to the scope of his learning. My father says that reading is the key to all knowledge.'

Dr Parrish gave a nod of agreement at this and murmured, 'Yes, indeed.'

Mr Yates said, 'And how far would you take your pupils, Miss Morris? – in their learning, I mean.'

'As far as it was possible to go, sir – within their capabilities.'

'Would you care to elaborate?'

She hesitated, not knowing what was expected of her. 'Well, the lives of the poor are so restricted,' she said. 'Generally they know nothing of what goes on outside their immediate vicinity. And they are kept down by their lack of knowledge. I – I would do what I could to change things for them. To open the world for them.' She was aware as she finished speaking of how pompous her words sounded, but she meant them; it was what she believed.

While the school inspector glanced about him with raised eyebrows, the Baptist minister spoke up. 'And what would be the point in that?' he enquired. 'In the countryside the men work as labourers on farms, and in the towns they operate machines in factories. What good could it do them to know about the finer points of the Poor Laws or the machinations of the French Revolution?'

'If they're kept subjugated then it certainly wouldn't do them any good at all,' Abbie answered. 'But surely a man has a right to the opportunity to better himself.'

'I'm afraid,' said Mr Yates, 'that that kind of philosophy could only lead to discontent. Or hasn't that occurred to you?'

'Oh, but a certain amount of discontent is surely necessary, sir,' Abbie replied. 'All progress and creativity are born out of frustration and discontent. It's complacency that is fatal to progress.'

Mr Yates and Mr Carstairs stared at her, eyes wide.

Dr Parrish said, 'So you would not, I imagine, agree with the recent words of the minister Robert Lowe when he was speaking on Education.'

'You mean,' Abbie replied, 'when he said that the lower classes "ought to be educated to discharge the duties cast upon them"? No, sir. If that's the philosophy behind all education then a man will never be able to better himself. Every child would be condemned to being no better than his parents.'

'And you,' said Mr Carstairs, now barely hiding his hostility, 'would like to be better than yours.'

'Well, sir. I would like to have the opportunity to do more with my life.'

'Your father, I understand,' enquired Mr Yates, 'is a labourer, is that so?'

'He's a bricklayer, sir. I would hope to gain more learning than he was able to, but I don't know that I could be a better person.' She paused. 'My father is the finest man I know.'

There was a brief silence, then Mr Carstairs continued, 'Well, Miss Morris, you've treated us all to an exposition of your philosophy on education. Though I don't know how well your ideals would work in the classroom. I fear you might end up rather frustrated. The government pays the schools by results and anything that won't help a child to pass his annual exams in the three Rs might prove rather counterproductive. Have you thought of that?'

'My aim would be,' Abbie said, 'to do whatever I could within the rules and the guidelines set down.' She knew, looking at his cold eyes and unsmiling mouth, that she had long ago lost any chance of winning him over to her side. Glancing at Mr Yates, she saw the same picture. She should have realized at the start that she had not had a chance. She shifted in her seat, preparing to rise and take her leave. At the same time she was aware of the squire taking out his watch; clearly he was anxious to be elsewhere on such a fine day. The interview was not quite finished, however.

'By the way, Miss Morris,' said the Revd Hilldew into the silence that had fallen, 'I'm pleased to see you regularly at church.'

Abbie smiled. 'Well, it's been a little easier for me since my two younger sisters left home.'

'Yes – in your mother's absence you've been caring for the family, isn't that so?'

'Yes, sir.'

A pause, then Mr Carstairs said, 'Your mother passed on, did she?'

Abbie hesitated. She felt quite sure that her examiner already knew the answer to his question. 'No, sir,' she replied, 'as far as I know she is in good health. I have no idea. My mother left us.'

'She – left you, you say?' The inspector's ignorance was to Abbie's ears clearly feigned.

'Yes, sir.'

'Why was that? If you don't mind my asking . . . '

'Not at all, sir,' Abbie said. 'It was common gossip in Flaxdown at the time. The fact is that my mother went

74

away with a local man – and we have not seen her since. She left six years ago.'

The silence was broken, after a moment, by the squire who mumbled, 'Yes – er – very sad, very unfortunate. But I don't think we need to dwell on such matters, what? That's not part of our brief.' He turned to Mr Carstairs as he spoke, and the latter, as if anxious to regain lost ground, said awkwardly, 'Quite. We have no wish to add to your distress and shame, for after all –'

Abbie interrupted, 'I feel no shame, sir.'

Carstairs gaped at her. 'I beg your pardon?'

She got to her feet. She knew she had lost, and knowing, she no longer cared what they thought of her. 'My mother did wrong,' she said. 'But I am in no way responsible for her actions. Her going away left us very unhappy for a time, but my father, my brother and my sisters – we live our own lives now and our mother has no part in them any longer. If anyone is waiting for me to bow my head in shame and do penance for the actions of someone else then I'm afraid he's going to wait for a very long time.' She adjusted her skirt and tugged at her gloves. 'Now, gentlemen, I think I have taken up enough of your time.'

A minute later she was being shown out of the house by the maid and was walking away down the drive towards the gate.

'Well,' said Beatie, 'I'm sure there are other things you can do besides teach.'

Abbie nodded. 'That's what I said to Jane.' She gave a resigned sigh. 'Anyway, I'm not going to fret about it.'

It was Saturday afternoon. Jane had that morning set off back to Trowbridge at the end of her holiday. And now Beatie was here, having not long since arrived from Lullington for her last weekend at home before she came back to prepare for her wedding. Her employers, the Callardines, were spending the weekend with friends in Bath and, with two nursemaids already there, Beatie's services would not be required. She had driven from Lullington in the trap of a local farmer on his way to Warminster and would be returning with him on Monday morning.

Abbie looked across the kitchen table at her sister. Only three and a half weeks remained before Beatie's wedding and her excitement was evident in the brightness of her eyes, her voice, in her whole carriage.

The wedding was to take place at the church of All Saints in Lullington on Wednesday, 7 October. Mr Morris had booked to hire the pony and trap from Mr Taggart at the Harp and Horses and, on the morning of the great day, along with Abbie and Eddie (Lizzie and Iris would be unable to attend) they would set off from the cottage for the five-mile journey to the Lullington church. Abbie was to be Beatie's bridesmaid. In the knowledge that she would have to wear her bridesmaid's gown afterwards, Abbie had chosen a very simple design in dark-blue cotton. The dress had been made for her by Jane's mother.

Beatie had made her own wedding dress. Styled from a pattern brought from London, it was of white linen, and muslin and lace given to her by her mistress. Beatie had brought the newly finished dress with her that afternoon, wrapped in sheets of brown and tissue paper, and in the bedroom she had put it on and pirouetted for Abbie's approval. Abbie thought she would never see a lovelier sight than Beatie that Saturday afternoon, standing there in her white dress with her red lips and blushing cheeks, and her chestnut hair hanging heavy and loose.

'Oh, Abbie,' Beatie breathed now as she put down her cup, 'd'you think my wedding day will ever come?'

Abbie laughed. 'For heaven's sake, it'll get here soon enough!'

'Yes, I know, but – oh, I suppose I'm just too happy. I can't believe it's to happen at last.'

When their tea was finished the two girls left the cottage and strolled leisurely onto the heath where Beatie picked some tall yellow tansies, pieces of fern and a few sprigs of holly, all of which, she said, she intended to turn into a pretty display as she had been taught by Mrs Callardine. Back home, she arranged her bits of foliage and then set about helping Abbie prepare the evening meal. At just past six o'clock Eddie came in from the farm and soon after greeting his elder sister launched into some good-natured teasing about the coming wedding. As far back as she could remember, Abbie reflected, Beatie had always been Eddie's victim when it came to his teasing and practical jokes. Now Abbie listened to his tormenting and then said with a groan, 'Oh, Eddie, give the girl a rest, will you!'

'It doesn't matter what he says, Abbie,' Beatie said, laughing. 'He can't spoil it for me.'

Not long afterwards their father returned from his work at Warminster and after he had washed they sat down to eat. Beatie had brought along a few little treats with her from the Callardines' kitchen and the meal that evening was a particularly pleasant and happy one.

As they ate, Eddie spoke of the fair that was on at Old Ford, a village about three miles away: 'You girls ought to go. You'd enjoy yourselves. Especially you, our Beatie, for once you're an old married 'oman you won't get much chance for pleasure.'

When dinner was over Abbie and Beatie washed the dishes and joined Eddie and their father at the table, where they played whist. Eddie would not be serious for long, however, and after a while they gave up the game and fell into conversation. In time the talk turned to the murder of a child that had taken place some eight years earlier in the nearby village of Road. It had been a most sensational case, not least because of the mystery that had surrounded it. Then, five years later, in 1865, the victim's half-sister Constance had confessed to the crime and been sent to prison. The house, Eddie claimed, had since been haunted by the little boy's ghost.

'You're making that up,' Beatie said. 'I don't believe in ghosts.'

'No, not until you see one,' said Eddie. 'Then you'll believe all right.'

'Well,' Beatie went on, 'when I do, you'll be the first to know.'

'Ah.' Eddie nodded. 'That's if you can talk for the screamin' vapours.'

Later, Beatie rose and took a match to light the lantern.

'You ain't goin' to the privy, are you?' Eddie asked.

'And what if I am?' she said.

'You ain't forgot what 'appened in the privy at Road, 'ave you?'

The fact that the Road murder victim had been found in an outside lavatory had been enough to put off many a child from using an outdoor privy at night. Beatie, however, was not to be daunted. 'Eddie,' she said with a superior smile, 'I told you, I don't believe in ghosts and Constance Kent is safely locked up in prison these three years, so she can't do me any harm.'

'Ah,' he countered, 'but what if she've got out and is on the rampage? You ain't thought of that, 'ave you?'

Beatie moved to the door, opened it and hesitated on the threshold.

'What's keepin' you?' Eddie said. 'Losin' your nerve?'

She turned to her father. 'Father, make him stop, will you?'

Eddie added quickly, 'All right, all right. I'm sorry. But just don't forget to leave the door open.'

This last was a reference to the fact that when visiting the privy during the hours of darkness, neither Beatie nor her sisters, as children, would ever close the door when they were inside. Rather than be shut in they would take their chances with immodesty and sit there with the door open onto the garden.

'Oh, shut up,' Beatie said and, with a haughty glance at him over her shoulder, she went outside.

Eddie remained sitting at the table for a few seconds, then got up, and Abbie glanced around to see him opening the door and going out into the backyard.

She was just taking up her sewing basket when the sound of Beatie's shriek came ringing out from the back garden. Then, as Abbie and her father got up and hurried towards the back door, Eddie came bursting in, carrying in his hands a sheet which, Abbie realized, he must have taken from the washing basket in the outhouse.

'What have you done?' Frank Morris asked, but Eddie was laughing so much he could not answer. Throwing the sheet down onto a chair, he snatched his hat from the hook and ran to the door. 'I'm off to the Harp,' he yelled and, still laughing, sped out into the night.

Beatie missed him by seconds. She came dashing in at the back door, hair and skirts flying, her expression a mixture of anger, outrage and lingering shock. 'Where is he?' she cried, spinning, looking around her. 'Tell me where he is.'

'What's up?' asked her father. 'What did he do?'

'What did he do! He just tried to scare me to death, that's all. Where did he go?'

'Out,' Abbie said, trying not to laugh. 'Said he was off to the Harp.'

'Just as well for him.' Beatie stood in the centre of the

room, getting her breath back. 'I'll kill him,' she muttered. 'I'll kill him.'

A couple of hours later it was Eddie's white handkerchief that came in first when the door was opened. Tied to a stick like a white flag in a sign of surrender, the handkerchief appeared and waved about a couple of times before it was followed by Eddie himself. Beatie merely gave him a contemptuous glance and bent her head to her sewing again. Eddie came in, closing the door behind him. As he detached the handkerchief from the stick he burst out laughing.

'Oh, my God, you should 'ave seen 'er. Sittin' there like some young queen, the door wide open and the old lantern next to her on the seat. And then up comes the old ghost, all wrapped in white from 'ead to foot. "Whooo whooo," he goes,' and he waved his arms in the air. '"Whooo whooo" – and she lets out a scream they must 'ave 'eard in Trowbridge.' He opened his mouth wide, mimicking Beatie shrieking. 'And her almost fell down the 'ole. I tell you, if she was constipated before, she wouldn't 'ave been afterwards.'

While Beatie, all dignity, sat silently over her sewing, Abbie and her father couldn't help but join in Eddie's laughter, at the same time protesting at his cruelty.

'And when I told 'em down at the pub,' added Eddie, 'I thought they'd laugh fit to die.'

'So,' Beatie said, 'you had to go and tell them down at the Harp, did you?'

At the expression on her face Eddie's laughter died. 'Ah, come on, Beat,' he said. 'It was only a joke. I didn't mean nothin' by it.'

'You never do,' she replied. 'Everything's a joke to you, that's the trouble.'

Sitting up in bed, Abbie watched in the light of the candle

as Beatie sat in front of the glass brushing her hair. When Lizzie and Iris had gone away the sleeping arrangements in the cottage had been changed. The two beds in the rear bedroom were now used by their father and Eddie, leaving the front bedroom with the double bed to Abbie. Tonight she would be sharing it with Beatie.

'Honestly,' Beatie said, smiling into the mirror at Abbie's reflection, 'I thought I'd die of fright. All that talk of ghosts, and then he goes and does that. Though I suppose I should have expected something. But the way he suddenly loomed up in the doorway, covered with the sheet – well, I thought I would die on the spot.'

Abbie was about to speak when Beatie whispered 'Sshh!' and waved her hairbrush in a gesture for silence. From the stairs came the sound of footfalls; either their father or brother was coming up to bed.

'Listen,' Beatie said. 'That's Eddie, isn't it?'

'Sounds like it.'

'We'll soon know for sure.'

'What d'you mean?'

'Just wait.'

Three or four minutes went by and then the quiet was broken by a howl coming from the other bedroom. Beatie burst into shrieks of laughter, one hand to her mouth while she sat rocking on the stool.

'What's up?' Abbie asked, bewildered.

The door was flung open and Eddie was standing there in his nightshirt. In one hand he had some pieces of holly. He held them out to Beatie, his face dark with anger. 'It was you, wunnit?'

I?' Beatie's expression was all innocence.

'Ah – you put this bloody stuff in my bed, under the sheet.'

Beatie and Abbie exploded into laughter.

'Well,' Eddie said, 'I reckon we're even now, ain't we?'

He looked from one to the other and slowly his mouth creased into a grin. 'Ah.' He gave a little nod of congratulation to Beatie. 'I reckon the shock you give me more than equals the one I give you.' He put the holly down on the dresser. 'I won't be needin' these prickles no more tonight. I've had me fill of the buggers for now.' He rubbed his right buttock. 'You'll be glad to know that they're really murder on the arse.'

Later, lying in bed, Abbie and Beatie were still giggling over Eddie and the holly when they heard their father's footsteps on the stairs. After that there came the sound of the bedroom door closing, then the house was silent.

'Shall we go to the fair tomorrow?' Abbie whispered. 'It would be fun.'

'It would,' Beatie agreed. 'Oh, yes, let's.'

Chapter Seven

The weather that Sunday remained fine. The sky was a clear blue, just touched here and there with small, hazy drifts of slow-moving cloud. Setting off from Flaxdown soon after an early midday dinner, Abbie and Beatie walked for part of the journey along the dusty road, then left it to take a short cut along a footpath over the fields.

In the grass beside the track scarlet pimpernel and clover grew. In the hedgerows the pink trumpets of the bindweed twined among the brambles with their ripe blackberries, and on the fine boughs of the crab apple trees the fruit was clustered. In the surrounding pastures sheep and cattle grazed, while in other fields the dull gold of the stubble spoke of the end of the harvest.

Old Ford was a favourite venue for travelling fairs, and a couple of times a year one would arrive and its people would set up its accoutrements on the edge of the village, their numbers soon swelled by others who came to set up their own stalls and sell their produce and services.

The excitement generated by the fair would be enormous and on a Sunday, when many of the men were free from their work, the folk would flock from miles around. Today was no exception, and as the pair emerged onto the road again they found themselves joining a stream of people making their way to the fairground.

For some distance before they reached it they could hear the sound of its music drifting on the breeze. As the noise grew, so did the girls' sense of excitement so that they hurried on, eager to be there. Then at last the fair was before them, and they left the road and moved over the grass towards the crowds and the colourful tents and marquees and sideshows. While a nearby barrel organ played 'Drink to Me Only with Thine Eyes' in a swinging, catchy rhythm, the two girls joined the throng of happy merrymakers, caught up in the thrill of it all before they had even drawn level with the first tent.

There were so many people there, among them several faces familiar from Flaxdown, and Abbie vainly cast her eyes about for Eddie who would surely be there with his friends. As usual, apart from the many poorly dressed farm labourers and their families who were there in abundance, there also were members of the gentry from various localities, the men looking uncomfortably hot in their suits and collars, the women dressed to kill in silks and ostrich feather boas, their sons running around in the constrictions of Eton suits and their daughters in embroidered white muslin. Vainly the adult gentry tried to enter into the spirit of the various amusements and pursuits, Abbie noticed, though rarely did they succeed in doing more than appear rather out of place, at the same time putting temporary dampeners on whatever proceedings they participated in.

Most strange of all the strangers there, though, were the gypsies, and the two young women eyed them warily, never allowing their glances to linger on the dark, swarthy faces with their black hair and flashing, arrogant eyes. And many were the children there that day who were told stories of babes being snatched by gypsies and never finding their way home again.

With their pennies, halfpennies and farthings in their purses, Abbie and Beatie wandered around, the air filled with the sounds of chatter and laughter, and the cries of the barkers – the pie sellers, the tinkers, the knife grinders, the cobblers. Briefly the girls hovered outside the tent of a fortune teller, but when the dark-haired gypsy woman pressed them to enter and learn their futures they took fright and, giggling, hurried on.

Moving from one sideshow to another, they watched the quoits-throwing, the horseshoe-tossing, the bowling for a pig. One man had tethered by a chain a dancing bear, a sad-looking creature with dusty, mangy-looking fur that took lumbering steps to the tune of a badly played fiddle. With Beatie crying, 'Oh, it's too sad,' they turned from the sight. The next stand was that of a tooth puller who advertised his service as 'painless'. The girls hovered on the sidelines for a few minutes, waiting vainly for some toothache sufferer to put the barker's claims to the test and then, disappointed, moved on again.

After some deliberation they took a ride on the swing boats, their skirts tucked up under their thighs while they pulled rhythmically on the tasselled cords and swung out over the fringe of the passing crowd. 'There's our Eddie!' cried Abbie as she was carried up into the air, and she called out, 'Eddie! Eddie!' but with the music and the general hubbub he did not hear and was soon lost to sight again in the crowd.

Afterwards, the girls stopped beside a coconut shy and watched a group of young blades hurling wooden balls at coconuts perched on the tops of poles. The young men, very much aware of the girls' passing interest, swaggered up to the line one after the other, showing off as they went through exaggerated motions of flexing their muscles and limbering up. They appeared to have more power than accuracy, however, and none was successful until the last, the fifth young man, who, with his fourth and final missile, sent a coconut toppling onto the turf. Amid cheers from his friends he was handed his coconut prize, and as he clasped it he looked at the girls and smiled. When they turned away, their steps were followed by hoots and laughter from the group of young men.

After standing by the merry-go-round to watch the dancing, prancing horses swing past, they entered a marquee where they bought cups of tea served with milk – an unaccustomed treat – and scones spread with butter and jam. Then, the refreshments finished, they rejoined the crowds once more. Outside one particular booth a stout man beat on a drum and called out, 'Walk up! Walk up! Come inside and see the tightrope dancers,' while along a narrow apron of a small stage behind him two young girls in spangled tights strutted and danced. To Abbie and Beatie the magic of the invitation was too powerful to resist and after a brief conference they stepped forward and handed over their pennies.

At first the interior of the tent was gloomy after the bright sun, but soon their eyes became accustomed to the subdued light. They sat on a bench among the other spectators, their boots planted in the sawdust while their eyes took in the wire that was stretched six or seven feet above the ground between two stout poles like the masts of a ship.

As the rest of the audience filed in, filling up the benches, the lamps were lit and the show began, and the two bespangled young dancers, now wearing silver crowns on their heads, skimmed nimbly up rope ladders onto small platforms encircling the poles. Then, to the accompaniment of the beat of a drum, and music from an accordion player, they tripped with ease along the tightrope, turning, bowing, bending backwards and forwards, their curls dancing, their pink-painted mouths fixed in smiles. And then, all too soon, it was over and the tightrope dancers were taking their final bows. Thinking their money well spent, Abbie and Beatie joined the other spectators and trooped back outside.

Emerging into the sunlight, they turned in the direction of some lively music and came to where a small group of musicians stood playing, one man a hurdy-gurdy, another a fiddle, and a young woman who played a tambourine. They were playing 'Love's Golden Dream' in a bright, rhythmic tempo. Several young people were dancing to the music, while some of the onlookers sang along with the instruments:

I hear tonight the old bells chime, their sweetest, softest
   strain;
They bring to me the olden time in visions once again.
Once more beside the meadow land, beside the flowing
   stream,
We wander, darling, hand in hand, and dream love's
   golden dream.

'Oh, come on,' Abbie said, 'let's join the dancing.'

Beatie demurred for a moment but then, unable to resist, took Abbie's hand and a second later they were dancing away, their feet skipping over the grass, their skirts swirling and bonnet strings flying.

As the dance came to an end a couple of minutes later, they saw on the edge of the crowd the familiar face of a red-haired young man, Manny, one of Eddie's friends. Abbie called out to him and he waited as they moved towards him.

'Your Eddie's over there,' he said, pointing, as they got to his side. 'He's tryin' 'is luck in the shooting gallery. Mebbe you should go and give 'im some encouragement.'

With Manny leading, the two girls moved through the crowd to where Eddie, his hat at a rakish angle, stood at the rifle range along with others of his friends. Nearby, watching, stood a young man holding a coconut, and Abbie realized that he was the one she had seen at the coconut shy, the one who had smiled at them.

As she and Beatie reached Eddie's side he took a final shot with the rifle. The shot went just wide of the target, however, thudding into the wooden board. As he straightened, shaking his head, he caught sight of his sisters. 'Come on!' he bellowed at them. 'Come and try your luck. You can't do worse than I 'ave.' He thrust the rifle towards Beatie, who shrank from it, laughing. 'Come on,' he repeated, 'you'll be wed soon and there might be a time when you needs to know 'ow to use one o' these on your old man!'

While there was general laughter from the group, one of Eddie's friends said, 'Seein' as your sister's to be married, Eddie, I'd 'ave thought you might try to win a little weddin' present for 'er.'

'What d'you think I been tryin' to do!' Eddie said. 'I can't afford to buy 'er nothin', that's for sure!' Then, bending closer to Beatie, he added, 'Though after what you done last night I ain't so sure you deserves anything.' Straightening, he gestured towards the shelves that displayed the various prizes to be won – cheap china mugs and plates, little ornaments of dogs and cats, dolls and gold-coloured lockets on chains. 'Matter of fact, our Beat, I was after gettin' you somethin' from that lot. But I'm afraid you'll 'ave to be content with the thought; I can't afford another try.'

'Why not?' Abbie asked. 'You've got more money in your pockets.'

'Oh, ah,' he answered. 'But I needs that for a drink. You wouldn't see a man die o' thirst, would you? A chap's sisters are all very well, but they mustn't be allowed to come between 'im and a drop of good ale.'

Beatie said, 'But I'm surprised at you, Eddie – missing

like that. You're so good when it comes to rabbits and rooks.'

'Yes,' Abbie added, 'not to mention the odd suicidal pheasant that throws itself in front of your sights.'

He laughed loudly at this. 'Ah, but that's with a good gun, ennit? – one with a straight barrel!' Contemptuously he set the rifle down, adding with a dark mutter, 'These damn things are fixed. Ain't nobody meant to win nothin' with one o' these.'

While the sideshow owner glared at the impugning of his rifles, Eddie turned to his companions again. 'Anyway, let's go and find the beer tent.' As he moved away he called over his shoulder, 'I'd ask you two along, but it ain't no place for tender young things like you.' Then, with a wave, he and his friends were disappearing into the crowd.

'So,' said a voice at Abbie's elbow, 'you're to be married, are you?'

Turning, she saw that the words, directed at Beatie, had come from the young man holding the coconut.

'Yes,' Beatie replied. 'On October the 14th to Mr Thomas Greening of Lullington. Do you know him?'

The young man shook his head. 'I'm afraid not. But there, I don't know Lullington.' He was in his mid-twenties, Abbie guessed. Dark-haired, he was smartly dressed in a crisp white shirt and brown corduroy suit with a pink in his buttonhole.

'You're not from round these parts, then,' Abbie said.

'No, my home's in Gravesend.'

'Gravesend? And where might that be?'

'In Kent. On the edge of the Thames.' He added, gesturing off, 'I've been visiting a friend in Frome for a few days.' He touched his cap. 'My name's Louis.' He pronounced it 'Lewis'. 'Louis Randolph.'

'I'm Beatrice Morris,' Beatie said, and this is my sister Abigail.'

The young man nodded. 'I'm very pleased to meet you.'

Abbie murmured a greeting then took a step away, preparing to move on. But the young man forestalled her.

'I was just about to try my own fortune with the rifles,' he said. 'Maybe if you stay around for a minute longer you'll bring me luck.' Then, without waiting for a response, he turned to the sideshow proprietor and handed him some coppers.

The girls – with Abbie showing a little impatience – stepped to one side while the young man set the coconut down at his feet and picked up one of the rifles. At the same time the sideshow holder, with a practised flourish, stuck a little paper target on to the board. 'Five shots,' he said as he stepped back. 'Four of 'em in the bull or in the inner ring gets you the pick of the prizes.'

Louis Randolph raised the rifle to his shoulder, took careful aim and fired. The lead pellet went *thwuck* into the upper left outer rim of the target. 'Darn it,' he said, frowning. 'It fires high and to the left.' He reloaded the gun and bent again. There came the sound of the gun's report and the second slug appeared just inside the ring that encircled the bull's-eye.

'He did it,' breathed Beatie, to which Abbie said drily, 'Yes, once. He's got to do it three more times yet.'

Hearing her words, the young man turned and looked at her over his shoulder. 'How right you are, Miss.' He reloaded, took aim again, and this time the pellet whacked right into the target's bull's-eye. 'Two to go,' he murmured and briefly raised his eyes to heaven in a silent little prayer.

He loaded the gun a fourth time, took careful aim and fired again. And another pellet appeared in the target's inner circle. He breathed a sigh of relief and reloaded the gun. About to take aim, he hesitated, turned to the girls and asked, 'Do you wish me luck?'

'Oh, yes, indeed,' Beatie replied.

He nodded his thanks then said to Abbie, 'And what about you, Miss Abigail? Do you wish me luck too?'

'I'm sure I do if it will help you,' she said.

He gave a little frown. 'No – no, say it.'

Abbie smiled. 'Good luck.'

He grinned at her, raised the rifle, took careful aim and fired.

'You won!' Abbie cried against Beatie's words of approval and congratulation. She could hardly believe the sight of the slugs embedded in the target – two in the inner circle and two right in the bull's-eye.

As Louis straightened and laid down the rifle, the sideshow owner said, 'Well, now you best choose your prize. What'll it be? The two vawses – made of genu-ine 'and-cut crystal? Or mebbe the pair of genu-ine Stafford-shire dogs, 'and-painted by artists?' He pointed to a shaving set with razor, brush and mug. 'Or mebbe this fine set, young sir . . .' He turned his attention to the spectators. 'There y'are, ladies and gentlemen – you can see as the prizes can be won all right. All this young gen'leman's got to do now is choose.'

Louis stood there for a moment, then turned to Beatie. 'Now don't take this amiss,' he said, 'but I'd like to give you a wedding present.'

'Oh, no!' she protested. 'I can't let you do that.'

'Please,' he said. 'And if you won't choose then I'll have to choose something for you – and I know I'd go and pick the wrong thing.'

'No,' Beatie said, 'you must choose something for yourself – or for your mother.'

'I haven't got a mother. Nor a sister – nor a young lady for that matter.' He grinned. 'Come on, what'll it be?'

'Go on,' Abbie urged Beatie, giving her a little nudge, 'choose.'

Beatie was almost hopping with happiness and excitement. 'But why?' she asked. 'Why should you do this for me?'

'Because I want to. Just say what it'll be.'

After a moment's hesitation Beatie pointed to one of the shelves. 'Oh – the teaset,' she said, almost breathless. 'Oh, yes! Yes! The pretty teaset with the pink roses.'

The china teaset and its box were brought forward and held aloft by the man to allow the crowd to see what a marvellous prize had been won for so little effort and outlay. There were six each of the cups, saucers and plates, a teapot, a little milk pitcher and a sugar basin. While Beatie ohed and ahed over it the man wrapped the pieces in newspaper, placed them in the box and tied the box with string. A moment later it was being placed in Beatie's eager hands. 'Now don't drop it,' the man said.

'Oh, no fear,' she said, clutching the box to her. 'I'd never do that.'

Louis picked up his coconut from the grass and the three moved away from the rifle booth. As they did so Abbie turned to Louis and asked whether he had come to the fair on his own.

'No,' he replied, 'I came with my friends.'

'They'll be wondering where you are. They'll think you've been stolen by the gypsies.'

He chuckled. 'Oh, I don't think they'll be fretting about that.' He pointed over to the marquee that the girls had visited earlier. 'Can I offer you some refreshment? Some tea or some coffee or lemonade?'

Feeling that it would be churlish to refuse his offer after

such generosity, Abbie and Beatie accepted, and accompanied him to the marquee. There they drank more tea and ate some little cakes with icing sugar on top. As they emerged into the sunlight some minutes later, Louis gave a wave to someone in the milling crowd, then said to the girls, 'Will you excuse me for a minute? My friends are there and I just want to have a quick word with them.'

Leaving Abbie and Beatie, he went over to where his friends stood at the entrance to a marquee. Moments later the girls heard a voice yelling out not far behind them: 'There you are, our Beat!' and turning, they saw Eddie coming towards them.

Snatching at Beatie's hand, Eddie said boisterously, 'Here – you're comin' with me!'

Beatie laughed. 'Where to?'

'I'm gunna give you a special treat. Though I dunno why – after that business with the 'olly.' He pulled her towards him. 'I'm takin' you on the merry-go-round and then on the swing boats.'

'And you're paying?'

'What? Of course I'm payin'.' He gave a rueful shake of his head. 'Seein' as I didn't 'ave no damn luck with that bent rifle.'

'What about me?' Abbie said. 'Do I get to ride on the merry-go-round too?'

'Eh? Bugger that!' Eddie laughed. 'You ain't gettin' married! No, and I ain't got money to waste, neither!' He turned back to Beatie. 'Come on, make the most of the offer. It ain't gunna last for ever.'

Beatie thrust the cardboard box into Abbie's hands. 'Look after my teaset, will you? And make sure you don't break it.'

'Don't worry,' Abbie said. Then as Eddie pulled Beatie behind him into the throng, she called after them, 'I'll wait for you here, by the tea tent.'

As Louis came back to her side a moment later she said to him, 'Beatie's gone off with our brother, Eddie. He's going to take her for a ride on the merry-go-round.'

Louis smiled. 'Would you like to ride on the merry-go-round too?'

'Me? Oh, no – no, thank you.'

'I'll happily take you.'

'No, really, thank you all the same – though it's very kind of you to offer.'

'The offer's not made out of kindness.' He was looking at her very steadily. 'Perhaps you'd like some more tea or something?'

'Oh, no, I couldn't drink another thing. What I'd really like is to sit down for a minute. My feet are near to dropping off.'

'Come on, then.' His hand touched her elbow. 'Let's find a little peace and quiet and a spot to rest for a minute.'

'I don't know,' she said, 'I should wait here for Beatie.' She was very much aware of his touch.

'She won't be back for a while yet. I could do with a rest too.'

Making no further protest, she allowed him to lead her away, passing between the outer stalls and caravans and tents to where the field was free of sojourners and the grass was still relatively fresh and untrodden.

'There we are, look.' Louis pointed towards the edge of the field, where willows hung over a stream. There they walked side by side, eventually coming to a stop where a fallen tree lay beside the running water. Louis put down the coconut, took off his jacket and laid it on the grass. 'There you are.'

After a moment Abbie sat and placed the boxed teaset beside her feet. 'That's better. I need a rest before we start back to Flaxdown.'

Louis sat down beside her, his back against the tree trunk. 'I'll walk back home with you and your sister if you like,' he said.

'To Flaxdown? Oh, no, thank you. That's very kind of you, but we'll be all right.'

'Like my offer just now,' he said, smiling, 'it's not made out of kindness.' He paused, observing her closely. 'I'd like to. See you home, I mean.'

'No, it's too far. You'd have a three-mile walk to Flaxdown and then another three to Frome.'

'That's all right,' he said with a shrug. 'I'm twenty-four, not eighty-four.'

Abbie chuckled. 'Yes, but even so.' Turning her head, she saw that over in the fairground two or three lights had come on. The day was dying. She gave a sigh. 'I love coming to the fair. It's just a shame it all has to end. Tomorrow everyone'll be hard at work again.'

'And that includes you, does it?'

'Yes. Though I just work at home. I look after my father and brother. What about you? What do you do for a living?'

'I'm still studying. At Guy's.'

'Guy's? What is Guy's?'

'It's one of England's top medical schools.'

'You're going to become a doctor. That's wonderful.'

'It's what I've always wanted to do.'

'Where is Guy's? In London, I suppose.'

'Yes.'

'My mother came from London.'

He gave a little nod. 'That accounts for it, then. Your accent.'

'What about my accent?' She knew, though, what he meant.

'Well – it's not quite like that of the other local people.

Though it's not like your sister's either. Her accent is not quite like yours.'

Abbie's light laugh sounded slightly self-conscious. 'Perhaps it doesn't need to be.'

'What do you mean?'

'Well –' She gave a little shrug. 'I have . . . worked at it, as you might say. I felt I had to – if I wanted to be a schoolteacher.'

'A schoolteacher? Is that what you're going to be?'

'That's what I was hoping.' She shrugged, bent and pulled a few blades of grass from beside her foot. 'But it's not going to happen now – at least not in the way I thought it might. Still, I tell myself, there's more to the world than Flaxdown.'

'Indeed there is.'

She saw that he was studying her, smiling. 'What is it?' she said.

'I was thinking of you – smoothing off the rough edges.'

'What?'

'Working on your accent.'

'Oh – that.'

'It shows a certain – dedication. Determination.'

Was he laughing at her? she wondered. But no, there was nothing negative in his eyes. Nevertheless there was a slight note of defensiveness in her tone as she said, 'Perhaps one needs to have a certain determination in life.'

'Oh, one does indeed,' he said.

She nodded. 'Well, otherwise you – well, you'd never get what you were after, would you?'

'No, I suppose not.' He paused, smiled. 'How did you do it? Work on your accent.'

'I suppose I just – just copied my mother. As I said, she

came from London. No one in the village spoke as she did.'

'And is your mother proud of you? I'm sure she must be.'

'She – she's not with us any more.' Then, quickly, lest he should misunderstand, she added, 'She went away. Back to London. She left us.'

'Oh – I'm so sorry to hear that.'

'It was a long time ago.'

A silence fell and, attempting to dispel the little shadow, she said with smile, 'So – now you know; I actually set out to change my way of speaking. I had to. I didn't think I'd stand a chance otherwise.' She shook her head. 'Mind you – the ribbing I got from my brother Eddie – I don't mind telling you, at times it was hard to take.'

He chuckled. 'Is that typical of him?'

'Oh, yes. Though I come off lightly next to my sister.'

'Beatrice?'

'Yes.' She laughed. 'With her he's merciless at times.'

She became aware of music drifting across the grass. 'Love's Golden Dream' was playing again. More lights had come on. Louis looked over towards the fairground. 'I like your sister. She seems a very fine young woman.'

'She is.'

'And very pretty.'

'I think so.'

'So must anybody. Her intended – he must feel he's a very fortunate chap.'

'Well, he ought to. But there, I'm biased. One thing I know – she'll make a very good wife.'

'And what about you?'

'Me?'

'D'you think you'll make a good wife?'

She laughed. 'Beatie's the one getting wed, not me.'

'But you will – one day.'

She shrugged. 'Maybe.'

'No doubt of it. A girl looking like you.'

'Oh . . .' Feeling herself blushing at his words she dismissed his compliment with a little wave of her hand.

'I mean it,' he said. 'You're one of the prettiest and grandest girls I ever met.'

She neither knew what to say, nor how to react. Self-consciously she touched at her bonnet, untied the strings and retied them. He was gazing at her, his expression half amused, discomfiting. One square, tanned hand was raised to his mouth, forefinger touching at his full lower lip. His other hand rested in the grass, not far from her own. She thought how strong his hands looked, and yet sensitive; they were just the kind of hands a doctor should have. She felt suddenly very much aware of his nearness. The feeling made her a little fearful, while some small voice inside her head said that she should get up now and make her way back to the safety of the fairground crowd.

'I'd like to see you again,' he said. 'Would that be possible?'

'With you in London and me in Flaxdown?'

'There are ways. What do you think?'

She wanted to say yes, but she did not. Instead, she looked about her and murmured, without conviction, 'If I don't go soon Beatie'll think I've been kidnapped.'

'By the gypsies?' He smiled, his teeth very white in the slowly fading light.

'I shouldn't wonder. No, really, I must go. Eddie'll be mad if he has to wait with Beatie when he could be off with his friends.'

'Oh – wait just another minute or two. Give them a chance to finish their ride on the merry-go-round.'

Looking back over her shoulder she saw that more and

more lights were coming on, twinkling more brightly by the second as the sun sank lower. Against the rippling of the brook the sound of the hurdy-gurdy came clear and sweet in the evening air. She was aware of Louis's hand, so close to her own in the grass. And then his hand moved towards hers and she felt his fingertips gently brush the side of her thumb. The touch, lasting no more than a split second, made her catch her breath. She looked down at their two hands, while her heart pounded in her breast to a degree that she could never recall happening before. As she continued to look down she saw his hand rise and close gently over her own. She flinched and for a moment began to draw her hand away, but his fingers closed around it and she ceased to move. Keeping her eyes lowered, she gazed at their two hands entwined.

'Abbie . . .?'

She raised her eyes. He was gazing at her with a burning intensity, his lips slightly parted.

'I'm so glad I came to the fair today,' he said. 'And I would so like to see you again. Tell me I can.'

Unable to trust herself to speak, she said nothing.

'Tell me I can,' he repeated.

She gave a little nod, then saw his mouth turn up at the corners in a brief smile and then become grave again. He leaned towards her, until his face was only an inch from her own and she could feel his breath. Involuntarily she closed her eyes and the next moment she felt his mouth upon hers.

The kiss was brief, his lips merely touching hers before he drew back slightly. Opening her eyes she looked into his face once more. *What's happening to me*? she asked herself. She had met various young men over recent years, young men from the village and beyond, young men with whom she had joked and laughed and flirted. And it had meant nothing. This feeling, though, was different; this was like nothing else she had ever experienced.

His hands came up now and touched her upper arms, turning her to him. He drew her towards him and she did not resist, nor did she when he kissed her again, this time a longer kiss. She had never known such a sensation – the feeling of being held this way, of his lips upon her own. And dimly there came to her also a feeling of surprise, not only at the happening, but at her lack of will to resist.

The kiss ended, and he released her, but only to untie the strings of her bonnet. When he had done so he took it off and put it down beside her. Then his hands were there once more, upon her hair, her cheek, her shoulders. He drew her to him again and once more pressed his lips on hers. And she gave herself up to him, gave herself up to the moment, melting into his touch.

Held in his arms, she felt his kisses on her forehead, her cheek, her chin. And then he kissed her mouth again, and her lips parted and she felt the warmth of his tongue and moved her own tongue against it, so sweet, so sweet. He spoke her name between his kisses and she responded, speaking his name in a little gasping murmur and a little sob of happiness. When his hand slowly brushed the swell of her breast she could make no protest, no attempt to draw away. Held in his arms, the night had become a swirl of twinkling lights, lilting music and the feel of his closeness, his lips upon her lips, his hand upon her breast. And she *wanted* his hands upon her, *wanted* to feel the touch of him; wanted the moments never to end.

Without being aware of how she got there, she was lying on the grass, on her back, and Louis was bending over her, his soft kisses touching her face. She became aware suddenly that he was undoing the buttons on the bodice of her dress. The urgent feeling went through her head that she must stop him, but her half-hearted words of protest died on her lips, cut off by his kiss, and she felt his hand touch her naked flesh and move over the swell of her breast. He drew his head back and groaned, and she opened her eyes and saw that his own eyes were closed tight. Then he opened them again and looked deeply, longingly into hers. 'Oh, Abbie, Abbie, Abbie . . .' The sound of her name on his tongue was the sweetest sound, and she lifted her face to meet his lips as he bent to kiss her again.

After the kiss he gave a deep sigh, then lowered his head and pressed his lips to her breast. As she felt his wet mouth cover her nipple she gave a little cry and put a hand to the back of his head, caressing him, while at the same time her lips parted in ecstasy at his touch. 'Oh, Abbie . . . ' he murmured, and in return she breathed, 'Yes, yes,' each word a little sobbing intake of breath, knowing that she had never before experienced such complete joy and ecstasy.

Suddenly there came the sounds of small explosions. Momentarily startled, wrenched abruptly back to the present, she turned her head towards the fairground and saw fireworks bursting above it, erupting into coloured showers of cascading sparks. The sight and the sounds came like a cold, drenching wave, and she suddenly saw herself as she was, lying on the grass, her hand on the back of Louis's head, his mouth upon her breast.

'No . . . no.'

This was not right. This was not the way. Now she used her hand to push his head from her, feeling the cold air touch her breast as his warm mouth released her. 'Please, no . . .'

He straightened, and at the same time she sat up. She could see herself, shockingly, as she must appear, sitting there in the grass with the stranger, her clothes rumpled, her hair awry, her skin damp with their combined sweat.

'Are you all right?' he asked.

She did not even register the sound of his voice, much less his tone of concern. She was moving, getting to her feet. 'I must go,' she said. How could she have done this? How could she? Turning from him, ashamed, embarrassed, she buttoned her bodice and straightened her skirts. Then, her hands trembling, she smoothed her hair and put on her bonnet. Across the grass the lights of the fair were brighter than ever in the gathering gloom. So much time had gone by. How long had she been there?

'Abbie . . .?'

She heard his voice, but did not turn to him. She glanced down one last time to check her appearance and then began to move away.

'Abbie – Abbie, wait – please.' Turning, drawn by the urgency in his tone she saw him moving towards her with Beatie's teaset in his hands. Quickly she took the box from him. Quite unable now to look him in the eye, she said with a hollow little laugh, 'Good heavens – Beatie would never forgive me if I left it behind.'

She turned and hurried on, and he walked beside her as she hurried across the turf. As they drew nearer to the lights of the fair she stopped and turned to him.

'Please, don't come any further.'

He frowned. 'Why not?'

'No, please. Please, don't.'

He nodded. 'All right. But shall I see you again?'

The passion that had held her such a short time ago might never have been. Now she was aware only of reality. Now she felt only guilt. 'Do you really want to?' Still she could not meet his gaze.

'Do you need to ask?'

She said nothing.

'Where in Flaxdown do you live?' he asked.

'Green Lane.' She moved from one foot to the other. 'I

must go. Eddie'll be going crazy.' With her words she turned and walked away.

As she drew near the refreshment marquee she could see Beatie standing by the entrance. A moment later Beatie caught sight of her and moved forward to meet her. 'Eddie got fed up with waiting,' Beatie said. 'He's gone off to the Woolpack with his friends. Where have you been all this time? I've been here for ages.'

'I'm sorry,' Abbie said, and then, forcing out the lie, 'I – I was looking for you.'

'Looking for me? You said you'd wait for me here.'

'Oh – did I? I'm sorry.'

Beatie took the teaset from Abbie and hiked it securely under her arm. 'Anyway, now you're here we'd better start back home.'

She linked her free arm in Abbie's, and together they turned and set off in the direction of the road. The light was dying swiftly now, the lanterns glowing ever more brightly in the gloom. Louis was nowhere in sight.

'Is anything the matter?' Beatie's voice broke into Abbie's thoughts.

'What?' Abbie looked at her sister.

'You look a bit flummoxed about something. Are you all right?'

Abbie shook her head. 'No, I'm not flummoxed.' She gave a little laugh. 'You've got too much imagination.'

They were just nearing the road when a figure came towards them out of the shadows. It was Louis.

'Mr Randolph, hello,' Beatie said. 'We're just leaving.'

'Yes,' he said, 'and I'm going to see you safely home.'

'Really?' It was clear that Beatie was not averse to the notion. Out of politeness, though, she protested. 'Oh, but it's so far out of your way.'

'It's no trouble. And I'd like to.'

Abbie still could not meet his eyes. What did he think

of her, after she had permitted such liberties so soon after their meeting? 'Thank you,' she said, 'but it's not necessary. It won't take us long to skip across the fields.'

'Maybe not, but I'd feel better about it if you'd let me come with you.'

'No, no. We shall be all right, shan't we, Beatie?' Then before Beatie could answer, she added, 'No, really, we couldn't hear of it. All that way to Flaxdown and then another three miles on to Frome.' She had put a little firmness into her voice now, trying to distance herself from him and the memory of what had taken place.

'It's not so far,' he said.

'What about your friends?' Beatie asked, '– won't they be waiting for you?'

'I told them I'd be making my own way back.' He looked from one to the other, his glance lingering on Abbie's averted eyes. 'Well?'

'Thank you, really,' Abbie said, forcing herself to look at him, 'but we'll be fine.' She linked an arm through Beatie's, preparing to move on.

'Well – all right, then.' He nodded. 'In that case I'll say goodnight.'

'Goodnight,' Beatie said, then added, 'And thank you so much for my wedding present.'

'It was my pleasure. May it bring you joy.'

'Oh, it will. I shall treasure it always.' Briefly smiling, she looked down at the box holding the teaset, then, looking up again, asked, 'What about *your* prize?'

'My prize?'

'You won a coconut, didn't you?'

He clapped a hand to his forehead. 'Oh, good Lord – I've lost it.'

Beatie laughed. 'How could you lose a coconut?'

He shrugged, spread his hands. 'I – I must have put it down somewhere – and forgotten it.' As he finished speaking he flicked a glance at Abbie and she lowered her eyes and turned away. In her mind's eye she could see him beside the stream, dropping the coconut into the grass . . .

'Let me wish,' he was saying now to Beatie, 'that you find all the happiness you want in your marriage.'

'Thank you. Thank you.'

He turned back to Abbie. 'And you, Miss Abigail – I was wondering – I'm thinking of coming round Flax-down way in the near future . . .'

Beatie said quickly, a little mischievously, 'Then you must come to number four Green Lane.' She flicked a smiling glance at her sister. 'I'm sure Abbie'd be only too glad to give you a cup of tea.'

'Is that so?' he said to Abbie.

Abbie shrugged. Was he sincere? She didn't know what to think. 'Well,' she said, her smile only just there, 'I've never been known to refuse anyone who's in need.'

'Oh, I'd be in need right enough.'

Briefly searching his face for some hidden meaning to his words, she could read nothing there. She pressed Beatie's arm. 'Beatie we must go.'

'Well,' Louis said, '– goodnight again.'

'Goodnight,' said Abbie.

'Goodnight,' said Beatie. 'And thank you again.'

They turned from him, stepped onto the road and set their feet in the direction of Flaxdown. Reaching a bend in the road they turned and saw the dark shape of him standing against the lights of the fair, saw him lift his hat to them in salute. Moments later and yards further on and he was gone from their sight.

'Well,' Beatie said, 'you certainly made a hit there. You've got an admirer, sure enough. Anybody could see that. But why wouldn't you let him see us home? He wanted to.'

Abbie did not answer.

'Anyway,' Beatie said, 'you've got an admirer, whatever you say.' She smiled. 'Yes, you've got an admirer, and I've got the most beautiful teaset in the world.'

Chapter Eight

'We shouldn't have stayed so long,' Beatie said, switching the box holding her teaset from one arm to the other.

'It was my fault,' Abbie said. 'But with so much happening you don't realize how fast the time's going by.'

The girls had left the road and were making their way along a footpath across a field. The remaining light from the sinking sun had all but gone now, while the clouded moon was rising in the sky.

Reaching the far side of the field, they crossed over the stile and continued on across another meadow. Beyond this their path led them beside a wood, deep in shadow. As they walked, Beatie reached out and took Abbie's hand. 'We should have kept to the roads,' she said. 'I'd feel a lot safer.'

'Don't worry,' Abbie said. 'This way is much quicker and it won't be long before we're home.'

They were still walking with the dark bank of the woods on their left when they heard the voices.

Abbie came to a stop, fingers pressing into Beatie's hand. Beatie stopped beside her. 'Listen,' Abbie murmured.

They stood side by side on the footpath, listening. At first they heard nothing, but then came the brief sound of a voice, a man's voice, whispering, startlingly close at hand. As one, the heads of the two girls moved in the direction of the noise. Silence again. No sound at all but the creaking of the branches of the trees and the distant hoot of an owl.

Abbie leaned her head closer to Beatie's. 'It could be our Eddie,' she whispered, 'trying to scare us.' Beatie said nothing. The girls remained standing there for some moments longer, then turned and began to move on, hastening their steps. Almost immediately they heard from their left the sounds of something moving through the wood, as if keeping pace with them. Their steps quickened even more.

All of a sudden, with a violent rustling of the foliage just ahead, a figure sprang out from the darkness of the trees and stood before them. Giving little cries of fright, the girls came to an abrupt halt.

The light of the moon shone behind the form of a tall man so that he stood in silhouette, a dark, unfamiliar shape. Abbie and Beatie moved closer to one another. As they did so they heard further sounds from the trees on their left and saw another shape detach itself from the dark mass and move to stand near the first. Both men wore hats pulled low on their foreheads.

For some seconds no words were spoken, then Abbie said, her voice seeming loud in the quiet of the night: 'What do you want?'

The first of the two men, the taller, took a step forward. 'We're not going to 'urt you,' he said. His words were slurred, as if from drinking.

Although he had moved in closer, Abbie still could not see his face in the darkness, though she was sure she had never met him before. 'What do you want?' she asked again, taking a small step back.

'Why're you in such a hurry,' the shorter man said. 'We only want to pass the time of day. We don't mean you no 'arm.' Like that of his companion, his voice gave evidence of his having been drinking.

'Well,' Abbie said nervously, 'I'm afraid we can't stop. It's late and we've got to get home.'

She gripped Beatie's hand more tightly. Damp with sweat, it trembled in her own. Abbie did not know what to do – to remain and try to get out of the situation with diplomacy, or make a run for it – though the latter course, she knew, would have little chance of success.

'Did you 'ave a good time at the fair?' asked the shorter man.

The girls remained silent.

'We saw you there,' he said. 'We saw you dancing.'

'Yes,' said the taller man, and then sang quietly, his voice soft and chilling in the stillness, 'We wander, darling, hand in hand, and dream love's golden dream.' His voice cracked on the high note and he gave a drunken little laugh at his inadequacy.

'Ah, it's a very nice little song, that,' his companion said and added, 'Yes, you looked as if you were 'aving a really nice time. Were you?'

Abbie nodded, not speaking. Her heart was thudding against her ribs. Desperately she looked about her. If only someone else would come by, on their way home from the fair. There was no one.

'What's the matter?' asked the shorter man. 'Can't you talk? Cat got your tongue, has he?'

'Please.' Abbie said, her voice shaking, 'Let us go. Don't hurt us. Let us go.'

'I told you we don't mean you no 'arm.'

'Do you want money?' Abbie said. 'We've only got a little. A few pence, that's all.'

He shook his head. 'We don't want your money. We're only asking you to be sociable. We only want a bit of fun.'

'That's right,' said the other. 'Just a bit of fun, that's all.'

'What's that you've got there?' the shorter man asked, gesturing to the package beneath Beatie's arm.

When she did not answer he stepped forward and moved to take it from her. With a little cry, she swung away from him, dodging his clutching hands and at the same time swinging out her free hand to ward him off. Her flapping hand accidentally caught him on the mouth. Violently knocking her hand aside, he said angrily, 'Don't you try to play rough with me,' and reached out and snatched the box from her grasp. In seconds he had it open and was holding up one of the little rose-patterned cups, squinting at it in the gloom. 'Well, now, ain't that pretty.' He held the cup out for his companion to see. 'Look at that. Really pretty, that is.' He tossed the cup into the air, and as it fell he swung at it with his foot, shattering it with the toe of his boot. Beatie turned her head, burying her face against Abbie's neck. The man watched her reaction, then drew back his arm and hurled the box as hard as he could against the bank of trees beside them. It struck the trunk of a tree with a shattering sound. He laughed again, adding in a tone of mock distress, 'Oh, my, it sounds as if something's broke. What a shame.' He stepped towards Beatie. 'Don't you fret about some bit of china,' he said. 'I've got something here that you're going to like a lot more.' As he spoke he pressed a hand to his crutch. Then with his other hand he reached out and snatched at her arm.

With a scream, Beatie shrank away, while at the same time Abbie stepped forward to try to ward him off. 'Leave her alone!' she cried. 'Leave her alone!'

'Shut it. Just shut up.' The shorter man abruptly turned his attention to her now and, stepping forward, drew back his arm and swung. The back of his hand connected with her jaw, the blow sending her staggering backwards. Her head spun, pinpoints of light danced before her eyes, and she could taste her blood in her mouth. Then, while she fought to regain her balance, the man was upon her.

As she struggled in his grasp she was aware that Beatie, beside her, was being held by the taller man and was fighting desperately to get away. The next moment, in a flurry of billowing skirts, and whimpering like a creature in pain, Beatie had somehow wrenched herself from her captor's hold and was turning, dashing back along the path.

'Run, Beatie, run!' Abbie screamed. 'Run! Run!' And then a hand came down on her mouth, mashing her lips against her teeth and cutting off her cries. The next moment she was falling, the man falling with her. As she fought, his weight on top of her, she heard from a distance a muffled shout from the other man, followed by Beatie's high-pitched squeal of terror.

Against Abbie's cries of fear, desperation and protest came the rough, muttered words of her attacker as he struggled to hold her down. He lay full length on top of her. He was not a lot taller than she and it took much of his strength to keep her writhing, pitching form pinned beneath him. He succeeded, though, no matter how she tried to push him off. Smelling his beer- and gin-heavy breath as he lowered his face to hers, she desperately wrenched her head aside in an effort to avoid his mouth, but his hands came up and gripped the sides of her head, holding her still.

'What are you putting up such a struggle for?' he said grimly. 'All I want is what you give that other fellow at the fair.'

Hearing his words, she realized that she and Louis had been observed as they had lain together in the grass.

'You weren't playing hard to get with him,' the man said. 'Why should you be so difficult now? I doubt it's anything new to you or your friend.'

And then his mouth was on hers, wet with his saliva, his tongue probing against her tightly-clamped lips. At

111

the same time one of his hands left her head and wrenched at her skirts, pulling them up around her thighs.

Unable to hold her breath any longer, she opened her lips to gasp for air and at once his tongue was inside her mouth. She bit down, and he cried out in pain, and she tasted his warm blood with her own. The man pulled back from her, clapping a hand to his mouth and in the same moment she wrenched her body to one side so that he was momentarily off-balance. It was enough. Using all her strength, she forced herself upwards and, with a heave of all the weight of her body, toppled him into the grass. A moment later she had struggled to her feet and was dashing away.

'You bitch,' he cried after her as she fled. 'You bitch, I'll kill you for this.'

Holding up her skirts, she ran as fast as she could, heading in no particular direction, only desperate to escape from her pursuer, yet knowing that she could not get far. After running along the path for a short distance she suddenly swerved, dashing off into the dark of the wood. As she did so she was aware that the man had taken up the chase and was not far behind.

With the sharp thorns of brambles tearing at her skirt, and low, overhanging branches and twigs scratching her face and snagging at her bonnet, she dashed on, her breath coming in gasps of exertion and terror. The man was now so close that she could hear his muttered oaths as the foliage scraped at his flesh.

All at once she was faced by a great bank of bramble. She hesitated, swung away to her right, and in the next moment found her wrist caught roughly in the man's grasp. Pulled up short, she was violently yanked around and flung back so that she staggered against the slender trunk of a tree. Her arm free of his grip, she half sank to her knees, the breath knocked out of her body.

As she recovered her breath she slowly drew herself straight again, the tree bole at her back. There was no way out for her; with the tree and the brambles behind her and the man's dark form before her, all routes of escape were blocked.

They stood facing one another. It was so dark beneath the trees that she could make out little more than the general shape of him. He was standing a few yards from her, one hand to his mouth, his chest and shoulders heaving as he regained his breath. He took a step towards her and she screamed.

He came to a stop. 'Go on,' he muttered, 'scream as much as you like. Nobody's gunna 'ear you.'

'Please,' she gasped. 'Please – don't hurt me.'

'Hurt you?' he said. 'After what you did I should fucking kill you.' Raising his hands, he lunged forward.

As he moved over the short distance of ground between them, she braced herself, her left hand clutching at the tree's rough bark. At the same time her right hand lifted her skirt, and she drew back her foot and swung, kicking up and out with all the strength she could muster, a strength charged with all the fear within her. Her foot connected with him as he threw himself towards her, arms outstretched, the toe of her boot thudding upwards into his scrotum with such force that she felt a jarring in her ankle. He gave a cry of agony and, clutching at his groin, fell heavily at her feet. While he lay gasping and writhing on the earth she pushed herself away from the tree, ran past him and dashed on among the trees.

Eventually emerging on the other side of the wood, she came to a stop and crouched, gasping for breath, a stitch tearing at her side, her head hanging down. After remaining there for a few minutes she staggered to her feet and ran on again, keeping the edge of the wood on her left.

When she could run no further she re-entered the trees and scrambled down into a deep hollow overgrown with brambles. There in the dank, earthy-smelling dell, with the brambles forming a roof above her head, she crouched, bent over, chest heaving, her gasping breaths so loud that she was terrified the sound would give her away.

Slowly, as the minutes passed, her breathing grew calmer. In her mouth she could still taste the blood from the blow she had received, while her arms and hands had been cut and scratched from her dash through the trees. At some point she had lost her bonnet. Fingers pressed into the soft, leafy mould that lined the dell, she listened for voices, for any sound of her pursuer. There was nothing; nothing but the cries of nightbirds and the rustlings of foxes and other creatures that moved past in their forays for food. All she could do was wait.

Beatie had not managed to get far.

On breaking from the taller man she had run a wild, zigzagging course along beside the wood, crying in terror, her pursuer only yards behind her and swiftly gaining. Veering off to the left, she headed towards a little thicket that grew in the middle of the field. The man caught up with her as she reached its edge. Throwing himself forward, he caught her skirt just below her waist and hurled her to the ground. She fell heavily, her head striking the turf, momentarily stunning her and knocking the breath out of her body. As she lay there the man was upon her.

When she became aware of his feverish hands clutching at her she screamed, but then a clenched fist struck her violently in the face, cutting off her cry and making her head spin. Held down by his weight, she felt her wrists caught, yanked up over her head and then held there by one strong hand. Next moment his other hand was pulling her dress and petticoat up around her waist, and she could feel the night air on her stockinged legs. She felt a warm wetness around the top of her thighs, and dully the realization came into her mind that she was urinating. The awareness was only fleeting. The next moment she felt fingers snatching at the waist of her drawers and pulling them down, and heard them tear as they were wrenched over her boots. Moments later the cotton fabric was at her face, being forced into her mouth, cutting off her cries.

It couldn't be happening, the thought flashed through her mind; it was all a nightmare. But it was all too real. Only too real the hands beneath her knees, lifting them, parting them; too real the rough hands on her vagina, clutching, probing; too real the feel and the weight of the body between her legs, the man's hot member pushing against her, entering her, tearing, thrusting into her.

Although the man's passions had been inflamed by his lust and the alcohol he had consumed, the latter had affected his potency and it took a long time before he finished, heaving into her with long, violent thrusts in the spasms of his orgasm. He withdrew, straightened, knelt there for a moment and then got up. As he did so, his companion appeared, unfastening his belt and trousers. Quickly he lowered himself before the girl and entered her. He lay on her, pushing forcefully and rhythmically into her body, grunting with his exertions. Then, turning his head to his friend he complained, 'She don't put anything into it.' Pausing in his heaving, he reached out and snatched the gag from her mouth. 'How're you liking it?' he said. 'Aren't you enjoying it?' As he spoke he slammed into her with such violence that her body moved on the grass. 'Good?' he said. 'Is it good?'

The girl did not answer. The man slapped her on the cheek, but still she made no response. 'Useless bitch,' he muttered, 'she's out cold.'

From the distance on the night air there came to Abbie's ears the striking of the church clock in Old Ford as it sounded the hour of ten. How long had she been there? It must have been well over an hour. She did not know where she was in relation to the men, though she knew she had run a considerable distance. And where, she wondered, was her pursuer? Was he still in the woods, searching for her? Lowering her head, she pressed deeper into the damp shelter of the dell.

When the church clock struck eleven she was still crouching there, still having heard no further sound of the men. Some minutes after the last stroke had faded she drew her courage together, slowly pulled herself up and gingerly raised her head above the rim of the dell.

The light of the moon was very bright now and she could see clearly. Facing in one direction, she found herself looking into the dense darkness of the wood. Turning the opposite way she looked through the straggling trees and shrubs of the wood's edge across a meadow. In the distance twinkled lights in the windows of a small group of cottages. There was no sign of the men.

She remained there for several minutes more, peering this way and that in the moonlight, and then, doing her best to avoid the thorns of the brambles, pulled herself out of the dell and onto the grass. On shaky legs she stood up, stiff in her joints from crouching for so long, and warily looked about her again. She had to find Beatie. Entering the trees, she moved slowly, carefully, heading

116

for the far side, all the while keeping alert for any sound or sign of the men. Eventually, after some time, she emerged from the darkness of the wood to face the meadow, some hundred yards or so from the point at which she and Beatie had met the strangers.

There was no one in sight. Stepping out onto the footpath, she turned full circle, gazing about her. No one. After a moment she set off along the path.

Further along she saw something shining in the grass, and on drawing closer realized that it was one of the pieces of the broken teacup. Over to her right under a tree lay the cardboard box and the shattered remains of the rest of the teaset. She moved on.

Reaching the stile at the edge of the field, she turned and started off back over the grass, all the while looking for some sign of Beatie's presence. She was afraid to call out for fear of alerting the men. Eventually, nearing the end of her search of the meadow, she approached, towards the far side, the little thicket. As she drew nearer to it she heard the chimes of midnight on the night breeze. Reaching the thicket, she hesitantly entered the darkness of its shadows and began to move among the trees. As she stopped to unhitch her skirt from the thorns of a bramble she heard a sound. She froze, listening. It came again, from the far side of the thicket, a sound like a little moan, the sound of a child, lost. Beatie's voice.

Palms damp, heart thumping in her breast, she spun, lurching away in the direction of the cry.

Beatie was sitting on the ground at the edge of the trees, her hands in her lap. As Abbie burst through the screen of trees and ran towards her, Beatie turned her head and looked around at her.

'Oh, Beatie – Beatie.' Kneeling beside her, Abbie gathered her sister into her arms. 'Beatie – oh, Beatie . . .'

Beatie remained silent in Abbie's embrace. After a few

moments Abbie drew back a little and looked at her through the distorting film of her tears. In the growing brightness of the moonlight she saw that her bonnet hung loose and that her dress had been ripped at the shoulder so that her right breast was visible. Beatie seemed unaware of her nakedness. Her dress had also been torn at the waist, the skirt partly ripped from the bodice, while the hem of the skirt, hitched up beneath her buttock on one side, revealed that her stockings were torn and her legs smeared with what appeared to be blood. Raising her eyes again to Beatie's face, Abbie saw that her hair was tangled and matted, with twigs and leaves caught in it. There was a dark bruise on her cheek, her mouth and nose looked swollen and there was blood on her lower lip and around her nostrils.

'Oh, Beatie – oh, my love . . .' Tears welled in Abbie's eyes, spilled over and ran down her cheeks.

Beatie remained silent, her vacant eyes looking unfocusingly past Abbie across the moonlit fields. Then, her voice small, distant, a shade touched with shame, she said, 'I wet myself, Abbie. How awful. I couldn't help it, though.'

'Oh, Beatie,' Abbie burst out in a sob. 'Oh, my darling!'

Sitting on the grass, Abbie held her in her arms, occasionally patting her, as she would a child. After a time she spoke again.

'Come on,' she murmured, 'let's go home.'

Chapter Nine

At times it seemed to Abbie that she and Beatie would never get home that night. Beatie was not only in great pain but also appeared to be mentally stunned. Stumbling along at Abbie's side, she rarely spoke, seeming to move as if in a dream.

After traversing the fields they eventually came out onto the road again. And then, after what seemed an age, they reached Flaxdown and started up the lane. As they drew near the cottage Abbie saw the figures of her father and brother emerging from the front door. Her father was carrying a lantern. Seeing the girls, the men hurried forward.

'Dear God', Frank Morris said, 'where have you been? It's after one o'clock. Eddie and I have been out looking for you. We were just starting out again.' Coming to a stop, he raised the lantern so that its light fell on the girls' faces. 'Oh, Christ,' he said, his voice full of horror and fear. Abbie gave a sob and ran to him. His free arm came up and held her. 'What's happened?' he said. 'Tell me what's happened.'

In the same moment Eddie came forward, and standing before Beatie with her bruised and bloody face, and her torn and dishevelled clothing, he raised his fists before him. 'Who did this?' he cried out. 'Who did this to you?'

Abbie had never seen such passion as that shown by her father and brother that night. For the first minutes they were like madmen – Eddie in particular charging this way and that, going nowhere, aimless and disorientated by the shock and his rage and impotence. As well as she could, Abbie told of their meeting with the men, though with certainty she could only speak of her own experiences. What had happened to Beatie could only be surmised, for while Abbie and her father wiped the blood from Beatie's face, Beatie herself sat in silence, giving no answers to their questions. After a while Eddie, at Abbie's suggestion, ran off to fetch Mrs Carroll from Tomkins Row.

When Mrs Carroll entered the cottage behind Eddie a little while later she and Abbie took Beatie upstairs where they gave further attention to her injuries. All the while as they worked, Mrs Carroll talked gently to Beatie and gradually, at last, she began to respond.

After a time, with Beatie in bed and Mrs Carroll sitting at her side, Abbie went back downstairs. There she told Eddie and her father what she and Mrs Carroll had learned.

Eddie cried, new tears springing to his eyes, 'Both of 'em? You tellin' me it was both of 'em?'

Frank Morris gave a sob and put his head in his hands. For a few moments he remained so, then he looked up. 'What were they like, these men? Tell us what they looked like.'

Abbie gave what descriptions she could, but these were mainly limited to their height and what she surmised as the men's age range, that she guessed them to be in their twenties. She had not seen their faces, she said.

'They said they saw you at the fair?' Eddie said.

'Yes.'

Eddie and his father looked at one another.

'Come on, son,' Frank Morris said.

With a nod, Eddie strode towards the stairs. At the

same time his father went to a cupboard and took out a horsewhip. When Eddie re-entered the kitchen a few moments later he was carrying his gun. His eyes glittering, he said, 'I'll swing for 'em. We'll find 'em, and when we do I'm gunna kill the bastards.'

Seeing their rage, their determination, Abbie said quickly, 'Please – oh, please, don't do anything. You'll only make things worse.'

'What d'you expect us to do,' Eddie said, 'just sit here and do nothing?'

'But you'll never find them at this hour anyway,' Abbie protested.

'Abbie,' their father said, 'you just do what's possible for Beatie. We'll be back as soon as we can.' Moments later he and Eddie were gone.

Left alone, Abbie washed herself, and cleaned the cuts and bruises on her hands and face. She put on the kettle for tea and then went upstairs, where she found Mrs Carroll as she had left her, sitting beside the bed. Beatie lay quiet, her eyes closed. As Abbie entered the room Mrs Carroll lifted a finger in warning. 'She's sleeping.'

'I'm just making some tea,' Abbie whispered.

Mrs Carroll got up from her chair. 'Good. I could do with a cup, and I think she'll be all right to be left for a while.'

In the kitchen Abbie and Mrs Carroll sat drinking tea at the table. 'Will you tell the police what happened?' Mrs Carroll asked.

Abbie sighed. 'I don't know. If you do that, then everybody'll get to know about it. And that's the last thing Beatie would want.' She was silent for a moment, then she added, 'I hope Father and Eddie don't find those men. There'll be bloodshed if they do. I'd like them punished for what they did, but even if they are it won't

121

undo what's done. Nothing's going to make it right again.'

Mrs Carroll left an hour or so later, soon after which Frank Morris and Eddie returned. It was too dark, they said; they would start out again when it was light. And when the time came they did so, returning just before noon, again despondent at their lack of success. This time, they told Abbie, they had gone to the fairground at Old Ford.

'But they'd 'alf of 'em packed up and moved out,' Eddie said. 'We 'ad a good look round but we didn't see anybody like you described.'

'Weren't you afraid?' Abbie asked. 'Going into that place alone? All those gypsies?'

'We wusn't alone,' Eddie said. 'We 'ad Mike Taggart and 'is son with us, and Manny from the farm.'

Abbie's heart sank. 'So people in the village know of it now.'

Eddie and her father did not speak for a moment, then Frank Morris said, 'It can't be helped, Abbie. People can't just sit back and let such things happen.'

It was quite apparent that Beatie would not be in any fit state to return to her work at Lullington for a while, and Abbie wasted no time in writing a letter to Mrs Callardine, saying that Beatie was ill and would be unable to return to her duties for a time.

What should be done about Tom, however, Abbie did not know. It would not be long before he learned that Beatie had not returned to Lullington, and he would have to be given a reason for her absence. Upstairs in their bedroom, Abbie said to Beatie, 'I'll write to him, too. He'll learn from Mrs Callardine that you haven't returned and he'll be expecting to hear. We don't have to say what's happened, but he'll have to be given some reason for your staying on here.'

Getting no response from Beatie, who merely turned her face away, Abbie went back downstairs and wrote a letter to Tom telling him that Beatie had come down with the influenza and would be returning to Lullington as soon as she was well enough.

As the days went by – still without success for Eddie, who spent most of his evenings searching for the men – Beatie recovered from her physical injuries. Her other hurts, though, were not to be easily healed.

For some days she remained in the bedroom, lying in or on the bed or sitting by the window. And although her father, brother and sister tried to persuade her to come downstairs she would not. She said nothing further of her ordeal, and after a little time nothing more was asked of her.

It wasn't until the Thursday following the assault, as Abbie was working in the kitchen, that Beatie finally came downstairs and into the room. Abbie made tea and they sat drinking it at the table. Over the rim of her cup Abbie looked at her sister. Wearing one of Abbie's frocks, and with her hair neatly braided, Beatie, despite her bruised face, looked a good deal better. There was no life, though, in her expression. She sat with her lips set, eyes downcast. Reaching out, Abbie laid her hand on Beatie's as it rested beside her cup.

Beatie looked up. 'Oh, Abbie,' she said, 'how are you? All these days I've only been thinking of myself. I've given no thought to you. And look at you – your poor face.'

'I'm all right,' Abbie said, putting a hand to her bruised mouth. 'Don't worry about me.' She pressed Beatie's hand. 'Everything will be all right, Beatie. I know what you must be going through. But in time it will pass. It will all pass.'

Sudden tears glistened in Beatie's eyes. 'I wish I could believe that.'

'It's true. And in a while you won't have time to think about it. The wedding'll be here soon and there won't be time to think about anything else.'

'Oh, Abbie,' Beatie said, 'how can I get wed now?'

Abbie leaned across the table. 'Beatie, look at me.'

Beatie raised her head and looked into Abbie's earnest eyes.

'What's happened isn't going to change anything,' Abbie said. 'Why should it?'

Beatie looked away again. 'D'you think Tom will still want me now?'

'What? How can you say that? Of course he'll still want you. Why shouldn't he? You haven't done anything. Dear God, after what you've been through I should think the man would love you all the more.'

'I – I suppose he has to be told.'

'That's up to you to decide. Though even if you don't tell him I should think that at some time he's bound to find out.'

'Why?' Beatie said sharply. 'How should he find out?'

'Well,' Abbie shrugged, 'what with Father and Eddie going off looking for the men – and getting others to help . . . We've got to face it, Beatie, word will soon get about. I wish it were not so, but I'm afraid it's bound to happen.'

Beatie bent her head and buried her face in her hands. 'Oh, God,' she murmured, 'that's part of it – the shame that everybody has to hear of it.' She raised her head after a few moments, then added, 'If Tom has to know then it's best he's told properly. Before he hears it as gossip, I mean.'

Abbie nodded. 'Perhaps so.'

'Oh, but, Abbie, how can I tell him? I can't. I couldn't bear to.'

A little silence, then Abbie said, 'Would you like me to tell him?'

'Yes. Oh, yes. If he has to know then let it come from you.'

Abbie got to her feet. 'All right. I'll go and see him. I'll go and see him today.'

Keeping to the roads, Abbie reached Lullington just after three o'clock. She went at once to the Leaping Hare public house and, going round to the side door, rang the bell. The door was opened by a maid. When Abbie said she wanted to see Mr Thomas Greening she was asked in.

The maid showed her into a large drawing room, somewhat overfilled with furniture and bric-a-brac. Abbie sat down on the sofa while the maid went away and after a few minutes the door opened and Tom came in. Abbie rose from her seat and went towards him. He smiled gravely at her, took the hand she offered and urged her to be seated again. He sat down in a chair facing her.

'You got my letter, did you?' Abbie said.

'Yes. How is Beatie now?'

'Better, thank you. Much better.'

Silence in the room but for the ticking of the clock. He was too quiet, she thought, and furthermore he had made no comment on her bruised face. She realized that he already knew what had happened.

After a few moments she said, 'I don't know whether you might have heard something, Tom. We all know how gossip spreads. But – it's not the influenza that's keeping Beatie at home.'

He said nothing, but looked away, avoiding her eyes.

'Something – happened,' she said. 'Last Sunday night,

125

when Beatie and I were coming home from the fair at Old Ford.'

Still he did not speak.

'She asked me to come and tell you,' Abbie went on, 'because she's afraid to tell you herself.' She paused. 'Last Sunday, when we left the fair we –' She came to a stop, then, with a sad little smile, said, 'I don't need to tell you, Tom, do I?'

'I – I did hear something,' he said after a moment.

'What did you hear?'

'As you said yourself, gossip spreads.' Still he did not meet her eyes. 'We were bound to know. My mother was told – and she told my father. I heard about it from him.'

'Oh, God.' Abbie gave a groan. 'How dreadful that you should learn like that. I was hoping to be able to tell you first. What exactly did you hear?'

He shook his head, sighed. 'Is it necessary to –'

'Please,' she broke in, 'tell me.'

'I was told that some men – two men – oh, I don't want to talk about it.'

After a while Abbie said, 'It would be good for Beatie to see you, Tom.'

'Yes. Yes, of course.'

'I can't tell you what this has done to her. She's in a bad way.'

He nodded. 'It must have been the most ... awful ordeal.'

'Yes.'

'But you say she's recovering from it now.'

'Slowly, yes.'

'That's good. I'm very glad to hear that.'

'But she'll need time, and support.'

'Of course.' He paused. 'Have they ... caught the men?'

'No. Eddie and Father have been searching, but they haven't found them. They won't now.'

'It's a dreadful thing,' he said. 'Dreadful.'

'Yes, it is. But Beatie will get over it in time.' A thought occurred to her. 'When did you hear? When did your father tell you?'

'Yesterday morning.'

'Yesterday morning? Oh, Tom, why didn't you get in touch with Beatie right away? She needs you so.'

'I was going to,' he said. 'I was going to write to her today.'

'Write? You were going to write to her? Tom, she doesn't need letters. She needs to see you. She needs for you to be there at a time like this.'

He looked slightly affronted at her words. 'Abbie,' he said stiffly, 'I know you mean well, but this is something that Beatie and I have to sort out for ourselves.'

'Sort out?' she said. 'What do you mean, sort out? What is there to sort out?' She waited for him to turn his face, to look at her, but he did not. 'Tom please,' she said, 'you're not going to let this come between you, are you?'

'Of course not.'

'A dreadful thing has happened, but Beatie was the victim, not the perpetrator.'

'You think I don't know that?' He looked at her now, but only for a moment, then his glance moved to the clock. 'Listen,' he said, 'please don't think me rude, but I shall have to go. I'm working with my father in the cellar and he'll be wondering what's happened to me.' He got up from the chair. Abbie rose too and followed him out into the hall. At the front door he turned back to her.

'Please,' he said, 'tell Beatie how terribly sorry I am. And tell her I hope she'll soon be feeling much better.'

'I will.' Abbie waited for him to go on. 'Are you coming

to see her?' she asked. No part of the enterprise was turning out the way she had hoped.

'Yes, of course. Just as soon as I can get away.'

'I'll tell her that. May I tell her when she can expect you . . . ?'

'Very soon, tell her. Over the next couple of days.'

'When? Tomorrow? Saturday?'

'Well – Saturday, yes. Tell her I'll be there on Saturday.'

'When? In the morning? In the afternoon? She'll want to know.'

'In the afternoon. As soon as I can after midday dinner.'

Abbie nodded. 'Is there anything else I should tell her? Any other message?'

'Tell her – I'm thinking of her. And tell her not to worry.'

He put out his hand and Abbie briefly took it in her own. Then he opened the door and she passed through onto the front step.

'Tom,' she said, turning back to him, 'I'm not interfering; please don't think that. But Beatie is my sister and her happiness is very dear to me. She's a good, kind, sweet girl – as you well know. It would be the most dreadful thing if she were made even more unhappy over this. She's suffering enough as it is.'

'I'm sure. I can imagine what she must be going through.'

He said nothing more. Abbie stood looking up at him for a moment longer, murmured a goodbye, then turned and started away.

Back in Green Lane in Flaxdown, Abbie had opened the front gate and was moving up the path when she heard a voice call to her.

'Miss Abigail . . . ? Abbie?'

She turned and to her great surprise saw the tall figure of Louis Randolph striding along the lane towards her. After a moment's hesitation she moved back to the gate and waited, seeing again his wide smile, the warmth in his gaze. To her surprise she became all at once aware of the beating of her heart. She could scarcely believe it. She had thought never to see him again, but here he was.

'Abbie . . .' He lifted his cap as he came to a halt before her on the other side of the gate. She thought how fine he looked, how white his teeth against the tan of his cheek. Nervously, uncertainly, she returned his smile, murmured a greeting and shook his outstretched hand.

'Well, what luck,' he said, 'catching you here. How are you? Are you well?'

'– Yes, I'm very well, thank you. And you?'

'I'm very well.' He eyed the bruises on her face. 'But you look as if you've been in the wars.'

'Oh – that. A little accident, that's all.' She dismissed it with a wave of her hand. 'So – what brings you to Flaxdown?'

He shook his head in a gesture of mock disappointment. 'Ah, how soon you forget. I told you I planned to come down this way. Don't you remember?'

'Oh – yes.' She remembered it very well, though she had not thought it would happen.

'I went back to London the morning after the fair,' he said, 'and I returned here late last night.' He grinned. 'And it's been a thirsty walk from Frome this morning, I don't mind telling you. Still, it was worth it – seeing you again.'

'You came from Frome to see me?' she said.

'I came from *London* to see you.'

'Really?' She could hardly believe it. She had told herself that his words at the fair had meant nothing, that he would have forgotten them as soon as she had gone out of his sight.

She became highly conscious of the closed gate between them, conscious that he must be aware of it too. But she could not invite him in. How could she, with Beatie as she was. 'Are you staying in Frome?' she asked him.

'Yes – but at an inn there. My friend's away.' He was waiting to be invited indoors to be given tea. Her mind was in turmoil.

A little silence fell between them, then he said, 'I was so pleased to meet you at the fair. So glad.'

'Oh . . .' No words would come to her.

Silence again. Then he said with a little laugh, as if trying to ease the moment, 'I left my prize behind, you know.'

'Your prize?' She had no idea what he was talking about.

He chuckled. 'The coconut I won. I left it behind, by the stream.'

'Oh – that's a shame.' Through her brain flashed pictures of the two of them together beside the brook, the lights of the fairground twinkling in the falling dusk.

'Is your sister well?' His voice broke into her thoughts.

Clearly he had no idea of what happened. 'Yes,' she lied. 'She's quite well, thank you.' She paused briefly, awkwardly, then said, her words coming out in a rush, 'I'm sorry – but I can't ask you in. I'd like to but – it's just not possible right now.'

The disappointment was clear in his face. 'Oh, well, now, that's a pity. But I should have written first, I know.' Then he smiled. 'But – perhaps we could take a little walk. Just for a while. Have a chat.'

She said nothing, only stood there.

'I don't have to go back to London right away,' he said. 'I can stay for a day or two.' He waited. 'No?'

'I'm sorry, it's just that . . .'

His smile faded. 'Me? Is it me?'

'What? Oh, no. *No*.'

'Are you sure? I know that – that when we met you must have thought me very . . .' He had difficulty finding the right word. 'I know I didn't behave as I should have and I –'

'No,' she broke in, 'it's not that.' She spoke quickly; she didn't want to be reminded of that time. 'Look, I have to go in. I'm sorry . . .'

He didn't move as she took a step back from the gate.

'I could write to you,' he said. 'Is there any point in my doing that?'

She stopped, turned to face him again. 'Yes.' She gave a slow nod. 'Write to me.'

'And if I do will you answer?'

'Yes, of course. Oh, I'm so sorry about today. I can't explain but . . .' She let her words trail off.

'It's all right. I told you – I should have written first.'

'I'm sorry.'

'It's all right.' He was looking at her intensely. 'You know – whatever you might have thought – I meant what I said just now. I was so happy to meet you at the fair. It meant so much to me.'

Briefly, amid all the inner turmoil, she felt her heart swell with happiness at his words, and then heard herself saying, 'Yes – I too.'

'Truly?'

She gave a nod.

'Anyway,' he said, 'I can see I've caught you at an awkward time. I mustn't keep you.'

Forcing a smile, she stepped back towards him and put out her hand.

Taking it, he said, 'You're sure you'll answer if I write?'

'I promise.'

'You promise?'

'I promise.'

His smile was back. 'Fine. Goodbye, then – Abbie.'

'Goodbye.'

She moved up the path, then turned to make her way round the side of the house. Just before she passed the corner of the building she glanced back over her shoulder. He had moved onto the green, had come to a stop and was looking back at her.

He waved. She returned his wave and entered the cottage.

Now she had to see Beatie. Tell her of her meeting with Tom.

Chapter Ten

Louis's promised letter arrived on Saturday morning. Standing in the kitchen, Abbie unfolded the notepaper. Beneath his London address and the date, he had written:

Dear Abbie,

I am sitting down to write this immediately upon returning to my lodgings. I had so hoped to have the chance to talk to you in Flaxdown, but obviously I did not choose my time well. Still, having had your assurance that it was nothing personal, I am telling myself that only my timing was at fault. I'll try not to make such a mistake again. I have to say, however, that you did appear somewhat preoccupied, and whatever caused it – assuming that it was not my presence – I hope it is past.

I am somewhat at a loss as to what to say next. If I were with you it would perhaps be easier, but faced merely with this sheet of notepaper I find it difficult to put my thoughts before you. Let me just say that I cannot get you out of my head and that I am so looking forward to seeing you again. I have never stopped thinking about you since our first meeting.

Please write back as soon as you can and reassure me – as lack of certainty makes me so full of doubts. I need to hear from you and to see again something of the girl I met at the fair. She was hardly evident in Flaxdown.

I shall leave it up to you, and I shall wait and hope

for a letter. If you write, as I hope you will, I can arrange to come and visit again. In the meantime I shall remain,

    Yours,
       Louis Randolph

Abbie read the letter through three times. He had meant what he had said. She was so afraid that he had been toying with her, or that, once back in London again, he would forget. Though, she told herself, the fact that he had travelled all the way from London to Flaxdown for the sole purpose of seeing her – that, surely, was proof of his feelings. She felt a strange, embracing warmth. She was so glad, so very very glad that he had written.

She folded the letter, returned it to the envelope and put it on the mantelpiece. She would answer it soon. For the time being she must give all her attention and consideration to Beatie.

Beatie was ready long before the time of Tom's expected visit and by noon, having dressed with the greatest care, she was almost pacing the floor in her anxiety to see him. She ate little of the food that Abbie put before her, only eager to get away from the table again, as if by doing so she could somehow bring forward the moment of his arrival.

But the hours passed, and Abbie knew that he would not come.

At five o'clock Beatie rose from her seat at the window and went upstairs. Abbie followed a few moments later and found her lying on the bed, gazing dully at the wall.

'Perhaps something happened to detain him, or prevent his coming,' Abbie said.

'It's over,' said Beatie. 'He doesn't want to see me any more.'

'Beatie . . .'

'It doesn't matter what you say, Abbie, I know. A week has gone by and I've heard nothing from him.' Abruptly she sat up. 'But he's *got* to come. He's *got* to.' Bursting into tears, she threw herself down and buried her face in the pillow.

That evening their father returned from Trowbridge where he had been working for the past week. When he and Abbie were alone she told him of her meeting with Tom Greening and of his failure to appear that afternoon. He bent his head and sighed. 'What's to be done?'

Abbie shrugged. 'I don't think there's anything to be done. Except wait and hope.'

Eddie's reaction, as Abbie could have predicted, was more volatile than their father's. 'I'll go and see 'im,' he said angrily. 'I'll find out what's 'appenin'.' And he would have gone to Lullington, charging over in his usual hot-headed way, had not Abbie persuaded him against it. It would solve nothing, she said, and certainly it would do nothing to help Beatie.

On Monday morning Beatie shut herself in the bedroom with writing paper and pen. When she came down a while later she told Abbie that she had written Tom a letter. 'He'll come and see me when he's read it,' she said.

Sorrowfully, and unconvinced, Abbie watched as she left the cottage to post it. Tom had had ample time and every chance to contact Beatie, and he had not done so. She could not imagine how Beatie's letter would make him change his mind.

Abbie's fears were realized. As the days passed, she observed Beatie's growing despair while she waited in vain for some response to her letter.

On Saturday morning Abbie saw Beatie watching from the window once again as the postman walked past the cottage gate. In silence Beatie gazed at the old man until he moved out of sight, then she turned quietly away.

Abbie was preparing to leave for the grocer's shop and do other errands in the village. 'Beatie, why don't you come with me?' she suggested. 'You should get a little air. It doesn't do you any good to stay cooped up in here day after day.'

Beatie shook her head. 'No,' she said dully, 'I don't want to see anyone.'

Knowing that it was useless to try to persuade her, Abbie left the cottage. When she returned some forty-five minutes later, she found the kitchen empty and, on going upstairs, saw that Beatie's cape was not in the wardrobe. Back downstairs, she busied herself unpacking the shopping and doing other odd chores while she waited for Beatie's return. Twenty minutes later, when there was still no sign of her, she left the cottage to go in search of her. After wandering around the village for a time she saw Mrs Carroll, who told her that she had seen Beatie some time earlier starting out on the road to Lullington. Abbie at once set out after her.

Later, as she approached Lullington village, she saw ahead of her the solitary figure of Beatie sitting by the roadside. Abbie hurried towards her. Beatie, seated on the stump of a fallen tree, did not look up as she drew near.

'Beatie,' Abbie said, 'I wondered where you'd got to. Then I saw Jane's mother and she said she'd seen you heading out this way.'

Beatie sat looking ahead of her. Abbie sat down beside her. After a little silence she said hesitantly, 'What are you doing out here, Beatie?' She paused, waiting. 'Are you – going to see Tom?'

'I've already been.' Beatie began to pluck nervously at

136

her skirt. Turning to Abbie, she added with a strange little smile, 'He didn't want to see me.'

Hearing the tone of Beatie's words, seeing the strange, humourless little smile on her lips, Abbie felt as if her heart would break. 'Oh, Beatie – I wish I could say something to –'

'There's nothing you can say,' Beatie broke in. 'There's nothing anyone can say that will make it right. Only Tom – and it's too late.' A brief silence, then she went on, 'I felt that if I could only talk to him it would be all right again. But he wouldn't see me. The maid said he'd gone away, to stay with relatives, and that she didn't know when he'd be back.' She turned to Abbie. 'What did I do that he should turn away from me like this?'

'You haven't done anything,' Abbie said. 'Of course you haven't.' She put her arms round Beatie's shoulders, hugging her to her.

Withdrawing from Abbie's embrace after a moment, Beatie said, 'What shall I do now? I don't know what to do.'

High in a tree nearby a blackbird was singing, his voice unbearably sweet in the stillness. Below him a squirrel darted, a flash of red among the branches. In the meadow beyond the opposite hedge a cowman was driving a herd of cattle. Untouched by Beatie's grief the world went on.

'Beatie – come on home now.'

'Home . . .' Beatie spoke the word as if she had never heard it before and remained sitting there. 'He doesn't love me any more,' she said, 'and I don't know what to do.'

'There's nothing you can do right now. But if it's true – if it *is* over between you and Tom, well – I can only say it shows he wasn't the right one for you. He couldn't be.'

'Don't.' Beatie gave a worried little shake of her head. 'Don't say that.'

'Oh, Beatie,' Abbie said, 'I can imagine how you must be suffering – but in time you'll get over it. I know right now you can't possibly see that it could be so, but I'm sure it will happen.'

Beatie put out a hand and laid it on Abbie's. 'Yes, perhaps you're right.' She pressed Abbie's hand, then rose, drawing Abbie up beside her. 'Come on, let's go home.'

They hardly spoke as they walked and the journey seemed to Abbie very long. Eventually, though, they came to Flaxdown. They made their way along Miller Street, past the Lamb and Flag and crossed over the green. As they neared the entrance to Green Lane, Abbie saw a figure drawing near and recognized the Revd Hilldew. In the same moment that she saw him he raised his hand, hailing her and bidding her to wait.

'I'll go on,' Beatie said quickly, already turning, starting along the lane. 'I don't want to talk to anybody.'

'All right – you go on indoors and put the kettle on. I'll only be a minute.'

Abbie watched as Beatie, head bowed, went along the lane and turned in at the front gate of the cottage. A few moments later the Revd Hilldew was stopping at Abbie's side.

'I was just on my way to see you, Miss Abigail,' he said, smiling. 'Though it looks as if I'm lucky I didn't call a few minutes earlier.'

'Yes,' Abbie said. 'I – I've just been out with my sister.'

The man nodded and cast a careful glance along the lane in the direction of the cottage, then said quietly, 'I was told what – what happened. What a dreadful thing.' He paused. 'How is your sister now, may I ask?'

'I don't know. I honestly don't know.'

He shook his head sympathetically. 'It will take her

some time to get over such a – such an experience. Tell me – is her wedding likely to be delayed?'

Abbie sighed. 'I can't tell you, Reverend. I just don't know what's happening. Perhaps there's not going to be any wedding. I don't know. We're all at sixes and sevens.'

'I wish there were something I could do. Would it help if I had a word with her? I might be able to give her a little comfort . . .'

'That's very kind of you, sir, but – I don't think she wants to see anyone right now. Outside of the family, I mean.'

He nodded. 'I understand. But you will let me know if I can do anything?'

'Yes, I will. Thank you.'

'They haven't found the men, I suppose.'

'No. We've got no idea who they are or where they came from. But I don't care if they're never found. I just want it all to be finished with – and for Beatie to get over it.'

'Of course.'

They stood facing one another a moment or two longer, then Abbie took a token step away, anxious to go and rejoin her sister. Observing her move, the cleric said, 'I don't want to keep you, but listen – your sister is not the main reason for my coming here today. I wanted to see you on quite another matter.'

'Yes . . . ?' She saw that his expression was calm. And now he was smiling gravely.

'You're still as keen as ever to teach, are you?' he asked.

'What? Oh, yes, of course.'

'Then I think you might get your wish very soon.'

'Oh . . . ?'

'Miss Beacham, the village schoolmistress, is to be married in January. And of course, as you know, married women are not employed as teachers. So – her post will

139

become vacant as from Christmas. There was a meeting of the Board yesterday and in the end it was agreed that you should be offered the post.'

Abbie shook her head in wonder. 'I can't believe it. Is it true?'

'Oh, it's true enough, all right.' He added quickly, 'Though you'll have to assist Miss Beacham in the classroom in the meantime, to complete a period of training, of course. But if that goes well – and I see no reason why it should not – then the post will be yours.'

'But I didn't think I stood a chance,' Abbie said, '– not after my interview.'

'Well,' he shrugged, 'it would be foolish of me to pretend that all the members of the Board were equally in favour of your appointment. But the majority were and that's what counts.' He paused. 'So – do I take it that you accept the offer?'

'Oh, yes, indeed. Yes – yes, thank you. Oh, thank you, Reverend.'

'You've nothing to thank me for. Of course I wanted to help you, but my first consideration is always for the pupils. I think you'll be good for them.' Here a touch of a smile lifted one corner of his mouth. 'As long as you use your best judgement and aren't tempted to try to change the world from your classroom.'

Abbie smiled back at him. 'Oh – no fear of that, sir.'

He put out his hand and, gratefully, she grasped it, shook it.

'I'll be in touch again in the next few days,' he said, 'to settle the details and arrange for you to start working with Miss Beacham.' He gave a nod of satisfaction. 'And in the meantime if there is anything I can do to help with regard to Beatrice then don't hesitate to let me know.'

'I won't. And thank you again.'

He bade her goodbye and started away. As if in a

dream she stood watching him as he walked back across the green, then, pulling herself together, she turned and headed down the lane. What an irony it was, she thought as she passed through the front gate to the cottage, that such a moment of happiness should come at such a time.

She called out Beatie's name as she entered the kitchen, but the room was empty. Moving to the stairs she opened the door and called up, 'Beatie? Beatie, are you there?' There was no answer. She called again. Still no answer. She had probably gone outside to the privy. She took off her bonnet and cape, stood before the mirror and ran smoothing hands over her hair. Through her mind ran the Reverend's words – *It was agreed that you should be offered the post* . . . If only Beatie had not suffered such a terrible blow; as things were she felt guilt for her own personal good fortune.

On the mantelpiece above the range stood the envelope containing Louis's letter. She took it down, pulled it out and read it once again. In her mind she had already composed so many replies. And yes, of course she would see him. She couldn't wait to see him again. He was in her thoughts so often, from the time of her waking until the time of her sleeping. She would write to him tomorrow.

She returned the letter to the envelope and replaced it on the shelf. Then she banked the fire, filled the kettle and put it on to boil. Her thoughts reverting to Beatie's difficulties, she said to herself that perhaps it was not all over and done with. Perhaps Tom had indeed had to go away from home for a while. And even if he had not, even supposing that he had chosen not to see Beatie when she called, then it still did not mean that it was over. After all, he must have been terribly shocked at the news of what had happened. Perhaps in time it would all come right again.

Moving to the door, she looked out and, after a moment, crossed the yard and moved down the garden path. The privy, its door slightly ajar, stood empty. Puzzled, Abbie turned and started back towards the cottage. As she drew nearer the door she suddenly quickened her pace.

She entered the cottage almost at a run, swiftly turning inside and starting up the stairs. 'Beatie . . .' Her boots clattered on the treads. 'Beatie . . . ?'

Her heart pounding, she reached the bedroom and flung open the door.

It was Beatie's shadow she saw first; her shadow thrown onto the wall. Then, turning, she saw Beatie herself.

She hung suspended by her neck from a rope that she had tied to a stout hook in one of the beams. Her body was swaying slightly. Beside her dangling feet lay the overturned chair.

PART THREE

Chapter Eleven

It was 21 July 1872. Abbie had reached her twenty-second birthday less than two weeks previously, and three and a half years had passed since she had begun her work as a teacher at the village school.

The schoolhouse was flooded with sunshine this summer Sunday as Abbie washed her breakfast dishes and tidied the rooms. It didn't take long. The little cottage was comprised merely of one bedroom upstairs, and a small parlour and kitchen on the ground floor. In addition there was a tiny rear garden with a privy at its foot, and an even smaller garden at the front. Her housekeeping was something she tried to do religiously every day, always aware of the chance – albeit slim – that a member of the Board of School Governors might, unannounced, call to see her.

Now, her chores finished, she looked at the clock. Time to get ready to meet Jane and go with her to church.

A little later, dressed in her bonnet and cape, Abbie picked up her bag and went out into the July sunshine. From the cottage's front door she turned right along a path across the front garden and entered the gate that led into the schoolyard. Moving past the pump, she walked to the door of the school, unlocked it and went inside.

Stepping first into a small vestibule holding rows of coat racks, she went on into the schoolroom where lines of desks stood waiting for the pupils who would occupy them in September – pupils who, for the most part, would be spending the summer working on the land and helping with the harvest. Abbie moved through the room, her eyes scanning the windowsills and the floor. The previous year she had found a dead starling that had got in down the chimney and then died of starvation. Her daily check of the premises since then was to try to ensure that such a thing did not happen again. Satisfied, she turned from the room and, after locking the main door behind her, crossed the yard and made her way along the lane.

At the Carrolls' cottage in Tomkins Row she found Jane ready and waiting, and after a few minutes' conversation with Mrs Carroll she and Jane set off for the church.

Jane was in Flaxdown for her annual summer holiday. She had arrived a week previously and had a further week before returning to London where for the past two years she had been employed as lady's maid in the household of a wealthy barrister. During her week in Flaxdown she and Abbie had met every day, sitting chatting in each other's homes, swimming in the nearby clay pit or going for leisurely strolls in the surrounding countryside. During their time together Abbie had swiftly realized that Jane's time in London had given her an air of elegance and sophistication that she had not previously possessed. It was apparent in her dress; looking at her friend, Abbie could not but be aware of how striking was Jane's appearance in her blue dress and matching bonnet. Indeed, for a moment Abbie felt very conscious of her own plain bonnet and simple gown of brown and black houndstooth check.

After the service the two girls made their way towards the village green. As they walked Jane talked of a trip on a Thames pleasure boat that she had recently taken with her mistress. 'Oh, Abbie,' she said, 'it was so exciting. It sails right through the heart of London. You can see it all.

And what a wonderful place. You can't imagine what London is like. For a start it's so vast. Just the part where I'm situated – Fulham – is bigger than six Flaxdowns. And Fulham is only one small part. Oh, there's so much there – the museums, the theatres, the parks – so many sights to see. It's a different world.'

Looking around at the dwellings of the little village Abbie said, 'Then you'd need a good reason to come back to live in a place like this, wouldn't you? A reason apart from your mother, that is.' She smiled. 'One wearing trousers, perhaps?'

Jane burst out laughing, then said, her expression serious, 'Perhaps you're right. I suppose for the right man you'd go anywhere, don't you agree?'

Abbie shook her head. 'I'm afraid you're asking the wrong person.'

'Oh, yes,' said Jane, 'I was forgetting – you're set on becoming an old maid.'

They talked for a little while longer, arranging to meet again that evening, and then parted, Jane to return home and Abbie to go back to the schoolhouse. There she changed her clothes, gathered a few items together in a basket and set out once more. On reaching the cottage in Green Lane she found her father sitting on the back step cleaning his boots.

'Hello, Father.' She bent and kissed his cheek

Gesturing back into the kitchen, he said, 'You'll find carrots and cabbage there. And I've peeled the potatoes and lit the stove.'

'Good.' She tapped the basket hung over her arm. 'I got us a nice little piece of brisket.'

She stepped past him into the kitchen, put on her apron and got to work preparing the meal. On taking up her position as village schoolmistress she had continued to do what she could for her father and brother, visiting the cottage most evenings to prepare supper for them and each Sunday to get their midday dinner. The previous summer, however, Eddie and Violet had married and gone to live in a tied cottage on the other side of the village. So now there was only her father to care for. Not that he expected it, he said. Indeed, there were many occasions when he told her that she should be thinking more of herself and less about him; he could manage to get his meals perfectly well. Abbie, however, would have none of it, replying that she didn't want to spend all her time alone, but wanted company, too.

While the dinner was cooking her father went down to the Harp and Horses to fetch some ale. On his return he poured two mugs, and Abbie left off her work for a few minutes and sat down to join him at the kitchen table.

'Did Jane go with you to church today?' he asked.

'Yes.' Abbie smiled. 'Though more to show off her new dress than for salvation, I think.'

Her father laughed. 'How's she enjoying her holiday?'

'Oh, all right, I think. Though I'm sure she must find it deadly dull after London.'

He studied her for a moment, then said, 'Wouldn't *you* be happier in a bigger place? I don't mean London necessarily – but some place with a little more life in it.' He paused. 'It isn't right for a young person.'

'What isn't?'

'Well – spending all your time either with children or with me. You need to mix with people your own age.'

'I don't think you mean people my own age,' Abbie said, smiling. 'You mean young men. Or rather, a young man.'

'Well, it wouldn't do you any harm. I think you need to widen your horizons.'

'Father,' she said, 'what's brought all this on?'

'Well,' he said, 'sometimes lately I – I can see a

restlessness in you.' He gave a little shake of his head. 'Oh, Abbie, you must try to find what you want out of life, for until you do you'll never be at peace.'

'Father,' she said, 'I've got all that I want right now.'

'Have you?'

She frowned. 'You're talking about – about some special person, aren't you?'

'Is there no one?'

'No,' she said, a slightly defiant tone in her voice. 'No one. No one at all.'

'But even around here you must have met some young men. There's no shortage.'

'Father, there's no one – truly.' And even as she spoke a picture of Louis Randolph came into her mind, and her thoughts went back four years to the afternoon of the Old Ford fair. She had met him again a week later – out there by the green, and then just before Beatie's death a letter had come from him, sent from his lodgings in London. She had not replied. Nor when he had written a second time. He had not written again, and eventually she had thrown his letters away.

'Really no one?' said her father.

She smiled, holding on to her patience. 'I told you – no one.' Then she added, 'Father, don't try to marry me off. I'm quite happy as I am.'

Moments later, looking at him as he packed tobacco into his pipe, she became aware again of the change that had taken place in him over the past few years. And it was mainly due to Beatie's death, she thought. Her mother's sudden departure had given him a new lease of life, setting his spirit free. But Beatie's death had done the opposite. It was as if her end had closed a window in his heart, and as if now, for all his warm and pleasant ways, his road had been cast in shadow. He did not, Abbie knew, love his other children any the less; a part of his

149

heart would always be theirs; it was simply that his heart had not recovered from its wounds. But there, Beatie's death had made changes for all of them.

Setting down her glass and getting up from her seat, Abbie said briskly, 'Anyway, enough of all this talk of young men. I must get on with dinner.'

Later that afternoon Eddie and Violet appeared. Violet was pregnant; the baby expected towards the end of November. Abbie served tea with some little almond cakes that Violet had baked and brought with her. The fact that the cakes were delicious, and better than any she herself could have made, came as no surprise. Abbie had early on discovered, to her surprise and pleasure, that there was more to Violet than her pretty face and pert ways. She had no doubt that she made Eddie a good wife and would, when the time came, make their child an equally good mother.

Abbie observed her sister-in-law as they ate. Looking even prettier in her pregnancy, Violet was her usual animated self – and, Abbie thought, a good match for Eddie, whose exuberance seemed to have been tempered not one bit by marriage. Sometimes, watching the two, observing their high spirits and listening to their chatter, Abbie wondered what their home life must be like. Rather loud and boisterous, she had no doubt. But no other way would have suited her brother. No milksop Sunday-schoolteacher type for him.

'Oh, yes,' Violet said, 'I almost forgot.' Putting down her cup, she took a letter from her bag. 'We heard from Lizzie yesterday.' She passed the letter over to Frank Morris who unfolded it and began to read.

Lizzie and Iris had recently been back to Flaxdown for their annual summer vacations, their holidays overlapping, so that for one week they had been together at the cottage. As always, Abbie had been delighted to see her sisters, and their visit had passed all too quickly. Lizzie was nineteen now, and Iris would be eighteen in the autumn. While Iris was still in service in Bath, where she had stayed more or less contentedly for the past three years, Lizzie had tended to move around. This year had seen yet another change for her; on leaving Flaxdown after her summer holiday she had gone to fresh employment in the home of a wealthy family who lived just outside Trowbridge.

'Well, she seems to be settling in,' Frank Morris said as he passed the letter to Abbie. 'Though sometimes I think the girl will never be content.'

Abbie read the short letter. Lizzie wrote that the first two weeks in her new post had gone well and went on to say that she was soon to be temporarily promoted to lady's maid to a visitor to her employer's house. Although a little nervous at the prospect, she was nevertheless pleased.

As Abbie passed the letter back, Violet said, 'I'll write to her next week. If I leave it to Eddie it'll never get answered.'

'Well,' Eddie gave a dismissive wave of his hand, 'I ain't got time for such things.'

Abbie smiled. Her brother didn't alter. Studying him now, she silently observed that the only change in him over the years had been a minor one in his physical appearance – a slight alteration to the shape of his nose.

That, the breaking of his nose, had taken place almost four years ago, just a month after Beatie's death.

Abbie and her father had been at the cottage one Sunday afternoon when Eddie had come in with his knuckles bruised and bloody, his eye blackened and his nose bleeding and hugely swollen. Abbie had tended to his wounds, but for all her persistent questioning she had got nothing out of him as to the cause of his injuries.

The following evening, however, while walking through the village, she had run into Manny Harper, one of Eddie's friends and workmates from the farm. On seeing Abbie he at once asked how Eddie was.

'He's not too bad,' she replied, 'though I don't think his nose will ever be the same again.'

Manny shook his head in a gesture of sympathy and sucked in the air between his clenched teeth.

'You were with him, weren't you?' Abbie said.

'Oh, yes.' Manny said with a nod. 'I was that.'

Abbie sighed. 'It must have been some fight, that's all I can say.'

'It certainly was.'

'Really.' Abbie nodded with pursed lips. 'You don't look any the worse for it.'

'Oh, I wasn't involved,' Manny said. 'I just stood by and watched.'

'You stood by – and did nothing to help him?' She gazed at him levelly. 'And you're his friend, Emmanuel?'

'What?' Manny frowned. 'I didn't give 'im no 'elp because 'e didn't want no 'elp.'

'He chose to suffer like that?'

'Suffer?' Manny's frown deepened. 'It wasn't Eddie who suffered. It was Greening.'

'Greening? Tom Greening?'

Manny looked at her gravely, as if aware of the pain that the name must bring. 'The same.'

Greening had indeed left Lullington shortly before Beatie's death and he had stayed away, lodging, Abbie had heard, with relatives in Bath. He had remained there during the time of Beatie's funeral and for many days afterwards. Then one day Eddie had quietly told her that the young man had returned to his family home. ''E realizes 'e can't stay away for ever,' Eddie had said. "E've got to come 'ome at some time.'

Looking into his face, Abbie had seen the naked loathing in his eyes. 'Eddie,' she said, 'what have you got in mind? You're not going to do anything foolish, are you?'

'No.' He shook his head. 'I'm not gunna do anything foolish; I'm gunna do something smart and sensible. I'm gunna find the snivellin' bastard and break 'is neck.'

'Eddie, no!' Reaching out, Abbie had clung to his arm. 'Don't, I beg you. You'll only bring more trouble. And think how much Father's suffering as it is. You'll only make it worse.'

In the end she had got him to promise – albeit very reluctantly – not to go after Greening.

And that, she had thought, was the end of it. Now, however, here was Manny Harper telling her that Eddie's injuries had come as the result of a fight with the young man.

When she had seen Eddie later that evening she told him of her conversation with Manny and taxed him with his broken promise. He listened to her outburst then said calmly, 'D'you want to know what 'appened?'

'Yes.'

'Well, I didn't go lookin' for 'im,' he said. 'I just 'appened to see 'im. Manny and me was on the road to Lullington when Greening come along. And that was it. I went for 'im.' Turning, he looked at his reflection in the glass, one hand touching at his swollen nose. 'Unfortunately for me 'e was carryin' a stick – and as I run at 'im 'e swung at me with it and caught me across the face. God, it rocked me, I'll tell you, but it didn't stop me. And 'e soon dropped it.' He gave a bitter smile, his strangely altered features looking even more distorted. 'I 'ad 'im crying out for mercy, I did.'

'Don't go on,' Abbie said. 'I don't want to hear.'

'No, listen,' he said. 'I want to tell you – because I'm glad. I'm glad. I don't care what 'appens, I'll never regret what I done.' He gave a nod of satisfaction. 'Well, I give him what 'e asked for – mercy. I was merciful. I was merciful in that I didn't kill the bastard. But I tell you, by the time I'd finished with 'im 'e might well 'ave wished I 'ad. I ended up pitchin' 'im into the ditch – which was brimful after the rain. He 'ardly 'ad the strength to pull hisself out.'

'Oh – Eddie – he could have you up for assault. You could go to prison.'

'I wouldn't care. It'd be worth the price. 'E threatened all of that anyway. But don't worry, it won't 'appen. 'E'd be too bloody scared of what might come out.'

Tom Greening, it was soon commonly known, had sustained a great deal of bruising, a broken nose, a broken jaw and the loss of a tooth. And, Abbie had to admit to herself on hearing the news, she was not sorry – although for a while she had continued to fear possible repercussions on Eddie. But Eddie had been right: apart from the gossip – which was rife and told with relish – nothing more was heard of the incident.

'But one thing I find very disappointing about the whole thing,' Abbie had said rather self-righteously to Eddie on hearing the catalogue of Greening's injuries, 'is that you broke your promise to me. You gave me your word that you wouldn't fight with him and you did.'

Eddie considered this for a moment, then, giving a little nod, said, 'Ah, that's right, I did. I broke me promise, didn't I?'

'Yes, you did.'

'And I s'pose you're waitin' now for me to apologize, are you? Well, you can go on waitin'. I admit, I broke me promise, and I'll tell you also that I'd do the same thing all over again.' One corner of his mouth turning up, he'd added, 'There's another lesson for you, our Abs. You can't depend on nobody, can you?'

Now, sitting facing her brother across the kitchen table, Abbie looked at his broken nose and remarked to herself that he would never be quite so handsome again. But there again, Thomas Greening would be even less so.

Later, as Eddie and Violet left the cottage to return to their own home, Abbie and her father stood at the front gate watching as the two of them walked arm in arm down the lane.

'They make a nice couple,' Frank Morris said, his eyes following the pair.

Abbie nodded agreement. 'Yes. A bit mad and a bit wild, but nice.'

Her father said, 'You were somewhat set against that girl, as I recall.'

'Indeed I was.' Abbie pulled a face at him and then smiled. 'Which just goes to show that occasionally even I can make a mistake.'

Chapter Twelve

After three days of almost non-stop rain the sun had come out again and the Saturday market at Warminster was teeming with people. Abbie and Jane were among them. They had driven into the town with Mr and Mrs Cole, a Flaxdown farmer and his wife, and were to meet them at four o'clock for the ride back. Now, having spent some time wandering around the stalls and the shops of the town, they wanted to get some refreshment before starting back.

On the main street they entered a small inn where they found a vacant space on one of the benches. From the maid they ordered bread and cheese and tea, and when it was served they sat eating and drinking while all about them the other customers came and went. Against the sound of the noisy chatter Jane sighed and said, 'I can't believe that my holiday is over. Two weeks. This time tomorrow I shall be on my way back to London.' She was to leave at first light in the morning, riding in a neighbour's carriage to Westbury, where she would then take a train on the first stage of her journey back to London.

With the last sip of tea drunk and the last crumb of bread eaten the two girls went back out onto the street. There they set off towards a chemist's shop where Abbie intended to buy a tonic for her father who was confined at home with a fever and a heavy cold. On reaching the shop they entered its small, cramped interior to find two customers already there, one of whom, a tall man, was being served by the elderly proprietor.

The tall man's transaction completed, he picked up his package and left the premises while the chemist turned his attention to the middle-aged man who was waiting his turn. The latter had begun to make an enquiry about a particular ointment when the proprietor interrupted him to ask, gesturing to an umbrella that hung on the counter's edge: 'Is this yours, sir?' The customer replied that it was not, at which the proprietor remarked that it must therefore belong to the man who had just left. After a moment's hesitation, Abbie said that she would go after him and, putting down her basket, took the umbrella and hurried out of the shop.

Emerging onto the narrow pavement, she looked about her and caught sight of the man some thirty or so yards away approaching a barber's shop. She started towards him, but as she did so he disappeared through the doorway. Moments later, coming to a halt at the open door, she glanced into the interior. A stout man with a white towel round his throat was reclining in the barber's chair, being shaved. The tall man, the man she had pursued, was sitting nearby, reading a newspaper. Hesitant to invade such an essentially masculine province, Abbie did not know what to do and merely hovered on the step looking in, hoping that the man would glance up and catch her eye. He did not, however, but remained as he was, dark head bent over his paper.

As Abbie stood there, feeling increasingly self-conscious, the barber moved around his supine customer, looked up and caught sight of her. He said with a wide smile, 'Yes, Miss. A nice haircut and beard trim? Don't be afraid. We don't bite.'

His words brought the attention of the other two men, and they looked towards her and chuckled. As the younger man caught her eye she held up the umbrella. 'Sir – I'm not sure, but I think you left this in the chemist's.'

He looked from the umbrella to the package and bag on the seat beside him, then said with a groan, 'Oh, I'll be forgetting my head next.' Getting up, he came to her and took the umbrella from her outstretched hand. 'Thank you so much,' he said. 'It's very kind of you.' Glancing past her head at the darkening sky, he added, 'And it looks as if I might need it very soon.'

Returning to the chemist's shop, Abbie made her purchase of cough mixture and tonic, then together she and Jane stepped out briskly in the direction of The Fleece. It was almost four, time for their ride back to Flaxdown.

On reaching the inn, however, they could see no sign of Mr and Mrs Cole, and when the couple had still not appeared by four thirty Abbie remarked that they had better think about making other arrangements. As she finished speaking the landlord, a burly-looking man, came over to them.

'Are you Miss Morris and Miss Carroll?'

Abbie and Jane said that they were.

'I got a message for you from Mr Cole,' he said. 'They've 'ad to go on back. His missus was took bad. Nothin' too serious, but 'e've took her back to Flaxdown. They left just on 'alf past one.'

The young women thanked the man and as he returned to his work they looked around in the hope of seeing a familiar face. There was no one and after a few moments they made their way outside. They had no choice now but to walk and, adjusting their shopping baskets over their arms, they set off.

They had been walking for some twenty-five minutes under an increasingly darkening sky when the heavens opened and the rain came teeming down. Skirts flying, they dashed for cover under an oak at the roadside, and stood there in the tree's shelter, watching as the rain fell.

After several minutes they saw a horse-drawn carriage, a phaeton, appear over the crest of a hill. As it drew nearer Abbie moved out from their shelter with raised hand. At once the carriage came to a halt and, as she walked towards it, stepping gingerly in the muddy road, she saw to her surprise that the driver was the man whose umbrella she had returned in the barber's shop.

'Well, well,' he said, smiling, 'so we meet again.'

As Jane came forward from the shelter of the tree he patted the seat beside him, urging the two to climb in, and with relief they did so.

'We're going to Flaxdown,' Abbie said as she settled herself and closed the door beside her, 'if it's not out of your way.'

'Not at all,' the man said. 'I shall be going through Flaxdown.' With his words he gave a flap of the reins and the carriage began to move forward once more. 'This is poetic recompense,' he said, turning to smile at Abbie. 'You saved me from a possible soaking and now I'm able to do the same for you.'

The little covered carriage jogged on, while the rain continued to lash down. The man asked the girls their names and in turn introduced himself. He gave his name as Arthur Gilmore. His voice was quite deep, his accent not of the West Country. Abbie was sure that she had never seen him before in the area of the village. Taking in his profile, she placed his age in his late twenties. Well-dressed, tall and slim, he was a good-looking man with clear-cut, regular features, brown eyes and dark-brown hair.

It eventually emerged in the conversation that he was employed by Her Majesty's government as an assistant factory inspector and had come down from London on temporary secondment as a substitute for an officer who had recently died. Jane asked how long his work would keep him in the area and he replied that as soon as a permanent replacement was found he would be returning to London. With Jane saying that her own regular employment was in the capital, the talk then turned to the subject of the city and the facilities it had to offer. Abbie, knowing nothing of the place from personal experience, left the conversation to Jane and the stranger, content to listen to them and relax in the rhythmic jogging of the carriage.

The rain was still falling, albeit far less heavily, when they came at last to Flaxdown. As they entered the village the man turned to the girls saying, 'You'll have to direct me to where you live, ladies. I'm not familiar with the village.'

At this Jane spoke up, saying that Abbie's home was the nearer, following which she proceeded to give him directions to School Lane. A few minutes later the end of the lane came in sight, and as they drew near it Abbie thanked the man for his kindness and asked him to let her down at the corner.

When he had brought the carriage to a stop, he got out and quickly moved around to the other side to help Abbie down. Taking up her belongings, she told Jane that she would see her later, then took the man's outstretched hand and stepped down. After thanking him once more she turned and began to hurry away along the lane. She had hardly gone ten yards, however, when she heard his voice calling, 'Miss Morris – just a minute,' and turning saw him hurrying after her, raising his umbrella as he came.

'I thought you lived in the house on the corner,' he said

as he came up beside her, lifting the umbrella over their heads.

'No,' she said, 'I live in the schoolhouse at the end of the lane. But, please – it's really not necessary. It's not very far.'

'Far enough for you to get wet,' he said. 'Anyway, I'm here now.'

As they walked side by side along the lane he said, 'Is your father the local schoolmaster?'

'No,' Abbie replied, 'I'm the local schoolmistress.'

'You?' He bent his head slightly, looking into her face.

'You sound surprised,' she said.

'Well, yes – rather.'

'Why is that?'

'I remember my own schoolteachers. They were not like you.'

She did not ask how they were different, and a moment later they had arrived at the gate of the schoolhouse.

'Thank you again,' she said.

'It was a pleasure.'

'Well – goodbye.'

'Goodbye.'

Taking her key from her bag, she turned from him, pushed open the gate and hurried up the short path to the front door. On reaching it she turned and saw him walking away, back down the lane.

Later, when she had changed her clothes and rested for a while she went to call on her father. The rain had long since finished and the evening air was pleasant. On her arrival at her old home she found her father sitting in his chair beside the range. At her enquiry he replied that he was feeling a good deal better, though to Abbie he appeared not much improved. She gave him some of the medicine she had brought and then set about preparing supper for the two of them, heating soup and setting out cheese, ham and bread. Her father had little appetite, though, and as Abbie cleared away he remarked that he might soon go to bed to have an early night.

Once the dishes had been washed and put away Abbie wished her father goodnight and set off for the short walk to Tomkins Row. There she found Jane and her mother folding Jane's newly washed, ironed and aired clothes, and packing them in her box in preparation for her early morning departure. The task was soon finished, then Jane made tea and they sat chatting over their cups, their hands busy with their needlework. Jane and Mrs Carroll were mending underwear while Abbie worked on a frock she was making for Violet's coming baby. Throughout the conversation Jane made no mention of Mr Gilmore and Abbie saw no reason to bring up the subject. At nine thirty Abbie packed away her sewing and, saying her goodnights to Mrs Carroll, got up to leave. Jane followed her out to the front gate.

'Well, I reckon it's goodbye again,' Abbie said. 'Though I expect you'll be glad to get back to all the excitement of London.'

Jane clicked her tongue. 'Get back to a lot of hard work, you mean. I wish I could stay on for a few more days.'

'So do I.'

After a moment's silence Jane said, 'Tell me – what did you think of Mr Gilmore?'

Abbie laughed. 'Oh, Jane – shame on you. He's the reason you'd like to stay on, isn't he?'

A frown of annoyance flashed across Jane's face. 'No, of course not,' she said. Then with a shrug she added, 'Well, all right, then, he is.'

Abbie nodded. 'I could tell you were smitten with him right at the start.'

'You couldn't,' Jane said, her frown reappearing. 'How could you?'

'Don't get cross,' said Abbie. 'But I could. For a start you were so anxious for him to drive you on home.'

'Oh, God,' Jane said. 'I hope it wasn't that obvious. To him, I mean.'

'No, of course not. But I know you.'

Jane smiled now. 'Oh, but Abbie, he's such a handsome man, don't you think?'

'Well – yes, I suppose he is.'

'You *suppose* he is? When did you ever see his like around Flaxdown? London either, for that matter. For all my living there I don't get a chance to meet men like him – Mr Gilmore. Personable men with responsible jobs. When I do meet them they don't look twice at somebody like me – somebody in service. A footman is about as high as I can aim. It's all right for you.'

'Why d'you say that?'

'Well, you don't intend to ever get married, so it doesn't matter if you don't get the chance to meet the right man or not. I do intend to get married, though – if I ever find the right man.'

'You'll find him.'

'Maybe. Sometimes I wonder. I shall be twenty-three next January. So many girls of our age are engaged, or already married with families.' After a moment of silence she gave a little shake of her head 'Anyway, I don't think Mr Gilmore was that interested in me.'

'Oh, don't say that. He talked to you all the time in the carriage.'

'Well – only because you didn't seem interested in conversation. Look at how he ran after you to shelter you with his umbrella.'

'He was only being – gallant.'

'You think so?' Clearly Jane did not support such a notion. After a moment she said, 'He's staying in Keyford, on the way to Frome. He's got rooms.'

'How do you know that?'

'I asked him. And he's an only child. And he has no parents now.'

'He told you all that?'

'Well.' Jane shrugged. 'I asked him about his family.'

'Did your mother see him?'

'No, he let me off at the corner. It wasn't raining then.' She was silent for a moment or two, then she added, 'He spoke about you after you'd gone.'

'Oh?'

'He said he wouldn't have guessed you were a schoolteacher. He asked whether we had been friends a long time. I told him we'd been friends almost since we were born ... The best friends in the world, I said.' She paused. 'Did you like him, Abbie?'

'Oh – he seemed nice enough.'

'Nice enough,' Jane repeated to the sky.

'What d'you want me to say?'

'No, it's all right. Anyway, what does it matter? I'm going back to London in the morning and that'll be the end of it.'

'How can you be so sure? He might still be here when you come back at Christmas.'

'Yes, and there again he might not.'

'True, but don't forget that when he leaves here he'll be going to London too. So you could well meet him there.'

'Abbie, have you any idea how big London is? And with him living in Notting Hill? We'd never run into one another.'

'How d'you know he lives in Notting Hill?'

'I asked him.'

'So what if you don't meet him again,' Abbie said. 'You'll get back there and soon forget all about him. Besides, he might already have somebody. He might already be promised.'

'Yes, he might at that. I didn't have the nerve to ask him.'

'Really,' Abbie said, 'you surprise me.'

Jane stared at her for a moment, then began to laugh. 'Oh, Abbie, what should I do without you!'

They laughed so hard that soon they were holding their sides, shrieking out into the night air. After a little while the door opened and Mrs Carroll's head appeared around the jamb. 'It's all right,' Abbie said between laughs. 'It's just that your daughter amuses me.' She and Jane burst into new peals of laughter. Mrs Carroll gave a nod and pursed her lips in an ill-disguised smile. 'I'm glad to hear it,' she said. 'And if you raise your voices just a shade more I should think you could amuse them in Trowbridge too.'

On returning to the schoolhouse, Abbie went to insert her key in the door but found to her surprise that it was already unlocked. Strange – she was sure that she had locked it after her. Turning the handle she pushed the door open and entered the little parlour. As she did so she started slightly as a figure rose from a chair.

'Lizzie . . .' She stood, staring at her sister. 'Lizzie what are you doing here?'

Lizzie returned Abbie's gaze in silence for a moment or two, then, stepping forward, threw herself into Abbie's arms and burst into tears.

Chapter Thirteen

'Lizzie – what's the matter?'

Lizzie did not answer but only sobbed, her tears wet against Abbie's neck. Abbie held her for a minute or two, then led her to a chair. After a while Lizzie said through her tears, 'I knew you kept a spare latchkey under the flowerpot in the yard – so I let myself in. I haven't seen Father yet. I didn't want to give him a shock – have me suddenly appearing on the doorstep.' She was growing calmer now. Wiping her reddened eyes, she added dully, 'Abbie, I've been dismissed.'

'Dismissed? From your position? What for? What did you do?'

'I didn't do anything. That's just it.'

'Tell me. What happened?'

'She accused me of stealing.'

'Stealing? Who did? Mrs Carling?'

'Yes.'

Abbie gazed at her in disbelief. 'Tell me exactly what happened.'

Lizzie sighed. 'Oh, I had such hopes for this position, Abbie. To be lady's maid for the first time. I thought – well – being lady's maid to Mrs Carling's visitor was a real step up. And I worked hard, I really did. And I thought she was so nice at the beginning – the visitor, Mrs Cresswell. But she changed. She became so demanding and pernickety. I was on the go from morning till night. I managed, though, and I did well. I know I did.

But then she lost a piece of jewellery – a brooch. But I didn't take it, Abbie, you must believe that.'

'Of course you didn't.' Abbie pressed her hand. 'You don't need to tell me that.'

'Both Mrs Cresswell and Mrs Carling questioned me – about the brooch. I told them I didn't know anything about it, but Mrs Cresswell said it had to be me; it couldn't be anyone else. It didn't matter what I said; she wouldn't believe me. She insisted that my box was searched – and then when she couldn't find it she said that I must have hidden it somewhere else. And that was it. Mrs Carling dismissed me. Oh, Abbie, I'll never get another position without references.'

'Well, that's something we'll have to think about.' Abbie got to her feet. 'Have you eaten anything?'

'Not since breakfast. But I couldn't eat. I'm not hungry.'

'Nonsense. You must be starving. I'll get you something.'

Abbie began to prepare tea and scrambled eggs. As she worked Lizzie sat quietly in the chair. Her tears had dried now, but still she looked the picture of misery. When the food was ready Abbie set it out and Lizzie obediently came to the table and ate. When she had finished, Abbie took away the plate and sat down facing her. 'Now,' she said, 'we've got to decide what to do.'

'What *can* we do?'

'Supposing I go and see her – Mrs Carling.'

'What good will come of that?'

'I don't know. But we must do something. It's so unfair. Why should you want the woman's stupid brooch. Either she mislaid it, or someone else must have taken it. Who else is in the house?'

'Three other maids and the cook. But I can't imagine that any of them would think of stealing.'

'Well, it must be somewhere,' Abbie said. Then she

added with a sigh, 'Perhaps you're right. Perhaps there's nothing we can do about it. In which case we'll have to think what to do about your references. I suppose you could apply to your previous employer.'

'Write to Dr Ellis?'

'Well, he gave you a good reference when you left to go to Mrs Carling. And I'm sure if you saw him and told him the situation he'd be happy to do the same again. And he knows you couldn't be capable of stealing.'

'D'you think I could?'

'Why not.'

Lizzie nodded. 'I'll write to him. And I'll go and see Father first thing in the morning.'

'Yes, you don't want him to hear from somebody else that you're back. Besides, he's not well at the moment. He's been home from work the past couple of days – which is unusual for him.'

'What's wrong with him?'

'A severe chill, I think. He'll be all right as long as he rests in the warm. Anyway, come on. Let's get to bed.'

The next morning, Sunday, Abbie accompanied Lizzie to Green Lane to see their father. Having passed a restless night, he had not long got up when they arrived. As Lizzie followed Abbie into the kitchen he looked at her in surprise.

'What are you doing here?'

When Lizzie told him her story he reacted with anger and amazement. 'What? Accuse my girl of stealing? Accuse my girl of being a common thief!' Getting up from his chair, he strode across the room and snatched his coat from its hook. 'I'm going to see that woman. I'm not standing for this!'

'Father, please,' Lizzie said, 'it won't help. There's nothing to be done.'

'Of course there's something to be done! She can't accuse you of theft and get away with it.' His face pale with rage, he stood in the middle of the room, perspiring, his breathing sounding harsh and laboured.

'Come on, Father,' Abbie said, 'you're not in a fit state to go anywhere.'

He remained standing there. 'Well, what do you suggest we do?'

Abbie was at a loss. 'Perhaps we could write Mrs Carling a letter.'

'A fat lot of good that'll do.'

'Well, then,' Abbie said, 'if you're set on going to see her, wait a day or two – at least till you're feeling a bit better. Then we'll go together.'

He continued to protest for a few minutes, then hung up his coat again and sat down. 'All right,' he said, 'but I'm not just letting this ride.'

After Abbie had insisted on preparing some breakfast for him she and Lizzie left for the schoolhouse, telling their father that they would be back to get midday dinner. However, when they returned just after twelve o'clock, they found the cottage empty. A hastily scrawled note from their father, left on the kitchen table, told them that he had gone to Trowbridge to see Lizzie's former employer.

Abbie groaned and shook her head. 'You wonder where Eddie gets his hot-headedness and then you find out. Well – there's nothing we can do now but wait for him to get back.'

Frank Morris had got a ride in a cart as far as Westbury, his benefactor one Fred Haroldson, a local tradesman who told him that he would be returning to Flaxdown that afternoon. 'If you wants a lift,' he said as Frank Morris got down from the cart, 'I'll be passin' by the crossroads 'ere again about quarter past three. If I see you waitin' you're welcome to ride back with me.'

Frank Morris thanked him and said he'd do his best to be there. 'If I look sharp,' he said, 'I can just about get to Trowbridge and back in time.'

He set off then to walk the remaining six-odd miles. The rain that had begun to threaten started to fall heavily when he was within a mile of his destination, but he pressed on; there was no time to stop for shelter. By the time he reached the Laurels, the family home of the Carlings, he was soaked through.

His ring at the back door brought a young maid before him. He told her his name and said he had come to see Mrs Carling. The girl glanced at him curiously for a second, then invited him to step inside while she went to inform her mistress.

As he stood holding his hat he realized what an unprepossessing sight he must present. With his hand-kerchief he dabbed at his cheeks and forehead, but he was so wet that as the minutes dragged by a small pool of water formed on the flags around his feet. He wondered again at his wisdom in making such a precipitate venture. Perhaps Abbie had been right, maybe it would have been wiser to have written a letter.

There came the sound of footsteps and the young maid was there again. 'If you'll come this way, sir. Mrs Carling will see you in the library.'

He thought of his boots on the soft carpets. 'I'm wet through,' he said. 'Wouldn't Mrs Carling prefer me to stay here?' The maid went away again and he waited, and after a few minutes Mrs Carling herself was coming into the room.

She was a tall, middle-aged woman with dark, greying hair, dressed in a blue housecoat. She gave him a somewhat nervous smile and asked him if he would care to sit down. He thanked her but said that if she didn't mind he would prefer to stand. 'You know, ma'am, why I've called, I'm sure,' he added.

'Indeed I do, Mr Morris. This incident concerning Lizzie has been a most unfortunate occurrence . . .' Reaching into her pocket she drew out a letter. 'I wrote to her just this morning. It would have been posted later today.' She gestured to one of the kitchen chairs. 'Do please sit down. It would make it –'

'Mrs Carling,' he said, interrupting her words, 'my girl is not a thief. Lizzie's a good girl. She would never dream of stealing anything.'

'I know that, Mr Morris,' the woman said. 'That's why I've written her this letter.'

He frowned. 'I'm afraid I don't understand . . .'

'No, and why should you?' She gave a sharp little sigh. 'Mr Morris, the missing brooch has been found.'

'It's been found?'

'Yes. That's what I've written to tell Lizzie. It was found last night. The clasp was not secure and the brooch had obviously come loose and fallen. I found it myself, caught on one of the cushions in the drawing room. There's no question of Lizzie having taken it.'

Frank Morris's sense of relief fought with his anger at the unnecessary distress that Lizzie had been caused. 'It was there all the time,' he said, 'and my girl was branded a common thief and dismissed from her post.'

'I don't know what to say,' Mrs Carling said. 'This is very difficult for me. But – well, I didn't know Lizzie. She'd only been with me a very short time.' She gave a helpless little shrug. 'I wish I could undo it all, but that's not possible. Though it goes without saying that if she would care to return here then I shall of course be very pleased to take her back. If, however, she should decide that she cannot, then of course I'll provide her with references for her next post.'

She held out the letter. 'Please – give it to Lizzie. I've explained everything.'

He took the envelope, glanced at it, then put it in his pocket. 'She'll be very relieved. As I am.' As he finished speaking he felt the room sway slightly and he reached out and clutched at the back of a nearby chair.

'Are you all right, Mr Morris?'

He nodded. 'Yes, I'm fine, thank you.'

She frowned. 'You're absolutely soaked. Let me get the maid to bring you a towel.' She waved a hand back towards the deeper interior of the house. 'There's a fire in the library. Wouldn't you like to get dry and rest for a while before you start for home? You've come all this way. I'll have the maid bring you some tea and something to eat.'

'No, no. Thank you anyway.' He shook his head. 'I must get back. I'm getting a lift at Westbury. Besides, my daughters will be wondering about me.'

'Well, at least wait until the rain stops.'

He turned, glancing from the window. 'It's nothing to speak of now.'

'How will you get to Westbury?'

'Walking.'

'But it's miles. Couldn't you take a train from here to Frome? You wouldn't have so far to walk.'

'Yes, that's true, but . . .' He shrugged, moving away, anxious to be gone. 'I'll manage all right.' In the open doorway he turned to her. He felt strangely light-headed and as he wished her good day his voice seemed to come from a long way off, echoing in his head. A moment later he was turning again and stumbling away across the yard.

As he emerged into the lane beside the house he looked

up at the sky. Furled, ragged clouds rolled heavy and dark, but for the moment the rain was light. He pulled down the brim of his hat, turned up the collar of his coat and started off for the main road. On reaching it he came to a stop. It would indeed be easier to take the train from Trowbridge to Frome and walk the three miles from there. But he had already made his arrangements, besides which he could not afford to throw good money away. He reached inside his coat and took his watch from his waistcoat pocket. Just after two o'clock. He had no time to waste if he was to be at the crossroads in time. Turning to the left, he started on the long and winding road that would eventually take him to Westbury.

The rain came on more heavily after a time, but he trudged on; he was still so wet from his previous soaking that he saw no point in taking shelter. As the continuing downpour turned the road into mud, his progress became slower and more difficult. The light-headed sensation that had briefly touched him in the Carling house returned, coming over him in waves, sometimes so powerfully that he became momentarily disorientated and staggered in his path. But then, after taking a few moments for recovery, he would press onwards.

A mile out of Eversleigh he left the road to take a short cut across fields, and still the driving rain came down, lashing his bent head and running beneath the collar of his coat. He had long since ceased to be aware of the discomfort it brought; he was only intent on reaching the crossroads and then getting back home with the good news for Lizzie.

The footpath he followed led for part of the route alongside a small wood where he was sheltered in part from the rain. It could do nothing, however, to diminish his growing fever, and as he made his way his walk became a staggering gait. With the sky reeling above him, he came to a halt, clutching at a tree trunk for support, and there he clung, trying to slow his gasping breath.

Pushing on once more, he took a few further staggering steps and then, catching his foot against the root of a beech tree, fell heavily onto the sodden ground. There he lay without moving, eyes closed, his only feeling one of relief at the chance to rest for a while.

It was nearly half past three when Fred Haroldson approached the crossroads. He had been delayed because of the storm. The rain had ceased now, however, and the sun had come out, burning fiercely, drying the mud of the road and drawing a fine haze of vapour from the verges and the hedgerows. Reaching the crossroads Haroldson brought the mare to a halt and looked around him. There was no one in sight. Frank must have got tired of waiting, he thought, and made his own way back to Flaxdown. After a while he flicked the reins, called out a command to the mare and the cart started forward again.

While Fred Haroldson continued on his way back to Flaxdown, Frank Morris lay beneath the beech tree at the edge of the wood. As his clothes dried in the warm sun, the bluebottles were already buzzing around him and settling on his flesh and crawling into his mouth.

Chapter Fourteen

Stooping over the grave in which her father now lay, Abbie made a final adjustment to the white roses in the little earthenware pot.

It was a bright Saturday afternoon, the last day in August. Five weeks had passed since her father's death. When he had not returned that rainy Sunday she and Lizzie had gone out searching for him – though without direction, for they had not known the precise way he had travelled. Then, early that evening there had come word that his body had been found. The letter in his pocket, addressed to Lizzie, had quickly led to his identification.

Since that time there had been so many occasions when, finding herself absorbed in thoughts of him, Abbie could do nothing but weep. She wept not only over the fact of his loss but also for his goodness, for the unrewarded struggles he had known in his life and for his disappointment in the loveless marriage he had known.

For those remaining life had, of course, to go on. The cottage in Green Lane had passed to Eddie – which, Abbie thought, was the way it should be (her father's books Eddie had given to her – which was all that she had wanted). Lizzie too, now, was settled. She had not returned to her former position – it was too uncomfortably bound up with her father's death – but with the aid of glowing references from Mrs Carling had found a new

175

post – this time in Lullington – and seemed to be reasonably content there.

Now, Abbie realized as she turned from the grave, her own ties to Flaxdown were far less strong than they had been. Apart from Eddie – who in any case was immersed in his own family and his own life – she now had no real bond with the village. Beatie and her father were dead; her mother had long since abandoned all connection with the place, and Lizzie and Iris were away in service and unlikely ever to return here to live – as likewise was Jane. It was only her own work at the school that kept Abbie in Flaxdown. As she made her way between the graves onto the gravel path she had a sudden picture of herself in twenty or thirty years, a mature woman, the archetypal spinster schoolmistress. The thought filled her with a strange, vague regret.

In the schoolhouse she made some tea and read for a while, then began to work on her knitting for Violet's coming baby. She could not relax, though, and after twenty minutes or so she put the half-finished garment in its bag and went outside. After standing at the gate for a while, she opened it and walked out into the lane.

At the end of the lane she turned away from the village, taking a narrow footpath that led across a field where sheep and cattle grazed. At the far side she crossed over a stile and followed the path beside a field of ripening wheat. She was aware of a strange restlessness within her, a feeling akin to that she had known in the churchyard earlier that afternoon. Leaving the cornfield behind her, she walked through a small thicket, coming to a halt at the far side where she sat on a stile to rest for a while before returning. As she sat there she heard footsteps approaching behind her and turned to see a tall figure coming along the path. As he drew nearer she recognized him as the man with whom she and Jane had driven back from Warminster a month before.

His smile as he came closer showed that he in turn had recognized her. 'Well, hello,' he said, touching his hat.

She got down from the stile and smilingly returned his greeting.

He climbed over and stood facing her. 'It's Miss Morris, isn't it?'

'Yes.' She gave a shake of her head. 'But I'm afraid I don't remember your name – forgive me.'

'Gilmore. Arthur Gilmore.'

'Ah – yes.'

'Are you well?'

She nodded. 'Yes, quite well, thank you. And you?'

'Oh, well enough. Are you on your way to Keyford?'

'No, I was just about to go back to Flaxdown. I only came out for a stroll to get a little air.'

'Good. Perhaps we can walk together. If you've no objection.'

She nodded – she could do nothing but acquiesce – and together they set off.

'You're bound for Flaxdown, are you?' Abbie said.

'Yes, I have an errand to do.'

'And no carriage today?'

'It's not my carriage. It belongs to my landlord. He kindly allows me to use it on occasion.'

They walked on. After a while he said, 'I'm so pleased to chance upon you like this. I was hoping to meet you again at some time.' He paused. 'I heard about your father. I'm so sorry.'

Looking up, she saw sympathy in his dark eyes. She nodded her thanks.

'Were you – close to your father?' he asked.

'Yes . . .'

'I'm sure you must miss him dreadfully.'

'Yes, I do.'

'I know how you must feel – what you're going through. My mother died three years ago. I understand, believe me.'

They emerged from the thicket onto the path that led beside the cornfield.

'You've got brothers and sisters, haven't you?' he added.

'An older brother and two younger sisters. My brother's married and lives in Flaxdown. My sisters are away in service.' She added after a moment, 'I have to be honest and say that I don't envy them their work.'

'I'm sure you don't.'

'No. I consider myself very fortunate to have the job I have.'

He nodded. 'You'll be busy again soon with the new school term starting.'

'Just a couple more weeks.'

'Are you looking forward to it?'

'Yes, I am. It's hard work but I like to be busy. What about you? Is your work going well?'

'Oh, well enough. I didn't expect to be staying here so long. And now there's talk of my remaining for a year or more.'

'How do you feel about that?'

'I don't mind the idea.'

Having left the cornfield behind them, they started along the path across the cattle pasture. They were close to Flaxdown now.

'Have you heard from your friend Jane since she returned to London?' he said.

'Yes, I've heard from her. She's well.'

They had reached the stile where the footpath emerged onto the lane, and Arthur Gilmore moved ahead of her and, murmuring 'Allow me . . .' stepped over the stile and reached out to help her over. She climbed up, took his outstretched hand and stepped down on the other side.

'Where are you off to now?' he asked as he released her. 'Back home?' They were heading now for School Lane.

'Yes. But please don't come out of your way,' Abbie said.

'I've got plenty of time.'

A few minutes later they came to the gate of the little schoolhouse. They stood in silence for a moment or two, then Arthur said, 'I was wondering whether you would care to come out with me some day soon.'

'Oh,' Abbie said doubtfully, 'I'm afraid I tend not to go out a great deal.'

'Then it might make a nice change for you. It's Sunday tomorrow. Perhaps I could call on you in the afternoon.'

'Well – I'm not sure about tomorrow.' She avoided his glance.

'You already have an engagement?'

'Well, no, but . . .'

'Then let me call for you tomorrow. May I? If I can get the carriage we could go for a little drive – if you'd care to.'

She said nothing, though she knew that with her silence she was committing herself.

'Three o'clock, then all right?' he said. 'I'll be here at three.'

The following afternoon Abbie put on her best dress and best straw bonnet, the former of dark-blue velvet, the latter trimmed with matching silk ribbon. She was so unaccustomed to dressing up, that although the garments were more than three years old she regarded them as new. When she opened the door to Arthur at three o'clock he greeted her with a smile and what was unmistakably a little nod of approval.

He had been unable to acquire his landlord's carriage that day and so they walked, wandering leisurely along the lanes. During this time Abbie learned that he was twenty-eight years old, the son of a clergyman, now dead, whose parish had been in Clerkenwell, London. His late mother had, before her marriage, been a governess in Brighton.

In addition to Arthur's agreeable appearance – no one could have denied that he was good-looking – Abbie found that he was well-informed and well-read, and they discovered much to discuss when the talk turned to topical matters or to various works of literature. He was interested in the theatre, too, and in the opera, and appeared to be well-travelled. Abbie, who had journeyed barely twenty miles beyond Flaxdown, listened with fascination as he spoke not only of his years in London, but also of trips to Edinburgh and Paris.

Later that day, after he had accompanied her back to the schoolhouse and left her to make his return to Keyford, she realized that in spite of any doubts she had harboured she had greatly enjoyed the excursion.

As summer gave way to autumn the new school term began and Abbie found herself once again immersed in her work. And she and Arthur continued to meet. Although he was away for much of the time in the course of his duties, travelling to various factories over the surrounding areas, when he returned he would make the two-mile journey from Keyford to Flaxdown, and he and Abbie would go walking or driving. She welcomed his visits and found herself enjoying his company. For a while she had wondered why he had not married – he was obviously an attractive marriage proposition – but then during one of their meetings he revealed that in the past he had had a relationship with a young woman in London which had ended when she turned to another. He spoke little about it, however, giving the impression that it was well and truly over, and rarely referred to it afterwards. On those occasions when he had to go away in connection with his work he kept in touch by writing to Abbie, sending her short missives with brief comments on his employment and his surroundings, and occasionally enclosing a cutting from a newspaper in which he thought she would be interested.

After Abbie had written to tell Jane of her renewed acquaintance with Arthur, Jane demanded to be informed of its progress. Abbie wrote that there was nothing to report; she and Arthur, she insisted, were merely good friends and nothing more. In spite of Abbie's protests, though, it was clear that Jane saw the relationship as the beginning of a romance – 'For which you should thank God,' she wrote. 'Eligible men as handsome and charming as Mr Gilmore are scarcer than hens' teeth.' Abbie laughed over Jane's words; she and Jane, she silently observed, wanted different things from life; it was as simple as that.

On the 19th of November Violet's baby was born, a daughter whom her proud parents named Sarah. Abbie, watching Eddie as he clucked and cooed over the baby, remarked that one would think that no man had ever been a father before. Eddie, laughing, told Abbie that for all her book learning she didn't know everything, but that one day, with luck, she would perhaps learn and understand a little more. Abbie found it a touching sight to see her brother with his small daughter in his arms; his large labourer's hands holding her with such sure tenderness and his usual loud, boisterous voice reduced to the gentlest of tones. At such times all of Eddie's accustomed roughness vanished as if it had never been.

Arthur, who had been away in London for almost two weeks, returned to Keyford the following Friday. The next morning he drove over to Flaxdown in the borrowed carriage, picked up Abbie from the schoolhouse and drove her back to Keyford with him. From there they walked to the nearby railway station at Frome and took a train for Trowbridge.

In the town Abbie bought a rattle for the baby. Afterwards, the late-November day being unusually cold, they were glad to retreat to the warmth and shelter of an inn where they ordered a simple meal of game pie and vegetables. With it Arthur asked for ale for himself and tea for Abbie. As they ate, facing one another at the scrubbed-wood table, the air filled with the clinking of pewter and china, and the chatter of voices, Arthur told her of his visit to Her Majesty's Theatre in London the week before when he had seen a production of Verdi's *Don Carlos*, the composer's latest opera to be seen in London.

'The music is just magnificent,' he said. 'It's so stirring. And the costumes and the spectacle ... Oh, Abbie, you would have loved it.' Doubtless she would have, Abbie thought, though her chances of getting an opportunity to do so were so slim as to be non-existent. The nearest she had ever come to hearing an opera was at a concert given in Warminster when an over-large, throaty soprano and a rather short tenor had sung arias from French and Italian operas.

'What are you thinking about?'

As Arthur's voice broke into her thoughts she smiled at him. 'Oh, nothing in particular.'

'Truly? Sometimes you're so far away, and I wonder what's going on in your mind.' He put his head on one side, studying her. 'Are you content with your lot, Abbie?'

She gave a little laugh. 'Content? Well, I'm a lot better off than many other people, I'm sure of that.' She paused. 'Though I could sometimes wish I felt a little more ... secure.'

'Secure? In what way?'

'In my situation. At the school. If truth be told I have to admit that I'm not there with the unanimous blessing of the School Governors. There are one or two who wouldn't be sorry to see me gone.'

'Why is that?'

'I don't know. Perhaps because I've refused to be awed by them.'

'But having employed you in the post for four years, surely they can't still have doubts about your suitability. You must have proved yourself long since.'

'You think so?' She gave an ironic smile. 'Not everyone sees it that way. I have no doubt but that certain members of the Board are just waiting for me to make a mistake. But until I do there's nothing much they can do to me. So – I have to be careful and watch my step.'

'And – how would you feel if you should have to leave?'

She frowned. 'Well – I would be very sorry to find myself without work, without means of supporting myself.'

'Yes, I'm sure. And apart from that?'

She sighed. 'Oh, I don't know. I suppose if I'm honest I just have to admit that it hasn't turned out the way I had hoped – the way I anticipated. It's wonderful to be able to teach children to read and write – when so many of their parents, having had no schooling whatsoever, are illiterate. But I'm so constrained. I have to be so careful all the time – not to impart any ideas of my own. "Make sure that you keep always to the three Rs, Miss Morris. It's what the results are counted upon." ' She shook her head. 'It's not easy.'

'Perhaps you hoped for too much.'

'Oh, I've no doubt that I did. As I recall, I promised the vicar not to try to change the world from my classroom – but perhaps in reality I hoped that I could. I must have had my head in the clouds.'

'So what do you want out of life, Abbie?'

'What do I want out of life?' She put down her knife and fork, and pushed aside her plate. 'You sound like my father.'

'Do I? But what do you want? I thought you were happy in your work – but I find today that you're not as content as I supposed. I've known you now for about three months. In that time I've learned what your interests are; I've learned about your political views; I know what kind of books you read and which artists you admire. But sometimes I feel I know nothing about what's going on inside you – in your mind and in your heart.'

Abbie gave an awkward little laugh. 'In my heart?'

He nodded. 'Yes, in your heart.'

'Oh, Arthur –'

'I'm curious,' he said. 'Do you want what other women want?'

'What's that? Marriage? Children?'

'Is there something wrong with such things?'

'No, of course not. I'm not sure they're for me, that's all.'

'How can you say that?'

'It's what I feel.'

'Then where does your happiness lie?'

'I don't know. It might be in my teaching.' It was as if in some way a nerve had been touched and she was aware that she was slightly irritated by the questions. 'All

184

right,' she said, 'I might not be totally content in my work at the moment, but that doesn't mean to say that I shall not be in the future. I don't have to stay at the Flaxdown school.'

'Well, my work wouldn't be enough for me, I know that,' he said. 'I want more out of life than that.' He paused. 'A home, a wife, children . . .'

Abbie said nothing. While all around them the common sounds continued, she became aware of a strange little fluttering of panic. Then into the quiet between them Arthur said, 'I think I shall be leaving soon.'

'Leaving? You mean leaving Keyford?'

'Yes. I think they've found a permanent replacement for me down here. I believe I'm to be based in London again before long. I'll know for sure in the next few days.'

'Does that mean you won't ever return here?'

'Not to work, anyway. I'll have no reason to come here where work is concerned.'

She gave a little nod. 'Oh.'

Arthur looked at her with an ironic smile. '"Oh?" ' he said. 'Is that all?'

'Well . . .' She did not know what to say.

After a little hesitation he asked, 'Will you miss me, Abbie?'

'What? Oh, yes – yes, of course I shall.'

Arthur considered her rather matter-of-fact tone, then said with a shrug, 'Ah, well . . .'

'What does that mean?'

He smiled. 'I'd hoped that you would react . . . a little differently.'

'I'm sorry.' She felt awkward. 'I don't understand. I just –'

'Oh, Abbie,' he said, 'for weeks now I've been calling on you. And I know that you've been pleased to see me, but –'

'I have,' she broke in. 'I have been pleased to see you.'

'Yes, but you've given me no encouragement, have you?'

'Encouragement . . . ?'

'I don't want to be just a friend to you, Abbie. I've been hoping for more than that.'

She looked at him in confusion. Her emotions were in turmoil.

'Surely you've realized that?' he said.

She sighed. 'Oh, Arthur, I didn't. I didn't realize. I truly didn't. I've been selfish. I'm sorry. I've been so happy to see you. I've so enjoyed our conversations, our meetings. But – well – I was never looking for anything more.'

'I understand that now,' he said. Then with a shrug he added, 'So perhaps it's just as well that I'm leaving.'

'I don't know what to say. I feel that I've been leading you on.'

'No, you haven't,' he said. 'The fault is mine. As I said just now, you never gave me the slightest encouragement, or any reason to believe that I should expect more from our relationship than friendship.'

'I'm sorry . . .'

'It's all right.' He glanced towards the window. 'The sky's beginning to look very heavy. I think perhaps we ought to start back to the station, don't you?'

On the train they kept the conversation on safe ground, talking of mundane matters while the rain lashed at the windows. When they got to Frome Arthur hired a fly to take them to Flaxdown. After a journey during which their conversation was desultory and self-conscious, they came at last to the village. At the entrance to School Lane Arthur asked the driver to wait and then walked with Abbie to the schoolhouse. The rain had stopped and the last of the dull daylight was fading. In the doorway of the cottage Arthur looked down into Abbie's eyes.

'It's such a shame,' he said. 'I had great hopes for us.'

She said nothing.

'Well,' he said, 'I must go. I'd like to kiss you goodnight – but I must think of your reputation.' He added wryly, 'And also of the possibility that you might not care for me to do so.' Briefly his hand came up, his fingertips lightly at her chin. 'Thank you for spending the day with me.'

Without another word he turned and stepped along the path to the gate. Abbie stood, watching his dark, shadowed figure as he walked along the lane. Just before he moved out of sight he stopped, turned and raised his hat. Next moment he had moved on and was gone from her sight.

Chapter Fifteen

Seated at her desk, Abbie glanced through the window at the grey afternoon sky, then turned her attention back to the children who sat working at their desks. There were twenty-four in the class, their ages ranging from seven to ten years. The older ones, Abbie knew, would probably not remain beyond the end of the autumn term. As it was, she could never be sure how many of them would be present on any particular day. Nearly all her pupils were the offspring of farmers or farm labourers, and when there was a conflict of priorities – the children's school work or helping their parents in the home or on the farm – it was always the school work that came second. Perhaps there would come a day, she thought, when education was compulsory for all children. At present, though, such a hope seemed to have little chance of becoming reality.

The sounds in the room were composed of the ticking of the clock, the scrape of the children's chalks on their slates and the occasional whisper or sniff. At the moment they were working on some simple arithmetical problems that Abbie had written up on the blackboard. In ten minutes or so, at two thirty, she would bring the arithmetic lesson to an end and they would start work on their history studies.

She sighed. There was a strange feeling of melancholy upon her today. Was it because of Arthur? She had half expected that he would call on her yesterday, Sunday, the day following their outing to Trowbridge, but he had not. Although, she said to herself, she could not really blame him; he now probably saw their whole relationship as having been a complete waste of time. Perhaps she would never see him again. She felt a pang of regret at the notion. Oh, why, she wondered, did things have to get so complicated? Why could they not simply have continued as they were?

Fifteen minutes later she had just got her pupils started on their history lesson when the door opened and to her surprise and dismay the school inspector, Mr Carstairs, entered. Her low spirits sank even lower. During her years at the school he had frequently made unannounced visits to the classroom, and always, she was sure, with the sole hope of finding some fault with her lessons. She had no doubt at all that this was his purpose today. As always, however, she was determined to give him no cause for complaint.

Now, as she and the children got to their feet, Mr Carstairs gave her a brief nod, his thin lips moving in a cold smile. With a curt wave of his hand to the children he instructed them to go on with their lessons, while to Abbie he added that it was not his wish to cause any disruption.

A chair was brought for him by one of the pupils and he took off his overcoat and sat down. The children, as awed and intimidated by his presence as ever, were on their best behaviour, so Abbie had no concerns in that respect. However, his very presence as he sat watching her every move and listening to her every word put her into an acute state of self-consciousness, and she was greatly relieved when he at last put on his coat, wished her a curt good day and left the room.

Five minutes later, when the children too had gone home, Abbie remained sitting at her desk. It was so unjust, she said to herself. She was good at her job, and she worked hard at it, yet for all her efforts she met only antipathy from the likes of Carstairs, and she was quite sure that as long as he held his post of school inspector her grasp on her own position would remain as tenuous as ever. How could it be otherwise when he was just waiting for her to put a foot wrong?

She sighed. She could feel the pricking of tears and only with an effort managed to keep them back. Impatient with herself, she got up from her chair and, after checking that the windows were closed and the stove was safe, she let herself out of the building, locked the door behind her and set off across the yard.

She passed a restless evening. She had intended to go and visit Eddie and Violet to see the new baby again, but she did not and remained alone. At nine thirty she put aside her book for the third time. She was trying to read Thomas Hardy's new novel *Desperate Remedies*, but she was finding it impossible to concentrate. She would do a little sewing for half an hour and then go to bed.

As she got up to get her sewing basket there came a knock at the door. When she opened it a moment later she saw Arthur standing on the step.

'Hello, Abbie.'

She returned his smile, aware of how very pleased she was to see him. 'Well – this is an unexpected pleasure.'

'Are you busy right now?' he asked.

'No, not particularly . . .'

'I'm sorry to call so late,' he said after a moment's hesitation, 'but I had to see you. I wanted to tell you that I'm leaving the day after tomorrow. I'm going back to London.'

'Oh . . .' Abbie knew she sounded disappointed. 'So soon.'

'I'm afraid so. I was expecting it, as you know. It's just

happening a little earlier than I anticipated. I learned of it just this morning.'

Conscious of her position not only as a single woman but also as the village schoolmistress, she hesitated about asking him in without a chaperone present. However it was too cold and too late for them to stand talking on the step or to go out walking. She glanced about her then stood aside. 'Please – come into the warm.'

He stepped inside and she closed the door behind him.

'How did you get here?' she asked as she put the kettle on to boil.

'I got a cab.' He set his lantern on the kitchen table, took off his coat and sat down on the sofa.

'So,' she said, as she busied herself with the cups and saucers, 'you're leaving on Wednesday.'

'Yes.'

Without looking at him, she said, 'I shall miss you. I've enjoyed our times together; our walks, our talks.'

'I shall miss you too. Very much.'

Suddenly as she stood at the table the tears that had threatened earlier came brimming over. Quickly he got up and moved to her side. 'Abbie, what is it?'

'Oh – it's just that everything seems to be going wrong,' she said. 'I've had a bad day at school and now you come to tell me you're going away.' Dabbing at her eyes with a handkerchief she added, 'Listen to me – making such a fuss. I'm sorry.' When Arthur took one of her hands in his she made no attempt to resist, only glad of the comfort she felt at his touch.

'Tell me what happened today at school,' he said.

She told him of Carstairs's visit that afternoon, of the way he had sat in critical observance of her.

Arthur listened in silent sympathy, and when she had finished said, 'Abbie, I didn't come here tonight simply to tell you that I'm leaving. After our conversation on

Saturday I thought everything had been said and that I might go off without seeing you again. But I realized I couldn't.' He appeared uncertain of how to frame his words. 'I want to ask you to think again on what I said to you – that I had hoped to be more to you than just a friend. I still want that. I still hope for that.'

She said nothing.

'You're not happy here now, Abbie, I know that. You're not, are you?'

'Well – not at present, no . . .'

'No. You're alone now that your father's gone, besides the fact that you're having these frustrating difficulties with your work . . .' He paused. 'You don't have to stay here, you know.'

'I realize that. I could try to find a position at a different school. Go somewhere else.'

'Well, yes, you could. But that isn't what I meant.' He hesitated, the moment stretching out, then added: 'You could marry me.'

She did not know what to say. In the silence the ticking of the clock was suddenly loud in the room.

'Truly,' Arthur said. 'Oh, Abbie – we get on so well. I've loved the times I've spent with you. Why shouldn't they continue? We could be so good together. We could build a new life for the two of us, a good life. I would look after you – you must know that – and you would never need to fear people like Carstairs ever again. Give it up, all of it. Marry me.'

He waited for her to speak; when she still did not he went on, 'I know how you value your independence and I realize too that you don't seem to set great store by marriage. But Abbie, you mustn't judge every marriage by those that have failed. There are so many that are truly happy. And we could be, I know we could.' He gazed at her intently. 'Oh, Abbie, tell me you'll marry me. Tell me you will.'

She did not know what to say. Her thoughts were in turmoil. She could not tell – how could she tell? – was it love she felt for him? This deep affection and respect – did they add up to love? But in any case, was love so vital to happiness? Her father had loved and it had brought him only misery in his marriage. Beatrice, too, had loved. And what had that love brought her? Perhaps love was not necessary. Liking, respect, understanding – perhaps other qualities mattered equally in the long run. Perhaps they mattered even more. She looked at him as he stood before her, tall and straight, an anxious, slightly eager expression on his handsome face.

'I didn't know you cared for me in that way,' she said. 'I didn't know you cared so – so deeply.'

'Oh, I do, Abbie. I think you're such a grand young woman. And I know we could be so happy together.'

After a moment she gave a nod, then heard her voice as if from a long way off: 'Yes, Arthur – I will.'

'Oh, Abbie.' He stepped to her side, drew her to him and put his arms around her. 'You won't regret it. I promise you'll never regret it.'

It was nearly midnight. The two hours since Abbie had accepted Arthur's proposal had flown by. She had made tea and served a simple supper of bread, cheese and pickles, and as they had eaten and drunk they had talked of their future together.

Now it was time for him to go, and with a taper lighted from the fire he lit his lantern again, picked up his hat and moved to the front door. Abbie followed close behind him.

'I suppose,' Arthur said, 'I ought to go and see your

brother; ask his permission; do the right thing. I'll go and see him tomorrow.'

Abbie smiled. 'He'll be so relieved. He's had visions of me remaining here for ever – his old maid sister the schoolmistress, getting more eccentric by the year.'

During their discussions it had been decided that they would marry in Flaxdown in the spring, at Easter time, Abbie being wed from Eddie's home. In the meantime she would formally give notice that she would be leaving her teaching post at Easter on the termination of the winter term.

'And then,' Arthur had said, 'after our honeymoon I'll take you back to London with me – to your new home. I should get a promotion soon. But even without that I can promise you a good life. My father left me fairly comfortable, financially. I'm sure you'll like the house too.'

'Is it a big house?'

'Well, not so big, compared with other houses. It has twelve rooms.'

'Twelve rooms!' Abbie said. 'Not so big? That's enormous.'

Arthur laughed. 'Anyway, you won't have the work of cleaning it. You'll have maids. And a cook, too.'

'Maids and a cook? What shall I do with my time?'

'It won't hurt you to have a little less to do. I don't want to see you working as hard as you do now. Besides, there'll be plenty to keep you occupied. But whatever you do, you're not going to have any more of these problems. There'll be no worrying in case your pupils don't pass their school tests and the Board docks your wages. Nor whether Carstairs is coming round to check up on you. No more wondering whether you'll still have a job come the next school term.' He took her hands. 'Abbie, I know we shall be happy. I know it. Our interests are so in tune.

How could we not be happy together?' He sighed, a sound of pleasure. 'I can't wait to bring you to London.'

He put on his hat, drew her to him again and kissed her on the mouth. For the first time in so long she felt needed, wanted. After a moment he broke away and stood looking down at her. 'I think I'd better leave now,' he said. 'For the sake of your reputation if not of my own.'

Another kiss, lingering this time, and then he straightened and stepped out into the night.

Later, upstairs, Abbie put out the candle on the little table beside her bed and lay back on the pillow, looking into the dark. How could so much have happened in one single day? Not so many hours ago she had been utterly miserable and now everything had turned around.

Had she done the right thing in accepting Arthur's proposal? she asked herself. And then the answer came to her – yes, of course it was right. He was a good man, strong, dependable and, more important than that, he loved her. And the love of such a man was something to be prized, to be treasured. But love, on her part . . . ? How important was that? Once again there came thoughts of Beatrice and her Thomas Greening – of her own father and mother. Beatrice had loved, her father had loved – and love for them had brought no happiness whatsoever. No, she said to herself, where she and Arthur were concerned, it was important that she had such affection for him – and not only affection, but great respect and admiration. So many, many marriages had succeeded on so much less. And her coming marriage to Arthur? Yes, that would succeed. She was determined on that. For one thing she was going into it with no illusions; she was a sensible woman with both feet on the ground – not some starry-eyed teenager who could be swept off her feet by the first kind word and handsome face. They would be good for one another, she was sure. And apart from that, how good it would be to leave behind all the present frustrations that had arisen through her work. There were other things she could do with her life. She would not be idle – perhaps she could help Arthur with his work in some way. In any case, together they would build their happiness. A happiness for which they surely had sound foundations. Yes. Yes. She gave a little nod in the dark – she was doing the right thing. She had no doubt now, nor would she in the future.

She closed her eyes. After a while she slept.

The following evening was the last before Arthur was to return to London. Following his arrival at the school-house he and Abbie went to call on Eddie and Violet. When told by Arthur of his wish to marry Abbie, Eddie said drily, 'Well, thank God for that. I was beginnin' to think it'd never 'appen.'

The day after Arthur's departure Abbie wrote to Jane, Lizzie and Iris telling them of her engagement. They responded with warm congratulations and expressions of gladness. 'And you,' Jane wrote, 'always swore that I'd be the first to wed. So much for all your protestations, all your determination to remain an old maid.'

As the days passed Abbie heard regularly from Arthur and replied promptly to his letters. They had little to relate to one another apart from the progress of their daily lives, but nevertheless she looked forward to hearing from him and was disappointed when the old red-coated postman did not call.

In mid-December Arthur wrote inviting her to spend Christmas with him in London. Anxious to do the right thing, he also wrote to Eddie, asking his permission for the visit and telling him that Abbie would be properly chaperoned during her stay. Eddie, pleased to be asked, replied that it was up to Abbie. Abbie wrote to Arthur that she would be delighted to go.

A few days later she stood in the classroom as her pupils left their seats for the last time that year, their calls of 'Merry Christmas, Miss' making a ragged chorus as they trooped out into the cold afternoon air. As always, she watched their departure with a mixture of regret and relief. They did not know it yet, she thought, but the next term would be the last they would spend with her. From next Easter they would have a new teacher. When she returned from her trip to London she would write her letter of resignation.

She could scarcely believe that she was to spend Christmas in London and was thrilled at the prospect of a visit to the capital. Not only would she see the huge London shops, perhaps visit the theatre and go to a museum, but she would see Jane, too. Having learned that Jane would have some time free from her duties over Christmas, Arthur had urged Abbie to invite her to come and see them, and arrangements for visits had consequently been made.

Abbie had spent several days getting things ready for her trip – including going to Trowbridge to buy some new clothes – and when the Sunday morning of her departure came she was up early to make last-minute preparations. She had intended to hire a cab to take her to the railway station at Frome, but Eddie had spoken to his employer and borrowed his carriage. When Eddie called just after nine o'clock Abbie was all ready and waiting. She was wearing a newly purchased grey ulster with dark-blue braiding, and a trim little jockey hat decorated with ribbons. She knew that she looked well in the outfit, but nevertheless she felt somewhat overdressed and self-conscious – particularly when Eddie whistled at the sight of her and said, 'Oh, plannin' to 'ave tea with the Queen, are we?'

At Frome station Eddie shouldered her box and carried it onto the platform while Abbie bought her ticket. As she joined him to await the arrival of her train he said, 'Now you're sure you're gunna be all right?'

She rather suspected that he had some misgivings about her trip; he didn't really approve of her going off to spend a week in the house of a single man, notwithstanding that she was engaged to be married to him and would be chaperoned. His anxieties were somehow bound up with Beatie, she felt; since Beatie's death he had become very concerned for the welfare of his sisters.

'Of course I shall be all right,' Abbie insisted, then added, 'Arthur is a gentleman, Eddie. I shan't come to any harm.'

'Oh, ah,' he said with a wry smile, 'there's many a maid 'ave believed that to 'er lastin' misery.'

The train came in and when Abbie's box had been safely stowed away in the guard's van Eddie saw her aboard. He gave her a quick peck on the cheek as she leaned from the window to him, then the train was starting off.

At Trowbridge she changed for the London-bound train. There were three other travellers in the compartment she entered, an elderly cleric and two middle-aged women. Abbie exchanged murmured good mornings with them, then settled into her seat for the remainder of the long journey ahead. Sitting at the carriage window, her book momentarily forgotten, she gazed out through the smoke-begrimed window at the fields, woodlands and villages. The train stopped at the stations of unfamiliar towns, too: Chippenham, Calne, Swindon . . . After a time she grew bored with watching from the window and turned to her book and to eat and drink some of the refreshments she had brought along.

Didcot, Oxford, Reading and finally, at last, the train was entering the suburbs of London. And the nearer it carried her towards the heart of the city, the stranger the scenery became. She had never seen so many houses, so many buildings – and built so close one upon the other. It was like a different world. The dusty, dirty, smoke-grey buildings rose up on either side of the track like a forest. Seen from such a viewpoint, London seemed a very ugly place.

At last the train drew into Paddington Station. She got off, moved to the guard's van to take possession of her box and, turning, saw Arthur striding along the platform.

Looking very handsome in his dark-brown chesterfield, he embraced her and kissed her on the cheek. Then, while the other travellers milled about them, he held her at arm's length and looked at her. 'Oh, Abbie,' he said, 'you're a sight for sore eyes and no mistake.'

With Abbie's box following in the care of a porter, they went out to where the hackney cabs waited for hire and minutes later were sitting in a carriage, moving through the London streets. Here again was something new for Abbie. Now her journey took her through streets lined by tall, elegant houses, through areas with huge shops with wide front windows. She had never in her life before seen streets so busy; even Trowbridge on a market day did not see so many carriages and people bustling back and forth. And the town was so vast – it seemed to be going on for ever – why one could live here for a hundred years, she thought, and never see the half of it.

'Where are we going to?' she asked. 'This city goes on for ever.'

'We're heading for an area known as Ladbroke Grove,' Arthur replied. 'We'll be there soon.'

When before too long the cab came to a halt, it was in a quiet, residential street. Arthur helped her down while the driver took up her box and carried it up a small flight of steps to the front door of an attractive terrace house.

'This is it?' Abbie said with a slight note of wonder, looking up at the tall building.

'Yes.' Arthur nodded. 'This is it.'

Once the coach driver had put Abbie's box in the hall, and taken his fee and left, Abbie was introduced to the resident cook-housekeeper, Mrs Appleton, and the young daily housemaid, Ida. Mrs Appleton was a pleasant-mannered widow in her fifties; Ida a shy, plain-looking girl of nineteen or so. Abbie found herself standing self-consciously while the introductions were made; she could not but be aware of her own very humble beginnings. Indeed, had things worked out differently, she herself could have been in the situation that Ida, the housemaid, was presently in. Could they see through her? the thought flashed through her mind. Were they aware that her present role was, in her eyes at least, part reality, part performance. But no, they spoke to her with respect and her moment of unease passed swiftly.

The introductions over, Arthur shouldered Abbie's box and led the way up to her room. While his own was on the first floor, Abbie, for propriety's sake, was to be installed on the second, just across the landing from Mrs Appleton.

With the maid Ida behind her, Abbie followed Arthur into the room, which was warmly and attractively furnished, and had a bright fire burning in the grate. As Arthur set down her box she looked about her in delight. 'Oh, Arthur, it's lovely.'

'You like it? I'm afraid it needs a little attention. But that will be a good job for you to take in hand once you're here to stay. Anyway, you'll be comfortable enough in the meantime.' Taking in the maid with a smile, he added, 'If you need anything I'm sure Ida will be only to glad to oblige.' He turned and moved to the door. 'Come down when you're ready and we'll have some tea.'

When he had gone from the room the young maid asked Abbie whether she should unpack her box for her. Abbie thanked her but said she could manage on her own. While the maid hung up Abbie's hat and coat, Abbie moved to the window that looked out over the back garden and, beyond it, to a large rectangle of lawn and shrubbery. 'Who does that belong to?' she asked. '– the little green area in the centre there?' Ida replied that it was a communal garden, for the use of the square's residents. What an odd concept, Abbie thought, and wondered again at the strange ways of London and its people. When Ida had gone from the room, Abbie moved to the bed and lay back across it. How luxurious it felt compared with her narrow little bed at the schoolhouse. And how luxurious the room itself when compared with those she had inhabited in the past, both in her family home and the little schoolhouse. Once again it came to her that she was entering a new world. And for all her dreams it was a world she had never foreseen as a reality.

That evening she and Arthur enjoyed a quiet, pleasant dinner together. The food prepared by Mrs Appleton was excellent, as was the wine   not an elderberry or dandelion wine such as Abbie had drunk on occasion in Flaxdown, but a wine from France. Afterwards, Arthur played for her on the piano and sang a couple of simple songs in his pleasant baritone. Warmed by a bright fire that burned in the wide fireplace, Abbie sat drinking her coffee while above her head the gas lamps glowed, reflecting in the crystal and the china that decorated the room.

She could not get over the newness of everything. It was almost as if it were happening to someone else, perhaps some heroine in one of the romances that her mother had used to read. But it was true enough. And, she reminded herself, such a way of life would soon become the norm for her. The realization brought, not for the first time, a little frisson of pleasure. What would her father have thought, she wondered, if he could only have seen her now?

'What are you thinking about?'

The music had come to an end. Arthur sat on the piano stool smiling at her. She smiled back at him and shook her head.

'Oh, nothing – and everything.'

'I'm sorry I shan't be able to spend much time with you tomorrow,' he said. 'Until the evening, anyway.' Like most other people, he would be working right up to Christmas Day. 'But at least Jane'll be coming here to see you in the afternoon,' he added, 'so you won't be bored.'

'Oh, no. It'll be wonderful to see her again.'

'What are the two of you going to do? Have you thought about it?'

'Not yet. We'll think of something. We might well just stay here and talk.'

' . . . And talk, and talk.'

Abbie laughed. 'Very likely.'

There was a little silence, then Arthur said, 'Do you think you could be happy here, Abbie?'

'Happy? Arthur, anyone could be happy here.'

'It's you I'm thinking of.' He got up and came to sit beside her on the sofa. After reaching into his waistcoat pocket he took her left hand and slipped a ring onto her third finger. 'Now,' he said, 'it's official.'

She held up her hand and looked at the ring. It bore a large diamond in an ornate gold setting.

'Do you like it?' he asked. 'We can always change it for another.'

'I wouldn't dream of it. It's beautiful. And it fits perfectly.'

'I want to make you happy, Abbie,' he said. 'That's all I want.'

Leaning forward he gently kissed her. Then he wrapped his arms round her, drawing her close to him. He kissed her again, softly at first, but then more insistently and then drew back, gazed at her for a few seconds and said, 'I think you should go up to your bed, Abbie. You've had a long day and you must be tired.' Then he gave a groan and, shaking his head, added, 'Listen to me – what a hypocrite! I'm not that much of an altruist. Please – go up to bed now before I make a fool of myself. I promised your brother he'd have no cause to worry where you were concerned.'

Chapter Sixteen

Arthur had left the house for work the next morning before Abbie was up, so she breakfasted alone, served by Ida, the maid. She did not linger over the meal. The previous day she had voiced a wish to see some of the London shops and it was arranged that this morning Mrs Appleton would accompany her into the West End. Abbie would never have dared make the excursion on her own and was extremely grateful for the company of Arthur's cook-housekeeper. A native of London, Mrs Appleton knew her way around, and Abbie felt herself to be in safe hands.

Among the bustling crowds, they walked together around the brightly decorated stores where Abbie did some Christmas shopping, buying little gifts for Arthur and Jane, and for Eddie, Violet and the baby. The excursion was a revelation; she had never before seen such vast shops or such an abundance of luxurious goods on display. Apart from the Christmas gifts, she bought a new dress, which although fairly modest by the current vogue, was more fashionable than anything she was likely to see around Flaxdown. Made in pale-blue and white striped satin and trimmed with silk bows, its sheath-like form fell at the back like a cascade into an elegant train. Looking at her reflection in the glass in the dress shop, Abbie thought she had never before looked so grand. The cost of the gown made a considerable hole in her savings, but she did not care.

At a little after one o'clock the two stopped at a small restaurant just off Regent Street and ate a simple lunch. Abbie enjoyed the company of her companion. Mrs Appleton, tall, straight and grey-haired, was a warm, considerate woman with a wry sense of humour. Widowed now for a number of years, she was the mother of four sons and a daughter, the latter living with her husband in Shepherd's Bush and expecting any day the birth of her first child.

By the time Abbie and Mrs Appleton returned to Nelson Gardens, Abbie felt tired, but nevertheless very satisfied with the day.

That evening she and Arthur were going to a concert. He had managed to get tickets for the Royal Albert Hall, a vast concert hall that had been opened the year before. When they were due to leave in the hired cab she came downstairs wearing the dress she had bought that morning. She saw at once by Arthur's reaction that she had chosen well.

It was an unforgettable evening. She had never heard an orchestra in her life before, and it was a revelation now not only to hear the sounds of Mozart and Haydn, but also to watch the large body of men playing their instruments so expertly. It was a magical experience. Afterwards she and Arthur went to a restaurant for supper, following which they took a cab back to Nelson Gardens.

The next day was Christmas Eve. Abbie spent the morning alone and after lunch prepared herself for Jane's visit. Jane arrived at the house just after three o'clock and over tea they talked with the excitement of seeing one another again while they caught up on the events of the past few months.

Dinner that evening was a very pleasant affair. It was the first time Jane and Arthur had met since the day of the Warminster market when they had all three driven back to Flaxdown in his carriage through the rain. Jane was at first rather subdued in his presence, but after a while she began to relax. At the close of the evening – Arthur sending her on her way back to Fulham in a cab – it was arranged that she would visit them the following day, Christmas Day, to join them for dinner.

After breakfast next morning Abbie and Arthur exchanged gifts. She had bought him tobacco, toilet water, macassar hair oil and some handkerchiefs. In return he gave her perfume, toilet water, a beautiful parasol and a pair of gloves of the softest kid. Jane arrived later, and after an excellent Christmas dinner the three sat in the drawing room and played cards.

Jane had been given permission to stay over that night and it was decided that she would share Abbie's bed.

'Do you suppose', Jane whispered into the dark as they lay there side by side, 'that certain people are meant for each other?'

'Oh – I wouldn't think so. I think a person's either lucky or unlucky – in finding the right one.'

'Yes,' Jane said, 'I think so too. And you're very lucky, you know that? Your Arthur's handsome, intelligent – and has a good position. You'll never want for anything.' She smiled. 'It hasn't happened at all the way we thought it would, has it? Here you are, looking forward to your wedding, when you always vowed you'd never marry. And here am I without anyone. Ironic, isn't it?'

'It will happen to you too. And probably when you least expect it.'

'Perhaps.'

Late the next morning Jane said her goodbyes and set off back to Fulham and her duties. She and Abbie would meet again in the spring, they said, when Abbie had come to London to live.

That evening Abbie and Arthur dined alone and afterwards relaxed in the drawing room beside the fire. The following evening they went to the opera, to see a production of Verdi's *Luisa Miller*. As with the concert, it was for Abbie a most wonderful experience. Not only was she deeply moved by the tragic love story, but she was overwhelmed by the colourful spectacle, and the beauty of the music and the singing. Afterwards they had supper at a restaurant near the theatre, following which they took a cab back to the house.

The following day was Abbie's last before returning to Flaxdown. During the afternoon she and Arthur went to visit the National Gallery, where they looked at some of the paintings. Arthur showed a surprising knowledge of the works on view, pointing out to her characteristics of the various artists' methods, and relating interesting anecdotes. Even without his accompanying comments, she would have been almost overwhelmed by the sights. Passing from one vast room to another – rooms that seemed to go on and on – she was astonished at the number of masterpieces on display. Let alone seeing so many, she had never conceived of such numbers being housed in one building. And the size of some of them. Several were so incredibly vast; no wall in her little Flaxdown schoolhouse could have accommodated as much as one quarter of their dimensions.

Later, she and Arthur went to a restaurant where they lingered over dinner. Then, back at the house he bade her goodnight on the stairs with a chaste kiss, though she could see in his eyes the longing for more.

Next morning she said her goodbyes to Mrs Appleton and Ida, and left with Arthur for Paddington, where she was to catch the 10.20 for Trowbridge.

The train was already standing at the platform when they got to the station. Arthur saw Abbie's box safely on board, then escorted her into a carriage where he sat beside her. For the moment they were alone in the compartment. From somewhere off in the distance a clock chimed the hour of ten. Putting his arm around her waist, he said, 'I don't want you to go.'

'I don't want to go either.'

After a little silence he whispered, 'I so wanted you last night. And had there been an opportunity I think I'd have thrown away my promise to your brother.'

At his words her feelings brought again that now-familiar warmth to her heart, a warmth to add to the thrills and the excitement of her short visit to the capital. Yet she did not know how to respond to his words, and she merely took refuge in banalities. Self-consciously she said, 'I'm afraid Flaxdown's going to seem very quiet after London.'

'Yes,' he said with a smile, aware of her feeling of awkwardness, 'I'm sure it will.'

'Oh, indeed, and I'll have so much to tell Eddie and Violet – and my pupils, too, when the new term starts.'

'Have you written your letter of resignation yet?'

'I'll do it in the next few days. There's time – so long as I hand it in at the beginning of the term.'

A little silence fell between them in the midst of the cacophony of the station's sounds: the shouts, the guards' whistles, the hoot of an approaching train.

'I'll miss you, Abbie.' Arthur drew her closer. 'Perhaps I shan't let you go. Still – it won't be long till you're here again – and next time for good.'

'Yes – for good.'

He bent closer and kissed her, and against the slightly stale odour of the compartment was the now-familiar pleasant smell of him: a faint trace of the tobacco he sometimes smoked, his cologne, the oil that he had used on his hair that day. Seeing his smile, she felt a rush of tenderness towards him. He moved to kiss her again, but at that moment an elderly couple appeared at the carriage door. Then, as the newcomers settled in their seats, there came the sound of the guard's voice, warning that the train was about to start.

'I must go.' Arthur gave Abbie a kiss on the cheek – rather chaste in deference to the other passengers – opened the carriage door and stepped out onto the platform. Abbie got up, leaned from the window and took the hand he held out to her. 'I shall go home and write to you straightaway,' he said. 'And I'll come to Flaxdown to see you as soon as I can.'

The final whistle blew and as the train began to move their joined hands parted. Abbie waved from the carriage window until, a few moments later, he was no longer in sight.

Reading ... Oxford ... Abbie mentally marked off the stations as the train moved on westwards. As they left Didcot she ate the sandwiches Mrs Appleton had prepared for her. Swindon ... Calne ... The journey seemed to be taking for ever and she was eager now to get home again. Chippenham ... Melksham ... and then, finally, the last stop on the line, Trowbridge.

Here she got out and a kindly porter placed her box beside her on the platform. Her connection for Frome was not due for another hour and a half. She refreshed herself in the ladies' room then drank a welcome cup of tea and settled herself to wait. At last her train drew in. As there was no porter in sight she herself bent to try to pick up her heavy box and move it across the platform. As she did so, however, a man appeared at her side saying, 'Are you getting on the train? – then please, allow me.'

Even as he took her box from her and she thanked him, a part of her mind acknowledged a recognition of his voice. But she was climbing into the carriage now and he was behind her.

Aware of him closely following, she turned to see him bending as he set her box down and pushed it under the seat. The next moment he was straightening before her and raising his hat. She opened her mouth to thank him again, then found her words dying unspoken on her lips.

'Yes, we've met before, haven't we?' he said.

His smile was warm, open and full of surprised pleasure. He was tall, in his late twenties, smartly dressed, with wide shoulders and a broad, handsome face. He had dark-brown hair and blue-grey eyes. Facing him, she at once saw him again as she had seen him that day over four years earlier – standing in the colourful bustle of the fairground, turning to smile at her just before bending his head over the rifle as he aimed at the target to win for Beatie her teaset. And for a brief moment she seemed to know again the sights, the scents, the sounds from that time – the bustle of the animated people, the smell of the food being eaten and the grass crushed beneath their feet; the sounds of laughing, happy voices and the music . . .

'Hello, Louis,' she said.

His smile was still there. She had forgotten just how white were his teeth.

'Hello, Abigail.'

A little moment of silence. They both stood there in the carriage, awkward. Abbie did not know what to say. He was the last person she had expected to see; indeed, she had not expected to see him again in her life.

Suddenly he had put out a hand and was taking hers. His hand seemed so large, so strong, her own so small within his firm but gentle grasp.

As she looked down at their hands clasped together in a formal handshake, she heard him say, 'It's been such a long time, Abbie,' and then, 'Oh, but it's so good to see you again.'

'Yes. Yes.'

Her hand felt so warm within his grasp and she felt so conscious of his touch. Quickly withdrawing her hand she gave a self-conscious smile and sat down on the seat. As she smoothed her skirt she was aware of him sitting down facing her on the opposite seat.

As he unbuttoned his coat and set down his hat beside him he said again, 'It's been such a long time,' then added, 'Who ever would have thought that we'd meet again like this.'

'Yes.' She gave a little nod, her voice only just there. She became aware of a slight pounding in her chest. *This nervousness – if that is what it is – is nonsensical*, she told herself. Why should their meeting again affect her so?

'Let me see,' he was saying, '– it's five years come next summer.'

'You wrote to me,' she said, 'and I didn't answer your letters. I'm sorry. You must have thought me very rude.'

'It's all right.' He brushed aside her apology with a little wave of his hand, then said gravely, 'Your sister – I learned some time later that she – she died. I was so sorry to hear that. She seemed such a lovely young woman.'

Abbie nodded. 'Yes.'

'I'm really so sorry.'

'Yes,' she said again. She didn't want to talk about Beatie. Changing the subject: 'What are you doing in these parts? I thought you were situated in London.'

'I'm bound for Frome.' He smiled. 'I'm living there now. I've been there for a couple of months.'

'Frome,' she said. 'Well – Frome is a very pleasant place.' With a little chuckle, born purely of discomfiture, she added, 'So we are almost neighbours.' She found herself dismayed by the banality of her words as she took refuge in small talk. But she could not relax with him – it was as simple as that. How, a fleeting thought went through her brain, could she allow him to have this rather disconcerting effect upon her? Was he aware of it? And was it something he set out to do? Where, she asked herself, was that pleasant and safe-feeling calm she knew in Arthur's company?

'Your medical studies must be long finished,' she said, aiming to get onto safe ground.

'Oh, yes, indeed.'

He then went on to say that he had spent some time in Bristol, working at a hospital, but had left to take up a share in a practice in Frome, where one of the general practitioners in a partnership had recently retired. He enjoyed his work, he told her. At that moment, he added, he was returning from a visit to his father in Gravesend.

When he asked Abbie about herself she told him that she was teaching at the village school in Flaxdown.

'So it happened after all,' he said. 'You *did* become a teacher. When we talked about it you thought it was not going to happen. Well done.'

'Thank you.' She was surprised that he remembered their conversation.

'Are you liking it, your work?' he asked.

'Yes, very much – when I'm allowed to get on with it.'

'But what are you doing here, on the train?'

'I'm returning from London.'

'You've been to London?'

'Yes.' Now there was a note of pride in her voice. 'I went there to spend the Christmas period.' She paused, then, looking away, unable to meet his eyes, added, 'With my fiancé.'

'Oh, Abbie – you're engaged to be married.'

'Yes.' Unable to read his tone, she looked back at him. He was smiling at her.

'So you're to be married,' he said. 'Oh – I'm so happy for you. Congratulations. When is your marriage to take place?'

'In the spring. At Easter.'

'Well – that will soon be here. Then you'll be a married woman. Would I know the gentleman?'

'I hardly think so. His name is Arthur Gilmore.'

'No, I don't know him – though I'm certain he's a lucky man.'

'What about you?' she asked. 'Are you married?'

'Me? No, I'm afraid not.' He smiled. 'Obviously I haven't been as fortunate as you.'

Darkness had fallen by the time they reached Frome, and to Abbie's disappointment there was no cab to be had when they emerged from the station. 'Well, I'll just have to wait,' she said, her breath vapouring in the cold air. She felt dirty and tired. She had set out from Arthur's house just after nine o'clock that morning and it was now after four.

'You can't wait around here in the dark in this cold weather,' Louis said. 'Come on.' He took up her box. 'I live close by. I'll drive you home.'

She protested for a moment, but he would hear of no other course and together they set off along the street.

He lived only five or six minutes' walk from the station, in a large grey-stone house set back from the road, and from the little Abbie could see in the gloom, surrounded by a fairly spacious garden. Louis invited her to take some tea before starting off for Flaxdown, but she declined, saying that if it was all the same to him she would prefer to get on home. He agreed at once and, after putting his bag in the house and collecting a lamp, he led the way to the small stable and coach house at the end of the drive. She stood watching as he hitched up the mare and then, shortly afterwards, muffled up against the cold wind, she was sitting beside him as they set off.

At last they drew into Flaxdown and he brought the carriage to a halt at the schoolhouse, helped Abbie down, picked up her box and followed her up to the front door. When she had unlocked it he went in after her and set her box down. She thanked him for his kindness and asked whether she could offer him some refreshment before he started home.

'Another time I'd like to very much,' he said. 'But I must get back now. I have a lot to do before I start work in the morning.'

When, after an exchange of handshakes he had left, Abbie hung up her cape and bonnet. It was warm in the cottage; Violet or Eddie had been round and lit the stove. She filled the kettle and put it on to boil. In the larder she found fresh milk, eggs, bread and cheese – again thanks to Eddie or Violet. After preparing a simple meal of bread, cheese and pickles she made a pot of tea and sat down to eat.

As she ate she became aware of a sense of dissatisfaction. She felt strangely low-spirited – yet she could not pin down the cause of such feelings. Once having departed from London, she had been eager to get home again, but now that she was here her eagerness had somehow gone flat. She looked around her. The cottage was so small and humble compared with Arthur's house in London ... Yet it was not that, she realized – not disappointment in her present surroundings. What, then? She thought back over her week in the capital. There had been so many things to see and do. And through it all Arthur had been so solicitous of her happiness. It had also been good to see Jane again. She thought of Jane's words to her when they had been lying in bed in Arthur's house: 'You're very lucky.' And it was true; she was lucky; in the spring she and Arthur would be married, and from then on she would want for nothing. She had, she told herself, absolutely nothing to be disappointed about.

She pushed aside her plate with the uneaten food and picked up her cup. As she raised it to her lips there came a knock at the door. It would be Eddie, she guessed, checking to see whether she had returned safely.

Moving to the door, she opened it and in the light that spilled out saw not the familiar figure of her brother standing there but a woman.

'Yes . . . ?' Abbie said.

The woman did not answer.

'Yes?' Abbie said again. 'Can I help you?'

The other nodded and the nod was not an answer to Abbie's question but a gesture of affirmation. 'Yes,' the woman said and nodded again. 'Yes, it is you. Oh – Abbie . . .'

Abbie frowned, perplexed; there was something in the woman's voice.

The other spoke again. 'You don't know me, do you?'

A moment of silence passed, then, her knees suddenly weak, Abbie breathed: 'Mother . . . ? Is it – is it you?'

Chapter Seventeen

In the kitchen Abbie sat and looked at her mother as she drank the tea and picked at the bread and cheese that had been put before her.

Now, without her cape and bonnet, her mother seemed smaller in height than Abbie remembered. At the same time she appeared heavier; there was a thickness about her chin and throat and about her waist that Abbie could not recall. There was a faint, musty, stale smell about her and she looked so much older too. The rather striking prettiness that Abbie remembered had gone for ever – not only in the coarsening of her features and the lines in her face, but also in the appearance of her skin; the flesh of her cheeks and nose was now covered with a fine mesh of broken veins – like the faces of some of the ale drinkers Abbie had seen standing around outside the pub.

Her mother's appearance had altered in other aspects also. Abbie remembered her having always taken great pains with her dress and her hair, but now it looked as if such concerns were things of the past. Her clothes were dirty and worn, her boots dusty and down-at-heel; and her hair, now thinning and greying, was unpinned and uncombed, and hung untidily about her cheeks. Her mother had been thirty-eight years old at the time of her departure. Ten years had passed since that time and they were all reflected in her appearance.

Elizabeth Morris had said little since her arrival, mostly confining herself to a few monosyllables. Now, though, raising her head from her cup she said, 'Oh, Abbie – you can't imagine how relieved I am to see you.' A pause, and then, 'I suppose you want to know what I've been doing all this time . . .'

Abbie shook her head. 'There's time. For now I think you should rest for a while. And I think I should go and let Eddie know you're here.'

'He already knows. I called there first. A young woman answered the door. I thought for a minute you'd all moved away.'

'The young woman – that would be Violet, his wife.'

'So I gathered.' Mrs Morris nodded. 'Anyway, I asked for him – Eddie – and he came to the door and . . .' The piece of bread fell from her fingers and she suddenly bent her head, her shoulders shaking while tears ran from her eyes.

Abbie went to her side and put a hand on her shoulder. 'Don't cry. Oh, don't cry.'

After a minute, a little calmer, her mother went on, 'He didn't want to know me. He wouldn't ask me in.' She dabbed at her eyes. 'So then I asked to see your father – and he told me that he – that he'd died.'

'Yes.'

'Please – tell me what happened.'

While her mother listened in silence, Abbie sat down again and told of Lizzie's dismissal and their father's subsequent death on his way back from Trowbridge.

When she had finished her mother briefly closed her eyes and said, 'I was not a good wife to your father, Abbie. I wasn't a good wife to him – nor a good mother to you children.'

Abbie remained silent. After a few moments her mother brightened a little and said, 'So – here you are, a grown woman and living in the schoolhouse. The village schoolmistress. Your father would be proud. Mind you, he was a clever man himself.'

'Yes, he was.'

A brief silence, then with a little wondering shake of her head, Mrs Morris said, 'I can't get over it – seeing Eddie standing there in the doorway. It was such a – a shock. He's all grown up now. And married too.'

Abbie nodded. 'His wife was one of the Neville girls. They lived on the other side of the green, if you remember.'

'Ah – yes.' Her mother gave a non-committal nod.

'And they have a baby now,' Abbie said. 'Sarah. She was born just last month.'

'Eddie – a father,' her mother said. 'Just fancy.' The corners of her mouth turning down she added, 'You should have seen his face as he looked at me. It was like stone. He hates me.'

'No,' Abbie said. 'He was shocked to see you, that's all. He'll be all right in a while, you'll see.'

'Perhaps.' Her mother did not sound convinced. 'He didn't even ask me in. I asked for you then, and he told me where I'd find you.' She broke into a spate of coughing – a chesty, painful sound. When the spasm had subsided she went on, 'And what about you? Are you going to send me away?'

'What? No, of course not. How can you ask such a thing?'

'I – I can stay here tonight?'

'Yes, of course. You shall have my bed.'

'Where will you sleep?'

'I'll be all right. I'll make up a bed for myself on the sofa.'

Her mother gave a sad little smile. 'Thank you. At least you're still my daughter – aren't you?'

'Oh – Mother . . .' At her mother's side again Abbie

218

bent and put an arm around her shoulders. As she did so she took in the tainted smell of her mother's breath and fought back a slight feeling of revulsion. 'Come on,' she said, 'you should get to bed now. You don't look that well and I should think you could do with a rest.'

Upstairs, her mother put on one of Abbie's night-dresses and got into bed. When Abbie had seen her settled, she moved to blow out the candle.

'No,' her mother said, 'don't go just yet. Stay with me for a minute.'

Abbie sat down on the side of the bed. After a moment or two her mother said, 'I can't get over it – you being a teacher. You've done well for yourself.'

Abbie smiled and gave a little shrug.

'And what about the other girls? What are they doing now?'

Abbie hesitated for a moment, then said, 'As I told you – Lizzie's in service. She's in Lullington now. As lady's maid to a Mrs Hazeldine. Iris is in service too – working as a kitchen maid at a house in Bath. They're happy enough, I think.'

'And Beatrice? What about Beatrice?'

A little moment of silence, then Abbie said, 'Beatie . . . Beatie is dead.'

After much weeping Mrs Morris had at last fallen asleep, and Abbie had left her and crept downstairs again. Now, sitting huddled over the stove, getting the last of the heat, she felt drained and too exhausted even to make the effort to make up her bed on the sofa.

Eventually, however, she stirred herself and went into the parlour. Later, lying awake in the dark room, she thought about her mother's return. What was going to happen now? What was her mother going to do? And what about her own plans? She had not yet told her mother of her forthcoming marriage. Tomorrow, she said to herself, she must go and talk to Eddie.

'I don't want to see her,' Eddie said.

He sat at the kitchen table of the little house in Green Lane, his face stony, his lips set. Behind him on the settle Violet tended the baby while she listened to the strained conversation.

'But she's our mother, Eddie,' Abbie protested. 'Whatever she's done she's still our mother. We can't forget that.'

'She's the one who chose to forget it,' he said. 'Our mother. Huh. You can look on 'er like that if you want, but I don't. I can't. And I never will be able to.'

'But she needs looking after. You can't just pretend she doesn't exist any more. Besides, she doesn't look at all well. If you ask me, I think she's ill.'

'I'm not asking,' he said shortly. 'And if she's sick then let 'er go and find one of 'er fancy men. Let one of them take care of 'er. Where's Pattison? Maybe 'e'd like to look after 'er.'

'Oh, Eddie, you know very well that that was all over and done with years ago.'

'Maybe so,' he said, 'and I don't doubt there've been plenty of others since.'

'Be sensible, Eddie – please.'

'I am being sensible.'

'She's got to stay somewhere.'

'Let 'er stay with you, then.'

Abbie sighed. 'For now she can. But what if the school Board find out and object? They might. There's no telling with them. And if they kick up a fuss she and I could both find ourselves without anywhere to live.' She paused. 'Besides, I'm leaving in the spring – to be married. Have you forgotten that?'

'That's all right,' he said, 'you can take 'er with you. If your Mr Gilmore's 'ouse is as big as you say there'll be plenty of room for one more. And I expect she'd like that. A grand 'ouse in London – it's what she've always wanted. She was never satisfied 'ere, that's for sure.'

'Oh, Eddie, how can I do that – take her to London with me?'

'Why can't you?'

'No, I just – I can't.'

'It don't look like you've got any choice. But whatever 'appens, she's not staying with us.'

'But you've got two bedrooms, Eddie. And she could help Violet about the place. She wouldn't be any trouble, I'm sure.'

'Oh, you are, are you?' His laugh was a brittle, humourless sound. 'She wouldn't be no trouble, you say? She'd never be anything but. She've been no trouble for the past ten years because she've been out of our sight. And as far as I'm concerned it can stay that way.'

'Eddie – listen –'

'No, you listen,' he said. 'She've come back because she've got nowhere else to go. Now she needs us; she needs us to look after 'er. Well, once there was a time when we needed 'er. And where was she then? She was nowhere to be seen. Where was she when our Lizzie and Iris were so lost without their mam that they didn't know what to do with theirselves? Where was she when they cried for 'er each night? She was gone off with Pattison. Where was she when Lizzie got the sack? Where was she when Beatie needed her so?' He swallowed, shook his head and went on angrily, 'When her children needed her she was not to be found. Well, now the boot's on the other foot. Whatever you do, our Abbie, is up to you, but I'm tellin' you that I don't want 'er back in my life, and that's that.' He got up from the table. 'I'm 'appy enough as things are. I've done without a mother for the past ten years and I don't need one now.'

'You'd see her in the workhouse – is that it?'

He shrugged. 'I won't see 'er anywhere. It don't matter to me where she goes. I just don't care.' He stood up, looked over to the stove and said to Violet, 'We needs more coal in. I'll go and get some.' In another moment he had gone from the room.

'How do you feel about it, Vi?' Abbie asked, turning to her sister-in-law.

Violet shrugged, avoiding Abbie's eyes. 'It's up to Eddie what 'appens,' she said. 'But if you wants the truth, I wouldn't exactly jump at the idea of having your mother here with us. I know it's hard on you, but – well, we're 'appy as we are. Still – it's up to Eddie. He makes the decisions.' Another shrug. 'Anyway, who knows? He might change his mind after a bit.'

'No, he won't do that. You know as well as I do that once Eddie's mind is made up it'll take the devil himself to make him budge.'

When Abbie returned to the schoolhouse she found her mother sitting at the window, waiting.

'Did you see him?' Mrs Morris asked.

Abbie nodded. 'Yes, I saw him.'

'He still doesn't want to see me, does he?'

'No, I'm afraid he doesn't.' Then Abbie added, not believing her own words, 'But wait a while – he'll come round.'

Her mother gave a sigh. 'What's to become of me, Abbie? I've got nowhere to go.'

'You'll stay with me, Mother, for the time being. There's nothing else for it. We'll manage.'

'You were always a good girl.' Her mother smiled now. 'I won't be any trouble to you, I swear I won't.'

'I'm sure of that.'

Mrs Morris reached out and briefly took Abbie's hand. The unaccustomed physical contact made Abbie feel awkward.

'I knew I could rely on you,' her mother said. 'You won't see me out on the street, will you?'

'Of course not.'

'I won't let you down, I promise.' Mrs Morris released Abbie's hand, paused, then added, 'We'll get on just fine, the two of us.'

'Yes, I'm sure we shall.'

'Oh, we shall indeed. You know, Abbie – you and me – we're alike in many ways.'

That evening Abbie wrote to Arthur. She told him once again how much she had enjoyed her stay in London and thanked him for his kindness, not only to herself but to Jane. However, she said nothing of her mother's return. She would tell him of that at a later time. And she would also have to solve the problem of where her mother would live once she had gone up to London. She sighed. No doubt it would all be sorted out in time.

The following morning she and her mother sat over breakfast, though Mrs Morris seemed to have little appetite.

'Try to eat a little more, Mother,' Abbie said. 'You need to get your strength back.'

'I will – in time. I'm just not that hungry right now.' After a moment's pause Mrs Morris asked, 'Aren't you curious to know what I've been doing all this time?'

'Well – yes. But I reckoned you'd tell me when you felt like it.'

'There isn't a lot to tell.' Her mother gave a short, staccato laugh. 'And certainly it's no tale of glory. But there, I don't suppose you thought it would be.' Abbie was silent. Her mother went on, 'Jack Pattison and I – we went to London. He got work there, but it was nothing to speak of. We didn't stay together long. The rows started and he soon got fed up and went running back to that mouse of a wife of his. So – I had to look after myself.'

'You – you could have come home again,' Abbie said.

'Yes, I suppose I could. But there you are – I didn't. For whatever reason, I stayed. I did various jobs and managed to keep myself, and then – then I met someone else.'

'You mean another man?'

'Yes.'

'Who was he?'

Her mother was about to answer, but then checked herself. 'What does it matter? What do their names matter? They're all the same.' She broke off to cough two or three times, then added, 'Anyway, that lasted a few years, but eventually it ended. Then – I met someone else. Another man. And that lasted for a little time. But it came to an end too. It always does. You can't put trust in men, Abbie. They always let you down in the end.' After a pause she smiled and added, 'You know, I was sure I'd come back to find you married. I'm glad to know you've got more sense.'

Abbie hesitated a second then said, 'I *am* to be married, Mother. Come Easter.' While her mother looked at her in surprise, Abbie continued, 'His name is Arthur Gilmore. He lives in London.'

'Well, I never. London, eh? So you'll be leaving here.'

'I'm going up to London to live.'

'You didn't tell me.' There was a slight note of resentment in her mother's tone. 'So that means come Easter I'll be out on the street again.'

'No, of course not,' Abbie said quickly. 'We'll get

something worked out. You know very well I wouldn't just go off and leave you with nowhere to live.'

'It wouldn't be the first time it's been done.'

Abbie found the conversation depressing. She got up from the table and moved to the dresser. 'I must get off to the post office,' she said.

From a drawer she took the letter she had written to Arthur, then reached down from the top shelf the little tin in which she kept her household money. After transferring a little of the cash to her purse she replaced the tin, put on her coat and muffler, her bonnet and her mittens. Her mother remained silent at the table.

'Now, don't you go worrying yourself, Mother,' Abbie said. 'You'll be all right, I promise.' She moved to the door. 'While I'm out I'll get you something for your cough.'

As Abbie set out along the lane she thought back to her talk with Eddie. Perhaps his was the answer to the problem. He had spoken in bitterness, but perhaps the only thing was for her mother to go and stay with herself and Arthur in London after their marriage. But what would Arthur think of such an idea? His house was certainly big enough, and surely he wouldn't see her mother abandoned. She had no doubt that her mother could be happy in such a situation; what Eddie had said was true – a fine home in London was what she had always wanted. Abbie let out a deep sigh, her breath clouding in the cold, crisp air. One thing was sure: their mother had no future with Eddie; whatever happened to her was in the hands of Abbie herself.

That evening, while Abbie worked at her knitting, her mother took up some of Abbie's mending. A few minutes later, looking up over her needlework, Mrs Morris asked

225

about Arthur. In reply Abbie told her how they had met, of the work he did and of his house in London.

A little silence followed, then her mother said hesitantly, 'Abbie – d'you think that in his house there might be room for me too?'

'Well – we'll see,' Abbie said with a smile. 'I intend to talk to him about it.'

'Well, if he's as nice as you say he is I'm sure he wouldn't want to see his wife's mother end up in the workhouse, would he?'

'You needn't worry about that, Mother. That's not going to happen.'

As her mother, with a little nod of satisfaction, went back to her mending, Abbie thought of the letter she must now write to Arthur. She would have to tell him of her mother's return and put to him the question of whether she could have a home with them after their marriage. She must write tomorrow. Yes, and she must also write her letter of resignation; the spring term would begin soon and she would have to hand in her notice at that time. Glancing over at her mother she saw that her eyes were closed, the mending lying in her lap. Abbie got up, went to her and gently touched her shoulder. 'Come on,' she said as her mother opened her eyes. 'It's late. Time for us to get to bed. And you know what today is, don't you?'

Mrs Morris frowned. 'It must be the – oh, yes, it's New Year's Eve.'

Abbie nodded. 'That's right. Tomorrow it's the start of 1873.' She looked off into the unknown future. 'I wonder what the new year will bring.'

Chapter Eighteen

Abbie had been up since six thirty. Now, glancing at the clock she saw that it was just after eight. All was quiet in the little schoolhouse. Her mother was still upstairs. Half an hour earlier Abbie had crept up and found her sleeping. Hopefully she would remain so for a while yet; it was what she needed.

Having finished her breakfast and washed the dishes, Abbie now sat at the kitchen table, trying to compose a letter to Arthur. Almost three weeks had passed since her return from London and the reappearance of her mother, and although she had written to Arthur several times she had not done so as frequently as before her trip. Neither had she yet made any mention of her mother's return. She must, though; she would have to. She couldn't keep putting it off.

When she had finished the draft of her letter she set down her pen and read it through. It would not do. With a sigh of frustration she tore up the page and added it to the other paper fragments on the table near her writing pad. Taking up her pen again she wrote '*Dear Arthur*' and then set down her pen once more. After a minute she replaced the cap on the inkwell, gathered up the scraps of paper and dropped them into the fire. She moved to the window and looked out. The snow that had fallen two days before still clung frozen to the hedgerows and covered the verges beside the lane. Up above, the sky was a dull yellowish grey. Nothing moved and all was silent;

not even the singing of a bird broke the quiet. Soon she would have to leave to begin her day's work at the school.

Into the quiet came the sounds of movement overhead. Her mother was getting up. Abbie plumped up the cushion on the fireside chair, put another log into the fire and set the kettle on to boil. After a little while she heard the creaking of the stairs and a few moments later her mother came into the room. Abbie greeted her and watched as she moved to the chair and sat down. 'Did you sleep well?' she asked.

A nod. 'Quite well, thank you.'

Abbie eyed her mother appraisingly. She did not look well; she was pale and there was a listlessness in her movements, though at the same time a strange restlessness, an edginess about her.

'I'll get you some breakfast,' Abbie said.

Mrs Morris shook her head. 'Nothing, thank you. I'm not really hungry.'

'Mother,' Abbie said, 'you must eat or you'll get sick.'

'Please,' her mother said with an irritable wave of her hand, 'don't fuss. I told you – I'm not hungry.'

Abbie insisted, however, and after some persuasion her mother ate a little porridge. Afterwards Abbie put on her coat; it was time to go to the school. 'There's plenty of wood and coal for the stove,' she said, 'so make sure you stay warm and keep the heat going under the stew.' She picked up her bag and moved to the door. 'I'll pop back at half past twelve. Will you be all right while I'm gone?'

'Yes, of course. Don't worry about me; you go and get on with your work.'

Abbie observed again her mother's lacklustre air. 'I must remember to get you some more of that tonic,' she said.

'Those patent medicines,' her mother said contemptuously. 'They don't do any good. Have you got such a thing as a little brandy? That might help me to pick up a little.'

Abbie nodded. 'I'll get you some.'

Abbie's morning passed slowly, but at last it came to an end. Those children who had brought their midday dinners ate in the classroom and then, putting on their coats, went out into the yard to play. Abbie was now free for a little while. Leaving the school behind her, she set off in the direction of the Harp and Horses. As she hurried along the street she saw Mr Hilldew, the vicar, coming towards her. She returned his smile of greeting.

'Miss Morris,' he said. 'And how are you this cold winter's day?'

'I'm very well, thank you, Reverend,' Abbie replied.

There was a brief pause, then he said, 'Miss Morris – I've heard that your mother has come back to Flaxdown.'

'Yes,' Abbie said, her heart sinking. 'That's correct, sir.'

'And she's staying with you at the schoolhouse, I believe.'

'Yes, sir. I hope the School Board has no objection.' She prepared herself for words of disapproval but to her surprise and relief they did not come.

'No, there's no objection,' Mr Hilldew said, 'certainly not on my part just so long as nothing interferes with your work at the school.'

'Oh, no,' Abbie said quickly. 'Nothing will interfere with that.'

'Good, good. And how is your mother?'

Abbie sighed. 'She could be better, sir. I hope, though, that she'll soon begin to pick up again.'

'Come the spring,' Hilldew said with a nod. 'Come the spring.'

When the Reverend had wished her a good day she hurried on to the Harp and Horses. A little later, back in the warmth of the schoolhouse kitchen she poured some brandy into a glass and gave it to her mother. Mrs Morris took a sip and nodded her approval. 'Yes – this will do me good.'

Another letter from Arthur had arrived while Abbie had been at school. Abbie read it through and put it in her bag. As she served the stew that she had left on the stove she told her mother of her meeting with the vicar. 'So, you see,' she said, 'everything's going to be all right.'

'Oh, yes, we shall be all right,' her mother said. 'Besides, we shan't be staying here much longer, shall we?' Her dull eyes had lighted up. 'Soon we'll be in London and it won't matter what the School Board thinks. They can go hang. For us it'll be goodbye to Flaxdown for ever.'

Her mother's words came back into Abbie's thoughts a little later as she crossed the yard for the afternoon's lessons. Clearly Mrs Morris had been thinking a good deal about the move to London and was looking forward to it. After all, why should it not work out for the best? Surely Arthur would not object. It was foolish to keep putting off asking him.

Later, while her pupils sat quietly at their work, Abbie took pen and paper and began once more to compose a letter to Arthur. After a couple of efforts she eventually drafted one which she thought would do. In it she simply told him of her mother's unexpected return to Flaxdown, of her delicate health and reduced circumstances. Would he, she asked, have any objection to her mother living with them after their marriage?

Once school was over for the day Abbie bade her pupils goodbye until Monday, saw them off the premises and then sat down to finish her drafted letter. When it was done she read it through one last time, addressed the envelope and sealed it inside. She would post it tomorrow when she went out to do the weekly shopping. Gathering up her belongings, she let herself out, locked the door behind her and crossed the yard. As she entered the schoolhouse a few moments later she came to an immediate halt.

'Oh – Mother!'

With a cry, Abbie dashed forward. Her mother lay sprawled at the bottom of the stairs, one booted foot resting on the lower step. Quickly Abbie knelt beside her.

'Mother . . . Mother . . .'

Mrs Morris opened her eyes. There was a bruise near her temple and she looked dazed. Near her head was a little pool of vomit. It was for the most part dark-coloured, like old blood. Frowning, she mumbled, 'My foot. I've hurt my foot.'

'Can you get up?' Abbie asked. With some difficulty she helped her mother to her feet, though Mrs Morris could not without pain put her right foot to the floor. Then, supporting her as best she could, Abbie led her to her chair beside the fire.

'What happened?' Abbie said. She pulled up another chair, laid a cushion on the seat and lifted her mother's injured leg onto it. 'Did you faint? Did you trip? What happened?'

'I don't know.' Mrs Morris's words sounded slightly slurred. Then, 'Yes,' she said, 'I – I think I must have tripped.' Putting a hand to her head, she touched at the bruise. 'I don't remember.' She gave a little groan and closed her eyes. Abbie laid a rug over her and, bending to adjust it, took in the scent of her breath. She smelled brandy and the thought went through her mind that perhaps her mother had drunk too much of it. But then she saw the bottle on the little table beside the chair. It was still four-fifths full. She looked into her mother's face. Mrs Morris, eyes closed, lay with her head resting on the back of the chair. She was very pale, her mouth and chin stained with vomit. Abbie took a damp cloth and dabbed at her mother's face. As she did so her mother opened her eyes and gave a vague little smile. 'Ah, Abbie,' she said, 'you've always been a good girl – and I don't deserve it.'

'Nonsense.' Abbie drew up a stool and sat down. 'Let me have a look at your foot.' With a frown she added, 'What were you doing with your boots on?'

'I put them on to go to the privy.'

Mrs Morris winced in pain as Abbie touched her ankle. With difficulty Abbie removed the boot. The ankle was quite swollen.

'I think you've sprained it,' Abbie said. 'I hope it's nothing worse. Perhaps we should get the doctor to look at it.'

'No,' her mother said sharply, 'I don't want any doctor coming here, poking and prying around. I'm all right.'

'But you're not all right,' Abbie said. 'It's obvious that you're not. You've hurt your ankle and you've been sick, too, and –'

'I'm all right,' her mother protested. Then a moment after speaking she gave a sudden heave, threw her head forward and vomited, the mess spilling down over her skirt.

'That's it,' Abbie said. 'I'm going for Dr Parrish right now.'

Mrs Morris did not accept Dr Parrish's arrival with any degree of welcome, but rather irritably protested that he was wasting his time as there was nothing wrong with her apart from her twisted ankle; and that, she added, would soon mend.

'Well, we'll see about that,' the doctor said. He set

down his bag and handed his coat and hat to Abbie. As he moved towards Mrs Morris she looked at Abbie who stood nearby. 'Abigail,' she said, 'I think it would be better if you left us alone for a minute.'

'Yes, of course,' Abbie said, a little surprised. She turned and moved to the door. 'I shall be in the front parlour when you've finished, Doctor.'

Without a fire, the parlour was cold, and Abbie was glad she was still wearing her outdoor clothes. She waited there for some time, then at last there came a knock on the door and the doctor entered, his bag in his hand.

'Yes, her ankle is sprained,' he said. 'I've bound it and put a little salve on the bruise on her head. I've also left her some medicine to help settle her stomach.'

Abbie thanked him. He looked at her for a moment in silence, then sat down on the settle, placing his bag on the floor beside him. Abbie sat on a chair facing him.

'Your mother's ankle will mend,' he said. 'It'll be painful for a while, but if she rests it'll soon be all right again.'

'That's a relief,' Abbie said. 'But what about her vomiting?'

He nodded. 'You must keep her on soft foods for a while. Nothing fried. And above all make sure that she keeps away from alcohol.'

'Yes, of course.' Abbie sighed. 'Oh, it was such a shock coming in and finding her lying there. I don't know how she came to trip like that.'

Dr Parrish shrugged. 'Well, when a person gets inebriated I'm afraid that kind of thing is only too likely to happen.'

'Inebriated?' Abbie looked at him in surprise.

'Yes,' Parrish said. 'Weren't you aware?'

'Well – well, no.'

'But – couldn't you smell the brandy on her breath?'

'Yes, I could. But – she hadn't drunk much of it. I only got the bottle today, just early this afternoon. She said she'd like a little. She thought it would do her good. You could see the bottle there for yourself; it's next to her chair. There's not much of it gone.'

'Well, that's as maybe,' Parrish said, 'but it doesn't alter my opinion. I'm afraid your mother is very much the worse for alcohol.'

Abbie frowned. 'But how could she be? On such a small amount, I mean.'

'Well, there's no doubt that she is. And she's certainly had no small quantity to drink – that I'm certain of.'

'I don't understand,' Abbie said. 'I just don't understand . . .'

Parrish looked at her keenly, then said with a note of sympathy in his voice, 'This has come as a shock to you, hasn't it?'

'Yes, it has. I'm – bewildered.'

He nodded. 'There's something else I should tell you. I'm afraid this isn't anything new.'

'What do you mean?'

'I'm saying that this is a problem she's had for some considerable time.'

'What?' Abbie's frown deepened. 'Dr Parrish, are you saying that my mother is a – a habitual drinker?'

He sighed. 'I'm sorry you have to learn of it like this. But there's no doubt in my mind whatsoever. As far as drink is concerned she has a very real problem.'

'But – but she's been back almost three weeks now and I've seen no sign of such a thing. She's had nothing to drink until today when I got her the brandy.'

'That doesn't mean anything. A person who's – well, a dipsomaniac, to use the proper term – such a person often goes several days without indulging. It's nothing unusual. It's a recurring urge.' He paused. 'You say she's been back nearly three weeks.'

'Three weeks come Sunday.'

'Did you know she was coming back?'

'I had no idea.'

'She'd been away for several years, isn't that so?'

'Ten years.'

'Yes. Well, after all that time it wouldn't be altogether surprising if she was – well – let's say, on her best behaviour. Do you understand what I mean?'

'Yes.'

'And so for the past three weeks, at least, she's abstained.'

'She hasn't had any choice – I never keep liquor in the house. As I said – I only got it today because she asked me to. I still don't understand how she could get in that condition on such a small amount.'

'I've told you – she's had a considerable quantity.'

'But how could she have?' Abbie was puzzled. She just did not understand how such a thing could have happened. She gazed off into the distance for a moment, then said, 'I – I've just thought of something. When I came in I found her wearing her boots. She wasn't wearing them when I left this morning. She said she put them on to go to the privy – but I'm not altogether convinced.' She got up from her chair and went into the kitchen where she found her mother fast asleep in the chair beside the range. Moving quietly so as not to disturb her, she went to her side and took up the bottle of brandy. She pulled the cork, sniffed at the bottle's contents, replaced the cork and set the bottle back on the table. Then, moving in silence, she began to look around the room. That done she went upstairs to the bedroom. She found the empty brandy bottle beneath her mother's pillow.

Coming back downstairs she went into the parlour. Holding out the empty bottle she said to the doctor, 'Here is the answer. She must have gone out this afternoon while I was at school and bought a second bottle.' She gestured in the direction of the kitchen. 'Which is the one in there now. The one I bought earlier – this one – she drank. All of it. And in the space of an afternoon.'

The doctor gave a little nod. 'So your questions are answered.'

'Yes. Now they are.'

'That was the cause of her vomiting, of course.'

'Was it?'

'Yes. As I said, she does have a problem. How long she's been drinking to excess, of course, I can't say. But it's obvious that she has – and for some time. I'm afraid the lining of her stomach has already been damaged. As for the state of her liver, who can tell.'

'Will she be . . . all right?'

'She will, yes, as long as she keeps away from that stuff.' He gestured to the bottle in Abbie's hand. 'She'll get better if she avoids alcohol. If she doesn't – well – I wouldn't answer for the consequences. It's in her hands.'

'And mine.'

'That's between the two of you.' He paused. 'Do you have much influence over her? Will she take notice of you?'

'I really don't know. I'll do my best, anyway.'

He nodded and got to his feet. 'I must get off. If you need me don't hesitate to call.'

'I won't. And thank you.'

He put on his coat and took up his hat and his bag. As he moved to the door Abbie said, 'Oh – Doctor . . .'

'Yes?'

'Dr Parrish – you're a member of the School Board . . .'

He nodded, waiting for her to go on.

'Well,' she said, 'with this happening to my mother, I –'

'Miss Morris,' he said kindly, 'you have no need to worry. If you're thinking that this – this difficulty might harm your position then put the thought out of your head. So long as your mother's presence doesn't reflect on the school in any way, and as long as you continue to do your work – which I might say I consider you've done admirably so far – there's nothing more to be said. My visit to your mother today is between the three of us. It need go no further.'

'Thank you.'

'Now –' He put on his hat and opened the door. 'Bear in mind what I said. And if you take my advice you'll get rid of the rest of that brandy.'

When he had gone and Abbie had closed the door behind him she went into the kitchen. Her mother was still sleeping.

Quietly Abbie took from the shelf the tin in which she kept her household money. It needed only a glance to see that some of it was missing. So the remaining part of the mystery was answered. From now on she must find another, safer, place in which to keep her money.

Moving across the room, she took up the bottle of brandy from the small table and went outside. There she uncorked it and tipped its contents onto the hard earth. The two empty bottles she threw into the trash bin.

She was stirring a pot on the stove a little later when her mother awoke.

'Oh, I've been asleep,' Mrs Morris said.

'Yes,' said Abbie, 'you slept for quite a long time. How are you feeling now?'

'All right, thank you.'

'How's your ankle?'

'Not too bad.'

Abbie gestured to the sofa. 'We'll do a swap. I'll make

up your bed down here tonight, then you won't have to struggle up the stairs. You'll be warmer too.'

Her mother gave a nod of acceptance.

'I'm making some soup,' Abbie went on. 'It's just about ready. Would you like some?'

'A little later, perhaps.' Mrs Morris turned and looked round at the small table at her side.

'If you're looking for the brandy,' Abbie said, 'I threw it away.'

'You did what?' For a brief moment a look of profound anger mixed with disbelief flashed across her mother's face. 'Why did you do that?'

'Do you need to ask?'

'I don't know what you mean.'

'I think you do, Mother.'

Mrs Morris gave a shake of her head. 'I don't. But if you've got money to waste . . .'

'You know I haven't. And by the way, I got rid of the other brandy bottle too – the empty one.'

Silence in the room. Taking up the bottle of medicine that the doctor had left, Abbie said, 'Come on – I think you should take a little of your medicine.'

She poured some into a glass and watched as her mother reluctantly drank it.

'It's just a bit of an upset stomach,' Mrs Morris said sulkily, at the same time pulling a face at the taste.

By the light of a single oil lamp Abbie sat at the kitchen table, her writing pad before her. Raising her head, she looked across at her mother where she lay on the sofa in the shadows. Earlier there had been tears of self-recrimination – and apologies and promises too. Never again, her mother had said, would she do such a thing. 'I don't know what got into me,' she said through her tears. 'But it just happens like that sometimes – the need to have something to drink.' Then, self-pity colouring her tone, she added, 'Don't be hard on me, Abbie. I haven't had an easy time, you know.'

'I'm sure of that, Mother.'

'And sometimes a little drink has made things easier to bear. Sometimes it's the only way to shut out the reality.'

'I understand.' Abbie had put an arm round her. 'Believe me, I do.'

'But no more. I promise you that.'

'It's for your own good, you must realize. Dr Parrish made that very clear.'

'I know. I know.'

Mrs Morris was sleeping now. Abbie gazed at her for a moment or two longer then turned back to her task.

Beside her writing pad lay the letter she had written earlier that day to Arthur – the letter in which she had asked if her mother could live with them in London after their marriage. She read once more what she had written and, with a little sigh, tore the paper in pieces. Then, taking up her pen she wrote:

Flaxdown

Friday, 17 January 1873

Dear Arthur,

Today I received your letter of the 15th. In fact I've received three letters from you this past week. I can understand your being disappointed that I have not written as often since my return from London. I can only ask you to forgive me, and hope that you will bear with me and try to understand. For one thing, I have been extremely busy. Added to which I have been back before my class over the past week, and the first week of a new term is always very demanding.

You asked me whether I have yet handed in my notice to the Board of School Governors. I have to tell you that as yet I have not. Oh, I wish I could see you face to face, instead of having to write these words to you. I do not really know how to say it, but I want to ask whether you do not feel that perhaps we are being a little hasty in planning our marriage for this coming Easter. I truly feel that it might be better for us to wait a little while – perhaps until the summer. What do you think? In that way it would give us both a bit more time to get all our arrangements made. As it is I feel that everything is happening so fast and I can't quite keep up with it all.

I beg you – please do not infer from my words that I care any the less; it is just that at present I feel that this would be the wisest course.

Please write back at once and tell me that you do not think too badly of me.

Ever your loving,
Abbie

She read the letter through once more. It was far from ideal, but it would have to do.

She posted it the next morning.

Chapter Nineteen

On Wednesday, when Abbie returned to the schoolhouse in the break between morning and afternoon classes, she found a letter waiting for her.

'From your young man,' said her mother from her chair by the range, 'going by the writing on the envelope.'

Abbie took it into the parlour, opened it and read Arthur's words.

London
Tuesday, 21 January 1873

My dear Abbie,

This must be brief as I have very little time. Simply I have to say that your letter of the 17th came as a great shock. I just don't understand what is happening. Anyway, if possible I shall travel down to Flaxdown this coming weekend, probably arriving late on Saturday. I'll get a room at the Harp and Horses. No more until then. I'll call to see you as soon as I can. I'll let you know later the time of my train and when I expect to be in Flaxdown. We can discuss everything when we meet. In the meantime I remain, as always,

Your loving
Arthur

Abbie stood for a moment or two, then thrust the letter into her pocket and went back into the kitchen.

'Oh, what it is to be in love,' her mother said with a

241

faintly cynical note in her voice. Then, giving a rather theatrical little shiver she added, 'I don't know whether you've noticed but it's freezing in here. The fire's almost out and there's no more fuel.'

Abbie went to the outhouse and brought in some wood. When she had fed the stove she put a pan of soup on to heat, and set bread and cheese on the table.

Leaning towards the fire her mother said, 'Oh, it'll be grand to get away from here. To get back to London again. To be able to enjoy a few real creature comforts.'

Abbie remained silent.

'Well?' her mother asked, 'what did he say, your young man?'

'He's coming down to Flaxdown this weekend.'

'Good. I'll have a chance to meet him at last.'

Saturday came, and Abbie found herself watching the clock more and more as the afternoon drew into the evening. At seven o'clock she donned her coat and muffler and pulled on her mittens. From her chair by the fire her mother surveyed her for a moment, then asked, 'Will he be coming back here?'

'I don't know,' Abbie replied. She was lying; she had no intention of bringing Arthur back to the schoolhouse. 'In any case I shan't be late,' she added. She gestured to the basket of firewood by the range. 'You won't let the fire out, will you?'

Her mother ignored this. 'I hope I'm going to meet him,' she said.

'We'll see.'

As Abbie let herself out the bitter evening air struck her so keenly that it almost took her breath away. Hurrying through the gate, she started along the lane. She had received a letter that morning from Arthur telling her what train he would take and that he would be calling on her around seven thirty. It was her intention to meet him before then, however; she didn't want him coming to the schoolhouse.

Reaching the end of the lane, she came to a halt. The sky above was clear; all the stars were out and shining with an icy crystal brilliance. The moon hung low, its light reflecting dully off the frozen snow that lay on the tops of the hedgerow. She would wait for him here, for he would have to come this way from the Harp and Horses.

In just minutes she could feel the icy cold creeping through the soles of her boots. She pulled up the collar of her coat, hugged herself against the chill, and began to pace back and forth. A couple of villagers passed by as she stood there and, recognizing her, called out cheery greetings. Abbie answered them, her breath vapouring in the cold air. At last, after almost half an hour, she heard footsteps and saw coming towards her the tall shape of a man. She waited until she was sure and then stepped forward to meet him.

'Arthur – hello.'

He came to a stop before her. 'Abbie. What are you doing out here? You'll catch your death on a night like this.'

'I was waiting for you.'

He smiled, then, reaching out, put his gloved hands on her shoulders and drew her towards him. He kissed her, drew back a little and looked down into her face.

'Well? What now? Are we going to your house?'

'Arthur,' she said, 'do you mind if we don't?'

He looked at her questioningly.

'It's – it's not really convenient,' she said. 'I'll explain later.'

He frowned. 'As you like. Then where shall we go?'

'Could we just – walk?'

'On a night like this? Abbie, you must be joking. Come

on, let's go back to the Harp. At least there we shall be in the warm.'

They set off together, walking through the village till they came to the public house. Entering the private bar they found it – to Abbie's relief – empty. She took off her coat, muffler and mittens, and sat by the crackling fire. Arthur ordered drinks for the two of them – tea for Abbie and a glass of ale for himself.

Seated beside her, he said, 'Now, Abbie – tell me what this is all about.'

'Oh, Arthur, I'm so sorry,' she said with a sigh. 'I've made such a mess of everything.'

He shook his head. 'I don't understand what's going on. Your letter came like a bolt out of the blue.' He paused, gazing into her eyes. 'Did you mean what you said about our waiting to get married?'

She nodded, turning away, avoiding his eyes. 'Yes.'

'Why? What's happened?'

She turned back to him. 'You remember I told you about my mother, don't you?'

'Yes. What about her?'

'Well – she's come back. To Flaxdown.'

'She's here?'

'She's at home right now, at the schoolhouse.'

'But – when did this happen? When did she come back?'

'She arrived the night I got back from London.'

'Why didn't you tell me before? Why wait until now?'

'I don't know.'

'And she's been staying with you since her return?'

'Yes. She has to. She's got nowhere else to go.'

The young barmaid appeared at their side, set down the tea and the ale and retreated to the bar.

Arthur said, 'It must have been a great shock to you, her coming back after all this time.'

'It was.' Abbie went on then to tell him a little about her mother's return, though she was careful to give away no details of the life she had been leading during the years of her absence.

When she had finished Arthur said, 'And is she the reason for your writing as you did?'

'Yes.' She paused. 'She – she needs me, Arthur. She's not well – and she needs to be cared for. She has no one else but me now.'

'What about your brother? Can't he help?'

'He refuses. He won't forgive her for going off in the first place. He won't even see her. So you see – it's all up to me now.'

'But I don't understand why her return should affect us – our getting married.'

'Oh, Arthur, how can I leave her? I told you – she's sick. I can't leave her at such a time.'

'What exactly is wrong with her?'

A moment, then Abbie said, though hating to lie to him, 'I – I think it's her heart . . .'

He spread his hands. 'Well, you don't have to leave her. She can come and live with us in London. Lord knows, the house is big enough and she'd probably be more comfortable than she is at present. The two of you crammed into that tiny little place – it can't be easy. And we can make sure that she gets the best medical attention available.'

Abbie did not know what to say. How could she with reason refuse his offer? As far as Arthur was concerned it was the obvious answer to the problem. After a moment she said, 'No – I'm afraid it wouldn't work.'

'Why not?'

'No – it just wouldn't.'

'Why not?' he persisted. 'It's the perfect solution.'

'No . . .' She picked up her teacup and took momentary refuge in drinking a little of the tea.

'Hadn't the idea occurred to you,' Arthur said, 'that your mother could come and live with us? Surely it must have.'

'It wouldn't work,' Abbie said.

'You keep on saying that. Why wouldn't it work?'

'I told you – she's sick. She needs attention.'

'Yes, and I said that she shall have the best attention. And you'll be at home all the time once we're married. You won't be out teaching school half the day. You'll have time to give her the care she needs.' He studied Abbie's face. 'Why don't we go and see her? Let me meet her.'

'No,' Abbie said quickly,' – we can't do that.'

He frowned. 'I don't understand you. I've told you that I'll do everything I can to help and you know I mean it. I've given you my assurance that she'll be well looked after if she comes to stay with us. I can't do more.' He studied her. 'There's some other reason, isn't there?'

'Of course not. What other reason could there be?'

'Is – Is it because you're . . . ashamed?'

'Ashamed? What do you mean?' Her voice was sharp.

'Because of what she did – going off and leaving you and your family.'

'Oh – that . . .'

'Because it needn't bother you. It's none of my business and no one else's either.'

'No,' she said, 'it's not that. I've told you – she's sick. And apart from that – oh, Arthur, she's not the easiest woman to get on with.'

He said nothing, but gazed steadily at her, as if trying to read something that was not immediately apparent. The only sounds came from the crackle of the burning logs and the distant murmur of voices from the other bar.

After a moment he said in a low voice, 'Are you sure, Abbie, that this is truly all because of your mother? Are you sure you're not using her return as an excuse?'

'What d'you mean? An excuse for what?'

Before he could reply the door opened and a young man and woman entered, strangers to Abbie, in high spirits and chuckling over some shared private joke. They took seats at the next table. With their arrival in the small room the privacy of a moment ago was gone.

Abbie and Arthur retreated into a common silence for a while, then Abbie said, giving him a somewhat uncertain smile, 'You haven't touched your beer . . .'

'What?' He looked at her as if coming out of a dream.

'Don't you want your beer?'

'My beer? No.' He shook his head. 'We can't talk here.' He reached for his coat on the bench beside him.

A few moments later Abbie followed him outside, pulling on her mittens as she went. In silence they walked for a while in the direction of the lane, then, coming to a stop, Arthur turned to her and said, 'Abbie, I must ask you again – are you sure it's your mother?'

'Oh – Arthur . . .'

'Perhaps – perhaps you're just not ready for marriage. I'm aware that it's all happened rather quickly between us . . . Or perhaps you're just not ready for marriage to *me*.'

'Please, don't say that . . .'

He stood waiting, but she did not go on. 'Anyway,' he said sadly and not without a trace of bitterness, 'I suppose it's as well to get things sorted out now – rather than try to do it when it might be too late.' He lifted a hand, as if to touch her, then let it fall back to his side. 'Come on,' he said wearily, 'I'll walk with you to your home.'

They did not speak again until they reached the

entrance to School Lane. There he came to a halt. 'I won't come any further, if you don't mind. You'll be all right, won't you?'

'Yes, of course.' She could hardly look at him.

'I – Is your mind made up?'

'Arthur – yes. Believe me, there's nothing else I can do. Mother has to stay here – and I have to stay with her.'

He nodded. And he remained standing there, waiting, as if even now she might say something that would change everything – make everything as it had been. But she said nothing.

'If you change your mind,' he said into the silence, 'you know my address.'

She nodded.

'Well.' He shrugged. 'There's nothing for me to stay here for, so I'll leave for London first thing in the morning.'

She looked down at her mittened hands clenched before her.

'Goodbye, Abbie,' he said.

He hesitated a moment longer, as if giving her a last chance to say something that would hold him, stop him going, then turned and started away. In just moments his receding figure was swallowed up in the dark of the night.

She remained there for a few moments longer, then set off along the lane. When she got to the schoolhouse she came to a halt, her hand on the gate, hovering, unde-cided. She could not bear to go indoors just yet. After a moment she turned and set off back the way she had come.

A few minutes later she had arrived at her erstwhile home, the cottage in Green Lane. Violet answered her knock at the door and quickly urged her to come in out of the cold. Eddie was out, she said as Abbie entered the warm kitchen, adding, 'Gone to the pub for his weekly pint. He hasn't been long gone.'

As Abbie took off her coat she declined Violet's offer of tea, saying that she had just had some. She moved to bend over the crib where the baby lay sleeping.

'She's beautiful, Violet,' she whispered. 'You must be so proud of her.'

'Oh, ah! But she's a little madam at times, I don't mind saying. She've got Eddie's spirit – which is the worse for 'er.' Violet's soft laughter belied the content of her words, though, and Abbie chuckled along with her. There was such a sense of normality and peace in the little cottage. It was a feeling that Abbie seemed to have been without for so long.

As Abbie sat down beside the fire Violet asked, 'How is your mam? Is she all right?'

'Yes – she's fine, thank you.'

'Is something wrong, Abbie?' Violet was looking at her intently.

'Wrong?' Abbie shook her head. 'No. No, nothing's wrong.'

Violet nodded. Taking up her knitting, she asked Abbie how her school work was progressing and for a while they spoke of mundane affairs. Abbie appeared calm as she sat there, though she was aware that the calm was only on the surface. After an hour or so she got up from the chair, saying that she must get on home. She reached for her coat. 'Mother will be wondering where I am.'

Having said goodnight to Violet she let herself out of the house. As she pulled the gate shut behind her she saw Eddie coming towards her.

''Ello, Abs,' he said as he reached her side. 'Been in to see Vi, 'ave you?'

'Yes.'

'You goin' 'ome now?'

249

She nodded. 'Yes.'

'I'll walk a way with you if you like.'

'I'll be all right. You don't need to trouble yourself.'

'It's no trouble.'

She set off and as he fell in step beside her he asked, 'Well – how is she?'

'She? Mother?'

'Ah – Mother.' It was clear that he found difficulty in saying the word.

'Do you care?'

He did not answer. They skirted the green, moving in the direction of School Lane. After walking in silence for a while, Eddie said:

'I saw your Mr Arthur Gilmore not long ago.'

Abbie said nothing. He turned, looking down at her profile. 'Not to speak to, though. I just saw 'im in the distance – going into the 'Arp. Staying there, is 'e?'

'Yes.' Abbie quickened her step slightly.

'What's up, Abbie?' Eddie said. With his words he reached out and took her arm, bringing her to a halt. 'What is it? Summat's up. Tell me.'

She just shook her head, unable to speak.

'Abbie . . .'

She went to turn, to move away, but his hand tightened on her arm. 'Come on,' he said, 'tell us what's up. Is it 'im – Arthur?'

She turned her head away.

'What've he done? Tell me.'

'He hasn't done anything,' Abbie said. 'Don't think anything like that.'

'What is it, then?'

She took a breath. 'It's just – well, I'm not getting married now.'

'What? Not gettin' wed? Why not?'

'I – I can't.'

250

'Why not?'

'I just – can't.'

He was silent for a moment, then he said: 'Is it summat to do with our mam?'

'Oh, Eddie –' She loosed her arm from his grasp. 'What does it matter anyway?'

'It matters. Tell me.'

She sighed. 'Yes – it is to do with Mother. I can't leave her, can I?'

'Well, can't you take 'er with you?'

'Not the way things are.'

'And 'ow are things?'

After a moment's hesitation she told him about her mother's fall, of the doctor's visit and what he had said.

'Why didn't you tell me before?' he said.

'I didn't think you'd want to know.'

'Point taken.' He gave a nod. 'But you say she've been all right since then?'

'Yes – but there's no telling for how long. She could start again at any time. Don't you see? I can't take her with me – not with her being like that. Neither can I leave her to fend for herself.'

A little silence, then, 'You – you makes me feel guilty,' he said.

'That's not my wish. You must do what you have to do.'

'Ah, I know, but . . .' He shook his head. 'You've 'ad it all to put up with.'

She shrugged. 'It doesn't matter now.'

'Why d'you reckon she started to drink?' he said.

'I don't know. Because she was unhappy, I suppose.'

'Unhappy?'

'Oh, Eddie – of course she was unhappy!'

'But she 'ad everything. And she chose to give it all up.'

'Well, you see her as having had everything. I don't suppose that's the way she saw it.'

'Ah, she's never been satisfied.'

'I don't suppose she has. But what can one do about that? People are different.' She gazed at him in the dull light. 'Eddie – why don't you come and see her. You were always her favourite. It would mean so much to her.'

He shook his head. 'I'm sorry.'

'But Eddie –'

'I vowed I wouldn't. I'm sorry.'

'You're sorry,' Abbie said. 'Well, I can't stand here. I'm getting cold.' Turning, she stepped away from him. This time he made no move to hold her.

As she entered the kitchen a minute later her mother looked up expectantly. 'Well, where is he?' she said. 'Where's your Mr Gilmore?'

'He's gone back to the Harp,' Abbie replied, not looking at her.

'I thought you were bringing him back here. I was looking forward to meeting him.'

Abbie, taking off her coat, said nothing.

'Shall I see him tomorrow?' her mother said.

'No – he's leaving for London first thing in the morning.'

'Leaving for London? But he only got here five minutes ago.' Her mother clicked her tongue in disapproval. 'Some way to conduct an engagement, I must say.'

'There isn't any engagement, Mother. Not any more.'

'What do you mean?'

'Just that. There's not going to be any wedding.'

The following Wednesday a letter came from Arthur in which he expressed his great disappointment at the way things had turned out. Though he had not, it appeared, completely given up. Towards the end of his letter he wrote:

> . . . If your situation alters and you change your mind you know well enough where to find me. At present you may believe that it is all finished between us but I know that it is not. One day we shall be together; and I will wait for that day . . .

Abbie read Arthur's words through many times. And each time her thoughts and emotions were warring inside her mind and her heart. Had she done the right thing? After all, she had been offered a life with a man who loved her, a life of comfort – and after so many years of insecurity, such an existence seemed a wonderful prospect. But then, yes, she would tell herself, she had done the right thing; in her particular circumstances she had done the only thing possible.

PART FOUR

Chapter Twenty

For the tenth time in twenty minutes Abbie leaned forward to look from the window, her breath clouding the cold pane. As the mist on the glass faded she saw the lane clearly again, bleak and chill, with traces of last week's snowfall still clinging to the verges. In the kitchen, though, it was warm. She had seen to that.

'For goodness' sake,' came her mother's voice from behind her, 'you won't make them appear any faster by standing at the window all the time.'

Turning to her, Abbie chuckled and said, 'I'm just so anxious for them to get here.'

It was close on noon, Sunday, 16 February, and Lizzie and Iris were coming to Flaxdown. With their mother having returned they had received permission from their employers to take the day off. Iris had written earlier in the week to say they would be arriving during the latter part of the morning. She had changed her place of employment the previous November and was now situated at Radstock. This morning she would travel from there to Lullington, where she would meet up with Lizzie, and from there the two sisters would make the journey to Flaxdown together. Their time of arrival would depend on what lifts they could beg and how much of their journeys would have to be made on foot.

Abbie, with a little help from her mother, had spent the morning cooking and cleaning. Now, with everything ready, she had changed into her second-best dress, over which she had put her apron. Mrs Morris too had put on her best clothes, recently bought for her by Abbie, and then sat patiently while Abbie dressed her hair. Now, as Abbie looked at her mother she could see the nervousness in her eyes. It was hardly to be wondered at; today she would be seeing her two youngest daughters for the first time in more than ten years.

If only, Abbie thought, Eddie would also come round – come and make it up with their mother. She had asked him to, using the occasion of their sisters' visit as an added reason. He would not, though; he still refused to have anything to do with their mother. 'Lizzie and Iris knows where I am if they wants to see me,' he had said and that, Abbie realized, was the end of it for now.

She could not understand how Eddie could continue in such cold determination. He and their mother had seen one another on just two occasions since her return and then solely by chance. In the small place that was Flaxdown such meetings were unavoidable. Mrs Morris, sorrowful and bitter, had later told Abbie of the encounters. On each occasion, she said, Eddie had merely nodded in a stiff, ungiving manner and continued on his way. Abbie tried to convince herself that in time he would unbend, and come to his mother and give her the recognition she so wanted. Until that happened, however, they would just have to get on the best they could.

Still, she told herself, at least Lizzie and Iris were coming – and that must be a real comfort to their mother. She herself was nervous at the thought of the imminent reunion. She so wanted it to go well and for everyone to be happy. Certainly she had done all in her own power to ensure its success. But with her mother there was no telling what would happen; there was no knowing what her mood would be. Since her return she had become more and more difficult to get on with, and there had been numerous ups and downs in the little schoolhouse. Mrs Morris had grown increasingly querulous and quarrelsome and hard to please, so that at times Abbie had despaired that they could ever be happy together.

Today, though, all would be well, she told herself, her mother was in a good mood.

Turning back to the window, she looked again along the lane, then gave a little squeal of joy. 'They're here! Oh, Mother, they're here!'

Abbie served roast lamb for dinner, followed by rice pudding. She and her sisters ate well, and even their mother ate more than was her wont of late. Now, with the meal ending, Abbie looked happily across the table as her mother laughed aloud at Lizzie's recounting of some amusing incident that had recently occurred at the house in Lullington where she was employed. Abbie's own laughter was not so much at Lizzie's anecdote, but from pleasure at the general atmosphere. Besides, it was so rarely that she heard her mother laugh, or saw any contentment in her face.

Abbie sighed. The reunion of her mother and sisters had been so much better than she could have dared hope for. At first there had been a restraint between them, but gradually it had died away and they had begun to relax in each other's company. Abbie had known then that everything would be all right between them. She was happy – not only for her sisters, but equally for her mother. It was what she needed – to find herself accepted by her children, to be forgiven and to feel close to them again. They could be a family once more – and even Eddie would come round in time.

Now, as Iris and Abbie cleared away the dishes and made the tea, the light-hearted conversation continued. Unable to get over the change in her younger daughters,

Mrs Morris remarked again in wonder at how fine they had grown. Abbie knew well enough what her mother meant. Looking across the table at Lizzie, Abbie took in her bright, animated expression. Lizzie wore a dress of pale-blue voile with a white lace collar. She would be twenty in May and was ravishingly pretty. She was very much like Beatie in her facial appearance – even prettier if that were possible – but taller, and her thick, luxuriant hair was a little darker. She was quite unlike Beatie in personality, though. Whereas Beatie had had a shy, gentle nature, Lizzie was more like Eddie. She had an exuberant, voluble way, and was inclined to be impetuous and headstrong.

From Lizzie, Abbie's glance moved to Iris as she came to the table bearing cups and the milk jug. Iris had reached eighteen that past October, and was as unlike Lizzie as it was possible to be. She was three or four inches shorter and not nearly as pretty. Her freckled face was too narrow, her jaw a little too long and her mouth a little too wide. Her hair, while being the prettiest corn colour, like Eddie's, lacked the rich abundance of Lizzie's locks. She was unlike Lizzie in personality, too, being more like Beatie. She did, however, own a cleverer mind than that of either Beatie or Lizzie – and perhaps even of Abbie herself, Abbie thought.

Having set down the cups, Iris began to remove the pudding dishes. As she went to take Abbie's dish Abbie reached out and briefly touched her wrist in a little gesture of affection. Iris looked at her with a warm smile on her plain little face, at the same time briefly widening her blue eyes in acknowledgement of the gesture.

'And I expect you girls have grown up in other ways too,' Mrs Morris said to Iris. 'I don't doubt but that you've got some young man hanging around, have you?'

Taking her seat at the table again, Iris smiled and shook

her head. 'Not me. I haven't got time for all that.' As she finished speaking she flicked a glance at Lizzie. Mrs Morris saw the brief communication and at once turned to Lizzie.

'But I suppose you have, Lizzie,' she said.

Lizzie gave a little shrug.

'Come on, then, tell us his name,' Mrs Morris said with a chuckle. 'I think I've got a right to know.'

Lizzie looked quickly from Iris to Abbie, then back to Iris. And in that moment Abbie saw panic in her eyes.

'Well, yes,' Lizzie said casually, turning back to her mother. 'As a matter of fact I do have a young man.'

Her mother nodded. 'I reckoned you would – a pretty girl like you. And what might be this young man's name?'

'His – his name is Adam. Adam Woodward.'

'And –?' her mother prompted. 'Tell us about him, then.' But before Lizzie could reply she turned to Iris. 'Have you met him?'

Iris nodded. 'Yes, I have. He's very nice.'

'And I suppose he's handsome, is he?' asked Mrs Morris to Lizzie. 'Well, he'd have to be, wouldn't he?'

'Ah, he is that,' Lizzie said. 'He's very handsome.'

'Well,' said her mother, 'you know what they say: handsome is as handsome does.'

Lizzie laughed, but it was an odd sound, and Abbie, hearing it, felt a sudden, strange little chill about her heart.

'And what does he do, this handsome Mr Adam Woodward?' their mother enquired.

'He's a farmer,' Lizzie replied.

'A farmer?' Her mother raised her eyebrows, impressed. 'He owns a farm?'

'No, no,' Lizzie said quickly, 'I mean he works on a farm. He's a farmhand.'

'Oh.' Mrs Morris nodded, disappointed. 'A farmhand.'

'But he won't always be,' Lizzie said quickly. 'He's got brains and he's going to do really well some day, I'm sure of it.'

Mrs Morris was looking at Lizzie appraisingly now. 'You sound as if you're quite smitten with him.'

Lizzie said nothing.

After a moment her mother added, 'Now don't take it amiss what I say, Lizzie, but don't you go and throw yourself away on the first young lad who sets his cap at you. You're a pretty girl and if you're clever about it you can go a long way.'

Lizzie, remaining silent, looked briefly at Iris who sat with the teapot in her hand.

'I've seen it happen more times than I care to recall,' Mrs Morris said. 'You act in haste and you'll repent at leisure, remember that.'

Abbie felt a sudden stab of resentment at her mother's words. She thrust the feeling aside – after all, she told herself, it was natural that a mother should want the best for her daughters.

'And how old is this young man?' Mrs Morris said now.

'He's older than I am,' Lizzie said.

'And how old is that?'

'Twenty-two.'

'Twenty-two. Well, that's not so much older – though it's old enough to start showing a little sense. And he comes from Lullington, does he?'

'Yes. His family lives there.'

'Have you met his family?'

'Some of them.'

'Some of them? How many are there?'

'Well –' Lizzie shrugged, 'there's his mam and dad, and his brothers and sisters.'

'How many brothers and sisters?'

'He's got six brothers and four sisters.'

Mrs Morris stared at her for a moment, then turned a wide-eyed glance to Abbie, as if seeking an endorsement of her own dismay. With difficulty Abbie dropped her gaze.

'Eleven children,' Mrs Morris observed. 'How can people do it? Have they no control?'

Iris spoke up at this. 'But Mother, there are plenty of families with more than eleven children.'

'I'm well aware of that,' Mrs Morris said. 'And I'm sure that they're well aware of it too. How could they fail to be? All those mouths clamouring to be fed. All those bodies to be clothed. It's no wonder they're as poor as church mice. You'd think people would have more self-control.'

Lizzie said nothing, but Abbie could see from her set mouth that she was growing increasingly unhappy. 'A lot of people like big families,' Abbie said.

'You truly believe that?' said her mother. 'You really think wives enjoy endless childbearing and living in poverty and squalor?'

Abbie shrugged. 'I don't mean everyone. But – well, look at the Queen.'

'Indeed look at the Queen,' said Mrs Morris. 'The Queen doesn't have to care for her children if she has no inclination, does she? If her children cry there're a dozen nursemaids to pick them up and comfort them. And she certainly doesn't have to scrape and save to clothe and feed them, does she?' She shook her head in deep disapproval, then to Lizzie she said:

'Don't you listen to your sisters, Lizzie. You just remember what I say – don't go and commit yourself to the first good-looking young man who comes along. I know what it's like, young love. You young people think

263

you're the only ones it's ever happened to. You think nobody older than you has any idea what it's like. You think you've discovered it all. But you have no idea in reality. You look at some young man and think you'll love him for ever – and that if you can't have him you'll die. Isn't that what you think? Oh, Lizzie, my dear girl, it isn't really like that at all. Believe me, the world's full of young men and if you don't have this Mr Woodward or whatever his name is there'll be another one come along who's just as fine, just as handsome. And no doubt doing better than a mere farmhand. A girl like you should be able to have her choice.'

A little moment of hesitation, then Lizzie said, 'I've already made it – my choice.'

Mrs Morris looked at her for a second in silence, then said, 'Well, you say that now. But you're so young. You wait – you'll get another position in another town and you'll meet somebody else. Then you'll forget all about this young man.'

'I shan't.'

'Believe me, you will. I know what I'm talking about.'

'I shan't be moving to another position. I'm not moving away from Lullington.'

'How do you know that? How can you be so sure what's going to happen? You can see into the future, can you?'

'Well, no, but – I know.' Lizzie shrugged. 'I – I just know.'

With these words another glance passed between herself and Iris. Seeing the exchange, their mother frowned, a flash of irritation touching her features. 'What's going on?' she said. 'Is there something I'm missing?'

Lizzie hesitated, then, said, giving a wide, forced smile, 'Well, I s'pose I may as well tell all of you my news.

You've got to know at some time . . .' She gave a little laugh. 'I'm going to be married. Next month, as a matter of fact.'

Silence in the room. Mrs Morris turned to Abbie. 'Did you know about this?'

Abbie shook her head. 'No, I didn't.'

'What about you?' Mrs Morris looked at Iris. 'It's obvious that you knew all about it.'

Iris nodded. 'Well – yes.'

Mrs Morris turned back to Lizzie. 'Next month, eh? It's all happening very quickly. And I don't suppose anybody'd need to be a genius to realize the reason for such a great rush.'

Lizzie said nothing, just stared down at her cup.

Her mother looked at her and slowly nodded. 'So I'm right about that. When is it to be?'

Lizzie raised her eyes. 'The wedding?'

'No, not the wedding. You've already told us that's taking place next month. I'm talking about the baby. When d'you expect that?'

Lizzie lowered her eyes again and gave a little shrug. 'I'm not sure. Probably around the middle of September.'

Her mother nodded. 'How long have you known this young man?'

'Just under a year.'

When Mrs Morris spoke again there was contempt in her voice and in her face. 'You're nothing but a little fool,' she said. 'I so looked forward to seeing you girls again and when I do I get greeted with this news. God – it's so depressing.'

Abbie herself had been taken aback at Lizzie's news and at the implication of it. Nevertheless she could not listen to her mother's words and remain unmoved.

'Oh, Mother – please,' she said, 'don't say that. If it's what Lizzie wants then we have to accept it.'

265

'What she wants?' her mother said. 'It isn't what she wants. The girl's got no choice in the matter. She's got herself into a pickle and there's no other way out of it.' She turned to Lizzie. 'You're a fool to go and get yourself in a mess like this. I hoped you'd have more sense.' She turned away in disgust.

Lizzie stared at her and then, suddenly dissolving into tears, burst out, 'I wish I hadn't come here today! I wish I'd stayed in Lullington.'

Iris got up, went to Lizzie's side and put an arm around her shoulders. 'It's all right, it's all right.'

'All right!' Mrs Morris said scornfully. 'You think it's all right, do you? Well, if you think that then it's clear you've got no more brains than your sister. And it's obvious that she's got none.'

'Mother,' Abbie said, 'let's not make this even more unpleasant.'

'You're a fine one to talk,' her mother said. 'You're even more foolish. You had it all and threw it away.'

'We're not talking about me,' Abbie said. 'We're talking about Lizzie. And where she's concerned there's nothing to be done about it now. It's happened and we have to make the best of it. Or rather, Lizzie has to make the best of it. It's what it all means to her that's important.'

'Well,' Mrs Morris said, 'you can see very well what it's going to mean to her. She'll be having a dozen brats around her feet before she knows where she is.'

Lizzie got up from the table. 'I'm not staying.'

'No, Lizzie – come on, now.' Abbie got up and joined Iris at Lizzie's side. 'It'll be all right. You just gave us a bit of a shock, that's all.'

'Why should it matter to anyone else what I do?' Lizzie said. 'It's my life and I can live it any way I like.'

'Oh, that's rich,' said Mrs Morris to the ceiling. 'She can live her life any way she likes. I think not. 'She turned to

Lizzie. 'You are not going to live your life the way you like – that's one thing you can be sure of. Your life's mapped out for you now, that's clear to anybody. From now on you haven't got any choice in what happens to you. It's going to be one lifetime's slog of trying to make ends meet – that's what it's going to be for you.'

'Abbie,' Lizzie cried out to her elder sister, 'make her stop. Please, make her stop.'

Abbie put her arms around Lizzie, drawing her closer. 'Mother,' she said over Lizzie's head, 'I think you're being cruel and very hard on the girl. At a time like this she needs all the support she can get.'

'Well, I'm sorry,' Mrs Morris said disdainfully, 'but if she expects me to condone her stupidity she'll have to wait a mighty long time.'

Breaking from the circle of Abbie's embrace, Lizzie turned to her mother and said passionately, 'I don't expect anything from you! I would be a fool to do that!' Striding across the room, she snatched her coat from the hook on the door. 'I'm going. I'm not staying here.' Looking back at her mother she added, tears shining in her eyes, 'I love Adam. I love him and he loves me. And we're going to be married. And we want to be married. So what does it matter to you or anyone else how we do it? And so what if we'll never be rich? We'll have each other and that's what we want. And anyway, it's *our* lives.' She turned to Abbie. 'Abbie, I'm sorry to leave like this after all the trouble you've gone to, but I can't stay.' To her younger sister she said, 'You stay if you want to, our Iris, but I'm going.'

Iris stood undecided for a moment, watching as Lizzie pulled on her coat, then said: 'I'll come with you.' She could not look her mother in the face.

Lizzie, putting on her bonnet, moved to the door. 'I'll see you at our Eddie's, Iris. I'll wait for you there.'

'That's right,' Mrs Morris said, 'you go to your brother's. At least you all know which side he's on.'

Lizzie looked at her for a moment, then turned and ran out, the door banging behind her. As Abbie started across the room after her, her mother said, 'Let her go.' Abbie came to a stop. 'Don't you care?' she asked.

Mrs Morris shrugged. 'The girl's made up her mind. You can see that.'

'Oh, Mother . . .' Abbie shook her head in despair. She turned to Iris who was taking her own coat down from the hook. 'Iris, tell her to come back. She mustn't leave like this.'

Tears glittering in her own eyes, Iris said, 'She won't come back now, Abbie. You must know that.' She glanced across at her mother. 'And I don't blame her either.'

Mrs Morris looked at her coldly. 'If you're going too, then get going.' To no one in particular she said, 'A fine day this has turned out to be.'

'Yes,' Iris said, 'and whose fault is that?'

Abbie looked in surprise at her sister – she who was usually so reticent.

'Oh,' said Mrs Morris, 'so the little mouse has got a voice after all.'

Iris and her mother faced one another across the room. 'Yes, I've got a voice,' Iris said. 'And I don't mind telling you that if you don't see Lizzie again you've only got yourself to blame.'

Mrs Morris was silent for a moment, then she said coldly, 'Aren't you going? Your sister will be waiting for you.'

Iris shook her head in sorrow. 'Mother, you don't know how nervous we were about coming to see you today. We weren't hoping for a great deal. Only that we could – well – that perhaps we could make a new start together.'

Mrs Morris turned her face away.

'It was easier for me,' Iris went on. 'You can't imagine how difficult it was for Lizzie. Not only were we seeing you again after so long, but she had her – her news to tell you.' Her voice was coloured by her tears. 'You don't know how she dreaded it – how worried she's been. If there had been a better time for you all to know then it might have been easier, but you can't plan these things. You had to know today. But Lizzie loves Adam and he loves her. And he's a good young man. It might be true that they've got nothing, but they'll manage somehow.' She took a step forward. 'Don't you see? She needed your understanding at a time like this. She wanted your love, not your condemnation. But how should we expect you to understand that?'

'Don't let me hold you up,' Mrs Morris said.

Buttoning her coat, Iris gazed at her. With a shake of her head she said: 'Oh, why should we have expected anything different from you? You haven't changed at all.'

While her mother visibly stiffened at the words, Iris went on, 'You never cared for any of us – never. You proved that ten years ago and you proved it again today.' She put on her bonnet and tied it beneath her chin. Stepping to Abbie, she put her arms around her and kissed her on the cheek. 'Thank you for a lovely dinner, Abbie. I'm sorry it all ended like this.'

Abbie held her. 'Iris – don't go.'

'I've got to.' Iris broke away. 'Lizzie's upset. She won't come back here today. When we've seen Eddie we'll start on back to Lullington.'

Without a further word or glance at her mother she crossed to the door and left the room. A moment later Abbie saw her hurrying away along the lane. After the briefest hesitation Abbie herself was reaching for her coat.

Her mother watched as she did up the buttons. 'You're leaving too, are you?'

Abbie took down her bonnet. 'I must. I can't let them go like that.'

Abbie could hear Eddie bellowing as she knocked and entered the cottage in Green Lane. In the kitchen she found Lizzie sitting with her face in her hands and Iris standing beside her. They both still wore their coats and bonnets. On the settle nearby sat Violet with Sarah in her arms. Eddie stood with his back to the window, glaring at Lizzie. He had just heard her news. Red in the face, he clenched his teeth over his indrawn breath. 'Adam Woodward's his name, is it?' he said. 'Well, I'll be going to see Mr Woodward! 'E ain't treatin' my sister like that and gettin' away with it.'

'Oh, Eddie, please,' Lizzie said, raising her tear-stained face. 'Don't go making trouble for us. We got enough to think about already.'

'I should damn well think you 'ave,' he said. 'I'll give 'im bloody trouble when I gets 'old of 'im. He'll be bloody sorry 'e laid 'ands on a sister o' mine. Well, I'll tell you summat, 'e better do the right thing by you – else 'e'll know what trouble really is.'

'Eddie,' Iris broke in, 'she already told you they're getting married next month.'

'And so they better be.' He glared at Iris, as if somehow it was now her fault. Turning back to Lizzie he said, 'And you tell 'im, your Mr Woodward, that I wants to know the date and the time of the weddin'. And you tell 'im too that 'e better be there. Cause if he ain't there 'is life ain't gunna be worth nothin'. You tell 'im that. 'E ain't playin' fast and loose with no sister o' mine and that's for sure.'

'He's not like that,' Lizzie said. 'He loves me.'

'Just as well for 'im, then.' Eddie looked around at

Abbie as if seeing her for the first time. 'What d'you think about all this, then, our Abbie?'

Abbie sighed and spread her hands. 'Oh, Eddie, does it matter what I think? Does it matter what any of us think?'

'Oh, ah.' He nodded. 'I might o' guessed you'd take that attitude.'

'It's only important that Lizzie does what she wants to do,' Abbie said. 'And if she wants to marry her Mr Woodward and he wants to marry her then I don't see what's wrong with that. Anyway, there's nothing we can do about it.'

'Oh, you think not, do you?' he said belligerently. 'Well, you just wait and see.'

'Oh, Eddie, for goodness' sake,' Abbie said impatiently. 'Stop behaving like this. It's always the way with you.'

'Well, with Father gone I'm the 'ead o' this family now. And I'm responsible for you girls.'

'Well, that's very commendable,' Abbie said.

He looked at her sharply at this, as if suspecting sarcasm.

'No,' Abbie said, 'I mean it, I do. But that being the case you've got to act responsibly. It's no use you going charging about like some dratted bull in a china shop. That'll only make things worse. Leave Lizzie and her young man to sort it out for themselves. She's a sensible girl, she'll be all right.'

'Sensible!' he said with a snort. 'She ain't got the sense of one of White's cows. If she'd 'ad any sense she wouldn't've got 'erself in this mess in the first place.' He snorted again. 'Sense, my arse.'

Iris spoke up again now. 'Eddie, listen,' she said gently, 'I've met Lizzie's young man and I tell you he's a right nice young fellow.'

'Yes, he is,' Lizzie said. 'He is.'

'It's true, Eddie,' Iris said. 'And he's that fond of her,

271

really. And I know he'll do right by her.' She put a hand on Lizzie's arm. 'Come on, dry your tears, Lizzie. Everything's going to be all right, you'll see.'

'Well,' Eddie said grudgingly, 'it damn well better be.'

A little silence fell in the room, broken only by the sound of the clock and Lizzie's sniffs while she dabbed at her eyes with her handkerchief. The wind was going out of Eddie's sails now and he was growing calmer. Though not quite ready just yet to give in completely, he added, 'Anyway, I'll be keepin' my eye on things and at the first sign of trouble I'll be in Lullington faster than Mr Woodward can spit. I 'ope 'e understands that.'

Iris and Abbie exchanged brief glances. Things would be all right now. Abbie looked at Eddie and gave an inward sigh – not untouched by affection. His reaction had been exactly what she might have predicted.

Eddie remained standing with his back to the window for a moment longer, then clapped his hands hollowly together and crossed the room. Bending, he took the baby from Violet's arms. 'Come on, babby,' he said. 'Come on to your dad.' After a moment or two, looking over Sarah's head, he said gruffly to Lizzie, 'You wants to take your coat off, my girl, or you'll catch a chill when you goes out. It's bitter cold out there.'

'Well,' Violet said into the silence, rising from the settle, 'how about a cup o' tea, then?'

Iris, Lizzie and Abbie, taking off their coats and bonnets, murmured their thanks. As Violet turned to the kettle on the range Eddie held Sarah out in his muscular arms.

'Would one of you aunties like to 'old your niece for a minute . . . ?' He addressed all three of his sisters, but held the baby out towards Lizzie. Lizzie gently took the baby from her brother.

'Am I the only one who knows?' Eddie said.

Lizzie looked up questioningly, while Abbie frowned and said, 'The only one who knows what? What do you mean?'

'Our mother,' he said. 'Do she know about Lizzie's baby comin'?'

Lizzie, nodding, said grimly, 'Yes, she knows.'

'What's up?' Eddie said. 'Why d'you look like that?'

'I'll tell you later, Eddie,' Abbie said quickly. 'Leave it for now.'

'Why?' he said. 'What 'appened?'

Abbie frowned at him. 'There was a – a bit of a scene.'

'A scene? You mean over our Lizzie and her baby?'

'Yes,' Abbie said, while Lizzie shook her head despairingly and said with a little groan, 'Oh, please, don't start it all again.'

'We ain't startin' nothin',' Eddie said. 'What's the matter, then?'

'It was Mother.' This came from Iris as she looked up over the cups. 'Well – she said some very cruel things to Lizzie. I don't like telling tales, but it's true. They were very cruel.'

'Tell me.' Eddie leaned forward ominously. 'What did she say?'

'Please,' Lizzie said, 'just leave it, can't you?'

'I wants to know.' He turned to Iris. 'Tell me what she said.'

Iris sighed, looked from Lizzie to Abbie, and then back to Eddie. 'She told Lizzie she was nothing but a fool and that she's wasted her life. That's why Lizzie came here. Mother told her she's going to spend the rest of her life in misery.'

'She what!' Now Eddie's outrage was back. 'I don't believe it!' He looked at Lizzie. 'She 'ad the gall to talk to you like that – to say that to you?' His eyes were wide as he looked one by one at his three sisters. 'Well, I'll go to

273

blazes! She goes off, leavin' 'er 'usband and five children to fend for theirselves. She don't send a single word to one of 'em in more'n ten years, and then when she's on 'er uppers she comes crawlin' back. And she've got the nerve to talk to you like that? Well, I'll be damned if that don't take some beatin', eh?' He shook his head, whistling through his teeth. 'You listen to me, our Lizzie' – he jabbed the air to punctuate his words – 'if our mother says anything else to you about it you just tell 'er to mind 'er own damn business. Because it ain't no bloody business of 'ern no more. She give up all right to what you does with your life when she went off all them years ago. And now it's no concern of 'ers what you do.' He shook his head again, still unable to believe what he had heard. 'Well, I'll be damned,' he murmured. 'That's the pot callin' the kettle black and no mistake.'

Abbie remained with Eddie and Violet and her sisters for a further hour or so, until it was time for Lizzie and Iris to set off back on the road to Frome where they would catch their ride to Lullington.

Abbie walked with them to the edge of the village and there came to a halt. A chill wind flicked at the girls' clothes. Taking Lizzie in her arms, Abbie embraced her.

'Don't you worry about anything,' she said. 'Eddie's right – it's not important what Mother thinks.' She hugged her sister to her and kissed her cheek. 'Let me know when the wedding is, won't you? You know I'll be there if I can.'

Lizzie nodded. 'I will. And thank you, Abbie.'

'There's nothing to thank me for.'

'I shan't come back again, Abbie. Well, to see Mother, I mean. I'll come and see you, but I don't want to see 'er.'

Abbie sighed. 'Well, that's up to you, my dear. But perhaps in time things will be easier between you both.'

'I can't see how.'

'Well – wait and see how things go on.' Abbie looked into her eyes. 'In the meantime you just look after yourself. And don't bother about what people say. If you and Adam are happy together then that's all that matters.'

She released Lizzie, stepped to Iris's side and put her arms around her. 'And you too, our Iris,' she said with a smile. 'You look after yourself too.'

Iris smiled back at her. 'I will.'

'And try to eat a bit more, will you? Hugging you is like hugging a sparrow.'

Iris laughed. 'It's the way I am, Abbie.'

'I know – and I won't quarrel with that.' Abbie bent, and as she pressed her cheek to Iris's she murmured, 'And keep an eye on Lizzie for me, will you? She confides in you.'

'I will.'

'Good girl. You let us know if she's in trouble or needs anything, won't you?'

'Don't worry.'

Abbie gave Iris a final hug and released her. 'Now you girls get back as soon as you can, won't you? Don't hang about on the road. And don't talk to any strangers.'

Lizzie and Iris nodded concurrence and then, calling out their goodbyes, started away. Abbie stood watching as they set off together along the road, waited until they had gone out of sight round a bend, then turned and walked off in the direction of School Lane.

On her return she found the schoolhouse empty and her mother's coat gone.

Mrs Morris returned just after eight that evening. As she entered the kitchen Abbie put her book aside and watched as her mother took off her coat and made her way unsteadily to her chair by the fire.

'I wondered where you were,' Abbie said.

'That's very thoughtful of you,' her mother said without looking at her. Her voice was slurred.

Silence, then Abbie said, 'Lizzie and Iris have gone back.'

Her mother nodded. 'I assumed they would have. Not that it makes any difference to me.'

'Oh, Mother –' Abbie shook her head and said sadly, 'It could have been such a lovely day – the four of us all together again.'

'If all you're going to do is reprimand me,' her mother said, 'then you can save your breath. I don't want to hear it.'

'No,' Abbie said, 'you only ever think of yourself, don't you. Lizzie was so upset. Why did you do it – talk to her in that way?'

'Why? Because I can't stand to see the girl make a wreck of her life. It's time somebody talked some sense around here.'

'All right, she might have made a mistake, but it doesn't help to berate her. You could have made a difference for the good. You could have helped her.'

Mrs Morris looked at Abbie with contempt. 'It's not my way to say things just to make folk feel good. I speak my mind, offend or please.' She got up from the chair again. 'I'm going up to bed.'

Abbie got up and stepped towards her. 'Mother, where did you get the money from – to buy liquor?'

Mrs Morris hesitated a moment, turned challenging eyes to her, then said, 'I'm not standing here to be questioned by my own daughter.'

With her words she passed through into the hall and closed the door behind her.

After the sound of her mother's footsteps had faded on the stairs Abbie went to her purse. In her hurry to go after Lizzie and Iris she had left it behind. On examining its contents she saw that some of her money was missing.

Chapter Twenty-One

Abbie set a bowl of potatoes on the kitchen table and sat down. As she took up her vegetable knife the bright July sun reflected off the blade. She glanced over to her mother where she sat, as was her wont, beside the range. Mrs Morris was still wearing her nightdress over which, despite the warm day, she had thrown her old coat.

'Mother,' Abbie said gently, 'why don't you get dressed. You'd be much more comfortable.'

'Abigail,' Mrs Morris said, 'will you just leave me alone. You do whatever you want to do, but just leave me alone. That's all I ask.'

Abbie silently got back to peeling the potatoes. After a minute her mother rose and went out of the room. Abbie heard her footsteps ascending the stairs. A few minutes later Mrs Morris reappeared in the doorway, crossed to her chair and sat down again. Seeing that she was still wearing her nightdress and coat, Abbie realized at once the purpose for her temporary absence. She was, Abbie said to herself, starting earlier than usual today.

After a few moments Mrs Morris took a bottle from her coat pocket and poured a little brandy into a glass. Catching Abbie's gaze, she turned to her with a long-suffering sigh. 'Don't go gawping at me with that critical expression. I know what you're thinking.'

'But you promised. You promised you wouldn't drink any more.'

'I need this.'

'You don't need it – and you'll only make yourself ill again.'

Her voice taking on a whine of self-pity, Mrs Morris said, 'For God's sake, do you begrudge me what little comfort I can get? Lord knows there's precious little else.'

'Are you really so hard done by?' Abbie said, irritated by the words. 'It seems to me you've got a great deal more than many people.'

'Really? Perhaps you'd be kind enough to tell me in what way I'm so well off.'

'What? Well, in case it's escaped your notice, you've got a home, and also –'

'Oh, yes, of course – a home. And by the good grace of my loving daughter.' She gazed around in mock-admiration. 'How could I not take account of such luxury.'

Stung by the injustice of her mother's complaining, Abbie said sharply, 'And also by the good grace of the School Board. And it may not be the epitome of comfort, Mother, but it's better than nothing.'

'How kind of you to remind me,' her mother said sarcastically. She gazed at her daughter for a moment in silence then added, 'You could have had everything. We could have been living in comfort – for the rest of our lives.'

'Please, let's not get on to that again.'

'I never thought you could be such a fool. You're even more stupid than Lizzie. At least she made her mistake by not giving any thought to her actions. You made yours after careful deliberation. We could have been really happy. But you chose to throw it all away. You won't get a chance like that again.'

'I'd rather not discuss it.'

'You never want to discuss it. But why did you do it?

Why did you send him away like that? Why won't you tell me your reasons?'

Still silent, Abbie resumed her task of peeling the potatoes.

'Is it that you were you ashamed of me?' her mother said.

'Please – don't be foolish.'

'I'm not being foolish.'

'I don't want to quarrel with you, Mother,' Abbie said shortly. 'There's been more than enough quarrelling already.'

'And that's my fault, is it?'

'Oh, for God's sake!' Abbie got to her feet, throwing the vegetable knife with a splash into the potato pan. 'There's nothing I can say to please you. Whatever I say it's bound to be wrong. Why are you always so disagreeable? Can't you even make an effort to be pleasant? To be happy?'

'Happy,' her mother repeated with a sardonic smile. 'I'm not sure I know the meaning of the word.'

'You think you're the only one with difficulties in this life. Don't you ever spare a thought for anyone else?'

'Why should I? Who ever spared a thought for me?'

Abbie shook her head. 'I can't believe you can say such things. What about your family? Have you forgotten them? You had a husband and five children – who all loved you. But it was not enough for you. You always wanted more.'

Her mother looked down into the contents of her glass. 'Love,' she said contemptuously. 'What good does love do? All the so-called love that's supposed to have come my way has done me no good at all.' She raised her eyes again to Abbie. 'What use is love if you end up alone?'

'You're not alone. There are many who are, but you are not.'

'I'm not alone?' Her mother's eyes widened in assumed

surprise. 'Tell me how I'm not alone. Are you talking about my children? Are you talking about my son who lives half a mile distant and refuses to acknowledge me? Are you talking about my two younger daughters who won't come anywhere near me any more?'

Abbie said quickly, 'You're not blaming Lizzie and Iris for that, are you? It was your doing.'

Her mother ignored this. 'Or perhaps you have in mind my other daughter – who begrudges me any pleasure – and never stops reminding me how generous she's been to me.'

Abbie stood there for a moment longer, then without a word moved to the door, went through the hall and let herself out into the bright summer air.

At the front gate she turned right along the lane and walked past the silent schoolyard – the children were all on their summer holidays – and, continuing on, let her steps take her to a footpath where she turned her back on the village and set off across the meadows. After several days of rain the weather had turned fine, and now the sun shone down out of an almost cloudless sky. Following the path, beside which cows contentedly grazed, she eventually came to the copse, at the far side of which was the stile. Here it was, last August, eleven months ago, that she had met Arthur as he was walking to the village from Keyford. How long ago it all seemed now, and how little she had to show for the intervening time. It had been almost seven months since she had seen him; seven months since that bitter January evening when she had told him that they could not wed; that she must remain in Flaxdown to care for her mother. A few days afterwards had come his letter in which he had written that he still believed that one day they would be together. When she had written back she had expressed her deep regret at the heartache she had caused him, and at the same time had

281

returned to him the ring that he had given her. It was her returning of the ring that had made it final. Since that time there had been no communication between them.

And now, at times such as this, she found herself looking back and wondering at her decision to break off her engagement. At the time it had seemed the right thing to do, but now ... She sighed deeply. The growing deterioration of her relationship with her mother continually brought up similar doubts, more questions. With Arthur she would have been free of all such worries. Not only would her mother have been cared for, but living in a fine London house she would have been a happier person – though given her mother's character, there could of course be no certainty about such a thing. But surely, Abbie thought, she herself would have been happier. She thought back to her brief time in Arthur's London house – and there was not only the comfort of the dwelling itself, with its large rooms and fine furnishings, but the added luxury of servants. Everything about it would surely have made her life a better one. And there was London itself. It was like a different world from this small village of Flaxdown. She thought briefly of some recent letters from Jane, in which Jane had spoken of this or that event that had taken place in the capital, and of the places she had visited at various times. All of it only served to point up the excitement offered by life in such a place and the dullness and predictability of her present surroundings. What was even more depressing was that, as things stood, she could not see any way out of the situation; she had made her bed and now she must lie on it.

Faintly on the breeze came the distant sound of a church bell, calling the villagers of Flaxdown to morning service. Abbie had not been to church in some months now. She had, she realized, lost the desire to attend even for the sake of appearances.

Careless of her skirt, she hoisted herself onto the top bar of the stile and sat there looking around at the summer scene. In the grass, now rich and lush after the recent rain, two blackbird chicks followed their father, begging for food. She could smell the clover blossom. There was peace everywhere about her, but within her there was nothing but turmoil. She would like to stay outside, she thought – stay out and never have to go back. But it couldn't be; soon she must return to the house – to that unhappy place that was daily becoming more and more like a prison.

She pictured her mother, sitting morose and discontented in the kitchen. After the initial bout of drinking in January when Abbie had called in Dr Parrish, her mother had vowed that she would never again touch alcohol. But following the visit from Lizzie and Iris she had begun drinking once more – and it had grown worse. On one occasion Abbie had returned from school to find her prostrate on the floor, a near-empty brandy bottle beside her. And she had been vomiting again – not undigested food, but the dark-coloured viscous fluid that she had brought up on the first occasion. As before, the situation had alarmed Abbie greatly and she had considered going for Dr Parrish. She had been reluctant to do so, however. She had never had occasion to summon him since that first time and there was a chance he would have concluded that her mother's drinking problem was over. Reluctant to revive it all, to reveal to him that her mother was no better but was in fact in an even worse condition, she had shrunk from informing him – not only because of the shame it would bring but also because of her very real fear that it would result in her losing her position at the school and, with it, her occupancy of the house. It was a very real possibility, she knew. On the other hand, if her mother was really ill then it was not something that could be ignored.

In the event it had not proved necessary to send for the doctor. Helping her mother to the sofa, Abbie had made her comfortable and generally cared for her. And as the hours had gone by Mrs Morris had begun to recover, and Abbie had realized that the worst was over and that she would be all right. The next day her mother had tearfully promised once more to be strong and to abstain. But as before the vows had not lasted – which was not so surprising, Abbie thought: there was little so fragile as a promise broken and remade.

And yet, she considered, perhaps she herself was partly to blame for what had happened. With the knowledge of Abbie's engagement, her mother had set her heart upon leaving Flaxdown for ever, had looked forward to living a comfortable life in London. But Abbie had broken her engagement and shattered the dream. And now her mother had nothing to look forward to.

With a sigh, Abbie let herself down from the stile and slowly set off back the way she had come. On reaching the village, however, she turned not towards School Lane but in the direction of Tomkins Row. A few minutes later she was knocking on the door of number three, and Jane's mother was inviting her in.

Seeing that Mrs Carroll had been busy at her lace-making, Abbie protested that she was interrupting her work, but Mrs Carroll brushed aside her protests. 'It's no matter. I was wanting an excuse to stop. Besides, it's nice to see you. It's been several weeks.'

Mrs Carroll made tea and they sat facing one another over the kitchen table.

'I meant to come round and see you before now,' Abbie said, 'but – well, what with one thing and another . . .'

'Oh, you must be very busy, I'm sure of that,' Mrs

Carroll said, 'what with your teaching and everything. But you're on holiday now, right?'

'Yes, thank heaven.'

'I heard from Jane in the week,' Mrs Carroll said. 'You know she's a lady's maid now?'

'Yes, she wrote and told me. I'm afraid I owe her a letter. When you write do please tell her I'll be in touch very soon.'

'I will.'

Abbie gave a sigh and glanced from the window. 'I've just been for a little walk over the fields. It's such a beautiful day.' Turning back to Mrs Carroll, she added, 'Did you know that Violet's expecting again?'

'No, I didn't. Well, that's nice. I'm sure Eddie makes a good father, doesn't he?'

'Yes.' Abbie smiled. 'Perhaps surprisingly, but he does.'

'It's amazing what fatherhood does for some men. It can be a great calming influence.' She paused. 'And how is Lizzie? She and her young husband going on all right?'

'Yes, they're fine. She and Adam have got a tied cottage now. She's still working for her same employers, but going in daily instead of living in. She'll keep on with her work as long as she can, she says.'

'Well, that's sensible.'

'Which won't be for much longer, though. Her baby's due in a couple of months.'

'It was nice that you were able to get to the wedding,' Mrs Carroll said. 'Shame, though, that she didn't get wed here in Flaxdown. I thought she might have got married from Eddie's. But still, you and Iris were there and that made all the difference, I'm sure. Though it's a pity your mother couldn't make the journey.'

'Yes.' Abbie nodded.

'Do you hear from Iris?'

'Oh, yes. She writes regularly. Not like Lizzie. They're

as different as chalk from cheese, those two. Yet they're very close.' She sighed. 'I don't know when I'll see them again. Lizzie won't be coming to Flaxdown this summer, I know that much.'

'Well, she's a married woman – and now she's expecting her baby . . .'

'Yes.' A little pause. 'Iris won't be here either.'

'Well, once they move away from home they begin to build new lives, don't they? They spread their wings. It's the way of it.'

'That's part of it, I suppose.'

Mrs Carroll was regarding her a little more keenly. Abbie, aware of the look, gave a shrug and said, 'To tell you the truth, it's because of Mother. It wasn't exactly a happy time for them when they came back in February to see her. There was a terrible row. Which was why Mother didn't go to Lizzie's wedding.' Abbie lapsed into silence. In the quiet she became aware of the ticking of the kitchen clock and the sound of birdsong.

'You look troubled, Abbie,' Mrs Carroll said.

'Oh – oh, it's just – just the way things are right now.'

Mrs Carroll gave a little nod. 'I've realized for some while that you've been unhappy – though I didn't like to say anything.' Then quickly she added, 'I'm not prying, Abbie. I just don't like to see you like this. But I'm always here if I can do anything to help, you know that.'

'Yes, I know – thank you.' At the woman's warm, sincere tone, Abbie felt like weeping. She said with a shake of her head, 'I feel so – so disloyal, but – well, I just don't know what to do any more.'

'About your mother, you mean.'

'Yes.' Abbie lowered her glance and looked into her cup. 'As I said, the last time the girls came home they had a miserable time. Mother behaved so badly. They were just small children when she left and you'd hope that now she's back everything would be so good between them.' She gave a deep sigh. 'I don't think I'll ever understand her. It was unfortunate that Lizzie had her – her news to tell just at that time, but you don't plan these things. I couldn't believe it – Mother being so harsh.'

'Well,' Mrs Carroll said, 'I don't suppose any mother likes to learn such a thing. They'd all rather it was different.'

'I know that, but she had no right to take on so. I mean, she hadn't been near us for years. She had no right to make Lizzie feel so bad. Nor Iris for that matter. I'd thought at the start that everything was going to be fine. And it seemed to be – but then Lizzie told us and suddenly – well, everything went sour. But it's not only that. It's Mother's attitude, her general behaviour. I shouldn't say it, I know, but – oh, sometimes I wish she'd never come back.'

And suddenly the tears that had threatened came spilling over and running down her cheeks. And as the tears flowed she spoke of her mother's drinking, her slovenliness and selfishness, her unwillingness to do any work about the house. It all came pouring out. 'What makes a person behave like that?' she said. 'I don't know her any more. Though maybe I never did.' She paused. 'The thing is, she just won't stop. The drinking, I mean. Or she can't stop. One or the other. She makes promises, but they never last. I used to believe her when she'd promise – but I don't any more. I suppose I have to realize now that she'll never change. And it isn't only her drinking – though that's bad enough.'

She fell silent. Mrs Carroll briefly leaned across the table and laid a hand on her shoulder. 'You poor girl. You've been carrying this around with you all this time.'

'How could I tell anyone?' Abbie raised her head. 'I feel bad enough coming to you with my sad stories. Eddie doesn't want to hear. He's long since washed his hands of her – and the way she is now, and with the way she behaved towards Lizzie, I can't see that he'll ever change his attitude.'

'So it all rests on you. What are you going to do?'

'What can I do except put up with it? And now, with each day that goes by, I just feel less and less able to reach her.'

'Oh, Abbie, I wish there was something I could do to help you.'

Abbie sighed. 'There's nothing.'

'How does she come by the money – to buy the drink?'

Abbie hesitated, then said, 'She used to steal it. She used to steal the money from me. I changed the hiding place for my money several times, but she usually managed to find it. Not any more, though. Now I keep it with me.'

'So how does she manage to pay for it now?'

'Well – when things are desperate I buy the drink for her.' A bitter little laugh. 'Can you believe such a thing?'

'But –'

'I know. Crazy, isn't it? On occasion I've actually gone out and got it for her. I've had to – otherwise she'd go and get it herself somehow – money or no money. It's happened. And I'm sure you've heard about it, haven't you?' She looked into Mrs Carroll's face with her question, but the older woman avoided her glance.

'Yes,' Abbie said with a nod, 'I can see that word has got back. But how could it not? It makes a good story for the village, doesn't it? My dear mother, going into the Wheatsheaf – cadging drinks from the locals. And it must have made a pretty picture too. How could I allow it to happen again? So – as I say – if she's that determined, then I go and get it for her. I'm just wondering when I'm going to hear about it from some member of the School

Board – Mr Carstairs or the Baptist minister. It's bound to happen. It's just a matter of time.'

Now Mrs Carroll faced her again. 'Does she – drink every day?'

'No. It goes in cycles. There are days when she drinks, but then there'll be several days when she doesn't touch a drop. That's when she's full of remorse, when she makes her promises to give it up. But it always starts again. And the expense of her drinking is something I don't know how I'll keep up with if it continues.'

'It must be an expensive habit, I'm sure of that.' Mrs Carroll paused. 'What do you feel for her, Abbie?'

'Feel? For my mother?' Abbie frowned, as if addressing the question for the first time. 'I don't know. Not affection, I know that. I suppose I feel a certain duty towards her. Well, she is my mother. Apart from that, though – sometimes I think I hate her.' She looked at the other woman, expecting to see a reaction of horror and disapproval. It was not there. 'Mind you,' she went on, 'I don't think she's that fond of me. She blames me a great deal for the situation we're in – or rather the situation she's in.'

'In what way?'

'Well if I hadn't broken off my engagement she'd be in London now – so she believes – living in a fine house with every possible comfort. What she's always wanted, in fact. I suppose I've denied her that. But how could I take her to London with me – the way she is? Though perhaps if I'd married Arthur and taken her to live with us she would never have got like this.'

'You can't blame yourself,' Mrs Carroll said. 'You can help others only to an extent, then there comes a time when they have to take responsibility for their own actions. They can't always be putting the blame on others.'

'No, I suppose not.'

After a moment Mrs Carroll asked, 'Do you ever hear now from your Mr Gilmore?'

'Oh, no.' Abbie shook her head and gave a melancholy little smile. 'And neither am I likely to, ever again. No, I'm afraid that part of my life is over.'

Chapter Twenty-Two

While Abbie sat at the kitchen table with Mrs Carroll in Flaxdown, Arthur Gilmore was sitting on a bench in London's Hyde Park. In his hand he held an open book, but with all the distractions around him it was not easy to concentrate and he had more or less abandoned his intention to read.

The park before him made a colourful scene. There were numerous children there, some playing – quietly or boisterously – while others walked, or sat with their parents on the benches or the grass. There were elderly couples, strolling sedately, and lovers walking hand in hand and arm in arm. About them dogs dashed after sticks or balls thrown by their owners. Arthur watched as a few children, taking advantage of the breeze, flew kites. Their shouts and cries rang in the summer air, while up above their heads the bright, dancing shapes rose and dipped in the blue sky.

Since the spring Arthur had taken to coming to the park on some Sunday afternoons – taking a cab from Notting Hill along the Bayswater Road. After spending the week inspecting working conditions in the factories in the East End it made a pleasant change. It was good to be away from the bustle, the noise, the heat and the grime, and instead to relax in green surroundings and breathe cleaner air.

Glancing to his left he saw that a young woman and a little girl of about seven had taken occupancy of a bench nearby. With her back to him the woman was bending, adjusting the lace on one of the child's boots. When the operation was finished she straightened and the child took up a brightly coloured ball, got down from the bench and ran a few feet away. Turning, she awkwardly tossed the ball to the young woman. It fell into the grass, several feet too short. With a shake of her head the young woman moved forward, picked up the ball and tossed it back to the child – who immediately tossed it back again – and again with no sense of aim, so that once more it fell short.

Arthur watched. His keen attention, however, was directed solely at the young woman. She wore a trim little jacket over a pale-lilac muslin dress that was trimmed with threaded silk ribbons and lace. Her corn-coloured hair was, as was the fashion, set in a chignon. Perched forward on her head was a small, neat lilac hat decorated with a white frill. Notwithstanding that she had her back to him, Arthur was quite sure that he had seen her slim, straight figure and blonde hair before. He waited for her to turn so that he could see her face.

And then came his chance as the child's ball came bouncing past her feet, and with a laughing groan the young woman turned to follow it. Seeing her face he at once got up from the bench, and as he did so she saw him and came to a halt.

'Arthur . . . !'

'Jane.' He smiled broadly. 'Well, I certainly didn't expect to see you here.'

'No,' she said, 'nor I you.'

She came forward and they shook hands. 'What a lovely surprise,' she said.

He nodded. 'It is for me.'

He saw that the child's ball had come to rest close to his

foot. He bent, picked it up and held it out to the little girl. 'Here you are, miss.'

The child took it from him and thanked him.

'Anne's a little shy,' Jane said, smiling. She turned to the child, 'Anne, this is Mr Arthur Gilmore.' To Arthur she said, 'This is Miss Anne Linden. I'm lady's maid to Anne's mama – but today I have the very pleasant task of bringing Anne to the park.'

Arthur nodded and smiled at the little girl. 'Hello, Anne. And how are you?'

'Very well, thank you, sir.'

Jane looked around her at the bright summer scene. 'Oh, it's so lovely here in the park when the sun is shining.'

'It is indeed,' Arthur said. 'I'm something of a regular weekly visitor of late. I like to get out in the air. Relax a little.'

'Yes, I can understand that.'

A moment of silence fell. Jane broke it by saying: 'Well – how have you been?'

'Very well, thank you. And you?'

'Yes, quite well.'

Another little silence, then Arthur said, 'Do you hear from Abbie?'

Jane nodded. 'We correspond regularly. Though of course she's kept pretty busy these days. She was very well the last time I heard a couple of weeks ago.'

He hesitated. 'I've heard nothing from her these many months. Not since January, in fact.'

After a little hesitation Jane said, 'I was very sorry to hear of what happened – between the two of you.'

'Yes.' His tone was non-committal. Then with a shrug he added, 'Ah, well – it's over now. And I trust she's happy.' He paused. 'Is her mother still living with her, do you know?'

'As far as I know.'

Arthur gave a little nod, while Jane turned to Anne who was showing signs of restlessness. 'This isn't what you came to the park for, is it, Anne – to stand around while we talk?' Turning back to Arthur she said, 'It's time we left. We're meeting Anne's parents at Marble Arch.' She put out her hand to him and he took it in his. 'It's so nice to see you again,' she said.

'It's very nice to see you.'

Abbie had walked through the village on her return from Mrs Carroll's and was just approaching the schoolhouse when she heard the sound of a horse and carriage. Turning, she saw a pony and trap coming up the lane. Curious, she waited, one hand on the front gate. The carriage came to a stop and the driver, a young man, jumped down. He was in his twenties, wiry and lithe, with reddish-brown hair and freckles.

Touching his cap he said, 'I've come looking for Miss Abigail Morris, miss. Would you happen to be her?'

Abbie dimly registered that his accent was not of the West Country but was more likely of London. She also noticed an urgency in his speech and movements.

'Yes, I am,' she said. 'What is it?'

'I'm groom and coachman to Mr and Mrs Pinnock, miss,' he said. 'I've just drove over from Radstock.'

'Radstock?' Abbie's heart began thudding in her breast. 'It's Iris, isn't it? My sister Iris?'

'Yes, miss. I'm afraid so.'

'What is it? What's happened?'

'She – she've had an accident, miss . . .'

'Oh, dear God . . . Is she – badly hurt?'

'She fell down the stairs, miss. Early this mornin' it happened. The missis sent me to tell you. Says I got to bring you back to the house if you'll come.'

'Oh, yes – yes, of course!' Abbie turned on the spot for a second, directionless in her sudden panic. 'How is she? Is she badly hurt?'

'I don't rightly know how bad, miss.' He paused, then added, 'The other maid – Mary – she told me Iris was insensible.'

'Oh, God.' Briefly Abbie put her head in her hands. Raising her eyes to the young man again she said, 'I'll just get my coat and put a couple of things in a bag. I'll only be a minute.'

'Right, miss. While I'm waiting I'd be glad of a drop of water – for meself and the horse. It's hot work, driving in this heat.'

'Yes, of course.' Abbie directed him to the pump in the schoolyard and then, in case he should have need of it, the water closet at the end of the small cottage garden.

As she entered the kitchen a few moments later her mother looked at her from her chair. 'You've been gone a long time,' she said. The level of the brandy in the bottle, Abbie vaguely noticed, had sunk considerably. She was not concerned about it now, however.

'Mother,' she said, 'I have to leave. I've got to go to Radstock. Iris has had an accident and Mrs Pinnock has sent her man to fetch me.'

'What kind of an accident?' Mrs Morris's voice, affected by the alcohol, was a little too loud, as if she had difficulty in controlling it.

'Apparently she fell down the stairs,' Abbie said. 'I must go to her.'

'Iris sent for you.' Now Mrs Morris's tone sounded rather aggrieved.

'What?' Abbie frowned, preoccupied.

'Iris – she sent word for you to go to her?'

'I don't think Iris is in any fit state to send for anybody. Apparently she's unconscious. It would be her employer,

295

Mrs Pinnock. Anyway, what difference does it make?' She took from a cupboard her little travelling bag – not used since her trip to London. 'Mother,' she said, 'why don't you come with me?'

'To Radstock?'

'Yes.'

'Oh . . .' Mrs Morris frowned, shook her head. 'It's such a long way.'

'But Mrs Pinnock's carriage is outside. And it'll bring us back – the young man said.'

'Oh, I don't think so.' Mrs Morris shook her head again. 'It's too far for me, Abbie, all that distance – and the way I'm feeling. Besides, what if we don't come back tonight? Where should we sleep?'

'I don't know but – oh, there'd be a hotel or something. We'd be all right.'

A silent moment, then Mrs Morris said, 'D'you think Iris would be that keen to see me?'

Abbie sighed. 'Listen, Mother, you've got to put all that behind you. Come with me. Let Iris know you care about her.'

Mrs Morris took a little sip of the brandy. 'She doesn't care about me. Not a fig. She made that clear enough.'

'Oh, Mother – for God's sake . . .'

'She doesn't. She chose to spend her summer holiday with Lizzie and that husband of hers.'

'His name is Adam.'

'She could have come here, but she chose not to. And for the simple reason that she didn't want to see me.' She shrugged. 'Well, if that's the way she wants it.'

'Mother, this isn't the time for these old – enmities. Come with me. Make it up with her.'

'No.' Mrs Morris took another sip from her glass. 'No, you go. I'm sure she'll be happier with just you there. And I'm sure you'll care for her as well as anyone can.'

'Mother –'

'I mean it. You go on alone.'

Abbie stood a moment longer, then turned and went into the hall and up the stairs to her bedroom. Since she had made the decision to stay in Flaxdown instead of moving to London, the sleeping arrangements in the cottage had been altered. She had borrowed a spare bed from Eddie and set it up in the front parlour, where her mother now chose to sleep. Abbie had been pleased, for it meant that she had her bedroom back again.

When she had finished packing her valise she went back downstairs and put on her cape.

'I'm going now,' she said. 'I expect to be back later today. Will you be all right while I'm gone?'

'Don't worry about me.' A little pause. 'Can you leave me a little money? Just a few pence – in case I need anything while you're gone.'

Abbie took a florin from her purse, put it on the table beside her mother's glass and moved to the door. There she stood helplessly for a moment, then murmured a goodbye and went into the hall.

The young coachman was waiting beside the horse. As Abbie got to his side he took her valise from her and helped her up into the trap.

'I must just call and leave a message for my brother,' Abbie said. 'His house is not far away.'

The young man nodded. 'Right, miss, you just tell me where to go.'

With Abbie directing him to Green Lane they set off, a few minutes later coming to a stop outside Eddie's cottage. Eddie was, of course, out at work, but Abbie left a message for him with Violet to the effect that she was going to Radstock to see Iris. A few moments later, with Violet standing watching at the open door with Sarah in her arms, Abbie was back in the trap and starting away again.

At last they came to Radstock, some ten miles to the north-west of Flaxdown. The house of Iris's employers, Mr and Mrs Pinnock, was situated on the northern edge of the town centre. Reaching it, the driver drove the trap into the yard, and even as it came to a halt Abbie was snatching at her valise and climbing down.

Mrs Pinnock herself answered the door to Abbie's ring. She was a small, stout woman with spectacles and a brisk but warm manner. After taking Abbie's cape and bag she led the way at once to the stairs.

'It was a very bad fall, I have to tell you,' she said over her shoulder. 'The poor girl had just started down from the top landing, carrying a tray' – she gestured upwards – 'and missed her footing. The stairs are quite steep.' They had reached the first landing now. Mrs Pinnock turned to Abbie. 'Anyway, the doctor came – I called him at once, of course. Iris has wrenched her ankle badly, and she's also severely bruised but fortunately there are no bones broken.'

In spite of her words, however, there was an anxious tone in her voice. Abbie said, 'Your driver told me she was unconscious.'

'Yes – I'm afraid that's true.'

'And now?'

Mrs Pinnock shook her head. 'I'm sorry to say there's been no change.'

'You mean she's still like it?' Abbie groaned. 'Oh, God . . .'

'Poor Iris,' the older woman said. 'She's such a good girl. Such a sweet, obliging little thing.' She hovered for a moment, then turned again towards the stairs ahead. 'Anyway – let me take you to her.'

They continued on up a third flight of stairs. Reaching the top floor Mrs Pinnock led the way along a narrow landing to a door at the end. Stopping before it she turned to Abbie and said, 'Iris shares this room with my other maid, Mary – who's sitting with her right now. I've arranged for Mary to sleep in another room for the time being and I've had another bed brought in here.' She gave a little shrug. 'Well – I thought that if you wanted to stay overnight with Iris then you could. And sleeping in the other bed you won't disturb her.'

Abbie thanked her. Mrs Pinnock softly opened the door and tiptoed in, Abbie close behind. The curtains had been closed against the summer light and the dimness of the room was relieved only by a small oil lamp. As they entered, a young girl of fourteen or fifteen got up from a chair beside the bed. Mrs Pinnock nodded to her and whispered, 'Mary, this is Miss Morris, Iris's sister. She's going to sit with Iris for a while now.'

'Yes, mum,' said the girl, giving Abbie a curious glance.

'Has there been any change?' Mrs Pinnock asked her.

'No, mum. She's about the same.'

Mrs Pinnock sighed, then said, 'Perhaps you'll go down to the kitchen and get Miss Morris some tea, will you?'

'Yes, mum.'

As the girl went from the room Abbie moved towards the bed.

With the bedclothes drawn up to her chin, Iris lay on her side in the double bed, her face away from the light of the lamp. She lay quite still, eyes closed, her knees drawn up. The sight of her injured face gave Abbie a clear indication of the violence of her fall. Her chin was bruised and grazed, added to which her right eye was discoloured and swollen.

'Oh, Iris . . . ' Abbie breathed. Afraid to touch her, she bent lower. 'Iris . . . Iris, it's me, Abbie . . .'

There was no response. Abbie tried again to rouse her, repeating her name several times. And then after a little while Iris stirred and opened her eyes. Abbie's spirits rose, and she bent to her again. 'Iris . . . Iris, it's me, Abbie. Wake up, Iris, my dear. Oh, please wake up.'

Iris frowned, looked unfocusing into Abbie's face and then closed her eyes again.

'Iris,' Abbie persisted. 'Iris, wake up, do.' Again Iris opened her eyes. She muttered something in an irritable tone and then closed her eyes and drifted off once more. Abbie straightened up, the tears running down her cheeks.

Mrs Pinnock said, 'I'm afraid she's been like this most of the time. It's possible to rouse her now and again, just briefly, but there's no getting any sense out of her.'

'What time did it happen – her accident?'

'Just after seven this morning.'

'And she's been like this ever since?'

Mrs Pinnock spread her hands in her helplessness. 'Dr Hinton says there's very little anyone can do except wait. He says to keep her in a darkened room – that and lay cold compresses on her head. Otherwise it's really just a matter of time. He says she's sustained a severe concussion to the back of her head. Though he doesn't believe there's any fracture. He thinks she'll be all right in time. Give it a little while, he says, and he thinks she'll come round all right.'

'He *thinks*,' Abbie said. 'Doesn't he know?'

Mrs Pinnock frowned and said a little stiffly, 'Miss Morris, we're doing all we can for your sister. But we can only rely on what Dr Hinton tells us.'

'I'm sorry,' Abbie said. 'It's just that I'm so – so worried.'

'I know you are. Of course you are.' Mrs Pinnock put a hand on her shoulder. 'Listen – you sit down and rest for a while. Mary will bring you your tea. I'm sure you'll be glad of a cup after your long drive.'

'Yes, I would – thank you.'

'I'll be about the house if you should need me. And Mary's always available to sit with Iris if you should want her to.'

'Thank you.'

Mrs Pinnock moved to the washstand and took up the jug. 'I'll get Mary to bring up some fresh cold water for the compress.'

Abbie murmured her thanks again. When Mrs Pinnock had gone she sat down on the chair that Mary had vacated, turned to the bed and gazed down again at Iris's bruised face.

'Iris . . .' she whispered close to Iris's ear. 'Iris, my dear . . .'

There was no response. With a deep sigh of sadness Abbie sat back in the chair. She continued to gaze down at Iris's unmoving face for some minutes and then, raising her head, took in the room.

So this was where Iris lived. This plain, simply furnished little room was now the closest thing to home that Iris knew. The bed on which she lay unconscious was where in better times sharing the space with her workmate, Mary – she rested after her long day's work and dreamed her dreams.

The small room held the other, narrow bed that Mrs Pinnock had spoken of. There was also a chest of drawers and a small wardrobe. On top of the wardrobe sat Iris's box. Seeing it, Abbie remembered the day when Iris had left Flaxdown to go to her first place of employment. That would have been in sixty-six. Iris had been twelve years old. Eddie had walked with her to the station at Frome, her box on his shoulder. Abbie recalled how Iris had wept at their parting – at the pain of leaving home and from anxiety at what might lie ahead. Abbie had stood at the gate watching as they had set out that July morning. Iris, wearing her best clothes, had looked so small and vulnerable.

Twelve years old. It was too young, Abbie thought, too young to have to go out and fend for oneself. She remembered how she and Jane had gone off to Eversleigh looking for a petty place when they had been the same age. In the event, Fate had decided against such a course for Abbie herself and she had had to stay at home to care for the rest of the family. It had been easier for her – not having to go out and face the world. Not like Iris and Lizzie, nor Jane; nor those countless other girls and boys who were sent away into service at such tender ages.

And now more than six years had passed since Iris had left Flaxdown to make her own way. Those six years had gone by so fast. During that time Iris had, as was the custom, changed her place of employment several times, each move having been made with the notion of betterment in mind. Betterment. The word was like a bad joke. How had Iris bettered herself? How, when for those six years of hard work she had nothing to show beyond a few possessions that would fit into her little wooden travelling box? Perhaps, the thought suddenly came to Abbie, it was this that had lain at the base of their mother's anger . . .

There came a soft little tap at the door. It opened and the young maid, Mary, entered, carrying the pitcher filled with fresh, cold water. As she set it down on the washstand she said, 'I'll be bringing up your tea now, miss.'

Abbie thanked her. When Mary had left the room Abbie poured some of the water into the bowl, dipped the compress in it, wrung it out and applied it gently to Iris's head.

After a little while Mary was back, now carrying a tray bearing tea and a plate with a slice of fruit cake on it. She set the tray on the chest of drawers. 'Can I get you anything else, miss?'

'No, thank you. The tea will be fine.' She added as Mary moved back across the room, 'Mary, have you been here long?'

'Since last summer, miss.'

'Are you and Iris good friends?'

'Oh, yes, miss. She looked after me when I come 'ere.'

Abbie nodded. Yes, Iris would do that, she thought.

Just after seven o'clock Mary brought up another tray to Abbie. It held a bowl of vegetable soup and a covered plate of roast lamb, potatoes and beans. Holding the tray on her lap, Abbie ate most of the food. As she put down her knife and fork Mary entered again with a little dish of rhubarb and custard. Abbie thanked her but said she had eaten enough. Soon afterwards Dr Hinton called once more. He was a short, bearded, middle-aged man with a bluff manner and a strong smell of tobacco about him. Mrs Pinnock accompanied him into the room and introduced him to Abbie. While Abbie looked on, he bent over Iris, lifting one of her eyelids and speaking her name. At his insistent voice Iris stirred, opened her eyes for a few seconds, muttered some unintelligible words in a fretful tone and then drifted off into unconsciousness again.

'Is this the way she's been?' the doctor asked.

Mrs Pinnock replied, 'Yes, it is,' to which Abbie added, 'She wakes like that from time to time if I try to rouse her. Sometimes she speaks. Though nothing she says makes much sense. Also when she wakes she's usually rather irritable.'

The doctor nodded. 'The symptoms are typical.'

'How long is it likely to last?' Abbie asked.

He gave a shake of his head. 'I'm afraid there's no knowing. Sometimes a few hours; sometimes days. In some cases it can go on for weeks.' He was picking up his bag again. 'You can only wait – that's all.'

Throughout the rest of the evening Abbie sat at Iris's side, periodically speaking to her and refreshing the cold compress on her head. At one point Mrs Pinnock came in accompanied by her husband who had just returned from his work. Abbie recalled Iris saying he owned a large draper's shop in the town centre. He was a stout, balding little man with a kind and solicitous manner, and was clearly concerned about Iris. The three of them conversed for a while in hushed voices, and then Abbie was left alone again. Later, after she had eaten a simple supper, she got undressed and put on her nightdress. She lit the nightlight on the chest of drawers, turned out the oil lamp and climbed into the narrow bed that had been placed a yard from where Iris lay.

It was strange lying there in the unfamiliar, dimly-lit room. From Iris's bed there was no sound, no movement. Head turned sideways on the pillow, Abbie gazed at the shadowy form of her sister. After a time she fell asleep.

Immediately upon waking, awareness of the situation came back to Abbie and she sat up and looked across at the other bed. Iris still lay on her side, her knees drawn up. Abbie got out of bed and moved towards her.

'Iris . . . ?'

As before, Iris briefly surfaced, opening her eyes and looking vaguely into Abbie's face. She spoke some words that made no sense, then closed her eyes again.

Abbie bowed her head in despair. The thought came to her once more – what if Iris should never waken? She had read of people injured in accidents, people who had been rendered unconscious and never recovered. Without ever waking they had gradually declined and died. She pushed the thought aside.

After renewing the compress on Iris's brow, Abbie moved to the window, drew back the curtain a fraction and gazed out over the sunlit front garden. She thought of Eddie and her mother in Flaxdown. Perhaps she should send Eddie a wire. But there was nothing she could say that would bring any encouragement or cheer. Yet she could not leave things as they were for much longer; sooner or later she would have to send Eddie word. And her mother too. And another thing – what was to happen about Iris and herself? They could not stay indefinitely in the Pinnock household. As kind as Mrs Pinnock had shown herself to be, there would be a limit to her kindness. If Iris remained as she was for any length of time, dependent upon her mistress, there was bound to be a strain upon such goodwill. Abbie sighed. She did not know what to do. Closing the curtains she drew back from the window. And as she did so she heard Iris's voice.

'Abbie . . . ?'

Swiftly Abbie looked round. Iris had turned in the bed and was squinting at her in the gloom. In another moment Abbie was at her side, bending to her, laying one hand gently on her shoulder. 'Oh, Iris – my dear . . . !'

Iris raised a hand from beneath the bedcovers and touched her mouth weakly. 'I'm thirsty, Abbie,' she said. 'Can I have some water, please?'

When Dr Hinton called later that morning he expressed great relief and satisfaction. He was sure, he told Abbie, that Iris would make good progress now. Abbie went with him out on to the landing and there, in answer to her enquiries, was told that it would be possible for Iris to be taken home to Flaxdown within a few days. When the doctor had gone Abbie re-entered the room and went to the bed where Iris lay.

'Iris . . .?'

At Abbie's voice Iris opened her eyes.

'I'm taking you home,' Abbie said. 'The doctor says that in a few days you'll be well enough to travel.'

That afternoon Abbie sat in the Pinnocks' library and wrote letters to Eddie and her mother, telling them that Iris was showing sure signs of recovery and would probably be well enough to travel back to Flaxdown later in the week. In her letter to Eddie she also suggested that as their mother was alone he might wish to go and call upon her. She did not, however, hold out much hope for such a move. When the letters were finished she went out to post them. Back in the bedroom she took off her cape and bonnet and sat down at Iris's side. Iris was awake again.

'I've just written to Eddie,' Abbie said. 'I told him I'll soon be bringing you home.'

Iris's smile of relief changed to a frown of concern. 'But – where shall I stay?'

'With Eddie and Violet. Eddie gave me strict instructions.' She bent lower and lightly kissed Iris's bruised face. 'You're not to worry about anything, all right? We'll take good care of you.'

Chapter Twenty-Three

The Pinnocks' young groom-cum-coachman was named Alfred – known as Alfie – Timson, and late Friday morning he came up to the attic, lifted Iris up in his arms and carried her down the stairs and out into the air. Abbie and Mrs Pinnock followed close behind. Having watched the young man negotiate the narrow, bending stair, Abbie said to him as they reached the waiting carriage, 'You did that wonderfully well, Alfie. Thank you.'

He smiled. 'Aw, it wasn't any trouble, miss. She don't weigh no more'n a butterfly.'

Mrs Pinnock had had a little feather mattress and some cushions placed in the carriage, and Alfie gently laid Iris down upon them. Mrs Pinnock handed a parasol to Abbie saying, 'You'll probably need this – to keep the sun off her face. The doctor said the light will continue to bother her.'

Abbie thanked her, checked that Iris was comfortable, then turned back to the woman. 'Mrs Pinnock – I don't know how to thank you for all you've done.'

'I've done nothing, my dear.'

'Oh, you've done so much.'

Mrs Pinnock put out her hand. As Abbie took it she said, 'When Dr Hinton sends you his bill, please send it on to me.'

'Well, we'll see,' Mrs Pinnock said. 'Now you take Iris home. And remember that as soon as she's well again her position will be open for her.' She looked into the carriage. 'Did you hear that, Iris?'

Iris smiled faintly. 'Yes, mum – thank you.'

Abbie thanked Mrs Pinnock once more and Alfie helped her up into the carriage. As she settled herself at Iris's side he took up the reins and a few moments later they were starting away on the road to Flaxdown.

In order to avoid jarring Iris more than was absolutely necessary, the young coachman drove without haste. For a little while Iris talked with Abbie, but she soon lapsed into silence and lay back with her eyes closed. Abbie, sitting beside her, did her best to ensure that Iris's face was kept in the shade and soon, with the rhythmic jogging of the carriage, Iris fell asleep. While she slept, neither Abbie nor the coachman spoke.

Iris awoke again a while later, saying that she was thirsty, and Abbie poured into a mug some of the water that Mrs Pinnock had provided in a bottle. Iris drank a little then settled back against the cushions. Seeing that she was not sleeping, but merely resting, Abbie turned her attention to the young driver. She was curious about him, and after making reference to his accent, asked where he was from. Obviously, she said, he was not originally from Radstock. No, he told her, he had worked for a London employer and accompanied him to Wiltshire to his country residence. Later, when his employer had planned to return to London, he, Alfie, had decided to stay.

'What was the attraction?' Abbie asked him. 'Why did you stay in this part of the world?'

'Well, for one thing, I got involved with the village band.'

'You play in a band?'

He turned in his seat and grinned. 'Yeh, I play the cornet. And the trumpet too on occasion.'

'Well,' Abbie said, 'I'm impressed.' She turned to Iris. 'Did you know that, Iris? Mr Timson is a musician.'

'Yes.' Still with her eyes closed, Iris smiled. 'I know.'

'Have you heard him play?'

'Yes. He's very good.'

'You hear that, Alfie?' Abbie said to the young man's back. 'You're getting some praise.'

'Well, that's good to hear.' She could hear the smile in his voice. 'A bit of praise is always welcome.' He gave a short laugh, 'Specially when it's deserved.'

Abbie laughed. 'Oh, and he's modest too. You hear that, Iris?'

'Yes.' Iris smiled. 'I heard it.'

'So,' Abbie said, turning again to the young man, 'what's your other reason for staying?'

'My other reason?' He didn't turn but kept his eyes on the road ahead.

'When I asked why you'd stayed, you said that for one thing you'd got involved in the band. So obviously there were other reasons.'

He nodded. 'Well, yeh, I suppose there are.'

'And . . .?'

At this he turned around in his seat and looked at her, a half-smile on his face. Abbie was about to speak again, but his glance quickly moved on and settled briefly upon Iris. Abbie, turning to her sister, saw that her eyes were still closed. Abbie grinned at him and gave a nod. Then, bending close to Iris's ear she whispered, 'You, Iris Morris, are a dark horse.'

Iris was not sleeping. After a moment, her eyes still closed, she smiled again.

A few minutes after entering Flaxdown they were coming to a halt outside Eddie and Violet's cottage in Green Lane, and almost at once Violet was there, coming out to

309

welcome them. They had received Abbie's letter telling them that Iris would be coming home, she said, and in preparation had made up a bed for her in the parlour.

Alfie gathered Iris up in his arms again, followed Violet into the cottage and in the parlour gently laid Iris down. Abbie drew the curtains against the light and got Iris settled while Violet took the young coachman into the kitchen and gave him some bread and cheese, a large slice of apple pie and some tea. By the time he was ready to leave again Iris was fast asleep. Briefly he looked in on her still, peaceful form and then Abbie followed him outside to wish him goodbye, to shake his hand and thank him for all his trouble.

'No.' He shook his head and nodded towards the cottage. 'Nothing's trouble where she's concerned.'

'Well – thank you anyway – for everything.'

'Don't mention it.' He swung up into the driver's seat. 'Say goodbye to her for me, will you?'

'I will.'

'She's going to be all right, is she?'

'Yes, she is. The doctor said the worst is now behind her. With complete rest, he said, he's sure she'll make a full recovery.'

'Good. That's good.' He smiled down at Abbie. 'Well, you just see she gets back to Radstock soon, all right?'

She returned his smile. 'Don't worry, Alfie, we shall do our best.'

Returning to the parlour with Violet she saw that Iris was still sleeping and together they crept from the room. Violet wanted Abbie to stay and drink some tea with her, but Abbie declined. 'I must get back home,' she said, then added, 'I don't suppose Eddie called on Mother while I've been gone. I suggested he might.'

Violet shook her head. 'No, he didn't.' She shrugged. 'But you know your brother as well as I do.'

The church clock was striking four as Abbie, carrying her valise, made her way along School Lane. She was looking forward to getting back indoors, into the comfort – such as it was these days – of her own home; to be once again among familiar things.

Looking up at the sky she saw that dark clouds were gathering and she quickened her step a little. She felt dusty and grimy, and also drained of energy. The anxiety over Iris's accident had taken its toll, added to which she still felt rather stiff from the long, slow journey. Nevertheless, she was aware of the most enormous sense of relief. Iris was going to be all right; that was the important thing.

As Abbie turned in at the gate of the schoolhouse she untied her bonnet and took it off. She wondered what kind of reception she would get from her mother. And how, she wondered, had her mother coped with being on her own for the past five days?

Going round the side of the house she let herself in at the back door. As she entered the kitchen from the scullery she opened her mouth to frame a greeting and then stopped in her tracks, her words freezing on her lips. The next moment she was letting fall her valise and bonnet, and hurrying forward.

'Mother . . .'

Mrs Morris lay sprawled on the sofa. Her face was deathly pale and there were dark stains over her bodice and skirt. Abbie bent over her. Her mother's breathing was harsh, her breath foetid. The stains were not only on her dress but on the sofa and the floor.

'Oh, Mother,' Abbie muttered distractedly, 'how long have you been in this state?' She raised a hand to her mother's pale cheek, and at the touch her mother's eyelids fluttered open, her lips moving as she struggled to speak. Abbie could just make out the words.

'I – I can't breathe . . .'

'Here – try to sit up a little.' Abbie put her arms around her and tried to pull her into a more upright position, putting cushions behind her back for support. Her mother's head lolled on her neck as she gasped for air.

Abbie fetched a little water and held it to her mother's mouth. Mrs Morris took a sip, but a moment later vomited, bringing up a heavy blackish fluid. Abbie straightened, frantic. 'Mother,' she said, 'I'm going for the doctor.'

'No . . .' The protest came in a faint, breathless groan.

'I've got to.' Abbie moved towards the door. 'I'll be back as soon as I can.'

She did not want to leave her mother, but she had no choice. Her cape flying out behind her, she ran from the cottage and down the lane. As she crossed the green towards the western side of the village the threatened rain began to fall and she realised she had come out without her bonnet.

At last she reached the house of Dr Parrish, and hurried up the drive, and rang the bell. To her dismay the maid who opened the door told her that the doctor and Mrs Parrish were out and were not expected back until later that evening. 'But if it's really urgent, miss,' the maid added, 'you best go and call on Dr Mason. He usually stands in for Dr Parrish. You know where 'e lives, don't you?'

'Yes – on the Warminster Road.' Abbie had never met Dr Mason; had only heard of him – that he was a dour, impatient man – but with Dr Parrish being out she had no choice. She thanked the girl and turned away. The rain was falling more strongly now. At the gate she turned towards the east, in the direction of Warminster, but when she came to Tomkins Row she ran and knocked sharply on the door of number three.

A few moments later it was opened and Mrs Carroll was there.

'Abbie,' she said, frowning, taking in Abbie's expression, 'what's up? What's 'appened?'

'It's Mother,' Abbie said, gasping and breathless. 'Oh, Mrs Carroll, she's so ill. She's having trouble breathing, and she keeps being sick. D'you think you could go round and stay with her for a while, please? Dr Parrish is out and I've got to get Dr Mason from the Warminster Road. I'm sorry to come running to you, but I don't know who else to ask. Violet's got the baby and now Iris as well to look after.'

Mrs Carroll did not hesitate. 'Of course, my dear.'

As the two left the cottage Mrs Carroll buttoned her coat and raised an old umbrella over their heads. 'You ought to have a hat,' she said. 'You'll catch cold in this.'

'I'm all right.'

'How are you going to get to Dr Mason's?'

'I'll go to Barton's stables and get a fly.' Abbie was already hurrying ahead. 'Please tell Mother I'll be back with the doctor as soon as I can.'

'Here –' Mrs Carroll said, 'take the umbrella. I don't have far to go.'

'No, thank you,' Abbie cried, and with a wave of her hand was dashing away.

Just past the Harp and Horses she went to the stables owned by the fly proprietor, Mr Barton. She found him just driving the fly out of the yard, and seeing her he brought the horse and carriage to a stop. He was a lean, short-sighted man in his early sixties, well-known to Abbie from her childhood.

'It's Abbie, is it?' he said peering down at her.

'Yes,' she said. 'Oh, Mr Barton, I've got to get to Dr Mason's on the Warminster Road. Can you take me there, please?'

'Well, I would, my dear, certainly,' he said, 'but I'm going to pick up a passenger from Frome station. I'm just off this very minute.'

'Oh, please – can't you help me? My mother is ill.'

'Well, I'm sorry to hear that, my dear, but I'm afraid there's nothing I can do. I'm already late.'

She groaned, shaking her head distractedly. She would just have to walk; there was nothing else for it. She started to move away, stopped, then turned back. 'Mr Barton,' she said, 'could I ride with you to Frome?'

'But you just said you wanted to go out Warminster way.'

'I've changed my mind. I'll pay you, of course.' As she spoke she realized that she had come out without her purse. 'When I get home again – I'll pay you then.'

'That don't matter,' he said, 'I've got to go to Frome anyway.' He beckoned to her. 'Come on – get in afore you gets drownded.'

A little less than half an hour later Abbie had reached Frome and was hurrying to Louis's house. The rain had eased during the journey, and now came to a stop as she ran up the drive to the front door and rang the bell. The young maid who answered told her yes, Dr Randolph was in, then showed her into the library, took her name and went away. Abbie glanced at the clock and saw that it was a little after six.

How, she wondered, would Louis receive her? They had not seen one another since their meeting on the train on her journey back from London. That had been just after Christmas. Due to her lack of transport he had then brought her back to Flaxdown in his carriage. And not very long after his departure her mother had appeared on the doorstep.

Now, months later, here was Abbie, again seeking his help.

She heard footsteps in the hall, and then all at once Louis was entering the room. 'Abbie!' he said, smiling. 'Well, this is a surprise. You're the last person I expected to see.' Having taken in her somewhat damp appearance he added, 'But what brings you out here on such a miserable afternoon?'

Quickly she told him something of the condition in which she had found her mother. 'And our local doctor is away,' she finished. 'So rather than go for the locum I came here – for you. I hope you don't mind.'

'Of course not. Wait here a minute and I'll get my coat and hitch up the horse. I've haven't long been back myself.' As he moved to the door he said over his shoulder, 'I'll get Lily to bring you a towel.'

He went from the room and a minute later the maid was coming to her with a towel. Abbie thanked her and dabbed at her face and hair. After a little while Louis returned, now wearing his coat and hat and carrying his bag.

'All right,' he said, 'let's be on our way.'

The rain had turned much of the road to mud, but nevertheless the horse and carriage made fairly good progress. As they rode, Abbie told Louis some of what had happened since their meeting in December. She spoke briefly of how her mother had come back into her life and had since been living with her. She then spoke of Iris's accident, of how she had gone to Radstock to see her and had returned home to find her mother prostrate and vomiting. Looking up into his grave face, she said earnestly, 'Can you help her? You can, can't you?'

'I'll do whatever I can – you can be sure of that. In the meantime, try not to worry too much.'

At last they came to Flaxdown and the schoolhouse, and even as Louis was reining in the horse, Abbie was getting down from the carriage and hurrying to the front door. As she reached out her hand for the latch the door opened and Mrs Carroll stood there pale-faced and obviously very distressed.

'It's all right, Mrs Carroll,' Abbie said reassuringly. 'Dr Randolph is here, and –'

'Oh, Abbie, my dear.' Mrs Carroll said, breaking in on Abbie's words. 'You're too late. Your mother – she died just a few minutes ago.'

Chapter Twenty-Four

It was August. Although Abbie enjoyed the annual school summer holidays, nevertheless there were times when she found herself looking forward to being back at her desk in the classroom again. Now, in these days of high summer her pupils were in all probability occupied with their usual seasonal employment – working in the fields to bring in the harvest. She looked from the window at the small, sun-drenched front garden, and beyond it to the lane, then turned back to the looking-glass and ran a smoothing hand over her hair. She was expecting Louis to call at any moment. He had written to say he had to be in the area, and that if she was not otherwise engaged he would like to see her.

If she was not otherwise engaged. No, that was not the case, and indeed was not likely to be. Turning from the glass she once again glanced along the lane. She felt strangely restless. She wondered at it, but told herself it was due to her absence from the schoolroom – and also to the loss of her mother.

A month had passed since her mother's death. On the day of the funeral Abbie, Eddie, Lizzie and Iris had gathered at the schoolhouse from where their mother's coffin was borne. Abbie and her sisters had wept. Perhaps, if truth were told, not so much for their mother's passing as at regret that they had never been close to her. Eddie – who was there mostly for appearances' sake – had remained dry-eyed.

After the funeral he had returned to the contentment of his family life with Violet and daughter Sarah, Lizzie back to her husband in Lullington to await the birth of their baby – due in mid-September – and Iris to her employment with the Pinnock family in Radstock. Abbie, whose life had been more strongly touched by their mother's return, was the most affected by her death.

Movement caught her eye, and looking further along the lane she saw Louis's tall figure coming towards the schoolhouse. Moments later there came his knock on the door and she moved to open it.

As he entered, taking off his hat, she said, 'I saw you walking along the lane. Didn't you come by carriage?'

'It's with the smith for repair,' he said. 'I had to take a fly.' He stood before her and gave a little – almost imperceptible – nod of approval. 'I must say you look very nice, Abbie.'

'Well – thank you.' She felt herself colouring slightly under his glance. Then, quickly, turning, without purpose, she gestured towards the window. 'Shall we walk, or would you like to stay in and have some tea?'

'Why can't we do both?' he said. 'Let's walk and then come back for tea.' He smiled. 'There's plenty of time – and after all, it's Sunday. I'm allowed the occasional time of rest.'

Abbie nodded. 'Absolutely – I agree. Have you finished your business in the village?'

'Yes, it didn't take long. So – shall we go for a walk?'

A few minutes later the two of them left the schoolhouse and set off along the lane, their steps taking them away from the village and into the deeper peace and quiet of the surrounding countryside. After following a meandering footpath through meadows they made their way onto the heath and there followed a rough track that skirted a small lake where willows grew along the water's edge. From across the water came the ringing sound of voices as a few of the village children swam and splashed in the sun-warmed shallows.

The day was very warm, the sun beating down out of a cloudless sky. Coming upon the remains of a fallen tree in a secluded spot in the shade of a willow, Louis suggested that they sit for a while. Abbie, glad to rest out of the sunlight, agreed with relief.

Taking off his jacket, Louis placed it on the fallen tree trunk and Abbie sat down on it. With his hat beside him, Louis sat on the tree trunk some few feet away while Abbie took off her bonnet and ran a cooling hand through her hair.

The two had met on more than one occasion since she had called upon him in the rain to minister to her mother. A couple of times since that day he had come to the schoolhouse without notice, and she had invited him in and given him tea. On two other occasions he had, as in this instance, written to suggest that they meet. In all of their meetings, however, nothing of any great importance had been said, but following her mother's passing she had found his company a great comfort, and was glad of his visits.

To a degree she had blamed herself for her mother's death, but Louis had insisted that she could not be held in any way responsible. The seeds of the tragedy had been sown long before her mother's return to Flaxdown, he had said. Specifically, he explained to her that her mother's death had been due to haemorrhage of the stomach lining, brought about by prolonged intake of alcohol. Dr Parrish had concurred in the opinion, and Mrs Morris's death certificate had been so endorsed.

Now, taking his handkerchief from his pocket, Louis

dabbed at the back of his neck and his forehead. Nodding out towards the sound of the children's voices, he said, 'I could envy them at a time like this.'

'Ah, yes. I know what you mean.' Abbie nodded. 'Jane and I used to come here and swim. They were lovely times. And so far away now.'

He turned to look more closely at her. 'It will get better, Abbie. Believe me, it will. It will get easier.'

'What do you mean?' she said.

'I thought you sounded rather melancholy – and because of your mother. Is it not that?'

'No. It's not that at all.' She smiled. 'I didn't mean to sound so down. I don't know; perhaps it's this particular time of the year – when the school is closed and all the children are away. One gets so accustomed to the routine; it's hard to get used to the difference. And with mother being gone ... well, I suppose I'm being thrown more and more onto my own resources.' She gave an ironic little chuckle. 'And obviously those resources are being found to be lacking, wouldn't you say?'

'No, not at all. I think it's quite understandable that you're at – well, at something of a loss. Your life has changed in the past weeks. It's bound to make a difference.' He put out his hand and patted hers as it rested on the tree trunk. Although his touch was brief, she could still somehow feel it on the back of her hand. The water, the fallen tree trunk – for Abbie they conjured up a picture of the two of them together that day beside the stream, when they had strayed from the fairground. She thrust the images away; that time was long past.

'Abbie,' Louis was saying, 'you mustn't be hard on yourself. You've been through a difficult time.'

He went on to ask after her brother and two sisters, and they spoke also of his work and of more mundane matters. And then, after a short pause in their conversation, he asked, letting his question fall like a stone into the still lake before them:

'And what about your Mr Gilmore?'

'What?' She had been looking out over the water, but now turned to him and saw the expression on his face, a look of gravity relieved only slightly by the trace of a smile.

'Didn't you hear me?' he said. 'Mr Arthur Gilmore.'

'What – what about him?' She felt somewhat flustered, discomfited by his question, and looked away again, back over the water.

'When we met on the train just after Christmas you said you had been to spend some time with him in London. That you were engaged to be married. You were to be married at Easter, you told me.'

She nodded. 'Yes. Yes . . .' A shrug. 'Unfortunately – things happen. Plans change.'

'I see. I think. Your plans changing – was this due to your mother's return?'

'Yes.'

'So you – postponed your wedding.'

A pause before she answered. 'Not quite. There's not going to be a wedding.' She turned to him at this. 'I couldn't do anything else. With my mother living with me and in the state she was in . . . I didn't know what else to do.'

'I see. So you and your Mr Gilmore are no longer engaged.'

'That would seem to be the position.' She looked away again. From the other side of the lake the children's shouts and laughter rang across the water. And suddenly Louis's hand was there once more, lighting on hers, his palm on the back of her hand.

'Abbie, that's so sad,' he said. 'I had no idea. The loss of your mother. The ending of your engagement. It's no wonder you feel somewhat low.'

Her hand was burning under the touch of his and, as casually as she could, she withdrew it. 'Oh, I'm all right,' she said. 'I told you, it's just the time of the year – with not enough to occupy my thoughts, my time.' She picked up her bonnet, moving to put it back on her head. The conversation had taken an uncomfortable turn. 'I think perhaps we might start back,' she said. 'I could do with some tea; I'm getting thirsty.'

Back at the schoolhouse Abbie made tea and they sat drinking it in the little parlour. Their conversation now, however, remained on safe ground; there was no talk of bereavement or broken engagements and gradually the mood between them lightened. Later on, when Louis left it was with the agreement that they would write and make arrangements to meet again in the near future.

Over the weeks, the months, they met from time to time. Sometimes, weather permitting, they walked or drove out into the countryside. On other, rarer occasions, they went to Trowbridge or another nearby town to look around the shops and perhaps take lunch or dinner at a restaurant. And as they continued to meet Abbie felt herself relaxing more in his company and looking forward to the times when they would be together.

Always, though, at the back of her mind, was the sense that there was something missing in her life. And she soon came to realize that its main cause had nothing to do with her work at the school. It must surely, she eventually told herself, be because of Arthur, and the unsatisfactory way in which their relationship had ended.

She said nothing of it to Louis or anyone else, however, telling herself that it was in the past, and best forgotten.

Neither did she speak to anyone of her renewed

friendship with Louis. Though if truth were told, she knew it could only be a matter of time before it was remarked upon. The time came when one Sunday afternoon she was visiting Eddie and Violet, and the subject came up. They had obviously discussed it, for Eddie said, smiling at her, 'I reckon you're something of a dark 'orse, our Abbie. Or a darker 'orse than I thought you were.'

'What do you mean?'

'Well, this young gentleman friend of yourn. You've never spoke of 'im.'

'And what gentleman friend would this be?'

'Oh, look at 'er!' Eddie's laugh was infuriating. 'Sittin' there like butter wouldn't melt in 'er mouth. You know who I'm talkin' about. Manny said he saw you in a carriage with the man a week or so back. And Violet saw you walkin' with 'im near the village.' He laughed again. 'Come on, own up.'

His teasing was so irritating that Abbie almost snapped back a reply. She bit her tongue, however, and said, hiding her annoyance, 'If you must know, his name is Louis Randolph. He's a doctor, living and practising in Frome.'

'A doctor, yet!' Eddie, impressed, gave a little whistle. 'A doctor. You're doing well for yourself, ent you?'

'And,' Violet broke in, 'a very good-looking doctor. Oh, very handsome indeed. You've got good taste, Abbie.'

Quickly Abbie said, 'Listen, it's not like you think it is. He's a friend and nothing more.'

'Oh, ah,' Eddie said nodding. 'We 'eard that one before, ent we?'

'It's the truth.' Now Abbie let her annoyance show. 'We met – well, years ago. And he was the doctor I called in to see Mother that time – though he was too late to help her. So please – stop making more of it than there is.'

'All right, all right.' Eddie raised his hands. 'You don't need to sound so damn rattled about it.'

'Well – the way you go on. I can't have a simple friendship without you making some huge affair out of it.' And it was true, she said to herself: her friendship with Louis was simply that, a friendship and nothing more. Granted, there were times when she had suspected that perhaps Louis wanted more from their relationship, but she did not, and he seemed to be content with things as they were. And that was the way it would remain. Neither one of them, she told herself, now expected anything other.

So the days, the weeks, the months had gone by – with little change showing in Abbie's life. And now here it was winter again.

From her seat at her classroom desk, she glanced up at the clock. A quarter to three. Not long to go now and school would be over for another day. She watched her pupils for a few moments as they worked, then got up from her chair, moved to the window and gazed up at the grey sky.

She sighed, aware again of a sense of restlessness. It was with her so much of the time now – like some constant companion. Here it was, mid-December; she had expected that such feelings would have long gone by this time, but instead they seemed to have been growing stronger. So much time had gone by. Was it a year since she had returned from London after spending Christmas with Arthur? Her plans at that time had been to leave Flaxdown in the spring for a life in London, but her mother had returned, causing upheaval in so many ways. Changing Abbie's life – changing it for ever.

Abbie remained standing at the window for a minute or two longer, then turned her attention back to her pupils. They were writing, some on slates, some on paper. The younger and less able ones were working on words, phrases and short sentences, the others on short compositions she had set them.

'Thomas? Thomas Gilpin . . . ?' She spoke the boy's name as she moved back to her desk and as he looked up from his work she beckoned to him, smiling. 'I'll see your composition now, Tom, if I may.'

The boy, just over nine years old, got up from his seat and came towards her, a paper in his hand. He was the son of a farm labourer from the other side of the village, a boy with a warm, pleasant manner and unexceptional academic abilities.

As Abbie took the paper from him his hand brushed against her own. 'Oh, Tom,' she said, 'your hand is so cold.'

'Yes, miss.'

'Do you feel cold?'

He did not answer. Not that she was surprised; he would not happily admit to such a thing. She took in his thin, darned woollen jumper, the frayed collar of his shirt. 'While I look at your work, Tom,' she said, 'perhaps you could do something for me?'

'Yes, miss?' His voice was low and grave.

'Go and put some more wood in the stove, would you?' She gestured to the old stove with its stack reaching up into the ceiling 'It might need a good old poke, too. I'm afraid I don't have the right knack with it.' She added as he moved away, 'And give your hands a good warm while you're there.'

'Yes, miss.'

He turned away. Abbie added: 'Take your time. And don't burn yourself.'

'No, miss.'

She watched him as he bent over the stove, his face set

325

in concentration. How little chance such children had, regardless of their abilities, she thought. Being from very poor families, most of them were doomed to follow in their parents' footsteps, rarely getting even a step further ahead.

She looked down at the paper before her. Christmas was only days away and her pupils were looking forward to it. Tom Gilpin, she saw, was no exception. In his small, surprisingly neat hand, he had written that Christmas was his favourite time of the year. On Christmas morning, he wrote, he and his brothers and sisters would find an orange in their stockings, and for Christmas dinner they would eat chicken or pork. Christmas was spelt with a small 'c'. He had continued:

. . . On christmas Day my Father doesn't have to work, but is with us all day long, even though it's not a Sunday. Last christmas when the pond was froze my Father went skateing on the ice. Sometimes he skates very fast, and sometimes slow. When he skates slow I can run beside him, holding his hand. My father says that when the yunion is strong there will be more days like christmas.

'Is it all right, miss?' The boy had finished tending the stove and was now standing at Abbie's elbow.

'Indeed it is, Tom. It's very good.' She smiled at him. 'You make it sound like a very special day.'

He nodded and smiled gravely. She turned back to the paper. There were numerous errors but she would not remark on all of them; there was no sense in discouraging him. 'Christmas must start with a capital letter,' she said, 'and there's no "e" in skating. Also there's no "y" in union. Apart from that it's excellent.'

He nodded, pleased. 'Yes, miss.' A pause, then: 'I'm not sure exactly what a union is, miss. What is it?'

'What is a union?'

'Yes, miss.'

'Well, a union, a trades union – which is what you're meaning here – is a band of men – a group of workers who stand together. They get together and say, "Look, we can do nothing on our own, but if we all stand together, side by side – if we form a union – stand united – we shall be stronger than if we're alone." Do you understand?'

'I think so, miss.' But he sounded uncertain.

Abbie said, 'In the case of your father – well, he works on a farm, doesn't he?'

The boy nodded.

'Right, so he was almost certainly speaking of the National Agricultural Labourers' Union. It was formed just last year – 1872 – by farm labourers – so that they could protect themselves.'

'Why do they need to protect themselves? Why do they want to be stronger?'

Abbie hesitated. The concept of trades unions wasn't something she wished to get into; still, the boy had asked. She glanced up at the class. While most of the children were working at their slates and papers, others were listening to the dialogue. She turned back to Tom.

'Let me try to explain,' she said. 'If you worked for a man and he took advantage of you – let's say he made you work too hard and too long for your wages – what would you do?'

The boy thought about this, then said, 'I'd tell him, miss. I'd tell 'im 'e was making me work too 'ard.'

A boy in the front row chimed in: 'Yes, miss, if it was me I'd tell him 'e'd have to give me more wages.'

'Yes,' Abbie said, 'but supposing he refused. What if he said, "No, I won't give you any more wages"?'

All the children were listening now. A small girl, from her seat in the second row, said: 'Miss, if he wouldn't pay me no more wages I'd tell 'im I wouldn't do 'is work.'

'And if he still said no?' Abbie said. 'What would you do then? And don't forget that if you're a farm worker you're probably living in a tied cottage – one owned by the farmer. If you left your job on the farm you'd have to leave the cottage, too, wouldn't you? And if you're a man with a wife and children to look after, what would happen then?'

Tom Gilpin said, 'Get another job, miss? And another tied cottage?'

Abbie shrugged. 'Perhaps you could – if you were very, very lucky. But your next employer might do the same thing to you. It could go on like that. And what would happen if you gave up your job and your home and couldn't find another, no matter how hard you looked? What would happen then?'

No one spoke for a moment, then Tom said, 'It'd be the workhouse, miss. That or starve, I reckon.'

Abbie nodded. 'There you are.' Her glance moved over the faces of the children. 'This same thing can happen to men in all kinds of work. Although they might protest at their conditions there's not a lot they can do about it – because so often their employer just turns round and says, "Well, if you don't like it, go and find another job." And of course, that can be a very difficult thing to do. So what happens is that the worker is forced to stay in his job and put up with the same conditions – no matter how bad they are.'

'But – how does a union help them, miss?' Tom said.

'Well, working together the members of the union try to decide what is fair – what is best for them, for all of them. And they can say to the bosses, "Look, if you don't play fair then *none* of us will work for you." And if they all say that, all those thousands of men, then the bosses have to listen. If just one worker refuses to work it doesn't make any difference to the employer, but if *all* the workers stop then the employer finds himself in a real pickle.'

'Going on strike,' one of the boys said. 'That's going on strike, isn't it, miss?'

'That's right,' Abbie said. 'When a body of men decide not to work it's known as going on strike. And they can stay on strike until the boss says, "All right, I'll listen to you." '

'But,' said another boy, 'if they go on strike they don't get any wages, do they?'

Abbie was about to reply when she heard the sound of the door opening. Turning, she saw appear the short, thin figure of Mr Carstairs, the school inspector. What was he here for now? She could feel herself touched with a little of that same fear and apprehension which always accompanied any sight of him. As he came across the room towards her she got to her feet, the pupils, as one, following suit.

'Miss Morris,' Carstairs said, acknowledging her with a slight nod. Turning to the class he motioned to the children to be seated. Obediently they sat, with the exception of Tom Gilpin who remained standing at Abbie's desk, looking undecided as to what to do. With a faint smile at the boy, Abbie murmured that he also might go and sit down. Needing no second bidding, he moved back to his seat.

She turned back to the man. There was no hint of pleasure in his cold eyes or his thin-lipped mouth. She wondered again what he was doing there. His visit was unannounced and she could only suppose that he had come in the hope of catching her out – of finding her to be wanting in some way. Well, let him go on hoping, she said to herself; the Board would have difficulty in faulting her teaching – she made sure of that – added to which her pupils' exam results had been generally very good under her tuition – better than they had been under the previous schoolmistress, Miss Beacham.

'And how are we, Miss Morris?' Carstairs asked, standing a yard or two away from her. Before she could answer he gestured with his hand. 'Do sit down, please.'

As Abbie sat, the man gazed somewhat appraisingly at her for a moment, then said, 'Is everything all right?'

She nodded. 'Yes, sir. Thank you. Everything's fine.'

'Good.' He briefly surveyed the class, then, turning back to Abbie, said, 'Don't let me interrupt you. What are the children doing right now?'

'Some of the children have been writing phrases and short sentences,' she said. 'The others have been working on English compositions.'

He nodded, glanced down at Abbie's desk and picked up the paper that Tom Gilpin had left. He read what was written, took in the name at the top of the paper and raised his eyes to the class. 'Who is Thomas Gilpin?' he asked.

After a moment's hesitation, Tom raised his hand. 'Please, sir – me, sir.'

'Stand up, boy.'

Nervously the boy got to his feet.

'Christmas has to be given a capital "c",' Carstairs said. 'And there's no "e" in skating.' He looked back at the paper. 'The word should be "frozen", not "froze", and the word union doesn't begin with a "y". Anyway, what do you know of unions, boy?'

Tom gave a little shrug. 'Not much, sir. Miss was just telling us about them.'

Carstairs raised an eyebrow. 'Indeed. And what exactly was Miss Morris telling you?'

'Well – about the unions, sir.'

'Go on.'

'About the bosses making the workers work too hard.'

'Go on.'

'Well – how in a union the workers get together, so that they're stronger and so that the bosses will listen. She told us that when –'

'Thank you.' Carstairs motioned with his hand. 'You may sit down.'

As the boy sat, Carstairs turned to Abbie, looked at her for a moment and then took out his watch. 'There's only a little while to go before classes end for the day,' he said. 'Might I suggest that you dismiss the children now?'

Abbie got to her feet. 'Thank you, children. Class is dismissed now. I'll see you all tomorrow morning. Don't be late.'

She remained standing as the children left their seats, took their coats from the hooks and went from the room. When the last one had gone Carstairs closed the door and turned back to her.

'Well,' he said, 'it would appear that I did right in stopping by the classroom this afternoon.'

Abbie said nothing.

'When you first came before the Board of School Governors,' he went on, 'it was made perfectly clear to you that this kind of thing would not be tolerated.'

'What kind of thing is that, sir?' Abbie said, though she knew full well what he meant.

'I think you know what I mean. I'm referring to this dissemination of your rather – modern ideas. Miss Morris, you are here to teach the children to read and write, not to fill their heads with so-called progressive ideas of socialism and equality.'

'Sir, I did not volunteer to speak on the matter of trades unions,' Abbie said. 'The subject came up when the boy wrote of unions in his composition. He asked me what a union was. I merely tried to explain.'

'Is that so,' he said sceptically.

'Yes, it is so. And if you wish to verify it I suggest you ask the boy concerned.'

Carstairs glared at her. 'Miss Morris, your tone is insolent. I have no intention of questioning the boy. I can rely on the evidence of my own eyes and ears, and to me the situation is perfectly clear.'

'I am not being insolent,' Abbie said. 'I merely wish to tell you what happened. The boy asked me what a union was, and I answered his question. Surely that's part of my reason for being here – to answer the children's questions – to try to enlighten them as far as I am able.'

'Ah, enlighten. An interesting choice of word.'

'Mr Carstairs, I'm only trying to do my job – to the best of my ability.'

'Which you think includes stirring up unrest, do you?'

'Unrest? I simply told them what unions are.'

'Unions! Huh.' Carstairs's tone made clear what he felt about such a concept.

'Yes, indeed,' Abbie said, growing angry. 'I know there are many people who would like to believe that such things as trades unions don't exist – for example, those rich employers who got their wealth by exploiting the poor – and their sycophants and hangers-on who would do anything to support them. But times are changing and the poor are demanding a voice. And unions do exist, whether some people like it or not – and as time goes on there will be more of them. And if they help to bring about a fairer and more humane system, then they can only be a good thing.'

She came to a halt, aware that her voice had been rising.

Carstairs was looking at her as if unable to believe his ears. 'Well, Miss Morris,' he said, 'perhaps I shouldn't be too surprised at such an outburst. After all, this incident doesn't mark the first time I've had occasion to doubt the wisdom of continuing to employ you in the classroom.'

Abbie was taken aback at this. What occasions did he mean? Since she had been employed at the school she had been careful never to put a foot wrong. She drew herself up. 'I have never failed in my work in this school,' she said stiffly. 'And I would remind anyone who is in doubt that my exam results have been better than those of any other teacher here over the past ten years.'

'In this instance,' Carstairs said, 'I was referring to the matter of your mother living with you in the school-house.'

Abbie's spirits sank lower. She was quite sure that he must be aware of the cause of her mother's illness and subsequent death; such knowledge would not have been kept from him. 'The Board of Governors gave their approval,' she said. 'I was given permission for my mother to live with me.'

'Indeed you were.' He nodded. 'Though not by me. I was not one of those who accepted – or condoned – such a situation.'

'You'd have had me turn her away, would you, sir?'

He avoided her eye. 'It is immaterial what I would have done. Though had the situation continued I rather think that the other members of the Board would have had second thoughts about the wisdom of allowing your mother to remain with you.' A pause, then he added: 'And you know, of course, what I mean. I'm sure you were even more aware than others of your mother's ... weakness.'

Her cheeks burning, Abbie remained silent while he moved away. In the open doorway he turned back to face her. 'You leave me in something of a quandary,' he said.

She waited.

'I am not unaware,' he went on, 'that your mother died only months ago, and it is not my wish to add to your difficulties. I could recommend your instant dismissal for what I've witnessed this afternoon – but I wouldn't wish to be thought lacking in humanity or sensitivity. However, there must never be another such episode as has occurred this afternoon.'

'Sir –' Abbie began, but he raised a hand in an imperious gesture for silence.

'On this occasion,' he said, 'I am prepared to let the matter ride. But, as I say, it must never happen again. And as an insurance I shall expect you to give me your word, in writing, that you will not again resort to this . . . unacceptable socialist indoctrination of your pupils. You know where I live, I believe? Fine. I shall expect your letter.' He raised an eyebrow. 'Understand – there are numerous young women who would be only too glad of the opportunity to step into your shoes.' He paused. 'It is Wednesday today. I shall expect your letter by Saturday afternoon at, say, five o'clock at the latest.' He gave a slight inclination of his head. 'I wish you good day.'

With his final words he turned and went from the room.

'Abbie . . . ?'

The voice came to her from out of the stillness and she gave a little start and pressed a hand to her breast. Louis stood in his overcoat in the open doorway of the schoolroom, his hat in his hand.

'Oh – Louis,' she said, '– you startled me.'

'I'm sorry,' he said, 'I called at the cottage but got no answer – then I saw a light burning in here.'

Abbie realized that some considerable time must have passed since Carstairs's departure. The classroom was quite dark apart from the area around her desk that was illuminated by the oil lamp. She realized too that the stove had gone out.

'The devoted schoolmistress.' Louis smiled. 'Working so late – and in the cold.' He set down his hat and sat on one of the children's desks, facing her. 'What are you doing – correcting your students' work?'

'No. I've been writing a letter. I wasn't aware how the time had gone by.'

'Am I disturbing you?'

'No, not at all.' She looked down at the envelope containing the letter. 'I've finished. I was just sitting here dreaming.' She placed the envelope, addressed to Mr Carstairs, in her bag and began to gather up her things. 'Would you like some tea?'

'That would be very nice.'

'I'll lock up here and we'll go home.'

He took up his hat. 'I've just been calling on one of my patients nearby and thought I'd take the opportunity to see how you are.'

'That's very thoughtful of you. And I'm very well.'

'Are you? You seem somewhat – preoccupied.'

'Oh . . . No I'm all right.'

With Louis carrying the lantern she put out the lamp, took up her coat and bag, and followed him to the door. When she had locked it behind them they made their way across the yard to the schoolhouse. Inside, Abbie lit the lamps, made up the fire and put on the kettle. It was almost six. They kept their outer clothing on while the room was getting warmer. Abbie, glancing up from placing a log on the fire, found Louis gazing at her. As

335

their eyes met he lowered his glance while she in turn straightened before the mirror and adjusted some of the pins in her hair.

After a time the kettle began to sing. They took off their coats and she made tea, and they sat drinking it while they spoke in a desultory way of unimportant things. Sometimes, during their more recent meetings, there had seemed to be a certain restraint between them that got in the way of the former ease of their conversation. It was the same this evening. In a very short time their talk became stilted and interspersed with silences, and Abbie became increasingly aware of his nearness. She could find no peace with him tonight. And following so soon after the scene with Carstairs, his presence seemed disturbing. She looked at him as he sat beside the fire, his tall, strong frame bent slightly towards the warmth while the glow of the flames reflected in his cheek. Before long, however, he put down his cup and got to his feet.

'I'd better go,' he said. 'I think you've got things on your mind.'

She rose and stood looking at him while he put on his coat. 'I wonder,' she said, 'if you would do me a kindness . . .'

'Of course . . .'

She moved to her bag and took out the letter. 'You'll be going past Hawthorn Lane, won't you? Could you deliver this at the Grange for me? That's the large house on the corner.' As Louis took the envelope she added, 'It's to Mr Carstairs. He's one of the School Governors.'

Louis was looking at her a little strangely. Then as if making a decision he took a breath and said, 'Abbie – I lied when I said I called on you while I was here seeing one of my patients.'

She barely heard him, and didn't register his words. The letter was in his hand; it was still not too late.

'I – I wanted to see you,' he was saying. 'I wanted –' He came to a stop. 'Abbie, are you hearing what I'm saying?'

'Oh, Louis, I'm so sorry.' She gave a distracted shake of her head. 'What did you say?'

He smiled. 'It's all right. Quite obviously this isn't the right time.'

'No, please – what were you saying?'

'It's all right. I'll wait till another time. It's quite clear that you have things on your mind at present.'

'I'm sorry,' she said again, 'I'm poor company right now, I know. My letter . . .' She gestured to the letter in his hand, hesitated, then said: 'Mr Carstairs came to my classroom this afternoon.'

'Yes . . . ? And . . . ?'

'He found that I had been talking to my pupils about the Agricultural Union.'

'Go on . . .'

'He was extremely angry. When the children had been dismissed he told me in no uncertain terms what he thought. Quite clearly he sees me as some kind of crusader who's intent on upsetting the country's social order.'

'That's unfortunate.'

'It is indeed.'

He looked down at the letter. 'Why are you writing to him?'

'He demanded it.'

'Demanded it?'

'Yes – he demanded that if I want to keep my position I send him a letter with a declaration that I will not in future – what were his words? – "resort to unacceptable socialist indoctrination . . ." So – I've written to him.'

Louis frowned. 'Are you sure you want to send this letter? I wouldn't have thought you'd allow anyone to bully you in such a way.'

'Nor would I.'

She held out her hand for the letter and he gave it to her. The envelope was not sealed and she opened it and took out the folded sheet of notepaper. Handing it to him, she said: 'This is my response to his ultimatum. You can read it.'

He looked at her for a moment, then unfolded the paper and began to read aloud the words she had written.

Dear Sir,

You asked me to write to you and I am doing so. You made it very clear this afternoon that unless I gave you a written undertaking not to 'resort to unacceptable socialist indoctrination' of my pupils I would forthwith be replaced in my post as schoolmistress. I tried to tell you that I have never attempted any kind of indoctrination of my students. In accordance with my instructions I have taught them the three Rs (to the success of which the annual examination results will attest) and, using my best talents and abilities, have attempted also to impart to them some knowledge of our history and of our place on the geographical map. I have also tried to instil within them some affection for the written word, in the hope that they will use it for their future pleasure and also as a means of bettering themselves and their situations. If this be regarded as sedition, then I must plead guilty to the charge.

My reason for writing this letter, however, is neither to plead my case (which I feel I have no need to do) nor to give you the undertaking which you demanded. I wish merely to give you formal notice of my intention to leave my post at the close of the next term.

Yours truly,

Abigail Morris

Louis raised his eyes to hers. 'Once he's read this you'll never work as a teacher in this area ever again. You realize that, don't you?'

She took the letter from him and replaced it in the envelope. 'Oh, yes. I could have said a lot more – told him what I think of him – but I shall need references and I mustn't burn all my boats.'

'But what will you do? Will you be happy giving up teaching? Which you'll have to do – unless you become a governess. But then you'd have to live with your employers, for you'll be forced to leave this cottage. Unless of course you go to live with your brother . . .'

She smiled. 'No, Louis, I have no intention of going to live with my brother – even if he invited me to.' She paused. 'Indeed – I don't intend to live in Flaxdown.'

'You – you don't?'

'No. By the time next Easter comes round I hope to be fixed up with a position in London.'

He gazed at her in surprise. 'You're going to live in London?'

'I intend to start looking for a position there right away.'

'But – why London? There are places closer at hand where you could find work. You don't need to travel so far.'

She shrugged. 'If I'm leaving Flaxdown I might as well go to London as anywhere else.'

'But you'll be so far away from – from your brother and your sisters.'

'I know that, but I don't play any major part in their lives any more. And I can still get to see them occasionally, I'm sure. Once I leave this post there'll be nothing to keep me in Flaxdown.'

'But why is it necessary for you to go to London?'

'It isn't exactly the end of the earth.'

'It's a very long way.'

'Yes – but anyway, I've got friends there.'

'Friends?'

'Well, yes – my friend Jane is there.'

'Oh, yes.' He paused. 'You said friends – plural.'

'I meant Jane. I shall try to find a place situated near her. It'll be lovely to see her again. It'll be like old times.'

'Is she the only reason?'

'What do you mean?'

'Is she the only reason for your choosing London?'

'Well, no – but I've been there. And there's no denying it's a wonderfully exciting place.'

'Oh, it is that, most certainly.' He gave a little smile. 'Is that what you're looking for – excitement?'

She laughed. 'A little excitement certainly wouldn't come amiss – not after living in such a quiet spot as Flaxdown all my life.'

'Well, London might be exciting, but it can also be a very lonely place. Wouldn't you be happier in a smaller town – somewhere nearer to your roots? You could go to somewhere like Trowbridge or Warminster.'

She frowned. 'Please, Louis – I don't need pessimism at a time like this. I need optimism and encouragement.'

'I certainly don't want to discourage you,' he said. 'I just wonder whether you're doing the right thing.'

'Oh, Louis – please. Don't play devil's advocate. This is difficult enough for me as it is without your depressing comments.'

'Am I depressing you? I'm sorry.' He stood there for a moment then took a step towards the door. 'It's getting late; I'd better be off.' He put on his hat. 'Whatever you do, Abbie, I just hope you'll be happy, that's all.'

'Thank you,' she said. 'It's what we all want, isn't it?'

'Yes.' He gave a little smile. 'And most of the time it's too much to expect.'

A moment later he had wished her goodbye and gone from the cottage. She stood there for some moments after his departure and then realized that she was still holding the letter. For a second she considered running after him, but decided against it. She would deliver it herself and without wasting any further time.

She put on her cape then left the schoolhouse and set off to walk the short distance to Hawthorn Lane. Reaching the Grange, the home of Mr Carstairs, she walked up the drive and inserted the letter through the letter box slot. It was done. And now there was no going back.

In the schoolhouse once more she ate a light supper then sat beside the fire, and all the while her thoughts kept going back to the events of the day and to her letter of resignation. She might have expected now to feel some sensation of relief, but she did not. Yet she had done the right thing, the only thing possible in the circumstances. Yes, and as for going to London, that would be all right too. She would find a place without too much difficulty. So why, she asked herself, was she fretting so? Was it due to Louis? Louis, sowing his seeds of doubt? But what did he know?

After school the following day she wrote to Jane, briefly relating what had happened and telling of her intentions to seek work as a governess in London. She would start searching the columns of the newspapers immediately, she said. In addition, if Jane should hear of any suitable position that was due to become vacant she should let her know at once.

After Abbie had put aside her pen she sat for some minutes deep in thought then got up and went to her bureau. From a drawer she took a letter in an envelope. It was the one she had received from Arthur after she had broken off their engagement. She sat down at the table, unfolded the sheet of notepaper and read again the last words that he had written:

... If your situation alters and you change your mind you know well enough where to find me. At present you may believe that it is all finished between us but I know that it is not. One day we shall be together; and I will wait for that day ...

She sat for a long time with the open letter before her.

Chapter Twenty-Five

All but one of Abbie's pupils had gone – wishing her their last goodbyes before hurrying out into the spring sunshine and the start of the Easter holidays. Only Tom Gilpin was left. He came to her where she stood going through the contents of her desk, stopped and looked up at her. He did not know but it was he who had been the catalyst in the situation that had led to her going.

'Yes, Tom . . .' She smiled at him as he stood silently before her.

'Miss,' he said, 'd'you know who we'll be having for our teacher next term?'

'No, I don't – but I expect she'll be very nice. And I'm sure you'll work hard for her, won't you?'

'Yes, miss.' He paused. 'I wish you wusn't going, miss.'

She did not know what to say. It was at moments like these that she wondered whether she was doing the right thing. But it was too late now – and in any case she could not have remained, with the situation as Carstairs would have it.

'They say you're goin' up to London, miss. Is that right?'

'That's right, Tom. I leave tomorrow.'

'Will you be glad to go, miss?'

'In some ways. In some ways perhaps not.'

'London's a big place, so they say.'

'Oh, it is indeed.'

'Are you going to be a schoolteacher in London, miss?'

'Well – not in a school, Tom. Not right away, at any rate. I'm going to be a governess.'

'To a rich family, miss?'

'Well, I don't know how rich they are.'

'D'you think you'll ever come back – to Flaxdown?'

'Oh, yes, no doubt of that. One day.'

He gave her a grave smile. 'Maybe I'll see you again, then.'

'I hope so, Tom.'

A little silence, then, 'Well – goodbye, miss.'

'Goodbye, Tom.'

They stood facing one another for a moment without moving, then she put out her hand. Solemnly he took it. 'You look after yourself, Tom.'

'Yes, miss. And you, miss.'

'I will.'

When he had gone Abbie continued clearing her things from inside her desk. Afterwards she stood looking around her. It was for the last time; she would never come to this classroom again. Gazing about her at the maps, diagrams and pictures on the walls, she thought of the happy times she had known here. After some moments she moved to the door, opened it and went outside into the yard. The March sun was bright, though there was a sharp east wind that caught at her hair and moved her skirt. The yard was quiet now, but this was not how she would think of it. She would remember it echoing with the voices of the children.

In the cottage she set down her things. The kitchen, like the other rooms, had a bare look about it. Over the past week she had packed her box and her trunk. She would be taking to London only those things she regarded as essential – the rest of her belongings she had given to Violet to share between herself and Lizzie and Iris. When she left tomorrow this part of her life would be at an end.

She made tea and sat drinking it at the kitchen table. Eddie would be coming for her in the morning, driving Mr White's pony and trap to take her to the station at Frome, where she would board the train for London. Everything was set now for her departure. At times over the past weeks it had seemed as if the end of term would never come. Yet at other times the days had seemed to pass too swiftly. She had had much to do – not least in the business of finding employment in the capital. She had achieved it without too much difficulty, however. Following correspondence with prospective employers and the submission of her references – Mr Carstairs had not been able to prevent the School Board giving her work a positive endorsement – she had travelled to the south-London suburb of Balham in mid-February to meet a barrister and his wife and two small daughters. It had been a satisfactory meeting and she had been engaged to begin her work there at Easter.

On her return to Flaxdown she had at once written to Jane telling of her new employment. Very soon, she had added, they would be meeting again. After finishing her letter to Jane she had taken up her pen once more and written to Arthur.

In her letter she told him that her mother had died the previous summer and that since that time her own situation had become intolerable – to the extent, she said, that she had been forced to leave her teaching post and seek employment elsewhere. As a result, she would be arriving in London at Easter to take up duties as resident governess to two children in Balham. She ended her letter saying:

I'm sure you must be surprised at hearing this voice from the past! Though I do hope that it is not a voice you have forgotten. I remind myself, however, that

345

little more than a year has gone by since last we met – though it is a year which for me has seen many changes.

Perhaps, once I am in London and settled to some little degree, we might meet for a chat – if you would like that. I know I shall be glad to see a familiar, friendly face.

Arthur had written back saying that he had been surprised to hear from her – though nevertheless pleased. He was very sorry to hear about her mother, he said, and yes, of course, once Abbie was settled in London they must find an opportunity to meet.

With her packing more or less finished, Abbie left the cottage to pay a visit to Eddie and Violet and the babies. After remaining with them for a while she set off for Tomkins Row to call on Mrs Carroll and wish her goodbye. On leaving she promised to give her love to Jane at the first opportunity.

She had crossed the green and was just about to turn into School Lane when she heard behind her the sound of a horse and carriage, then the sound of her name. Turning, she saw that the driver was Louis.

She stopped, smiling at him, at the same time feeling a slight sensation of guilt; she had not been in touch with him since her trip to London when he had called on her and she had told him the result of her interview. When they had parted at that time she had promised to write to him so that they could meet again before her departure for the capital. She had not done so.

Now Louis brought the cob to a halt beside her, gave a theatrical sigh and said with an ironic smile, 'I've concluded that if Mohammed won't come to the mountain, the mountain must go to Mohammed.' With a sad shake of his head he added, 'You were going to write to me to arrange a meeting.'

'Oh, Louis,' she said, 'you're reproving me.'

He nodded. 'Am I wrong to do so?'

'No, you're quite justified. It's simply that I've been so busy with all my preparations.'

He glanced up at the sky. 'It's a lovely evening. Would you care to go for a drive?'

'But – oh, I've got so much to do.'

'Just for half an hour or so.'

'Well, all right – just for half an hour. Then I must get back.'

'I guarantee it.'

He helped her up into the carriage and they set off. As they drove he turned to her and said, 'So would you have gone off to London without even saying goodbye? Shame on you.'

'No, of course not,' she protested, though as she spoke she could not look him in the eye. 'Oh, Louis,' she added, smoothing her hair, 'you can't imagine how the time has flown.'

'Ah, Abbie . . .' He shook his head. 'Excuses, excuses.' He turned, took in her expression and said, 'Oh, come on, there's no need to look like that.'

'Like what? How do I look?'

'Forget it. Let's not pursue it.'

Abbie could think of nothing to say, and in a rather awkward silence they skirted the western border of the green and headed towards the edge of the village. As they left the dwellings behind them Louis said without looking at her, 'I shall miss you, Abbie. And I still can't think for the life of me why you have to go and live in London.'

'Well, I have a job there,' she said.

'You do now, yes. But I'm sure you could easily have

347

found employment nearer at hand. It isn't as if work for governesses can only be had in London.'

'Perhaps so, but what is there to keep me here?'

'That's a question only you can answer. And if you can ask it in the first place then I suppose the answer is clear.'

'I – I've got to make something of my life,' she said after a moment. 'I must.'

'And you think you'll do that by becoming a governess in London?' Then he added quickly, 'I know I shouldn't be talking like this. It's just that I can't understand why you have to go running off this way.'

'Running off?' she said. 'I'm not running off.'

'Perhaps I was wrong in my choice of words.' A moment, then he added, 'Are you sure there's no other reason for your going to London? Apart from your general intention – of making something of your life, I mean.'

'Of course there's no other reason – although my friend Jane is there.'

'Is there no reason apart from that?'

'Louis,' she said, feeling her irritation growing, 'why are you asking all these questions? I'm leaving tomorrow; can't we just enjoy the drive? Please?'

'Of course,' he said, 'your Mr Gilmore's in London, isn't he?'

She stiffened slightly. 'So?'

He turned to her, his expression bland. 'It just occurred to me, that's all.'

'It didn't just occur to you.'

'Abbie – Abbie, stop sounding so cross. Why are you being so prickly today?'

'Well, perhaps I have reason to be – prickly, as you call it. For one thing, you appear to be impugning my reasons for going to London.'

He pulled the mare to a halt at the side of the road and

turning to her said, 'I'm not trying to be disagreeable, but – well, just tell me one thing . . .'

'Yes?'

'Has your Mr Arthur Gilmore got anything to do with your going up to London?'

Her nostrils flared in growing anger. 'Louis,' she said, 'I'd be glad if you'd turn the carriage round and drive me back. Would you mind?'

'Abbie, don't be angry. Can't we talk without your getting so cross all the time?'

'Please – turn the carriage round.'

'Abbie, calm down . . .'

He reached over to touch her hand, but she snatched her arm away. 'Well,' she said, '– if you won't drive me back then I'll walk.' She made as if to get out of the carriage, but he said quickly, 'No, no. Stay where you are.' Then, shaking the reins, they started off again.

Later, at the entrance to School Lane he brought the carriage to a stop, jumped down and helped her down onto the road.

'I'll walk with you to the cottage,' he said.

'No, that's all right, thank you.'

'You're still angry with me. Please. You're going away tomorrow; we can't part like this.'

She looked up at him now. His expression was earnest. After a moment she put out her hand. 'No, we can't. Let us part friends.'

He took her hand. 'I hope you mean it. It's what I want – if we have to part at all.' She moved to withdraw her hand, but he held on to it. 'Don't go to London tomorrow,' he said.

'What? Not go? Of course I must go. It's all arranged.'

'You can write to your employers. Tell them you've changed your mind.'

She stared at him. 'Why on earth should I do that?'

'Please – stay here.'

'Why?'

'Because I care for you. Very much.'

I don't want to hear these words, she thought, and turned her face away. She had a sudden picture of him as he had been at the fair that day. She heard again the music of the hurdy-gurdy and saw herself sitting with him beside the stream. Other images flashed through her mind. She saw him firing at the target, saw Beatie holding her teaset.

'I must go in,' Abbie said. 'I still have so much to do.'

'Is that all you have to say?'

'I'm sorry . . .' She shook her head distractedly. She could not meet his eyes. 'I'm just not good company this evening.'

'Perhaps that's my fault. Obviously I'm not the one to bring out the best in you. Perhaps your Mr Gilmore will have better luck.'

She stared at him for a moment or two in silence, then, turning, set off along the lane.

'Abbie . . .'

Louis's voice came to her as she strode away, but she did not falter, and she entered the cottage without looking back.

That night she climbed into her schoolhouse bed for the last time.

Lying there in the dark, she knew a sense of frustration and disappointment – when she should have felt excitement at the knowledge that in the morning she would be embarking on a new life. But Louis's words kept coming into her mind: *Has your Mr Gilmore got anything to do with your going up to London?*

He had no right to say such things. It was none of his business and in any case it wasn't true. Besides, Arthur was not just any young man: they had been engaged to be married. Why did Louis have to complicate things so – not only with his references to Arthur and questioning her motives for going to London, but telling her that he cared for her. There were times in the past year when he had proved himself such a good friend. Why could he not remain so? Though she could not say why, anything other – deeper – than friendship where he was concerned left her feeling unsettled and uneasy. Aloud into the dark she muttered, 'Oh, Louis, why do you have to start upsetting things?' As she lay there the thought came to her that once she had left Flaxdown she and Louis would never meet again. He was a part of her life that was now about to come to an end. With the thought a little stab of sorrow and loss touched her, but then she told herself that it was better this way. He was a part of the past and must remain so. A clean break with the past – that was what was needed. It must make no difference to her, the fact that he cared for her, that she would miss him. Their relationship was over. In less than a day they would be more than a hundred miles apart.

'Mama says you're going out, Miss Morris. Is that so?' Florence Hayward, eight years old, stood beside her sister Mabel, nine, in the doorway of Abbie's room. They were as alike as two peas, each with small, bright, dark eyes, and dark curls framing their round, rosy cheeks. Standing at the mirror, Abbie smoothed her coat, touched at her hair and made a final adjustment to her hat. Her glance caught that of the smaller Hayward girl in the glass and she nodded. 'Yes, that's right, Florence.'

'Where are you going to?' Florence asked.

Her sister Mabel spoke up at this. 'Florrie, Mama says you're not to ask so many questions.'

'It doesn't matter, Mabel,' Abbie said. 'It's no secret. I'm catching the train into the West End of London.'

'Whereabouts in London?' This again from Florence.

'To Victoria – then I shall get a cab to St James's Park.'

'Mama says,' said Mabel, 'that you're meeting your friend there.'

'Yes, that's correct. Her name is Jane. We're from the same village in Wiltshire. We haven't met for rather a long time and I'm very much looking forward to seeing her again.' Abbie moved to the window and looked out onto the drive and the front lawn, immaculate and green in the early April sunshine. The house was a tall, early-Victorian building, standing halfway up Bedford Hill. To the right at the hill's foot was the village of Balham proper, while at the top spread the green stretches of Tooting Bec Common. 'I'm not likely to need an umbrella, am I?' Abbie asked vaguely, then shook her head, answering herself. 'No, I think not.'

'Can we go with you?' Florence asked. 'I'd like to go into town. And Mabel would too.'

'I'm sorry, Florence,' Abbie said. 'Not this time.'

'Maybe some other time?'

'Maybe some other time.' She smiled at them. 'We'll see.'

She had been two weeks now in the Hayward household, and was getting to know her young charges. After several days when they had set out to test her, they had proved to be fairly agreeable children, reasonably well behaved, and not greatly taxing – and in any case she was not exactly a novice when it came to handling children.

Glancing at the clock she saw that it was almost two thirty. She moved back to the glass for a final check, then picked up her bag and crossed to the door. With Mabel and Florence following her down the stairs she stepped into the hall just as Mrs Hayward appeared from the drawing room.

'You're off now, are you?' the woman asked, her hands fluttering to her hair.

'Yes, ma'am.'

Mrs Hayward was a small, rather plump woman in her mid-thirties, with a round face and dark curls. Abbie could look at her and see exactly what her two daughters would look like when they had matured – though they appeared not to be like her in their personalities. Perhaps, she thought, they took after their father in that respect; though she could do no more than guess; Mr Hayward spent so little time at his home that she had only seen him on a few occasions.

That the girls were unlike their mother in their ways, however, was all to the good as far as Abbie was concerned. Mrs Hayward seemed to be incapable of relaxing. She always appeared to be harassed by one thing or another – whether it was her daughters, her servants, or the general vicissitudes of her rather humdrum life. She was one of those women who, no matter how uneventful their lives, always manage to find it a strain. Perhaps, Abbie thought, it was not so surprising that Mr Hayward spent so much time away from home, for surely he could find little there in the way of relaxation.

Now Mrs Hayward's flickering smile fought with a frown as she said to Abbie, 'You won't be late back, will you?'

'No, I shan't,' Abbie replied. 'I'll try to get here between six and half past.'

'Good. I shan't be able to manage the girls without you. They're such a handful.'

Looking from Mrs Hayward to the two quiet little girls, Abbie wondered briefly how Mrs Hayward would have coped had she had two boisterous sons to raise – perhaps a couple of boys cast in Eddie's mould.

At Balham Station Abbie took the train to Victoria and from there walked along Buckingham Palace Road, past the Palace itself and on to Birdcage Walk. A few yards along she came to a stop. She did not have to wait long. Just three or four minutes after her arrival she turned and saw Jane coming towards her. With a little cry of pleasure she hurried forward, while at the same time Jane quickened her own steps. A few seconds later they were clasping one another in a warm embrace.

'Oh, Abbie,' Jane said, 'it's so good to see you again!'

'And you!' Abbie said. 'And you haven't changed a bit.'

They drew back, looking at one another and then, linking arms, strolled away. They went into the park where beside the lake they found a vacant bench and sat down.

'Oh, Jane,' Abbie said happily, 'I've been waiting for this moment for weeks. Ever since I made my decision to come here.'

'I've been looking forward to it too,' Jane said. 'It's a shame we couldn't arrange it earlier – but as you'll learn, when you're in service your life is not your own.'

'Oh, yes, indeed,' Abbie said. 'I've learned that already.'

'Oh, dear, that doesn't sound so good. Do I infer that you're not altogether happy with your situation?'

'I expect I'll get used to it in time. I hope so, anyway.'

'What are your girls' names?'

'Florence and Mabel. Oh, they're no trouble.'

'Is it their father who's the problem?'

'He's hardly ever there. No, it's Mrs Hayward. She's such a fusser. And I don't seem to get any time to myself.

354

She always wants something done. She has maids, of course, but if it's to do with the girls or anything that personally concerns herself she calls on me. I never expected such a loss of freedom. Teaching in school was very different.'

After a while they decided to go in search of some refreshment and from the park they made their way to the Strand. Near Trafalgar Square they found a teashop where they sat down at a table and ordered tea and pastries. As they waited for the waitress to bring their order Abbie said, 'So, what has been happening to you outside of your work? How is your social life?'

'My social life? Oh – it ticks along, I suppose.'

'You make it sound very unexciting. Is there no one special? You haven't mentioned anyone in your letters for some time now.' With a chuckle Abbie added, 'You must make an effort. At this rate we'll both end up old maids, and we can't have that.'

'No,' Jane said, smiling, 'that would never do.'

Abbie said nothing for a few moments, then, taking a deep breath, she said, 'Jane, I – I want you to tell me what you think. Tell me as a friend, I mean.'

'What about . . . ?'

'As you're aware, you're not the only person I know in London. I do have another friend here.' A pause, then she went on, 'You realize that I'm talking about – about Mr Gilmore. You remember him, don't you?'

Jane nodded. 'Yes – of course . . .' She looked suddenly very perplexed. 'Abbie –' she began, then stopped.

'Yes, of course you remember him,' Abbie said. 'You came to his house when I was staying there the Christmas before last. Anyway, I – I wrote to him. Telling him I was coming to London.'

The waitress appeared with a tray and began to set out

355

the tea and pastries. When she had gone Abbie continued, 'I hesitated before writing, I don't mind telling you. I mean – not knowing whether I was doing the right thing. I still don't. But after all, we were engaged to be married and it was only through circumstances beyond our control that we – I was not able to go through with it.'

Jane, eyes lowered, poured the tea. She handed Abbie a cup. Abbie sipped from it, then went on, 'Well – he wrote back saying he looked forward to our meeting. And I wrote again last Tuesday, telling him that I was getting settled in. I haven't heard back yet, but I expect to very soon.' She looked down into her cup, then raised her eyes to Jane. 'Do you think I'm being terribly foolish?' She gave an awkward little laugh. 'Not to mention somewhat forward?'

When Jane did not answer, Abbie said, 'What do you think? Tell me what you think.'

Mechanically stirring her teacup, Jane said, 'Well – I don't know. What is it you're hoping for? What do you hope to get out of it – eventually, I mean?'

'Oh, Jane, when you put it like that it sounds so – I don't know – so calculating. But after all, it's not so long since – since we ended our engagement. Just over a year, that's all. And – he truly cared for me, Jane. He really did.' She looked keenly at her friend. 'I suppose I want to find out if he still does. Care for me, I mean.' She looked at Jane's downcast face and said, frowning, 'What's up? Is something the matter?'

Jane did not answer.

'What's up?' Abbie said. 'You've hardly said anything – though I suppose I haven't given you much chance, have I?'

With a distracted shake of her head, Jane said, 'Oh – Abbie – can we get out of here?'

'What? Why – yes, but . . . What's wrong?'

356

Jane was taking coins from her purse. 'I just – just want to get outside. Do you mind?'

'Of course not.'

Jane beckoned to the waitress and paid the bill. Then together she and Abbie went out into the air. Side by side they stood on the pavement while the pedestrians and the carriages passed by.

'What's wrong?' Abbie said. 'Do you feel ill?'

'No – I simply felt I – I had to get out of there.' Then quickly Jane added, 'Let's walk for a minute, shall we?'

'If you like.' Abbie slipped her arm through Jane's and together they walked along the street and then crossed over into Trafalgar Square. 'I mustn't be late,' Abbie observed as they reached the fountain. 'Mrs Hayward gets into a panic when I'm not there. God knows what she did before my arrival.'

Jane said nothing, but walked with her head bent, her lips set. At the foot of some wide steps Abbie drew her to a stop, withdrew her arm and said, concern in her voice, 'Jane, what is it? Tell me what's wrong.'

Jane lifted her hands, bent her head and covered her face. 'Oh, God . . .' Her words were muttered, her tone full of anguish.

Abbie laid a hand on her arm. 'Jane – what is it? Please – tell me. I'm your true friend. There's nothing you can't tell me.'

'You say that now,' Jane said without looking at her. 'Oh, Abbie, I'm so afraid you'll hate me.'

'Hate you?' Abbie looked astonished. 'Are you mad? How could I possibly hate you? I love you. You're my friend for life. You know that.'

Jane shook her head. 'Oh – Abbie . . .'

'Jane, look at me.'

Jane shook her head. 'I cannot.'

'Dear God, Jane, tell me what it is.' Abbie paused. 'Is it – something to do with me?'

Jane nodded.

'With you and with me?'

Another nod.

'What, then? I can't think of anything that –'

Jane broke in: 'It concerns a third person, too.' A moment of hesitation. 'Arthur.'

'Arthur?' Abbie looked bewildered. 'You mean *my* Arthur? My Mr Gilmore?'

Jane said nothing; did not move.

'What – what about him?' Abbie said. And now she suddenly felt her heart beating harder in her breast. 'You're going to tell me something dreadful, is that it? Is there some awful news about him?'

Jane looked into Abbie's eyes, then lowered her gaze. 'Forgive me, Abbie.'

'Forgive you? What are you talking about? Jane, what is there to forgive?'

They stood in silence, untouched by the sounds all around, the cooing of the pigeons, the voices of the children who played beside the fountain.

Jane sighed, took a breath and said, 'I love him.'

'What?' Abbie stared at her.

'Arthur. I – I love him.'

'You – love him? Arthur? Is this – some kind of joke?'

'No.'

'You love him? Do you mean this?'

Jane nodded. 'Yes.'

'You've seen him? You've met him here in London?'

'Yes.'

Abbie's mouth was so dry she could barely form her words. 'Does he know how you feel?'

Jane nodded again. 'Yes.' A pause. 'He – he loves me too.'

Abbie ran her tongue over her lips. 'I can scarcely believe you're saying these words.'

'Oh, Abbie – Abbie . . .' Jane reached out towards her, but Abbie drew her own hand away.

'So,' Abbie said, 'how long has this been going on behind my back?'

'Oh – don't say that, Abbie. We –'

Abbie interrupted, saying: 'It obviously didn't begin yesterday. When did it start?'

'– Last summer. I was in Hyde Park with Anne, my employer's daughter. And Arthur was there also. We met quite by chance. And the next week he was there again. And the week after that too.'

'How romantic.'

'Oh, Abbie – I didn't plan it.'

'No? You didn't go there hoping to see him again?'

Jane said nothing to this. Abbie nodded. 'I see. After that first time you hoped he'd be there.' She paused. 'Didn't you?'

'I never wanted to hurt you.'

'But you never once mentioned it to me – in your letters. You wrote about everything else, but not about that – the most important thing that was happening to you.'

'How could I?'

'You tell me.'

'Well – I was afraid to. I was afraid of hurting you.'

'Thank you. I'm touched.'

'Yes, I was afraid,' Jane said, 'even though I knew it was over between you both. You had told me that and so did he. He hadn't heard from you in a long time. After all, you'd made your decision, and he thought he'd never see you again.'

'You believed it was all over between us, yet you were

afraid to mention the fact that you were seeing one another.'

'Well – how could I know how you would respond? Though eventually, of course, I knew you would have to know. One or other of us would have to tell you.'

'That's very considerate of you.'

'Abbie, please – don't hate me.' There were tears in Jane's eyes. Abbie watched dispassionately as they brimmed over and ran down her cheeks.

'You've betrayed me,' she said. 'After all we meant to one another. You, of all people.'

'Don't say that.'

'It's the truth.' Abbie shook her head. 'And you let me tell you how I'd begun writing to Arthur again – that I was renewing our friendship.' Her own tears, of hurt and anger, were close to the surface. 'Did it amuse you? Will you tell Arthur about it later and have a good laugh together?' Abbie took a step away and stood looking out over the square. 'You've betrayed me – and humiliated me into the bargain. I can never forgive you for it.'

'Abbie . . .' Sobbing, Jane stepped closer to Abbie's side. She moved as if she would touch her shoulder but stopped and let her hand fall back to her side. 'I love you, Abbie,' she said. 'And I would not have hurt you for the world. But I thought it was over between you and Arthur. And as I said, he thought so too. God knows I didn't plan to fall in love with him. Nor did he plan to love me. It just – happened. Please, try to understand.'

'I understand only too well.'

Abbie stood there for a moment longer, then turned and walked away.

Chapter Twenty-Six

Abbie's preoccupation did not ease over the following days, but grew stronger. She went through the hours in the schoolroom with Mabel and Florence efficiently enough, but it was as if she were working in a fog; not for many minutes at a time did she find herself free of her disturbing thoughts.

On Thursday evening when the girls were in bed she sat alone in her room thinking over the situation. She could not continue as she was and just try to reconcile herself to it. Something would have to be done. In the end, after wrestling with the problem, she decided she must see Arthur and talk to him.

She sat down to write to him that same evening and, after several attempts, finished a letter asking him to meet her at Victoria Station on Sunday afternoon at three o'clock. There would be no time for him to write back so she would simply go there in the hope that he would appear. She would wait for him for one hour, she wrote, after which time she would return to Balham. As soon as the letter was finished she left the house, hurried down the hill and posted it.

She had done the best thing she could, she told herself as she walked back up the hill. If it was indeed true that Arthur had turned to Jane then he must have done so purely in the belief that he had no future with Abbie herself. Knowing that he could have would surely make all the difference.

Sunday arrived wet and squally. After lunch – of which she could eat little – she left the house and made her way to the station while the rain-spotted wind whipped at the skirt of her coat and threatened to turn her umbrella inside out.

As she sat on the train bound for Victoria she looked at her watch a dozen times, feeling as if she would never get there. But at last the train drew in to the station and came to a halt. She got down and saw Arthur standing at the end of the platform. He came towards her as she passed through the ticket barrier and briefly took the hand she offered in his.

'Thank you,' she said, 'for coming to meet me.'

For a moment or two they stood in silence facing one another while the other travellers moved about them.

'Arthur,' she said, 'we have to talk.'

'Yes, of course. Let's go and have some tea somewhere.'

At a nearby hotel they sat in a secluded corner of the lounge where they were served by a maid in a crisp, starched uniform. As Abbie poured the tea Arthur asked how her journey from Ballham had been. She replied that it had been quite agreeable, and asked whether he had been waiting long.

'Not so long. Fifteen minutes or so.'

A moment's silence, then Abbie said, 'Arthur, what are we doing? We're sitting here indulging in small talk as if there's nothing at all on our minds.' She glanced at a couple who sat some feet away at the next table, assured herself that they would not overhear her, and added, keeping her voice low, 'As you must know, I met Jane last Sunday. She'll have told you what was said. I had no idea that you and she had been seeing one another. The news came as quite a surprise. She had never mentioned it.'

'Abbie –' Arthur began, but she went on, 'I don't

understand Jane at all. She knew it was through no fault of my own that our engagement came to an end and still she –' She came to a stop and looked down at her fingers as they worked in her lap. 'Oh, Arthur, this is so difficult. You can't imagine how hard it is.'

He remained silent.

'I had to come here to see you,' she said after a moment, 'to tell you – that it's not too late.'

'Too late?' He frowned. 'I don't understand.'

She could feel her heart hammering in her chest. 'Oh, please, Arthur, don't be obtuse. You know what I'm saying.'

'I – I'm not sure that I do.'

'I'm saying it's not too late for us. For you and me. All those – difficulties are in the past. There's nothing now to keep us apart. We're both free and we –'

He interrupted her. 'Abbie, please. Don't – don't say these things.'

She would continue, though. It was as if she were driven to leave nothing unsaid. 'Don't be a goose,' she said, 'I'm telling you that things are different.' She paused. 'Arthur – please give me back the ring.'

'What?'

'The ring you gave me – that I returned to you. I want to wear it again.'

A little silence, then he said, 'I don't have it any more. And even if I did I . . . Oh, please, Abbie, don't go on.'

She looked at him in silence for a moment, seeing him lower his glance and turn his face away.

'Is it too late for you and me? Is that what you're trying to say?'

'Yes.' He gave a brief nod, still avoiding her gaze.

'That's not true. You don't mean that.' She paused. 'Are you saying that it really is serious – between you and Jane?'

'Serious? Yes, it's serious. Of course it's serious.'

She gave a deep sigh and briefly closed her eyes. 'Oh, God . . .'

'Abbie – I'm sorry. I don't want to hurt you but you must know that – well, I love Jane. And she loves me.'

She set down her cup and drew her bag towards her. 'I can't listen to this.'

'But – but you have to know the truth.'

'But you loved *me*. I was the one you loved, Arthur. We were to be married.'

'Abbie –' He shook his head. 'Abbie, all that is ended. Anyway, you didn't really care about me.'

'What? I – I loved you. You know I did.'

'Did you?'

'How can you doubt it? You know that I –' She came to a stop, watching as the couple at the next table rose from their seats and started away. Then she went on, 'You know I loved you. You must know that.'

'I don't know that at all. But whatever I thought – whatever I believed, I'm afraid it doesn't matter now. It's all in the past now.'

'It doesn't matter? It's in the past? Can you switch off your feelings just like that?'

'Abbie, when Jane and I met again last summer, quite by chance, I hadn't heard from you in ages. You had returned my ring to me and had made it clear that it was finished between us. For all I knew, you had gone out of my life for ever.'

'I had my mother to care for, Arthur. My life was not my own. I had my work, and I had the responsibility of my mother as well.'

'Is that truly all it was, Abbie? Was it truly because of your mother's return that you broke off our engagement?'

'Of course it was. What other reason could there be?'

'Well, I thought –' He broke off, then said, 'Abbie – all

this talk is only making everything more difficult. I don't want you to be hurt any more.'

'Are you telling me now that you care how I feel?'

'Of course I care.'

'I wish I could believe that.'

'Abbie, please . . .'

'I shouldn't have come here today,' she said. 'But I came to tell you that – that I love you.' She watched for his reaction to her words. 'Did you hear me?'

He nodded. There was pain and perplexity in his face. She frowned. 'Have you nothing to say?'

He shook his head, distress in every line of his face.

'Arthur,' she said, 'why do you think I came to London in the first place? I came because of you. I could have gone anywhere but I came here. Because I thought we could – make things up and – and be happy together. And this time for always.' She turned from him, looking through the window. Rain was falling now. 'I know what you must be thinking. You're thinking, my God, is there no end to the lengths this girl will go to in order to humiliate herself?'

'Oh, Abbie, please – for God's sake –'

'Yes, it was for you, Arthur. That's why I took the post of governess in Balham.' Tears spilled over and ran down her cheeks. She turned back to him. 'Oh, Arthur, I can make you happy if you'll give me the chance. I know I can.'

'Abbie,' he said, 'it's too late for all that. I love Jane. And she loves me. We're going to be married.' He paused, then added, 'Soon. Very soon.'

'Married.' She gave a little nod. 'And when exactly is the great day to be?'

'In just a few weeks.'

'So soon.' She studied him for a moment, then said, 'And when do you expect the happy event?'

'The happy –'

'The baby, of course.'

His silent glance told her that she had been right. It could make no difference now, the fact that she had told him she loved him. She had played her last card. She sat there, the tears streaming from her eyes. Apart from her sense of humiliation she felt abandoned, discarded. She felt purposeless, directionless. She had invested all her last hopes in this meeting and it had been a disaster. If Jane was expecting his child, then she, Abbie, did not have a chance.

'You're making a mistake, Arthur,' she said brokenly. 'And someday you'll realize it.'

Snatching up her bag, she got to her feet, turned from him and hurried away.

As she emerged onto the rainswept street she realized that she had left her umbrella behind. She could not go back for it. With the rain beating down she ran for the station where to her relief she found a train standing at the platform. Just before she got on board she turned and looked back to see whether Arthur had come in pursuit of her. There was no sign of him. She got into the carriage and sat down, and seconds later the train was starting away.

Abbie sat in her room, waiting.

Three months had passed since her meeting with Arthur, and now it was midsummer. She had no tuition duties on this July Thursday, nor would she have for the next nine days or so. Florence and Mabel had left on Saturday to spend a fortnight's holiday with their aunt in Brighton, Abbie and Mrs Hayward escorting them there on the train and returning to London the following day. Without the girls the house was quiet.

Following the recent weather pattern the summer day

had been very warm. But now in the early evening a little breeze had sprung up and the air had grown cooler. Abbie, sitting near the window, was glad of the change. She was awaiting the arrival of a visitor. Louis Randolph was due to call at the house to see her.

In spite of her belief that she and Louis would have no further communication she had heard from him on two or three occasions since her departure from Flaxdown. In a recent reply to one of his letters, Abbie had written that while the girls were away she would be taking the few days' holiday that were due to her, and Louis had at once written back to say that he had to come to London about the same time – to take care of some business and also to visit his father. So, he had suggested, it might be a good opportunity for them to meet again. She had readily agreed, since which time she had found herself looking forward to his visit. Inwardly remarking on her surprising happiness at the prospect of their meeting again, she told herself that it would be a welcome interruption of the monotony of her present dull existence, and would lift her out of her depression and general sense of unhappiness.

Adding to that unhappiness Jane had written to invite Abbie to her wedding in Flaxdown. In her letter she had gone on to ask Abbie for her understanding and her blessing, saying:

... I had always taken it as a matter of course that when the time came for me to wed, you, Abbie, my dearest friend, would be there to support me and wish me happiness. And it would complete my happiness now to know that you will be with us on the day of our wedding. Or, should that not be possible, at least to know that you do not hate me – indeed that you care

367

for me still and wish happiness for me in my life with him whom I love.

Abbie had not replied to Jane's letter, but had torn it up and thrown away the pieces.

Jane and Arthur's wedding had duly taken place at St Peter's church in Flaxdown, the couple then leaving for a honeymoon in France. Eddie's wife Violet had attended the marriage service, and had afterwards stood at the lych-gate watching as the pair had emerged from the church. Unaware of Abbie's frustrated aspirations, Violet had later written telling Abbie about it.

And, Abbie wondered now, would Louis also know of the wedding? It was possible. She thought of his words to her at Easter just before her departure from Flaxdown, when he had asked whether Arthur had anything to do with her moving to London. His question had made her angry. Well, if he had suspected her motives at that time he might also now guess at her present humiliation.

Interrupting her thoughts a knock came at the door. Abbie called, 'Come in,' and Mrs Hayward entered.

'No sign of him yet?' the woman asked.

'Not yet.'

Mrs Hayward's question was an irritation, as was her presence. Since leaving Florence and Mabel in Brighton Abbie seemed to have had barely a minute to herself. Mrs Hayward was constantly calling on her, asking her to do some task or other, which more often than not was merely an excuse to get Abbie's company. The promise of the diversion of Louis's visit, therefore, was doubly welcome.

'Perhaps he won't come,' Mrs Hayward said with a doleful sigh. 'Men can be so unreliable. That's one thing I've learned from life.'

Not allowing her irritation to show, Abbie said, 'Oh, he'll be here.'

'Well, I hope so, dear.'

Abbie was by no means convinced of the sincerity of the sentiment. On the contrary, she could not escape the feeling that Mrs Hayward would be mightily if secretly pleased if Louis failed to arrive. Abbie was convinced that her employer, determined as she was to find so little pleasure in her own life, was reluctant to see it in the lives of others.

Mrs Hayward had given instructions that when Abbie's friend arrived he should be shown into the library. Abbie knew that Mrs Hayward was impressed by the fact that Louis was a doctor – though slightly disapproving in other ways, for it was not quite in the order of things for a mere governess to make friendships above her station. At the same time this did not prevent Mrs Hayward from enquiring as to any possible marriage plans. Abbie had brushed aside the idea. 'Dr Randolph is an old friend,' she had said. 'I've known him for many years and there's nothing at all between us of a – a romantic nature. Nor is there ever likely to be.' Disappointed or relieved, Mrs Hayward had had to be content with that.

When Louis arrived just after six thirty, he came not by carriage but on foot, walking up the hill from the station. As he turned in at the gates Mrs Hayward, looking from the window, said, 'Here he comes now.' Then she added, 'You didn't mention that he was so tall – nor that he was so handsome.'

Mrs Hayward left her then, and after a few moments the parlourmaid appeared to tell Abbie that her guest was waiting in the library. Abbie pinned her hat in place, took up her cape and went downstairs. On entering the library she found Louis in conversation with Mrs Hayward. Louis smiled warmly at Abbie, and came forward and embraced her. And for a brief moment as his arms encircled her she felt once again those old familiar warring emotions: the comfort of his touch, and at the same time a strange reluctance to be close. It did not last more than a moment before they broke apart and Mrs Hayward, clearly eager to keep him there, was pressing him to take some refreshment. He graciously declined her offer, however, and after having helped Abbie with her cape they said their goodbyes and left the house.

In the pleasant air they made their way up the hill and onto the common where horsemen rode, children played and people walked their dogs. Louis told her that he had arrived in London the evening before, and was staying at a small hotel in Paddington. He intended, he reiterated, to attend to some business matters in London and then to travel out to Gravesend in Kent to see his father, whom he had not seen for some time.

'So,' he said, 'how does it feel to be free of your charges for a while?' They had now wandered into the wide area of woodland that stretched as far as the railway line.

'It's good,' Abbie said. 'And if I could be free of their mother too I'd be happier still.' She shook her head. 'Be thankful that you don't have an employer. Particularly one like mine. I've never known anyone to fuss so much. With her the merest problem becomes a crisis. There's no calm in the house. It's no wonder her husband's never home.'

'Perhaps his absence is the cause of it.'

'I doubt it. Though whatever it is, it's hard to live with.'

'Perhaps you need a vacation.'

'Not much chance of that, I'm afraid.'

'Have you seen your friend lately? Jane, isn't that her name?'

'Yes, that's right.'

'I believe she recently got married, in Flaxdown. Somebody told me, I forget who.'

Abbie, silent, did not look at him and was relieved when he returned to the former subject.

'If you're unhappy where you are,' he said, 'why don't you look for another post?'

'I intend to. Though Mrs Hayward will have a fit when I do. She's already told me that the previous governesses had no sense of loyalty. It seems none of them stayed long. And I can't say I blame them.'

They ate a rather mediocre dinner in the restaurant of a hotel near Streatham Hill railway station. At the end of the meal Louis pushed aside his empty coffee cup and said apologetically, 'I'm sorry it wasn't better.'

'It was fine. It was very nice.'

He shrugged. 'Anyway – I hope there'll be other times. When do your little charges get back from the coast?'

'Saturday the 25th. We're to go to Brighton to collect them – that's if Mrs Hayward isn't having the vapours. If she is I'll be going alone.'

'So you still have a few days of relative freedom before they get back.'

'Relative is the word.'

'Perhaps we can meet again while I'm here.'

'How long will you be here?'

'Till the weekend. I must get back to Frome by Sunday at the latest, or my patients will think I've forsaken them.' He paused. 'So that leaves just two days. Are you busy tomorrow?'

'Mrs Hayward has asked me to go shopping with her in the morning. I'd better go to keep her sweet.'

'Then perhaps we could meet in the evening. I could try to get tickets to the theatre or the opera or something.'

'Thank you. Yes, I'd like that.'

'Good.' He gave a nod of satisfaction. 'On Saturday I want to go to Gravesend to see my father. Why don't you come with me?'

Abbie looked doubtful. 'Oh – well – I don't know . . .'

'We could go down by train and if the weather's fine we could come back by steamer on the river. It could be a lovely day out.'

'But your father won't be expecting me.'

'I shall write to him at once. He'll get my letter on Saturday morning. Please say yes. He'll love to meet you. And I know you'll like him, too.' He paused. 'Will you come?'

'Well – if you're sure it'll be all right.'

'Of course it'll be all right. Good. That's settled, then. Now' – he raised a hand to summon the waiter – 'I'll pay the bill and take you home.'

It rained for a short while the following morning, only lightly, yet enough for Mrs Hayward to postpone the shopping trip. 'Oh, dear,' she cried, hands fluttering, 'everything conspires against me, I swear it does!' Abbie, who had not looked forward to the excursion, was relieved at the reprieve. Not for long, however, for in the afternoon Mrs Hayward announced that they would after all set out.

So – and most reluctantly – Abbie accompanied her to the Army and Navy department stores in Victoria. And as the time wore on she found herself growing more and more anxious; Louis was due to call for her at six o'clock and she was afraid that she would be late getting back. Mrs Hayward, however, seemed intent on dawdling over every possible purchase and to be quite incapable of making up her mind over the most trivial thing. Abbie felt her anxiety and irritation growing, and eventually

372

Mrs Hayward turned to her with wide, uncomprehending eyes and said, 'Miss Morris, why do you keep sighing so? And this constant shifting from one foot to another ... Are you ill? Have you got St Vitus's dance or something?'

'I'm sorry,' Abbie replied, 'but I'm getting anxious about the time. As you know, Dr Randolph is calling for me at six.'

'Well, didn't you tell him you were coming shopping with me today?'

'I did, yes – but your original plan was to come out this morning.'

'So?' Mrs Hayward's eyes widened in an overdone expression of surprise. 'You saw the weather, didn't you? It was raining. I can't control the weather, can I?'

From that moment on Mrs Hayward seemed to take as much time as she could to make her purchases, at the same time appearing to mock Abbie's anxiety by asking her views on particular colours and designs. By the time they emerged from the store – with far fewer purchases than could warrant the time spent within – Abbie was seething.

It was five thirty-five when they got back to the house, and Louis arrived promptly at six. By the time he and Abbie left again it was six twenty.

With great good luck he had managed to get tickets for the opera at Covent Garden. It was the last night of the season, and a special benefit performance of Bellini's *I Puritani* was to be given, with Emma Albani as Elvira. Madame Albani had made her debut there in 1872 and had since become a much admired prima donna. Abbie and Louis arrived at the Royal Italian Opera House with little time to spare. As they waited for the performance to begin Abbie could not help but think back to her visit to Arthur that Christmas when he had taken her to the opera, and also the concert at the Royal Albert Hall. But now, here, the curtains were parting, and as the performance began she was at once caught up in the music, the colour, and the beauty of the singing. At the end, after the lovers were reunited and the curtain fell, she joined in the rapturous applause that greeted the many curtain calls of the principals.

Afterwards she and Louis went for supper at a nearby restaurant, following which they made their way onto the street again where he called a cab.

'Please,' Abbie said as the vehicle came to a halt beside them, 'don't come all the way to Balham with me.'

'Don't worry about me,' Louis said.

The cab driver appeared not exactly overjoyed to be asked to drive all the way out to Balham. However, when Louis promised him an extra large gratuity it was a different matter.

'But, Louis,' Abbie protested as he helped her into the cab, 'it'll take you ages to get back to your hotel and you'll be so tired. I shall be quite safe, truly.'

'I'm sure you will be.' Louis climbed in behind her and closed the door, and the cab started off. 'But it so happens that I have to go your way myself.'

'What d'you mean?'

'I changed my hotel. I moved from Paddington. Tonight and tomorrow night I shall be a close neighbour of yours in Balham.'

'You've moved to a hotel in Balham?'

'Well, in Streatham, actually. The Regent.' He smiled, pleased with himself. 'When I leave you tonight I shall have only a short walk to my own bed.'

It had been past midnight when they left the restaurant and it was one o'clock before they reached the Haywards' house in Balham. It had been a pleasant ride, with little

374

other traffic on the road, and Abbie had relaxed into the gentle rocking of the carriage. As the miles had passed beneath the horse's hooves she realized that she was feeling calmer and more at ease than for some time.

After paying the driver Louis walked with her to the front door. She was tired now. 'I shall sleep well tonight,' she said as she took out her latchkey.

He nodded. 'I too. And I must say it's so good not to have to make that long journey back to Paddington.'

They looked at one another in the dim light. 'Thank you again for a lovely evening, Louis,' she said.

'The pleasure was mine.' He waited as she unlocked the door. 'I'll see you in the morning. Can you be ready at, say, half past eight? Or is that too early?'

'I'll be ready.

'Goodnight, then.'

'Goodnight.'

He turned and started back towards the street. From the open doorway Abbie watched as he reached the gate and turned to face her again. She waved and he raised his own hand in return.

After silently closing the door she located the candlestick and matches on the hall table, lit the wick and moved towards the stairs. As she did so she heard a sound, that of a smothered cough, coming from her left. She hesitated, then stepped quietly towards the partly opened door of the library. Pushing wider, she heard the rustle of clothing. She looked into the room and in the pale light from the candle saw Mrs Hayward sitting in a chair by the window. She heard the sound of steady breathing. Was the woman asleep? Silently Abbie backed out of the room and crept upstairs.

Minutes later she stood at the closed door of her own room, hearing the creak of the treads as Mrs Hayward came up the stairs. The woman had not been asleep. She had just been sitting there in the dark, waiting for Abbie's return.

Chapter Twenty-Seven

The following day, Saturday, dawned bright and clear, and at eight fifteen Abbie was ready and waiting when Louis called at the house. A few minutes later they were sitting in the cab and heading for Lewisham Station. A further half-hour and they were boarding a train for the first part of the journey to Gravesend, the small Kentish town set on the south bank of the Thames.

They arrived in Gravesend some little time after eleven thirty and set off to walk the short distance from the station to the home of Louis's father. The day was warm, but there was a refreshing breeze. Abbie enjoyed the walk. She had never been to such a place before, and she found it attractive and picturesque. After a while they turned into a narrow street and then Louis was leading her up a short garden path to the front door of a spacious house fronted by a green lawn with herbaceous beds and borders.

Bearing out the truth of Louis's prediction, the senior Mr Randolph appeared delighted to meet Abbie. He had received Louis's letter and had been eagerly awaiting their arrival. He was a handsome, grey-haired man in his late sixties, sensitive and intelligent. Still upright, he was only a fraction shorter than Louis. They were alike too in their facial features, Abbie observed, having the same broad-shaped face, the same blue-grey eyes.

While Mrs Willett, the cook-housekeeper, was preparing luncheon the three sat chatting of this and that, during which conversation it became clear to Abbie that Louis's family had been close-knit and loving. After lunch the three rested for a time and then left the house to take a leisurely stroll. At Louis's suggestion they went first to St George's church inside which Louis's father pointed out to Abbie a particular tomb. On moving closer she saw that it was the tomb of the Indian princess Pocahontas who had died in 1617, shortly after setting out on a voyage to Virginia, USA.

Following this excursion they made their way towards the river where they sat on a grassy bank looking out over the water, watching as the ships and boats crossed in their passage to and from London.

Paddles churning, a large steamboat glided by not far from the bank, just having left the Rosherville pier and now bound for the capital. Abbie could see that her decks were thronged with people, while over the water came the sounds of a band playing, of voices singing.

'They sound as if they're having a good time,' she said.

'They do, don't they?' said Mr Randolph. 'The boat will have come from Sheerness. Most of the pleasure boats go there on their day trips.'

Louis said to Abbie, 'Shall we take a steamer back to London? Or would you rather go by train?'

'Oh, let's go by steamer,' she said. 'It looks such fun.'

He nodded. 'Fun, yes – and very crowded too, if you don't mind that.'

'I shan't mind at all.'

Some time later, after they had returned to the house, Mrs Willett served tea along with delicious little scones and strawberry jam. Afterwards Abbie murmured to Louis that she would like to go and sit out in the garden for a while. 'It'll give you and your father a chance to talk,' she added.

She wandered outside and, in the shade of an apple

tree, sat on a wooden bench on the edge of a small, neat lawn. Forty-five minutes later Mr Randolph emerged from the house and came towards her. It was almost six, he said, and Louis was anxious to start back. As she got up she thanked him, adding that she had had a lovely day.

'Thank *you*,' he replied. 'It's been my pleasure.' Turning, he glanced back towards the house. 'It's good to see my son looking happy and relaxed again.'

She followed him into the house then, where she and Louis gathered their things together and said their goodbyes.

'You must come again, Abbie,' said the elder Mr Randolph.

'Thank you,' she replied. 'I'd like to.'

He smiled. 'I don't get enough visitors – of the kind I like, anyway.'

A few minutes later Abbie and Louis had left the house and were setting off back in the direction of the river. Arriving at the Rosherville pier they found a saloon steamer, the *Duke of Teck*, lying alongside and in the act of taking the Gravesend passengers on board. Joining the short queue, Louis bought tickets and, taking Abbie's arm, led her up the gangplank onto the boat.

There were already hundreds of other travellers on board. The sound of music was in the air, coming from a brass band that played on the saloon deck. There was a bright, happy atmosphere, and added to the noise of the churning paddles and the music of the band came the sound of some of the passengers singing.

Abbie realized that for many there the trip would hold no real novelty, for a journey down the river probably formed a regular part of their leisure pastime. For herself it was something quite new. She had never before been on a boat of any kind, and to be a passenger on such a large paddle steamer was quite a thrilling experience. With Louis beside her she stood at the rail as the vessel cast off her lines and swung out into the river, moving slowly and majestically against the powerful force of the ebbing tide.

'Ah,' Louis sighed, 'now there's a little breeze getting up.' As he spoke he put his arm around her waist. It was the first time he had made any attempt to touch her beyond the most casual instances of contact that had come in the course of their being together over the past days. She froze very slightly in the first moment of his touch, but then forced herself to relax.

'So,' Louis said, 'how are you enjoying your first riverboat trip?'

'I love it,' she replied. 'In fact, I think I might apply to the steamship company to see if they require any stewardesses.'

'Oh, dear, no,' he said. 'I'm afraid you wouldn't do at all. If you look at the stewardesses on board you'll see that they're all past the age where they might prove attractive to the rest of the crew. You'd be far too much of a distraction.'

He smiled down into her eyes. He had taken off his hat, and the river wind was ruffling his dark hair. His face was slightly flushed from the sun, making his teeth appear even whiter. Now as his smile faded she became aware that his blue-grey eyes remained fixed on her own, a little intense, and at odds with the lightness of his expression. She lowered her glance, turned her head and looked out over the swiftly flowing water again.

Later they went into the saloon bar for lemonade. It was a little too crowded, however, and after a while they made their way back onto the deck, where they found seats, and remained there for the rest of the journey.

Close on eight o'clock the boat called at Woolwich

where many of the passengers disembarked. From there it sailed on to London Bridge, the last port of call.

It was just after nine thirty when Louis and Abbie eventually arrived back at Balham.

'Are you tired?' Louis asked her as they emerged from the station.

'Not really.'

'No?' He sounded surprised. 'It's been a long day.' He stood casting his eyes about for a cab.

'Are *you* tired?' she asked.

'A little – but in a pleasant kind of way.'

'Well, now you can go to your hotel and rest.'

'I'm not *that* tired. Besides, if I'm going back to Wiltshire tomorrow I have to make the most of the little time I've got left to me here.'

A cab came into view and Louis hailed it. When it stopped he gave Abbie's address, then helped her inside and climbed in after her. As they set off he turned to her and said, 'Do you want to go back now? To Mrs Hayward's? We have to eat at some time. Shall we find somewhere . . . ?'

When she hesitated he said, 'I'll be leaving in the morning. I don't know when I might see you again . . .'

She looked at him but was unable to make out his expression in the dim light. 'All right,' she said, and then: 'Yes, it would be nice to have supper together.'

He nodded. 'Good. We can eat at my hotel.'

The supper at the Regent was simple but good and their hunger made it taste even better. On their entering the dining room there had been four tables occupied, but by the time they finished eating they were alone. In the silence Louis took a sip from his coffee cup, lighted a small cigar and leaned back in his chair. 'Have you missed your charges?' he asked. 'Your little girls?'

'I don't think I've given them a thought.' She sighed. 'This has been such a wonderful day. And I loved meeting your father. He's such a fine old gentleman. In some ways he reminds me of my own father. You would have liked him, I know you would.'

'I'm sure I should.' Louis drew on his cigar. 'It was a good day for me, too.' He paused. 'I don't want to go back tomorrow.'

'What time are you leaving?'

'I must be gone from here about eight. Nine at the latest.'

'And so back to Frome and back to work.'

'And back to work.' He looked at his watch and sighed. 'It's almost midnight. I must take you home.'

'Yes – I suppose so.'

A little later they emerged into the air once more. It was a fine, balmy night. From Streatham High Road they walked down to Tooting Bec Common and started across it by one of the many footpaths. At one point Abbie stumbled slightly and Louis said, 'Careful now,' and put his hand under her elbow. She was very conscious of his touch.

In silence they moved across the common. There was no one else about. The wide expanse of grass was silver-grey in the moonlight. Halfway across, Louis gestured to the trunk of a fallen tree a few yards from the path. 'Let's sit down a minute, shall we?' he said. For the briefest moment Abbie had a flashing vision of the two of them sitting side by side on the willow beside the stream, and saw the lights and heard again the music of the fairground. She thrust the images away, moved to the tree trunk and sat down. From somewhere over to the right came the sound of a nightbird's singing. 'I mustn't be too late,' she said.

'You're already very late. I'm afraid where Mrs Hayward is concerned your reputation will already have suffered a mortal blow.'

She shrugged. 'I'm really not that bothered by what Mrs Hayward thinks of me.' Tilting back her head she looked up at the cloudless vastness above, where all the stars were out in the milky way. 'Oh, Louis,' she said, 'what a magnificent sky. It makes you feel almost – insignificant. As if in the great scheme of things you can't be any more than – than like a little grain of sand.'

'Yes,' Louis said, gazing up. Then, turning to her, he asked, 'Are you very tired now?'

'A little. What about you?'

'Not any more.'

'Well, at least you won't have far to go tonight in order to get to your bed. Though come the morning when you've got to make that trip across London for your train you'll wish you'd stayed in Paddington.'

'No, I shan't wish that.'

'I know that your staying here was more convenient with regard to my being at Balham, but didn't it make for difficulties with your business in London?'

He did not answer at once, then he said, 'I had no business in London, Abbie.'

'You didn't? But you said –'

He broke in: 'It was a pretence. I came up to London to see you.'

She did not speak. In the silence the bird went on singing.

'Has it meant anything to you, Abbie, my being here?' he said. Then immediately he had spoken he shook his head and waved a dismissing hand. 'Don't answer that. I have no right to ask you such a thing.'

'Oh, Louis, it's meant a lot to me to see you again – to have spent this time with you.' And even as she spoke she realized that her words were nothing less than the truth. She had so enjoyed these hours in his company. 'It's been wonderful,' she added.

He looked at her for an instant, and then his arms came around her, drawing her to him. For a moment she was moved to pull away, but she did not. She was aware of the strength of his arms and also of how good it felt to be held, to feel safe again after so long. Another second and he was bending his head and his lips were pressing on hers.

Some feeling within her made her begin to draw back, briefly, quickly, away from him. But he would not brook her resistance and his mouth was there, still there, warm and persistent upon her own. After a moment or two she found herself letting go and giving herself up to his kiss, his touch. And while a part of her mind protested, she found herself returning his kiss and with a passion that she had not known in so long. She was revelling in the warmth and softness of his mouth on hers, the strength of his arms that held her.

'Abbie . . .' He drew back only long enough to speak her name, then kissed her again. After holding her for a moment longer he drew back once more. The sound that came from his mouth was a little laugh touched with a sigh of relief – like a man who had thirsted and been given water. 'Oh, dear God, Abbie,' he said, smiling down into her eyes, 'you can't know how I've wanted to do that.'

She did not know what to say. No words would come; she was only aware of his arms still around her and strange feelings and thoughts that warred in her mind and her heart. He held her closer and kissed her again, then looked into her eyes in the pale light and said:

384

'I love you, Abbie. I love you.'

'No, no,' she said, the words tumbling from her lips. 'Don't speak like this.'

'No?' He gave a little laugh. 'Why not? I want everyone to know. I love you. And I'm so proud of it.'

She looked up at him, even through the shadow seeing the tenderness and the joy in his expression, his darkened eyes.

'Oh, Abbie,' he said, 'I think you must have got into my blood that first day – that day at the fair. I've met a number of women so far in my life, but somehow you were always there. You'll always be there now.' He looked at her as if waiting for her to speak. When she did not, he went on, 'At Easter, when you said you were leaving Flaxdown, I was miserable. We'd just made contact again and then out of the blue you told me you were going away. I couldn't believe it.' He gave a rueful smile. 'I was angry too. I had the idea you were leaving because of your friend Gilmore . . . I'm sorry I said that when you were going away. About him. I was jealous. Of course I know now that I was wrong. When I heard not so long ago that he and your friend Jane had got married I realized I'd been barking up the wrong tree where you and he were concerned.'

Abbie kept her eyes lowered.

A little silence, then he said, 'You know, I shall be thirty next month.'

'Poor old man.' She grasped at the opportunity to try to make the conversation light.

'How old are you, Abbie?'

'I was twenty-four just over a week ago.'

'Really? Just over a week ago?'

'July the 3rd.'

'I wish I'd known. But I shall remember from now on.'

He reached down, lifted her right hand and clasped it between his own. 'I want to marry you,' he said.

'Oh – Louis . . .' She could not marry him, of course she could not. In spite of the passion she had known just moments ago, she knew that it was not right. Such an idea was out of the question. He was not the right one for her; he never could be. But how could she tell him? She frowned, searching for words that would not come.

'Don't say anything for a minute,' he said, as if sensing that she was about to refuse him. 'Hear me out.' He went on after a moment, 'I won't ask if you love me, as I'm afraid I mightn't like your answer. Though I should prepare myself for that too, I suppose.' He looked at her, studying her. 'Without false modesty, Abbie, I consider myself a good man. And while I might never be rich, I can offer you a comfortable life. You'd never want for anything for the rest of your days, I promise you that. And I would love you. I love you now and I would love you for as long as I live.'

'How can you be so sure?' she said.

'Oh, I am.' A moment's pause, then he added, 'You haven't mentioned anyone, so I'm assuming there's no special person in your life . . .'

She gave a shake of her head.

'Good.' He studied her for a moment in the moon's light. 'You do care for me, don't you? I'm working on the assumption that you do, anyway.'

'Oh – of course I do.'

He nodded. 'But your answer also tells me that you don't love me.' Then he added, 'But you would in time – I know it. Given time I can make you love me. I'm sure I can.' He pressed her hand. 'Well . . . ?'

She frowned. 'Oh, but Louis, I –'

He released her and raised his hand against her words. 'Please, don't tell me no. At least not till you've really had a chance to give it some thought. But remember what I say: I can make you happy. You won't want for anything for the rest of your life. That goes for my love and for everything else that I have to offer.'

'Is that everything else within reason?' she said with a smile, still trying to avoid the seriousness of the situation.

He grinned and gave a helpless groan. 'No. Out of reason as well. Oh, Abbie, I love you so much I don't think I could refuse you anything.'

Silence fell between them. After a time she said, 'Louis – I thank you so much for what you've offered me. I don't take it lightly, I can assure you. It's a great honour. And I'll do as you ask – I won't give you my answer now; I'll think about it. And think about it very seriously. And I'll write to you very soon, I promise.' She let out her breath in a deep sigh. 'Now – I really think I should get back before I find the doors bolted against me.'

In the hall of the Haywards' house Abbie closed and locked the front door and then stood quite still, listening. All was quiet. When she had lit the candle she was tempted to glance into the library to see whether Mrs Hayward was there again, keeping her watch. But she continued on up the stairs; it was getting on for two o'clock; Mrs Hayward would surely have been asleep for hours by now.

In spite of the lateness of the hour, Abbie could not sleep. Lying in her bed she thought back over the day – the train journey to Gravesend, the meeting with Louis's father, the trip on the Thames pleasure steamer, the supper at Louis's hotel. It had been such a full and pleasant time. And throughout it all Louis had been such fine company. But could there ever be more than friendship between them? He wanted it so. He loved her; he had told her so.

And over the next few days she must, as she had promised, write to him with an answer to his proposal.

Marriage to Louis ... To become the wife of a country doctor. She was aware that in the eyes of many she would be in an enviable situation. And she had no doubt that Louis would be true to his word; he would, she was sure, do all in his power to make her happy. She sighed, turning restlessly on the pillow. It was a fine and wonderful thing to be loved – and indeed to be loved by such a man as he. But even so it was not enough. It could never be enough. When she married it must be not only because she was loved, but also because she loved in return. There was nothing else for it, but over the next day or two she must write to Louis and tell him of her decision – that she would be unable to marry him.

Into her mind came a picture of Arthur, bringing with it a sharp pang of bitterness. Arthur had loved her too. And he still loved her, she had no doubt of that. It was only through circumstances, because he was now tied to another, that he could not declare his love for her. And never would be able to. At the thought she gave a little groan of anguish and frustration. There was no way out of the situation. Arthur would never be hers now. She had lost him – first because of her mother, and now through Jane. And this time the loss was irretrievable.

Softly on the night air came the striking of a church clock. Three o'clock. She must get to sleep or she would be fit for nothing. Restless and exhausted, she turned over, trying to seek out some new position that would offer her sleep. But still it would not come. When at long last she drifted into her disturbing dreams it was almost four o'clock.

She was awakened by a knocking on her door. Sleepily,

with her head pounding, she raised herself in her bed. 'Yes?' she called.

The door opened and Esther, the housemaid, put her head into the room. 'I'm sorry to disturb you, miss,' she said, 'but the missis wants to see you.'

Abbie glanced at the clock and frowned. 'You mean now?'

'Yes, miss. She's in her room.'

Abbie yawned. 'But it's not yet six o'clock.'

'I know, miss. I'm sorry.'

When the maid had gone away, Abbie sighed. What on earth could Mrs Hayward want at this time of the morning? She yawned again. She felt desperately tired from her lack of sleep . . . She closed her eyes again . . .

There was a knocking on the door. Abbie opened her eyes with the realization that she must have fallen asleep after Esther had awakened her and – horrors! – it was ten minutes to seven. Quickly she got out of bed, pulled on her dressing gown and opened the door. Esther stood there again.

'I know, Esther,' Abbie said, pulling a conspiratorial face. 'I went back to sleep.'

Esther leaned closer. 'She's getting really mad, miss.'

'Right. Thank you, Esther. I'll be there in a minute.'

When Abbie had washed and dressed she went down to the first floor and knocked on Mrs Hayward's door. Mrs Hayward called for her to enter, and she opened the door and stepped into the room.

Mrs Hayward was sitting up in bed, the pillows banked high behind her head. There was a wan, rather pathetic look about her. Gazing at Abbie with something not far short of a glare, she pursed her lips and looked down at her fingers.

'So,' she said, 'at last you deigned to come. How very kind of you.'

'I'm sorry, Mrs Hayward,' Abbie said, 'but I inadvertently went back to sleep.'

'So it would seem.'

Abbie made no response to this, but waited a few moments, then asked: 'What was it you wanted me for, ma'am?'

'It doesn't matter now.' The tone was clipped, petulant.

Abbie gave a little sigh, hesitated for a second, then started to turn away.

'I haven't dismissed you,' Mrs Hayward said, raising her glance.

'I'm sorry.' Feeling somewhat affronted at the imperious tone, Abbie turned back to face her. 'When I asked what you wanted you said –'

'I know what I said,' Mrs Hayward broke in. A brief pause, then she added, 'I was feeling exceedingly unwell.'

'Oh . . . I'm very sorry to hear that.'

'I'm sure you are.' Mrs Hayward lowered her gaze once more while a plaintive note of self-pity came into her voice. 'With Mr Hayward being away so much I've no one to turn to. I should have thought you'd realize that. I thought at least I could rely on you. I certainly can't depend on the other servants. Now it seems I was wrong about you, too.'

'Mrs Hayward, I'm sorry,' Abbie said. 'As I said, I fell asleep again. I didn't mean to, but I was very tired and – well – it just happened.' She paused. 'Anyway, how are you feeling now? Is there something I can do for you?'

'I had a dreadful night,' Mrs Hayward said. 'My heart was fluttering and pounding so. I was in a dreadful state. I felt sure I was going to have a heart attack. God knows the last thing I wanted to do was disturb you from your sleep, but I just didn't feel I had anyone else to turn to.'

Unimpressed, Abbie said, 'Would you like me to send for the doctor?'

'No, I would not like you to send for the doctor. I'm better. All I really need now is someone I can rely on. Somehow, though, I have the feeling it's not *you* – certainly not by the way you stand there with that rather cold expression on your face.'

'Mrs Hayward,' Abbie said, 'I don't know what to say. I don't know what you want of me.'

'A little sympathy wouldn't come amiss. A little sympathy and understanding.' A pause. 'I wanted to see you.'

'Yes, I know. But after Esther came and –'

'I'm not talking about when Esther came to wake you; I'm talking about a much earlier time than that.'

'Earlier? I don't understand.'

'Of course you don't understand. Half past one this morning – that's the time I'm talking about. I was ill and I wanted someone. I needed someone. I came and tapped on your door, but got no answer. When I opened the door I found your room empty and your bed not slept in.'

'Yes, I'm afraid I was a little late getting in last night.'

'A little late?' Mrs Hayward's eyes widened in mock surprise. 'A little late? You were gadding about at half past one in the morning and you say you were a little late? Dear God.' She gave an incredulous shake of her head. 'I won't ask what you were up to at such a time.'

Stung, Abbie retorted sharply, 'What I was up to, Mrs Hayward, is none of your business. And furthermore I resent the implication of your words.'

Mrs Hayward put a hand to her breast. 'So you resent my implication, do you? And what, pray, am I implying?'

Abbie waved the subject away. 'It doesn't matter.'

'Oh, but it does matter,' said the other. 'What do you think I'm implying?' She paused. 'Well, if the cap fits, my dear . . .'

'Mrs Hayward,' Abbie said angrily, 'if you –'

'Enough!' Mrs Hayward raised a hand, palm out. 'I've never heard such insolence from an employee in all my life, and I'm not going to lie here and listen to any more of it. I think you'd better go back to your room. And while you're there perhaps you'd do well to reflect on your position. For I'm certainly not going to employ someone who is insolent and impertinent, and who doesn't know her place. When you've had a chance to think things over perhaps you'll see your way to coming to me with your apology.'

'Mrs Hayward,' Abbie said, measuring her words, 'it's quite obvious that the two of us can no longer remain under the same roof. Therefore, rather than you use your energies to rant and rave at me, I suggest you put them to use in finding a new governess for your children.'

Mrs Hayward's mouth fell open. Then, quickly composing herself she said, 'You mean – you're quitting your post?'

'I mean exactly that. And I might also remind you that I was employed as a governess to your two little girls, not as a nursemaid to their mother.'

Mrs Hayward drew herself up in the bed. 'How dare you speak to me like that!'

'I do dare. With Florence and Mabel away I'm supposed to be on holiday. But if it were up to you I'd have very little time to myself. Look how you were the day before yesterday when we went shopping. You knew I had to get back to meet Dr Randolph, but you took all the time you could. And I know quite well that you were spying on me the night I got back from the theatre. When I opened the library door and saw you sitting there you were only pretending to be asleep. You were waiting for me to get back, weren't you? And that's why you went to my room this morning, too. It wasn't because you wanted my help. Not a bit of it. You merely wanted to – to catch me out, as it were.' She gave a contemptuous shake of her head. 'And did you think that having done so you would now find me all guilt and contrition? Well, I'm sorry to disappoint you, for I feel neither.'

Mrs Hayward opened her mouth to speak but Abbie went on, raising her voice, overriding her, 'Why should you be so concerned about what I do in my own time? Why? Did you envy me going out, enjoying myself? Good heavens, it's a rare thing for me in this house. When I'm not looking after Florence and Mabel I just seem to be at your beck and call. Well, it's finished now. And as regards my staying out late, all you need to know is that I wasn't bringing any kind of disgrace on your own good name. That you can be assured of. And that being understood, the rest is no concern of yours whatever.'

'I've never been spoken to in this manner in all my life,' Mrs Hayward said, her chin quivering.

'Well, more's the pity,' Abbie said. 'Because I'm sure it must be long overdue. I could say a lot of other things, but I think perhaps I've said enough. And now I'll be going.'

As Abbie turned away Mrs Hayward said, 'If you leave now you mustn't think I'm going to pay you.'

Abbie turned back to face her. 'I don't care. It's enough for me that I'm leaving your employment.'

'Without references?' said the other with a note of triumph in her voice. 'Surely you don't think I shall be giving you any kind of reference, do you? If so, you'll wait till apples grow on pear trees.'

'I wouldn't dream of asking. And I'll manage without them.' With her words Abbie strode from the room.

Inside her own room she closed the door and stood leaning against it. Her heart was thumping so hard, while her knees felt weak, and as she pressed her hands together she realized that her palms were damp with perspiration. Outwardly she had been very brave with Mrs Hayward, yet inwardly it was a different story. For a moment she almost felt that she might cry, and she choked back the threatening tears; this was no time to give way; it was a time for action. She had just talked herself out of a job, had in effect talked herself out onto the street – and without references.

She sank down on her unmade bed and remained there in deep thought for some moments. Then, with a look of resolve, she got up and reached for her boots. Two minutes later she had left the house and was hurrying up the hill.

The dew was still on the grass as she crossed the common by the footpath – the path she and Louis had taken so leisurely in the small hours of that morning. Leaving the common, she hurried up the street that took her onto Streatham High Road and eventually, close by Streatham Hill railway station, to the Regency Hotel. Please, she prayed, let me be in time.

There was a hackney cab outside the hotel, and as she entered the vestibule she saw Louis standing at the desk. At the sound of her footsteps he turned.

'Abbie!' His expression was half-smile, half-frown. 'What are you doing here?'

'Oh – Louis . . .' She was so out of breath she could hardly speak.

He moved to her side. 'Abbie, are you all right?'

'Yes. Yes, I am – now.' Her words came out in bursts. She gave a gasping little laugh. 'I had to catch you before – before you left. I was so afraid I would be too late.'

'Oh, Abbie. Sit down, do – before you fall down.' He led her to a velvet-covered sofa at one side of the vestibule. 'Are you sure you're all right?'

'Yes – absolutely.'

'Is there anything you want? Can I get someone to bring you something?'

'No, I'm all right.' She gestured towards the desk. 'You finish your business. I'll sit here for a minute.'

'I'm just paying my bill. I shan't be a moment.'

She sat getting her breath back while Louis attended to his business at the desk. Turning her head, she caught sight of herself in a long mirror that hung nearby. The strings of her bonnet had come untied and her hair was coming down. What a sight she was, she thought. As she retied her bonnet strings Louis came back to her side. 'You just got here in time,' he said as he sat down next to her. 'That's my cab waiting at the door.' He frowned, looking intensely into her eyes. 'Are you sure you're all right?'

'Yes – apart from looking an absolute fright. I just got a look at myself in the glass. Not a pleasant sight first thing in the morning.'

He smiled. 'You'd be a pleasant sight for me at any time.' He paused, still eyeing her intently. 'Well, tell me – what is this all about?'

'Oh, Louis . . .' She looked away from him. 'You'll think I'm mad – appearing out of the blue like this.'

'I couldn't ask for a nicer vision.'

'Do you mean that?'

'Of course I mean it. Abbie, what is this all about? Are you in trouble of some kind?'

'No, but – oh, can you spare a few minutes before you leave for the station? I have to talk to you . . .'

He nodded, looked at his watch, then got up, raised a hand to the porter and said, 'Please – will you go and tell my cab driver that I'll be out in five minutes? Thank you.' With that he took Abbie's hand and led her into the lounge. There was no one else present and they sat facing one another on a soft, overstuffed sofa.

'Now,' Louis said, 'tell me what it is.'

'You did mean it, didn't you?' Abbie said. 'What you said last night?'

'What was that? We said many things as I recall.'

'Oh – Louis . . .' She gave a deep sigh. 'I shouldn't have come, I know it.'

'For goodness' sake, Abbie, what are you talking about?'

She took a breath. 'Last night you asked me to marry you . . .'

'And you told me you needed time to think it over.'

'Well, I have – thought it over.'

He said nothing – just waited for her to go on.

'I have,' she said again, '– thought it over.' She took another deep breath, then laid her hand over his own. 'I came here to say that I've thought it over, and I will marry you, Louis. I'll marry you just as soon as you like.'

'Oh, Abbie,' he breathed, 'you've made me so happy. When I saw you I couldn't imagine what it was that had brought you here so early. It did cross my mind that you had brought an answer to my proposal – but I didn't really dare to hope.' Putting his arms around her, he drew her to him, holding her near. Feeling his closeness, the strength of his arms, Abbie felt again that sense of safety and secureness that she had known when he had held her last night on the common. It was such a good feeling – not only in itself and for its own sake, but also coming after all the recent uncertainty in her life. And why should it not always be there, she said to herself. It could. For she would forget Arthur – indeed, she had no choice, for he was now a part of her past. And commitment to a new life, a life with Louis, would be in part an affirmation of her determination to find a different future for herself. Yes, marriage with Louis . . . it was, she told herself, the best thing – the right thing – for her to do.

And even as she remained in the circle of Louis's arms she found herself stabbed by guilt. He deserved to know the truth. He had to. Abruptly drawing back out of his grasp, she said, 'Louis, this is no good – I haven't been totally honest with you.'

'What do you mean?'

'I – I have to tell you what happened.'

'I don't understand . . .'

She told him then of the scene with Mrs Hayward and that she had quit her position in the household. 'This isn't the way you'd want it,' she said, '– my acceptance of your proposal. I mean – if I don't marry you I'm out on the street with no job and nowhere to stay. You could say I wasn't faced with the most difficult choice. Please – forget it – forget that I said yes. It's not right. It's just not right.'

'Right?' he said. 'Oh, Abbie, we'll make it right. Listen, I'm just glad that you're willing to marry me. Don't change your mind.' He took her hands in his. 'Believe me, I do realize that your decision hasn't been prompted by any wild passion for me. More's the pity, but there it is. I didn't expect it to be. And if it took a little push from your Mrs Hayward to concentrate your mind and get you to reach the right decision then I'm not going to be critical. I might even send her some flowers.'

'Louis – be serious, please.'

'Of course.' He gave a little chuckle. 'Abbie, you must allow me some levity. After all, you're going to marry me. I've got what I wanted.' He gazed at her for a moment or two longer, then said, 'Now – we must be practical. I think we should marry soon, don't you?'

She nodded. 'All right . . .'

'Well, I don't see any point in waiting. I'll take you back to Mrs Hayward's house now, so that you can pick up your things. Then we'll go to Paddington and get the first available train to Frome. Can you stay with your brother in Flaxdown while the banns are called?'

'Yes, I should think so.'

'Fine.' He got to his feet, drawing her up beside him. Holding her close, he kissed her briefly on the mouth. 'Now,' he said as he released her, 'we must get busy. We have a great deal to do.' Taking her arm he linked it in the crook of his own and led her towards the vestibule. As they reached the doorway he smiled down at her. 'Oh, Abigail,' he said, 'you've made me the happiest man.'

PART FIVE

Chapter Twenty-Eight

'Oh, Mama, can't I come with you?'

Abbie was sitting at her dressing table, doing her hair when Oliver's small, pleading voice came to her. She turned and bent to him.

'I'm sorry, darling. It's too cold out today. You stay home in the warm with Maria.' As she spoke she glanced at the young nursemaid who hovered in the background. 'I shan't be late back.'

She smiled encouragingly and the child gave a resigned sigh and turned away. Oliver was two years and eight months old. He was a bright, clever little boy in whose dark hair and blue-grey eyes Louis could clearly be seen.

Louis entered the room, wearing his overcoat and hat. 'Are you nearly ready?' he said to Abbie. 'I've hitched up the carriage.'

As Abbie murmured that she was ready but for her hair he turned to his son and lifted him up. 'And a little kiss for your papa? To keep him warm on the road?'

Oliver pressed his lips to his father's cheek, then asked, 'Can I come with you?'

Abbie smiled. 'I've already told him it's not possible.'

'I'm sorry, Ollie,' Louis said. 'We'll go out another day.' He set the boy down on the carpet and Maria came, took his hand and led him from the room. Louis checked his watch with the clock. 'Abbie, we must go or I shall be late.'

She sighed. 'Don't you think they could manage without you for once?'

'They're expecting me and I must be there.'

'Of course you must be there. When are you not.'

Louis said with a little sideways smile, 'If I didn't know you better I might think you wanted to spend the time with me. Fortunately, I've learned not to be so foolish.' He looked at her as she finished pinning her hair; she was studiously ignoring his remark. 'I'll wait downstairs,' he said.

When he had gone from the room Abbie sat there while the sound of his footfalls faded on the stairs.

Letting fall her hands, she gave a deep sigh. Things were not getting better between them. The situation seemed to her to be deteriorating by the day. And Louis must feel the same way, she thought. He had to; it was obvious even to someone less perceptive than he.

Last night had marked another turning point. She had had one of her nightmares. The same dream, the dream where the weight was in her arms, and she had been unable to put it down. She had cried out in her sleep, 'No, no . . .' waking and sitting bolt upright. Then Louis's arms had come around her. But tentatively, not with certainty, as would once have been the case – for now he was never sure that there would be no rebuff. And true to her form of late, she had given him the rebuff that he had half expected, brushing aside his would-be comforting arms with a frown of irritation. 'It's all right. I shall be all right.'

'Would you like some water? Anything?'

'No, I told you: I shall be all right.' *How can I be like this?* she had asked herself, but the question had brought no answers. Or at least none that she had cared to dwell upon.

Later, just before she had fallen asleep again, with her back to Louis in the bed, she had been aware of his breathing. He was not sleeping, she was sure. His breathing was not that of a sleeping man.

She did not know what to do. Now gazing at her reflection in the glass, she felt almost as if she were seeing the face of a stranger. She looked different too. The young girl she had known had long gone, and gone for ever. She was twenty-seven now. And she could see in her face the passage of those twenty-seven years. She was still good-looking, but studying herself closely she could see the signs and scars of tensions and dissatisfaction. It was there in her eyes, in the set of her mouth.

And sometimes, at moments such as this, she would find herself wondering at her situation, pondering on her feelings of dissatisfaction. For she had so much; so much more than she had ever dreamed of having. How different was her life from those of her brother and sisters. As things were they could never hope to have the comforts that she now took for granted. She had none of the financial concerns that touched their lives, and which had touched the lives of her parents. Not for her a daily struggle to make ends meet, to work hard all day with so little monetary reward. She knew that in the eyes of Eddie, Lizzie and Iris she had everything. Yet at the same time, on occasion she viewed their comparatively poorer circumstances with something approaching envy; Eddie and Violet were extremely happy, she knew – as were Lizzie and her Adam. As for Iris and her young man, she knew that they were well suited and planned to marry before long. Such comparisons did little good in the long run, however, she was well aware; considerations of others' lack of ease and comfort could not for one moment take away her unhappiness with her own situation. And the realization simply made her ask herself again and again, why? Why?

From the foot of the stairs Louis's voice came calling

up, breaking into her thoughts: 'Abbie, we must go. I did tell you that I mustn't be late.'

'I'm coming.' She pushed one last pin into place, gave her hair a final pat and reached for her hat.

A few minutes later Louis was helping her into the carriage. As they drove away she looked back and saw Maria and Oliver at the nursery window. She waved to them and they waved back.

The mid-January day was crisp and cold. The pony's hooves rang on the hard road while his breath vapoured in little clouds above his rhythmically jogging head. Abbie kept her eyes on the road ahead as they drove, as did Louis, with only an occasional brief remark disturbing their silence. Reaching Flaxdown, Louis pulled the carriage to a halt near the entrance to Green Lane and helped Abbie down. 'Shall I call for you when I'm through?' he asked.

'No, I don't want to be too late so I'll get a cab. You go on home when you're finished.'

As she turned away Louis flapped the reins and the cob set off again.

Eddie and Violet and the children were all at home, as they usually were on a Sunday afternoon, and as Abbie entered the cottage the two girls came running towards her. Sarah was five years old now, and her younger sister, Eveline, was three.

'Did Louis bring you?' Eddie asked as Abbie took off her coat and hat.

'Yes. He's assisting at a post-mortem examination at Keyford, just off the Frome road. I shall take a fly back home.'

While the children played on the hearthrug the three adults sat around the fire.

'Oh, I forgot,' Abbie said, 'I heard from Iris in the

week.' From her bag she took a letter and gave it to Eddie. He opened it and read it, then passed it to Violet.

Iris, very much in love with young Alfred Timson, he who had been so solicitous at the time of her accident, had recently left Radstock for London. She had gone there solely to be with him. On the death of his employer, he had returned to the capital to live, having been offered work there as a musician with the London Steamship Company.

In her letter Iris had written to say that she was getting on well in her new position in Bayswater, and was looking forward to the summer and the day of their wedding.

'I wouldn't want to live in London,' Violet said, handing the letter back to Abbie. 'But I s'pose I would if I had good enough reason to.'

'No doubt Iris thinks she has,' said Eddie. 'Though why the two of 'em couldn't have stayed in Radstock beats me.'

'Alfred's family's in London,' Abbie said. 'Besides, he's a musician. That's what he's happiest doing. And where would he find employment as a musician in Radstock?'

'Could you go back to living in London, Abbie?' Violet said.

'I don't know,' Abbie replied. 'Though there's so much to do there – not like Frome or this place.'

With Eveline beginning to be fretful, Violet scooped her up and set about getting her off to sleep in a corner of the sofa. At the same time Sarah climbed onto Eddie's lap where, cradled in his arms, she was soon asleep. Violet observed the scene of relative peace and said, 'While I've got a minute I'll go upstairs and finish making the beds. Then I'll come down and get us some tea.'

When Violet had gone from the room Eddie said, 'You reckon you'll 'ave any more kiddies, Abs?'

'No,' she said at once, 'I shouldn't imagine so.'

'I reckon it's best to 'ave more than one,' he said. ' 'An only child gets lonely. And it's best to 'ave 'em when you're young, too, if you can. How long you been married now? Must be about three and-'alf years, eh?'

'That's right.'

'Don't you want any more children?'

'No, I don't.' She waved a hand, dismissing the question and the subject along with it.

Eddie gazed at her in silence for a few moments then said: 'You don't sound that 'appy.'

'What makes you say that?'

He gave a half-smile. 'Abbie, I might not 'ave the learnin' you've 'ad, but that don't mean I'm blind nor stupid. I know you of old – and I can read the signs.'

'Oh, yes, Mr Clever,' she said, smiling.

Frowning, he studied her in the firelight. 'Why are you so dissatisfied, Abbie? And I don't mean just lately; I've seen it for a good while now.'

'Eddie – you're imagining things.'

'No, I ain't,' he said, then added with a sigh, 'You and Louis, right?'

After a moment she gave a reluctant nod, sat for a moment staring into the fire, then said, 'I don't know what went wrong, Eddie. I had such hopes. But – I don't know – nothing turned out the way I thought it would.'

'And why was that, d'you suppose?'

She gave a shrug. 'I don't know. I thought we would be happy. Particularly when Oliver came along. And we were for a while but . . . it didn't last. I don't know where or how it went wrong.'

'Are you sure you don't know?'

'Of course I'm sure. If I knew I could do something about it.' She frowned. 'What exactly are you trying to say?' Then before he could reply she gave an awkward-sounding little laugh and said, 'I don't think I like this conversation.'

'I'd like to 'elp you, Abbie.' He paused. 'You don't still think about 'im, do you – the other one?'

'Who?' She forced herself to keep looking at him.

'You know who I mean. Arthur Gilmore.'

'Oh – him.'

'Yes – 'im as you promised to marry – and then didn't.'

'I didn't have any choice in the matter.'

'No?'

'You know I didn't. In case you've forgotten, Mother came back. To live with me. And she depended on me. Totally.'

He gave a little shrug.

'Well, you know she did,' Abbie said. 'You wouldn't help.'

He nodded. 'Well, you're right there, sure enough.'

'Anyway, what's any of this got to do with Arthur? You're imagining things.'

'Am I?' he said drily. 'Look, I know why you went to London when you left the village school here. You could have gone anywhere, but you chose to go to London because he was there. You thought everything would go back to the way it was before our Mother returned, didn't you? Only it never did.'

'Oh, for goodness' sake, Eddie,' she said – she could almost feel herself flushing with embarrassment – 'you don't know what you're talking about.'

'Don't I? I think I do. And you know I do. I 'ear you tellin' me that your marriage hasn't worked out the way you'd hoped, and I'm just looking for reasons why.' He eyed her carefully. 'Does Louis know?'

'Does he know what?'

'About Gilmore? Your going up to London in the hopes of marrying him.'

407

'Don't say such things,' she said sharply. 'You're so sure of yourself, aren't you? Suddenly you know everything.'

'Well, I know that you were so desperate to get to London that you wusn't even particular what job you took – taking the first one offered and getting yourself in with that crazy woman. Oh, I guessed what 'ad 'appened. One minute you're off to London and just four months later, after Gilmore's wed another, you're back with plans to marry somebody else. It don't need a professor's brain to understand that picture. Either you fell suddenly and desperately in love with Louis – which I find a bit hard to believe – or else you made use of 'im.'

Abbie got up from her seat. 'I'm not listening to this!'

'Not too loud,' Eddie said calmly, 'or you'll wake the girls.' He shook his head. 'I feel sorry for Louis, I really do.'

As Abbie's anger rose higher she felt tears welling in her eyes. Furiously she fought them back. 'I came to spend a pleasant hour or two with you and Violet, and instead I get these accusations. One day you're going to be too sharp for your own good.' She reached for her coat, pulled it on. 'I'm sorry, but I can't stay for tea. Please give my apologies to Violet. Tell her I'll come and see her again soon.' She added, 'And that'll be at a time when I can sit and relax without being accused of I don't know what.'

At that moment there came the sound of footsteps on the landing above. Not wishing, in her present state, to face her sister-in-law, Abbie moved to the door. 'I'll see you some time, Eddie,' she said. 'Goodbye.'

Outside she hurried along the lane, not looking back, not wishing to see whether Violet was standing at the open door.

Making her way to Barton's stables, she was just

drawing level with the Harp and Horses when she heard Eddie calling her. Glancing back she saw him running towards her, pulling on his old overcoat as he came. She ignored his call and kept going.

He soon caught up with her. 'Hang on,' he said, a little breathless after his dash from the house. Catching at her arm, he brought her to a halt. 'Give a chap a chance, will you?'

She saw that he had come out without a hat. Tight-lipped, she said, 'What do you want?'

'Come on back to the house, Abbie.'

'No, thank you, I've heard enough for one day.'

'Vi's wonderin' what I've said to upset you.'

'No doubt.'

'Oh, Abs, come on – don't be like this. I didn't mean to upset you – honest. And I couldn't let you go – not in this mood.'

'I wasn't in this mood when I arrived.'

'Yeh, well, I'm sorry about all that. But I didn't tell you anything you didn't already know, did I?'

She shook her head in exasperation. 'There you go again.'

'Aw, come on, Abs.' He put his head a little on one side. 'You and me was always able to talk in the past. 'Ave that changed? I only want what's best for you. You must know that.'

After a moment she gave a grudging nod. 'Maybe – but you've got a very strange way of showing it.'

He ignored this. 'Where were you off to? Barton's?'

'Yes.'

'I'll walk with you.'

Thirty yards along Carter's Lane they turned into Barton's stable yard, but on enquiring found that Mr Barton was already out on an errand to Warminster. He would be back in half an hour or so, Mrs Barton said, at which time the cab would be free for hire again. Abbie thanked her and said she would return a little later.

Out in the lane Eddie said, 'Come on, it's too blasted cold to 'ang about 'ere. Let's go into the 'Arp and get summat to drink. Though you'll 'ave to pay as I come out without any money.'

In the pub they took seats in the saloon bar. Eddie got a tankard of ale for himself and for Abbie a cup of coffee. There was no one else in the room. A bright fire was burning, while from the adjacent public bar came the murmur of voices and the clink of glasses. Brother and sister sat in silence for a moment or two, then Eddie said, 'You know, if you ever want to talk about anything, I'm always ready to listen.' When she said nothing he added, 'People should try to talk to each other more.' He turned and looked into the glowing fire. 'I always think – well, if our Beatie 'ad talked to somebody when it mattered she'd be 'ere today.'

'Perhaps you're right.' Abbie didn't want to talk about Beatie; didn't want to think about her. She remained silent for a moment, then she said wearily, 'Oh, Eddie, it's true . . . what you said about me and – and Arthur. My going up to London as I did. It was because of him – there's no point in my pretending otherwise.' She gave a deep sigh and added, 'I don't know what to do, Eddie.'

'About what?'

'Everything.'

'What d'you mean?'

She glanced around to ensure that no one could hear, then said: 'I think sometimes we should never have married, Louis and I. It was a mistake.'

'As bad as that, eh? What – what's the trouble, exactly?'

She hesitated for a second then said, 'Well, for one thing we hardly seem to spend any time together these days. Seven days a week, it seems, he's out all day, seeing to his patients – and often in the night too. Yet at the same time I don't have enough of interest to keep me occupied. I get so bored. His work is everything to him. I come a very poor second. And it's not necessary for him to do as much as he does. Yet even in his free time he makes commitments, volunteering for one thing or another. He doesn't seem to care. We can't go on like it.'

She looked down into her cup. She had not spoken the complete truth. Boredom and neglect were not the real reasons for her dissatisfaction, the causes of the failings in her marriage. The fundamental reasons went far deeper – and she herself was not sure that she knew the true nature of them. And trying to identify them and pin them down was like trying to catch shadows. All she could be sure of was that the hope with which she had begun her married life had faded and died, like a flower deprived of sunlight and rain.

Eddie's voice cut through her thoughts: 'What about taking more interest in Louis's work? A practical interest, I mean. Wouldn't that be possible?'

'Go calling on his patients, you mean? Dishing out soup and comfort? I don't think that's the answer.'

'How does Louis feel about all this? Is he happy?'

Abbie shook her head. 'Of course he isn't. And I don't see how he could be.' She stirred her coffee. 'Sometimes now we – we're like two strangers. Sometimes I think it's only Oliver who keeps us together. I don't know what to do any more.'

'Maybe,' he said, 'you've just got to try and make the best of it.'

'That kind of talk is no kind of comfort,' she said.

'Oh, it's comfort you want, is it?' He studied her. 'What *do* you want, Abbie?'

'Not much. And yet everything. Just to be happy.' She shrugged. 'I know. It's all everyone wants, isn't it? – from the richest to the poorest. And it's the thing that's most difficult to achieve.' She paused. 'I think I had a chance of it once.'

'With Gilmore, you mean?'

She did not answer.

'You do mean Gilmore, don't you?'

'Well, everything was fine until Mother came back and put an end to it all.' She sighed. 'Arthur loved me, you know. He really did.' She turned, looked at Eddie. 'I'm sure he still does.'

'Abbie, what are you talking about?' Eddie said. 'It's time you faced the facts and stopped livin' in the past. He's married to somebody else now. And so are you.'

'I'm perfectly aware of that,' she said sharply. 'But it doesn't change anything.'

'You sound mighty sure.'

'I *am* sure.'

'You're still 'ankerin' after 'im, ain't you? Arthur Gilmore.'

'Eddie,' she said, trying to hold her patience, 'you have a very – a rather blunt way of speaking at times.'

'I'm just telling the truth, as I see it. Pity you can't admit it to yourself. Far as I can see, it's crystal clear.'

'Oh, yes? And what exactly do you see?'

'Well – to give you your due, I suppose you wed Louis with the best of intentions, some of which were to forget all about your Mr Gilmore. But 'e won't be forgotten, is that it?'

When she said nothing in response to his words, he gave a little nod. 'Ah, I thought I was right.'

'Oh, Eddie, you'll never understand.'

'No, maybe I won't. All I know is that you've got a good 'usband, yet 'ere you are 'ankerin' after a man who belongs to somebody else. Excuse me for sayin' so, but he can't 'ave loved you that much, can 'e?'

'What do you know about it?'

'He chose to wed another. I don't need to know any more.'

'For your information, he didn't exactly choose to.'

'Oh, 'e was dragged to the church in chains, was 'e? Abbie, it don't make sense what you're saying. The man's married to Jane.'

'Yes, he got himself into a – a situation with her and he couldn't back out.'

'You think that's the way it was?'

'Absolutely. Jane was determined to have him.'

'You make her sound like some – I don't know. But however she got 'im, she've got 'im. And they've got a little kiddie too – so you better get used to the idea, and make the best of what you've got.'

Abbie drank the last of the coffee. 'When I think how close Jane and I used to be – what good friends we were . . .' She paused. 'I don't think I can ever forgive her for what she did.'

Eddie stared at her. Catching his gaze she said, 'Why are you looking at me like that?'

'Strong words, Abbie.' He put down his empty mug. 'I reckon we'd best go and see if Barton's back.'

They got up and left the pub. On arriving at the stable, they found that the fly proprietor had still not returned. They hung around in the yard for some minutes while Abbie's impatience grew, then she said, 'Eddie, I can't just stand here getting cold feet. I'm going to walk. It's not far. Only three miles.'

'As you like. I'll walk a little ways with you.'

They left the stable yard and set off through the village in the direction of the road leading to Frome. After a while Eddie said, 'You're gunna 'ave to give this up, Abbie.'

She came to a halt and they stood facing one another. 'Give what up?' she said.

'Tormenting yourself the way you are. Over Jane and Arthur and Louis.'

'I'm not tormenting myself,' she said. 'Besides, you don't understand.'

'So you keep tellin' me. After all, I'm just a dull-witted farmworker. Who am I to understand the way clever people go on.'

'Eddie, you're determined to quarrel, aren't you?'

'No, I'm not. I just don't understand 'ow a woman who's got everything can carry on like she's got nothin' at all.'

'I'm tired of all this talk,' she said. 'And in any case, it's none of your business.'

'I know it's not – except that you're my sister . . .'

'And I'm also a grown woman. I don't need a big brother to look out for me.'

'In that case,' he said, 'for God's sake start actin' like one. You don't know when you're well off. You don't 'ear me complainin'. And why should you? I got a nice wife and two grand little girls. And I'll tell you summat: you got a lot more. Not only 'ave you got a lovely little boy and a kind 'usband who's well thought of, but you got a fine 'ouse, an 'orse and carriage, and enough money so you don't ever need to worry about anything. And still none of it's enough. You don't know what the 'ell you do want, do you? Just like our mother.'

'What are you saying?'

'Well, reality was never good enough for her, was it? She was always after what she couldn't have, wanting what wasn't real. It blinded her to everything else, I reckon – everything that could have made her 'appy.' He looked at Abbie and gave a slow nod. 'Yeh, you remind me more and more of our mother every time I see you.'

It was the final insult. Abbie glared at him for a moment, then turned and strode away along the street.

The last house of the village was behind her now; before her stretched the winding road. She looked up at the pale, dull sky. In another half-hour or so the light would begin to fail. But she would be well along the road towards home by then. Home. Well, a home of sorts. At least Oliver would be there, sweet and dear and welcoming. If no one else did, Oliver made it all worthwhile.

A wave of hopelessness came over her and she almost groaned aloud into the cold air. Why could she and Louis not make it work? For most of the time at the beginning of their marriage she had pretended that everything was all right between them. But it was not so. It had never been right. Not truly right. At the start she had put on an act – and it had got them a certain distance. But it had not been strong enough or convincing enough to carry them for long. She was aware that the failure of their relationship showed in everything. It was as if she could no longer truly relax with Louis. She recalled how it had been on the first night when they had lain together – the tension she had felt when he touched her, the feel of his hands on her naked body, the feel of his own nakedness, the feel of him inside her.

But why should it be like that? She had entered into the marriage knowing that she did not love him. Though she had liked him so much, added to which she had enormous respect for him – not only for his work but for the kind of person he was. In addition he was so fine-looking. But all of this had not been enough. Her liking and respect for him had driven her to try harder to accept him in other ways, but she had not succeeded, at least not for very long.

And so, sadly, it had continued. And had become

worse. And of course it had not been long before he had become affected by her lack of warmth. And with the seeds of their failure having been sown, the pair had carefully nurtured them over the years with feelings of resentment, bitterness and guilt. For most of the time now they got by on politeness, generally managing to give to their marriage a satisfactory image, an appearance that all was well. But it was a mere patina. They both knew that not far beneath the surface the waters were far from smooth.

As she thought of Louis there came into her mind a picture of him as he had been on that day of their first meeting. How young they had been then. Once again she saw him bent over the rifle, taking aim at the target. She saw him too as they had sat together by the stream, and again as she and Beatie had turned and seen him standing against the lights of the fairground, his hand raised in farewell. Not long after that had come the men, the attack . . .

Such memories did no good. Putting them from her mind, she quickened her pace on the road.

A hundred yards further on she felt the discomfort of a stone under her heel and at the next field gate she stopped, took off her boot and shook the small pebble out. She had just finished fastening her boot when, on the periphery of her vision, she caught sight of an approaching solitary figure. A second later she saw to her astonishment that it was Arthur.

Chapter Twenty-Nine

Arthur was coming from the same direction, from the village. And seconds later she could see that he had recognized her. He half smiled as he came to a stop a couple of yards before her, his head inclining, his hand rising to touch his hat. He was wearing a chesterfield coat with a dark-blue muffler around his neck. They stood looking at one another, awkward and uncertain.

'Hello, Arthur.'

'Abbie . . . Well, this is a surprise.'

'Indeed it is.'

'I've been sent to do business in the area,' he said. 'So we're staying with Jane's mother for a few days.' He gestured ahead along the road. 'Right now I'm off to Keyford to enquire about the hire of a carriage for four or five days. Are you here visiting your family?'

'My brother, yes. I'm on my way home to Frome now.'

A little silence between them, then he said, 'Well – shall we walk together?'

'I see no reason why not.'

A hundred yards down the road they drew near a stile with a footpath leading across a field. It formed the first part of a short cut to Keyford and Frome.

'Would it help your journey if we took the footpath?' Arthur asked. 'Or would it be too hard on your boots?'

'Indeed it would help,' Abbie said. 'As for my boots, they'll have to look out for themselves. Besides, the earth's like iron today; they won't come to any harm.'

Without further hesitation Arthur climbed over the stile and helped her across to the other side, remarking as he did so, with a glance up at the heavens, that there was snow in the offing. The sky had taken on a heavy, dull yellow tinge that seemed to grow darker by the moment. Briskly the pair set off along the footpath that dissected the arable field.

'I must say, Abbie,' Arthur said, 'you're looking remarkably well.'

'Thank you. You also.'

'Oh, I'm tolerably well.'

'And your family?' She could not bring herself to ask after Jane. 'Your little girl?' Arthur and Jane's daughter, Emma, had been born some few months before Oliver.

'Oh, Emma's blooming. And your little boy? Oliver, isn't it?'

'Yes. He's very well, thank you.'

'How old is he?'

'He's just over two and a half.'

'Ah, yes.'

The whole thing was almost farcical, she thought. With all that had happened between them, here they were indulging in small talk as if they were mere acquaintances.

They came to another stile and, as before, Arthur climbed over and then assisted her onto the other side. They walked on, moving downhill now, a distance of a yard between them. In the well of the valley before them nestled a farmhouse, smoke rising from its chimney. In the fading light one could see that its lamps had already been lit.

Looking up once more at the sky, Abbie said, 'It's getting so dark.' She smiled. 'Perhaps this wasn't such a clever move of yours, Arthur, coming out on your errand at this time. You'll be wishing you'd stayed indoors.'

As they walked the sky grew darker still and now a keen wind sprang up at their backs. 'Arthur,' Abbie said, coming to a stop and glancing up again, 'it's looking very bleak. If you want to turn back, please do so. I shan't be in the least offended.'

'And leave you to go on alone?'

'I shall be all right. Anyway, I don't have a choice. I've got to get to Frome.'

'Then come on,' he said. 'While we stand here we're wasting time.'

They were nearing the far edge of the field when the first snow came drifting down, and very soon large flakes were falling thick and fast, so that the two were swiftly enveloped in a swirling white haze. As the wind strengthened to a furious pace Abbie halted in her tracks and turned to look back, but found she could barely open her eyes against the fury of the blizzard. With the cold flakes of snow melting on her tongue she cried out, her voice small and muffled in the fury of the wind-driven snow, 'We can't keep going in this.'

Arthur pointed to the cluster of farm buildings further down in the valley, now barely visible beyond the curtain of driving snow. His voice raised, he replied, 'We could go on down there and try to find some shelter. I'm sure no one would begrudge us a roof in weather like this.'

'I'm afraid you don't know Cassin, the farmer,' she said 'He has no reputation for neighbourliness. By all accounts he'd sooner see a person freeze than trespass on his property.'

'Are you afraid of him?'

'Not in the least.'

'Then come on.' After a moment's hesitation he reached out and took her hand in his own. Then, their heads bent, driven on by the blizzard, they made their way onward down the hill.

Abbie felt so conscious of being alone with Arthur, of her hand held fast in his. The whole strange episode seemed unreal, like something from a dream. Here she was, walking through a blizzard in the middle of a field with a man who had once been her intended husband. She was alone with him, cocooned in a strange, almost magical environment. It was as if the world outside this swirling, hazy white landscape did not exist, as if she and Arthur were the only two people left on earth.

Reaching a stile beside a five-barred gate Arthur carefully helped her over, and for a moment as he set her down he was holding her in his arms. Abbie saw that snowflakes had settled thickly on the brim and crown of his hat. And then he was releasing her once more and they were turning, moving off again before the storm.

As they neared the farm buildings at the foot of the hill the snow was falling more thickly than ever. There was no one in sight and they made their way to an old barn a little distance from the farmhouse. There, under Arthur's hand, the door creaked open, and the next moment, in a flurry of swirling snow, they were inside.

Sighing with relief, Abbie looked at Arthur as he closed the door and turned to face her. As with her own, every fold and crevice in his clothing was filled with snow. 'Well,' he said, 'we made it.'

'Yes.' Avoiding his eyes she turned, looking about her. The barn was spacious and there was hay in abundance. The high windows were small and dusty and the light shone in, filtered through the dusty pane, the blizzard beyond appearing pale and grey. No matter, the place was dry and relatively warm, and they would be sheltered for a while.

When they had taken off their coats, Arthur shook the snow from them and hung them on a nearby hook. His hat he placed with Abbie's on an upturned barrel. As she smoothed her hair back in place he took his watch from his waistcoat pocket. 'What time is it?' she asked.

'Ten past two.' He snapped shut his watch, replaced it, glanced towards the window at the storm and said, 'We might as well make ourselves comfortable. We're going to be here for a while yet.' He looked about him then moved to a large bale of hay and sat down. After a second she came and sat on the hay a couple of feet from him. For some moments they sat looking out at the snow that swirled past the dust-begrimed window, then Arthur shifted his gaze, looked at Abbie in the dim light and said, 'You're not concerned about the farmer – Cassin, or whatever his name is – are you?'

'Not in the least.'

'Will your husband be worrying? Wondering what's become of you?'

'He's working. He won't be home for a little while yet. He's not expecting me back at any specific time, anyway.'

'That's fortunate.'

She gave a rueful smile. 'Fortunate indeed. Though whether he'd notice if I'm there or not I don't know.'

'Abbie – that's a melancholy thing to say.'

She shook her head, avoiding his gaze. 'Oh – what does it matter, anyway?'

'What do you mean?'

'Nothing. It's not important.' Then she added, 'Nothing seems to be that important any more.'

'You sound rather low, somewhat defeated,' he said, frowning. 'It's not like you.'

She turned to him. He was so near. 'Arthur, how do you know what is like me and what isn't?' For some reason she could not discern she felt full of tears.

'Abbie, what is it?' he said. 'Tell me.'

'Tell you? Oh, Arthur – don't you know? It's partly to

do with – don't you know that?' And the tears that had threatened spilled over, running down her cheeks.

At the sight of her tears he gave a little groan and took her in his arms. 'Don't,' he said. 'Don't cry. Oh, Abbie, please don't cry.'

She clutched at him and the next moment she was lifting her head to him as he bent to her, meeting his mouth as it came down. He kissed her, his lips soft and urgent. She felt his warm tongue wet against her own, and then gasped slightly as his hand moved over her body and cupped her breast. 'Oh, Arthur,' she gasped as they broke from the kiss, 'tell me you love me.' She had to hear the words that would help to make it right. 'Please – tell me you love me.'

Still with his hand on her breast he looked at her for a long moment without speaking. Beyond his head the snow whirled past the window. They were wrapped in a pale, silent world, the only sounds the sounds of their breathing, the rustle of their clothing on the hay. 'Arthur, you know I love you,' she said. 'Tell me you love me too.'

But instead of speaking the words she wanted to hear, he was releasing her, drawing away, his expression clouded with anguish.

'What's wrong?' she said.

He got to his feet. 'This. Our being here like this.'

She didn't want to hear the doubt in his voice, the beginnings of his guilt.

He turned from her, gazing unseeingly through the window. 'I shouldn't have done that.'

'Please, don't say that. It was right. It was the right thing.'

'No.' He shook his head. 'No.'

'Arthur, you love me. We love one another. You know that.'

He turned to face her now. 'I love Jane.'

'But – you kissed me. You just kissed me.'

'I know.'

'You're not trying to tell me that it didn't mean anything. I know better.'

'I shouldn't have done it.'

'Arthur, don't keep saying that. You make it sound like something – something bad, something wrong.'

'It *was* wrong.'

She got to her feet. 'You keep saying that. You just kissed me, touched me – and now you tell me it meant nothing.'

'Abbie – this isn't getting us anywhere,' he said. 'Let's not pursue it. We have to forget that it happened.'

The fury of the snow had lessened. There was a little more light in the barn and she could see his face more clearly, see remorse there. 'And you can do that, can you?'

'You have a husband and son. I have a wife and daughter,' he said. 'And nothing could make me hurt Jane. I wouldn't do such a thing for anything on earth.'

'But you just kissed me.'

'I'm sorry. I shouldn't have. But it's done now and I can't take it back. But you must understand that it doesn't change a thing. Our lives are different now. When Jane and –'

'Jane,' she said bitterly. 'Jane Jane Jane.'

'Abbie, don't. Please don't speak her name like that. She loves you, you know that.'

She brushed wisps of hay from her dress, took her coat from the hook and began to put it on. 'I've had a demonstration of that love.'

'Abbie – please. Jane didn't scheme against you. What happened between us was something that – that just happened.'

'Yes – life is like that.'

423

In silence she put on her bonnet while at the same time he brushed himself down, shook his overcoat and put it on. When they were both dressed again he reached out and touched her gently on the cheek. 'We must go.'

Her chin quivered while the tears in her eyes blurred the image of him standing before her. As she dabbed at her eyes he moved to the window. 'The snow's almost stopped now.' He stretched up on tiptoe and looked out. 'There's no one about.' He turned back to her. 'Come on – I'll walk with you to the main road. You'll get a ride from there.'

Dumbly she nodded. They stood gazing at one another for a moment and then together moved towards the door. 'Let me go first,' Abbie said, 'in case anybody's near. We mustn't be seen together.'

While he lingered in the doorway she made her way across the snow-covered yard. There was no sign of anyone else about, and no sound disturbed the quiet but for the crunch of her boots in the snow. Keeping as far from the farmhouse as she could, she eventually located what she supposed was the footpath leading to the main road. As she made her way along it she looked back and saw Arthur following some fifty yards or so behind.

Well out of sight of the farmhouse and also of the road ahead, she stopped in the shelter of a little holly thicket and waited for him to catch up with her. In a little while he was at her side. They stood in silence. Everything around was clad in white, only the path they had trodden showing any disturbance of the virgin snow.

'You'll be all right now, will you?' Arthur said. 'You won't have to walk far, and once on the road you'll soon find someone who'll give you a ride into Frome.'

'Don't worry about me.' Silence between them again, then she added, 'We'd best say goodbye, then. I – I wish you good fortune, Arthur.'

'Thank you. You too.'

'Thank you.'

'Well – goodbye.'

'Goodbye, Abbie.'

She put out her gloved hand and he took it briefly in his. 'Before we go,' she said, 'I'd just like you to tell me one thing.'

'If I can.' He looked slightly anxious, as if fearing what was to come.

'Oh, you can. And honestly.'

'Honestly, certainly.'

'Tell me – when you and Jane decided to marry, were you truly in love with her?'

'Abbie – why are you doing this?'

'You're avoiding my question, Arthur. Please, tell me: were you truly in love with her?'

'Abbie, don't do this.'

She gave a little nod. 'And you're still avoiding my question. But it doesn't matter. I think I have my answer. Oh, what we will not do for decency's sake . . .' She gave him a trace of a smile, then turned and, picking up her skirts, moved on along the snow-deep path.

A little while later, as she walked along the edge of the road towards Frome, a carriage approached, moving in the same direction. To her relief she saw that it was a cab driven by a Frome fly proprietor. She hailed it, it drew to a halt beside her, she got in and moments later they were setting off. Just before the carriage turned a bend she looked back over her shoulder and glimpsed Arthur's distant figure moving through the snowy field towards the road.

Entering the house, she found to her relief that Oliver was asleep in the nursery and that Louis had not yet returned.

She washed, changed her clothes and went to lie on the bed in the main guest room. There she lay, thinking of her meeting with Arthur and their time together in the barn. Covered with a rug, she slept for a while.

She dreamed as she slept. It was a dream similar to the one she had had in times past. Before her was a dark, shadowed shape that slowly moved and changed its form as she watched. And then there was a weight in her arms. Heavy, so heavy. She must set it down, she told herself; she must; but she could not; she was compelled to bear it still. When she awoke she found that there were tears on her cheek.

A little later Louis came back. Darkness had long since fallen. As he entered the room she closed her eyes, feigning sleep, and was relieved to hear him creep away again.

He returned to the room half an hour later and came to the bedside. 'Are you awake?' he said softly.

'Yes, I'm awake.' She looked up at him as he lit the lamp on the bedside table. 'Did you just get back?' she asked, already knowing the answer to her question.

'No, I got back a little while ago. And you?'

'I got home a couple of hours since.'

'Were you all right?'

'All right?'

'I wondered whether you might have got caught in the snow.'

'Oh – well – just briefly.'

'You managed to find shelter, did you?'

'Yes.'

'How were Eddie and Violet?'

'Fine. They're fine.'

He frowned. 'Are you ill?'

'Ill? No – though I've got a bit of a headache.'

'What are you doing in here? Why didn't you lie on our own bed?'

She responded with a shrug. He gazed down at her for a moment longer, then moved to the window. He looked out into the dark for a second then closed the curtains.

'I hope you didn't catch a chill in the snow,' he said as he turned back to her.

'No, I'm perfectly fine.'

'You didn't stay that long with Eddie and Violet if you got caught in the storm. You can't have done.'

'No.'

'It didn't last such a long time, but it was very fierce while it lasted. Where did you find shelter?'

She frowned. 'Oh, for goodness' sake, Louis, all these questions.'

A little silence. Avoiding his eyes and at the same time trying to appear casual, she said, 'I think I'll sleep in here tonight, Louis, if you don't mind.'

He studied her for a moment then gave a brief, slow nod. 'As you like.'

'Well,' she said, 'it's just that I . . .' Her words came to a halt.

'You don't need to explain.' He paused. 'Shall you be getting up for dinner?'

'Yes, I'll be down soon. I've got to see to Oliver, anyway.'

As he turned away something on the carpet caught his eye, and he stooped and picked it up. He straightened, holding a little piece of hay. Abbie saw it shining in the light of the lamp. He placed it on the bedside table, then turned and made his way from the room.

Chapter Thirty

'Mama?'

'Yes, darling?' Abbie, sitting on the stool beside the bed, came out of her reverie and looked down at Oliver. 'What is it?'

'Shall we ever go to the seaside again?'

'Maybe – when the summer's here. We have to get through spring first.'

Oliver nodded his head on the pillow. Another thought came to him. 'And shall we go and see Grandpa again one day, and sail on the steamer on the river?'

'Perhaps. I should think so.' Gazing down at Oliver in the dim light, she thought how fine-looking he was; and also how much like Louis – both in his colouring and his features.

'Will you tell me a story, Mama?'

'Aren't you tired?'

'No.' A little shake of the head, followed by a yawn.

'Well – perhaps just a little story. What would you like?'

'*Roger Proudfoot*.'

'But that's one of Daddy's stories. You tell me you don't like the way I tell it.'

'Where did Daddy go?'

'I don't know. To look after one of his patients, I expect.'

'When he comes in tell him to come and see me before I go to sleep.'

'I will.' Abbie gently brushed his cheek. 'Are you going to close your eyes now? Just for a while.'

'All right. Just for a while.'

Abbie watched as his right thumb moved to his mouth and his eyes closed. Two minutes later he was asleep. She continued to sit there for a minute then got up and moved to the window. Moving back the curtain a little, she looked out into the April night where the lights of Frome twinkled in the newly fallen dark. After a time she let the curtain fall back in place and turned, looking down at the sleeping form of her small son.

Where did Daddy go? Oliver had asked, and she had replied that he had very likely gone to see one of his patients. Which was a lie – certainly in the way she had implied, anyway; whatever interest he had in the person he was going to see, it was not a professional one. After dinner he had wasted no time in going out again. Abbie had been sure of his purpose. She had come to recognize certain signs: the extra care taken with his appearance, his evasiveness. Why it should matter to her, she did not know, but there were occasions when she found herself consumed with jealousy. At such times she remonstrated with herself that she should be so disturbed by it. After all, his liaison kept him away from her bed – and wasn't that, she asked herself, what she wanted?

Since her meeting with Arthur in January she and Louis had not slept together on one single occasion. And it had been her doing, she could not deny that. For a time she had feared that he might insist on his rights, but he had not and they had continued to sleep apart. After a while the situation between them had – on the surface, anyway – come to be accepted. They did not quarrel. The unacknowledged understanding between them now led to fewer reasons for disagreement. They were polite and outwardly friendly with one another, but there was no warmth, no closeness. And then, a month or so ago he had – so Abbie believed – begun to find solace elsewhere. The realization had at first caused shock – apart from other emotions – not least it emphasized the growing divide between them. When the shock had diminished she was left nursing feelings of jealousy and resentment.

It was almost ten thirty when Louis finally returned. When he came in, Abbie was sitting in the drawing room, working at her mending. Having left his coat and hat in the hall, he came into the room and moved at once to the fire.

'Is it still cold out?' Abbie asked.

'Yes – quite.'

He sat down in his chair facing her and picked up the book he had been reading. He had no wish to read, she was sure, only a wish to avoid conversation. His face looked slightly flushed and she had a sudden memory of her mother, all those years ago, getting back to the cottage after her secret meeting with Pattison of the post office.

When Louis had returned from his rounds in past times, Abbie reflected, he would first have asked her how her evening had gone and would then have remarked on his visits to his patients. Of late, though, as he did tonight, he would sit silent in his chair, avoiding her eyes. She felt bitter at the situation; she was denied having what she desired, while he indulged himself whenever he chose.

'Oliver wanted a story,' she said, '– one of your stories.'

'Well,' he said as he put aside his book, 'I'll make it up to him tomorrow.'

'I also told him I'd ask you to go up and see him when you got in.'

'I will, a little later.'

'We see less and less of you these days, it seems. Your

patients are becoming even more demanding of your time just lately.'

He said nothing.

After a little silence she went on, 'Oliver was talking about our going to the seaside again. And also of going to see his grandpapa.'

'Well, why not?' he said readily. 'There's nothing to stop you.'

'I told him we must wait for the summer.'

'You don't need to do that. You can go any time.'

'I suppose we could. But he wants you to go as well.'

He spread his hands before him. 'If I could get away I would. But you know how difficult it is for me.'

'So you tell me.'

He frowned. 'What does that mean?'

She stared at him, biting back the words that sprang to her lips. The room was suddenly so quiet that she was aware of the faint hissing of the gaslight.

'Anyway,' Louis said, 'I should have thought you'd welcome the chance to go away with Oliver on your own for a while. Certainly you don't seem to find much joy around here.'

She nodded. 'You'd like me to, wouldn't you? Go away? That would leave you a clear view for a while: no commitments, no wife to see what time you leave and what time you come in.' Then, unable to stop herself, she asked almost in the same breath, 'Who is it you're seeing, Louis? And please don't insult my intelligence by denying it. You're seeing someone, I know it.'

When he did not answer she said, 'Well, I just hope you're not being too foolish. Doctors who consort with their patients are not highly regarded, I'm sure you're aware of that. Just try not to bring disgrace down upon all of us.' She glared at him, waiting for him to speak. 'Well – aren't you going to say something?'

'Do I need to?' he said, 'You already seem to have all the answers. Though I will say,' he added, 'that she is not one of my patients – so you have no need to worry on that particular score.'

She shook her head in wonder. 'It's amazing – you can be so cool about it all.'

'You just said there's no point in my denying it.'

'Just – tell me who it is.'

'It's no one you know. Anyway, what purpose would it serve, your knowing?'

'Don't you think I have a right to know?'

'Oh, Abbie, please,' he said, a note of contempt in his voice, 'spare me your self-righteousness – that holier-than-thou tone. And don't let's start talking about rights. In the eyes of the law there are certain rights I've been deprived of for a good while now.'

'Ah,' she said, stung. 'I wondered how long it would be before you threw that up in my face.'

'Abbie, you're the one who started all this. If you insist on opening this Pandora's box you mustn't be surprised at what comes out. You brought up the subject in the first place.'

She leaned forward in her chair, the half-mended stocking lying forgotten in her lap. 'How can it be avoided when you creep off to see your – your paramour like this?'

'Listen,' he said evenly, 'in case you're in the least interested, let me remind you that I'm still a relatively young man, and I have a man's usual desires. Although I've been denied a place in my marital bed I have not yet settled for celibacy. If you choose to turn away from me, then you shouldn't be surprised if I go to someone who will not.' He got up from his chair and stood looking down at her. 'In any case, I hardly think it behoves you to castigate me for my behaviour. What about your own? Or are you of the opinion that if no one knows what you yourself have done it counts for nothing?'

She frowned, momentarily taken aback. 'What are you talking about?'

'I'm talking about you and your Mr Gilmore.'

'What?'

'You heard what I said.'

'I never heard such nonsense,' she said. While her heart was pounding she tried to put contempt into her voice. 'And why do you call him *my* Mr Gilmore? And what has he got to do with anything?'

'Oh, Abbie, he's got everything to do with it – to do with everything.'

'I'm not going to listen to such foolishness,' she said. Bending her head, avoiding his accusing glare, she picked up her mending.

'You began this,' he said, 'and if it goes a little further than you would have wished then you have only yourself to blame. You should have let sleeping dogs lie. I'm talking about last January.'

'Last January? What about it?'

'The Sunday you went to see your brother in Flax-down. When I went to assist with the Marston post-mortem. Do you remember it?'

'Vaguely.' She kept her head bent.

'If you recall, there was a short, but rather violent snowstorm.'

'And –?'

'I remember that later on I asked you a few casual questions about your afternoon. And if I recall, you took me to task for being too inquisitive. I was aware, of course, of the reason for your – sensitivity.'

Her heart still thumping, she raised her head. He was looking down at her, his eyes steady. He held her gaze as

433

he said, 'You were with Gilmore that afternoon, weren't you?'

She got up, throwing down the stocking as she did so. 'I'm not listening to this. I'm going to bed.'

She made to walk by him, but he stood up, reached out and took her by the wrist. Then as she moved to free herself, he clasped her other arm. 'You have to listen.'

They stood glaring at one another. 'I can't of course know for certain what happened between you that afternoon,' he said, 'but I'm sure one doesn't need a very wild imagination to get near the truth. Human nature being what it is.' She opened her mouth to speak but he added quickly, shutting off her words, 'You see, when the snowstorm was over you were seen – the two of you – coming out of a barn. A barn on the property of a farmer on the Frome Road.'

Her cheeks burning, she was dimly aware of him releasing his hold on her. 'What liar told you this?' she said.

'No liar.'

'Who told you?'

'No one told me. It was I who saw you.'

'– You?'

He nodded. 'The post-mortem didn't take that long, and when Dr Grimmond and I had finished he asked me if I'd be kind enough to accompany him to see one of his patients who lived nearby, a certain Mr Cassin. He'd been ill for a couple of weeks and wasn't responding to treatment as well as Grimmond had hoped. And Grimmond wanted a second opinion.'

'What has this got to do with me?'

'I'm coming to that. Grimmond left his carriage at the Marston house and we set off in mine to Cassin's farm. The snow started to come down as we got near the farmhouse. I examined Mr Cassin, and afterwards his

434

wife made us tea while we waited for the snow to ease. When it had stopped I went to look through the window – and to my great astonishment I saw *you*.'

She remained silent in the face of his accusation while panic flashed through her.

'Yes,' Louis went on. 'I saw a figure in the distance – a woman's figure – walking away from the farm in the direction of the main road. And although you were quite some distance away I recognized you at once by your coat. I realized of course what had happened – you'd been on your way back from Flaxdown and had taken shelter from the snow. Nothing wrong in that. Anyway, I was just about to get my coat and go after you, when I saw him, the man. He was a couple of minutes behind you, but he was walking in the same direction.' He came to a halt, waiting for Abbie's reaction.

'You said I was seen coming out of a barn,' she said. 'But now you say I was just seen walking near the farm.'

'I know you'd been in the barn,' he said. 'I know it because a little later I went out into the yard – to all intents and purposes to go to the stable to check on the horse – and I walked up towards where I'd seen you and the man going by. I saw your footprints in the snow. And his. And I saw that they all came from the barn. Later, when Grimmond and I drove back out onto the road there was no sign of you. Obviously you'd found your cab by then. I did see your friend, though, walking alone at the side of the road. I didn't know who he was, but Grimmond put me wise. He knew the man by sight, and told me his name was Gilmore. Arthur Gilmore.' A pause and a nod. 'I'm glad you're not foolish enough to deny it.'

Staring down at the carpet Abbie said, 'I'm not denying it. But why should you assume that because we took shelter in the barn together something – took place between us?'

435

He said nothing for a moment, then he reached out, put a hand under her chin and lifted her head. 'Will you swear to it?' he said.

She made no answer, but with a sudden, violent blow dashed his hand away.

'I thought as much,' he said.

'It wasn't like that. It wasn't like that at all.'

'Was it not?' He gave a faint smile. 'Have it your way, my dear.'

'Louis, please –'

'Abbie,' he broke in, 'I really don't care that much any more.'

'But we didn't – we didn't . . . ' She let her words tail off.

'You didn't what? What are you trying to say?'

'We didn't – things didn't – go that far . . . '

He gave a short, humourless laugh. 'Oh, so things didn't go *that* far, huh? That's rich, that is. Well, things obviously went some way. Or why else should you be so secretive, so guilt-ridden, so defensive.' He shook his head. 'And you have the nerve to be moralistic with me – to remind me of my position and tell me not to bring shame upon you. You're astonishing, Abbie. That night – the night after you had been with him, Gilmore – you insisted on sleeping in the guest room. I didn't say anything, but I don't mind telling you that that, coming on top of what I had just that day discovered, hurt me very much.' He frowned, as if in bewilderment. 'This thing you've got for Gilmore – I don't understand it. When we married I thought it would be only a matter of time before you got him out of your system. I thought that if I did all the right things you would surely come to love me in time. I thought I would earn your love. But I was wrong, wasn't I?' He sighed. 'I wonder now whether you'll ever be free of him. I feel as if I don't know you any more. It's as if I'm married to a stranger.' He put a hand on either side of her face and stood gazing at her, his eyes burning into her own. 'Where have you been these past three and a half years? Not with me, that's for sure.'

She said nothing.

'You love him, don't you?' he said.

'Please, Louis.'

'Tell me. Then I'll know what it is I have to fight. You love him, don't you? Tell me the truth.'

She did not answer, and he released her, letting his hands fall to his sides. 'Go on, then. You're so anxious to get away. Go on to your celibate bed. Get out of my sight before I do something I might regret.'

Summoning all her dignity, she turned and moved towards the door. As she reached it his voice came:

'I don't think I can fight it, Abbie. Sometimes I don't even feel that he's real. Sometimes I feel you're obsessed not with him but with a ghost. And how can I fight that?'

Over the days following, Abbie did her best to avoid Louis. Her feelings were an uncomfortable mixture of resentment, bitterness and guilt, and she despaired of the situation ever improving. She toyed briefly with the idea of going away – of just taking Oliver and leaving – but stopped short of any serious consideration of the act. For one thing she had no idea where she could go. And even if there were a ready refuge she could not remain there. For how would she support Oliver and herself? Besides, her own desires apart, such a course would be too cruel. Oliver and Louis loved one another deeply and she could not in all conscience separate them.

Then, several weeks later, on a Sunday afternoon in late June, matters came to a head.

Oliver, in the care of Maria, had gone out for a walk in the sun. Abbie had just seen them off and was sitting in her room, reading. There came a tap on her door and when she called out Louis entered.

'Abbie,' he said immediately, 'we have to talk.'

'Oh, Louis, must we?' she said. 'This is all so upsetting and –'

'You think I enjoy it?'

'No, of course not.' She closed her book and put it on the table at her side.

Louis said, 'You don't think I've been happy these past weeks, months, do you? I assure you I have not.'

'I don't imagine you have been.'

'Not for a moment. And neither have you.' He moved to the bed and sat down. 'We've got to be adult about this. We can't just keep running away from the situation.'

'No, I suppose not.'

'We have to try to reach some sort of understanding. For Ollie's sake if for nothing else. Don't you agree?'

'Of course.'

'Who knows, we might even be able to find some degree of contentment if we try hard enough. It can't be worse than this. The silences between us; the cool politeness when we're together. Wouldn't you like things to be easier?'

'It goes without saying.'

He gave a little nod. 'Then just tell me something. Tell me what it is you want.'

'What do I want?'

'Tell me. Because I don't know. I'm not being melodramatic. I'm just trying to find out what we should do – what's best for the three of us.'

'Oh, Louis,' she said, 'do you think this is getting us anywhere? It's not only me. It's obvious that the whole thing has turned out to be a bitter disappointment to you. Perhaps the simple truth is that we're just . . . not right for one another. Perhaps you expected too much.'

He frowned. 'I? Expected too much? Abbie, with the love I felt for you I –'

'Ah,' she said, 'you speak of the love you *felt* for me. You speak of your love for me in the past tense.'

'For God's sake,' he said, 'what do you expect from me? Do you want to reject me and still have me protest undying devotion? You can't have it all ways.' When she said nothing he added, 'It wasn't always like this. Before we were married we were such good friends. And with our marriage I had such high hopes – particularly when Oliver came.' He paused. 'Most people would think we've got everything we need to make us happy. But for you it's not enough, is it?'

She remained silent.

'You must get rid of this obsession, Abbie,' he said.

'What obsession is this?'

'You know what I'm talking about. What are you going to do, spend the rest of your life hankering after something that's never going to be yours? Because Gilmore will never be yours. Never. You don't think he's going to give up his wife and child, do you? Give up everything in order to set up house with you – in a state of unmarried bliss?'

'Don't be tasteless,' she said. 'It's not becoming.'

'Abbie, for your own sake you must give it up. It's a wild-goose chase. And if you're not careful it will destroy you and you'd better watch out that it doesn't destroy others as well.'

'I thought you said just now you didn't want to be melodramatic.'

'I'm not. But what's left of our marriage? Tell me. We can't keep avoiding things just because they're not pretty to look at. I don't know where we go from here. I don't know what to do for the best any more. I only know this is no good for either one of us or for Ollie. If we go on like this we'll end up hating one another. I don't know about you, but I'd like to save our marriage. To that end, for what it's worth, I forgive you. And I –'

Her voice heavy with irony, she said, 'Oh, that's most kind of you. How magnanimous you are.'

'Please,' he said, frowning, '– let me finish. I was going to say that just because you've been at fault doesn't make it right for me to transgress also. And I have been at fault too. I can't pretend otherwise.'

'I'm glad you admit it.'

He shook his head. 'This isn't easy, you know. If we are to salvage anything then I think we have to start with forgiveness of past wrongs. Don't you think so?'

She gave a grudging nod of acquiescence. 'Yes.'

Looking at her steadily he said, 'I might as well tell you, Abbie, that I would never give Oliver up.'

She bridled. 'Why should you? Why do you say that? Have I ever asked you to consider such a thing?'

'No – but I want to put my cards on the table ... so you'll have less chance of misunderstanding me.'

'I think I understand you well enough,' she said.

'I wonder.' He was silent for a moment, then he said, 'Anyway – think about things. Perhaps you need a little time.'

'Time?'

'Yes, without me being around. I thought it might not be a bad thing if you and Oliver took a little vacation.'

'Oh? Where?'

'That's up to you. Wherever you want to go. Perhaps to the coast. Maybe Brighton or Southend. Go to a hotel somewhere for a month or so, or rent a house. It's up to you. He's keen to go, you said so.'

'If I do go away how do you think it will help us?'

'Well – at least you'll have time to think things over. And I think you need that.'

440

'What are you hoping will come out of it, my going away? That I'll be like St Paul on the road to Damascus? There'll be some great revelation and I'll suddenly come to my senses?'

'I'm trying to help us, Abbie,' he said. 'I don't know about you, but I'd like to try and save our marriage before it's too late. But if you've got different ideas . . . ' There was anger now in his face. 'I'm trying to offer a solution to a very real problem. But perhaps I'm just wasting my energy; perhaps I'm simply flogging a dead horse.' Turning, he stalked out of the room.

That night Abbie, wearing her dressing gown over her nightdress, sat in the drawing-room, a tray of tea beside her. It was almost two o'clock. The house was very quiet. The servants had gone to bed long ago. Feeling restless, she had been unable to sleep and in the end had come downstairs. She was waiting now for Louis's return. Just before eight he had been summoned by a local midwife to the bedside of an expectant mother, the young wife of a farmhand.

Since their talk that afternoon Abbie had thought a great deal about the situation between Louis and herself, and she realized that he had been right in so many of the things he had said. Why, then, had she been so disagreeable in her response? No wonder he had stormed out of the room. There was an old saying that guilt turned to hostility. Is that what had happened with her? Had the hostility she had shown been born out of her sense of guilt? Whatever it was or whatever its cause, it had solved nothing – that much she was sure of. Left alone to think things over, she had come to realize that much of what he had said made sense. They had to make an effort now or their marriage would soon be beyond saving.

She had been sitting there for close on an hour when

there came the faint sound of the carriage on the drive. A little while later she heard the front door opening and closing. There were footsteps in the hall, then the drawing-room door opened and Louis, his coat over his arm, looked in. He seemed surprised to see her still up.

'I saw a crack of light under the door,' he said. 'I thought the maid had left one of the lamps burning.'

'No,' Abbie said, 'I couldn't sleep so I came back downstairs.'

He nodded, stood there for a moment, then said, 'Well – I'm very tired. I'm going to bed. Goodnight now.'

As he started to back out into the hall Abbie spoke his name. He came to a stop. 'Yes?'

'Would you like some tea?' she said. She was very much aware of the awkwardness between them.

He hesitated for a second, then said, 'Thank you.' Closing the door behind him, he put down his coat, crossed to the fireside chair facing her own and sat down.

'Have you eaten anything?' she asked.

'I'm not hungry. The tea will be fine.'

In the kitchen she made fresh tea and, back in the drawing room, set it down on the small table beside the fire. Glancing at Louis as she straightened she saw that he had fallen asleep. She sat in her own chair and looked at him. She noticed the dark circles under his eyes, a deep crease between his eyebrows, and lines running from the outer edges of his nostrils down beside his slightly open mouth. Hands resting on the chair arm, his fingers twitched spasmodically a couple of times. He looked utterly exhausted. Loath to wake him, she poured herself a cup of tea and sipped at it, watching him. A few moments later he opened his eyes.

'You fell asleep,' she said. 'You must be terribly tired.'

'I am, rather.'

'I'll pour your tea.' She poured him a cup and passed it

to him. He drank from it, then placed it beside him. 'You were gone so long,' she said. 'Did everything go all right at the Tippets'? Was it a boy or a girl?'

He shook his head then bent forward, putting a hand to his forehead. 'A boy. But I lost them both – mother and son.'

'Oh, Louis . . . ' When he raised his head she saw the shine of tears in his eyes. 'Louis,' she said. 'Oh, I'm so sorry.'

He nodded and wiped his eyes. 'Twenty-three years old and looking as if she'd find childbirth the easiest thing in the world. But nothing went right. She was in so much pain, too. And there was nothing I could do. She struggled for all those hours – and after all that fighting she just . . . slipped away.' He shook his head. 'I've seen my share of death over the years, but there are some things that one just doesn't seem able to get used to. Her husband, poor man, he's inconsolable. And there's nothing to be done.'

They sat in silence for some while, then he said wearily, 'You say you couldn't sleep?'

'Yes, but – also I wanted to talk to you.'

'Oh?' he said carefully. 'What about?'

'I've been thinking about what you said.' She shook her head. 'I got so – tense this afternoon when you tried to talk. That's the way I am so much of the time lately. And it's not your fault – and I'm sorry.' She looked down into her cup. 'I want what you want, Louis. I'd like things to be better between us – if they can be.'

'They can be,' he said, 'if we both want it badly enough.'

'Yes, I know.' She paused. 'And as you suggested, I think it would be a good idea for me to go away for a while. I think I'd like to do that. Ollie and I, we could go

to the coast for a few weeks. As you said, it will give us –
you and me – an opportunity to think things over.'

'Yes.'

'So – I'll make arrangements, shall I?'

'Very good.'

'And when I come back I'll –'

'Please.' He raised a hand. 'Don't make me any
promises. Just see how things go. For the moment let's
not ask more than that.'

Chapter Thirty-One

The July sun was very warm. Before lunch Abbie, Oliver and Maria had gone bathing in the sea. Now, however, the tide was ebbing, so while Abbie rested in the shade of a large beach umbrella Oliver and Maria – obeying instructions to keep always within Abbie's sight – had gone exploring further along the beach. Every now and again Abbie would glance up from her book to check on the safety of the pair. After a time she saw them turn and start back along the beach towards her. As they drew nearer Oliver raised his arm and waved. Abbie waved back, observing with an inward groan that he had pulled out the front of his shirt before him and was carrying something in it. More seashells.

'Look, Mama, look!' Oliver called a minute later as he came across the sand towards her. 'We found lots more shells.'

'Yes,' Abbie replied, 'so I see.'

As she put her book to one side Oliver knelt beside her and spilled a cascade of shells onto the rug.

'Oh, my! They're beautiful,' Abbie said, flicking a little smile at Maria as she sat down nearby.

'They're for Daddy.'

'But you've already got so many for him at the hotel.'

'But he'll like them,' Oliver protested.

'Oh, I'm sure he will. He'll love them.'

'He can't get any for himself, can he?'

'No – that's true.'

'I mean, he's had to stay behind and work.'

'I know. Well, he's going to be very pleased, I'm sure.'

Oliver gathered up the shells and put them into an old straw basket. Then, his task finished, he brushed the sand from his hands. 'Maria and I are thirsty, Mama,' he said.

'Really? In that case you'd better have some lemonade.' From a makeshift picnic basket Abbie took a bottle of lemonade and poured some into two beakers, handing one to Oliver and the other to Maria. She watched Oliver as he drank. The vacation, she thought, had been such a good thing. They had been in Weston-super-Mare for over two weeks now, and so far everything had worked out well; the hotel was comfortable and the weather had been good to them, for the most part sunny and warm – a condition that was reflected in their glowing cheeks and tanned limbs. In such fine weather they had been able to come to the beach to bathe and relax nearly every day, and – a thrilling development – under Abbie's tuition Oliver, after less than a week, had learned to swim. From this point on there had been no holding the child; he wanted to be in the water at every opportunity available.

When Oliver and Maria had finished the lemonade Abbie replaced the beakers in the basket. Oliver was getting to his feet again. Looking out at the receding waterline he said, 'I don't suppose the tide will be back for a long time yet, will it?'

'I'm afraid not, darling. There'll be no more bathing today.'

He turned to Maria. 'Shall we go for another walk, Maria? But the other way this time.' He pointed off down the beach in the opposite direction.

Maria looked at Abbie for an answer. Abbie nodded. 'Yes, but don't go too far away. And stay within my sight so that I can keep an eye on you.'

Already Oliver was reaching out for Maria's hand. 'Come on, Maria.'

'And keep your hat on,' Abbie called after him.

Smiling after them, Abbie lay with her chin on her arm, watching as they wandered along the beach, every now and again stopping to look at something in the sand. Oliver could come to little harm here. Maria was a sensible girl and with the tide going out the beach offered no intrinsic dangers. They couldn't get lost, either, as they were now familiar with the spot where they had made their little settlement. They had chosen it on the first day – a place relatively secluded and sheltered from the breeze – and had come back to it nearly every day.

Abbie watched the pair for a minute longer then closed her eyes. From further off she heard the shouts of children playing, from above the crying of gulls, while from behind, beyond the promenade, came the distant sounds of carriages and horses' hooves. At her side her book lay forgotten.

Louis came into her mind – as he had so many times since leaving Frome. She felt that the night he had come in following the death in childbirth of Mrs Tippet and her baby son might well have marked something of a turning point in their lives. While they had not got back to any degree of intimacy, still they had begun to develop once more a little closeness, a little more trust – evident in so many things that passed between them. From then until she and Oliver had left for their vacation they had had ten days together – and as those days had passed Abbie had become more and more aware that perhaps after all they might be able to find some lasting common ground that would enable them to live together in some degree of harmony.

At this time on a Friday, she reflected, Louis would most likely be out on house calls. She had a sudden picture of him as he had been at the station on the Wednesday morning of their departure. When he had picked Oliver up in his arms to say goodbye the child had clung to him, arms tight around his neck. 'Daddy,' he had said, 'I want you to come with us. Why won't you come with us?' And Louis had replied that he had to work, that he could not leave his patients. Later, when the train was in, Abbie had been at the open carriage window, facing Louis as he stood on the platform.

'Now you two have a good time,' he had said. 'I know it'll do you good to have a change of scene.'

'Yes . . .'

'And stay as long as you like.' He smiled. 'Within reason.'

'Yes, within reason.' A pause. 'I'll drop you a line in the next day or two. Tell you how we're getting on.'

'I'll look forward to hearing. Look after yourselves.'

'We will.'

The whistle blew and the train began to move, and with Oliver standing waving at her side, Abbie watched until Louis was no longer in sight.

Since their arrival in the resort Abbie had written to Louis several times, reporting on their pastimes and conveying to him affectionate and newsy messages from Oliver. He had written back expressing happiness at their continuing pleasure.

Now, lying in the warm air, Abbie thought back over the time of their stay at the resort. Since leaving Frome she had felt almost tangibly the weight of her problems falling away. She had of course found much contentment in Oliver's happiness, but it went deeper than that. With the passing days she had found a growing sense of peace. Being so far from the scene of recent conflicts, perhaps she was seeing things more clearly, getting them in perspective. And viewed so, the problems seemed some-how less potent than they had been. Most vital of all, they no longer appeared to be insurmountable.

As far as her life with Louis was concerned, she knew she had either to accept it or reject it. There could be no compromises. She must commit herself to her marriage and all that went with it – or turn her back upon it. And she could not contemplate the latter. For one thing it would mean that she would lose Oliver – which was unthinkable. Louis had made it clear that he wouldn't give up his son and she couldn't blame him for that. Besides, Oliver's life in Frome was a good life. He had love, security and comfort – all that a child could need.

She sighed. Raising her head, she looked out over the water and saw near the horizon the darker shape of a steamer going by. This time, this place, she reminded herself, did not constitute her reality. They had been here over two weeks and soon she must start to think about returning home – which would mean that choices and decisions had to be made. But in truth, she realized, she did not really have a choice. Whatever her hopes might once have been there were no options available to her now. Arthur could no longer be a part of her life. He had made his commitments – and he could not give them up. There was nothing for it but to accept her present situation and make the best of it. And after all, her situation could, with effort and thought, bring her some happiness. She had a comfortable home and wanted for nothing materially. Even more important, she had a young son whom she adored. Yes, she determined that from now she would make the best of everything as far as she could. Louis was a good man and whatever lack there might be in their relationship she could not in all honesty see that it was due to any fault of his. The lack was in herself; contrary to her expectations, she had simply found it impossible to return his love.

From some distant place came the sound of a clock striking the hour of three. When Oliver and Maria returned it would be time to start back to the hotel for tea. Afterwards Oliver would sleep for an hour and Abbie could indulge herself in a soothing bath. She stretched on the rug. Her bare feet, outside the umbrella's shade, were warm in the sun.

While Abbie lay relaxing, Oliver and Maria, fifty yards along the beach, were attempting to build a sandcastle. They had only their hands as tools, however, and the task was not easy.

As they worked there came from the promenade a familiar voice:

'Oliver . . .'

Oliver and Maria turned to the sound and a moment later Oliver was giving a wild yell of delight. 'Daddy! Daddy!' At the same time Louis climbed over the rail and jumped from the promenade onto the sand. Moments later he was striding forward and sweeping his son up in his arms. He held him close for a second or two, then set him down and crouched before him.

'Well, look at my little boy! He's the colour of an Indian!'

'Daddy,' Oliver said, 'we didn't know you were coming.'

'No,' Louis replied, 'neither did I until a couple of days ago. Then I decided I had to come and see how you were.' He gave him another hug. 'Have you missed me? Or have you been having so much fun that you've hardly given me a thought?' Without waiting for an answer, he turned to Maria, who stood shyly a yard or two away, and asked whether she was having a good time. She replied that she was enjoying herself very much.

'Good.' He turned back to Oliver. 'Well – let's go and find your mother, shall we?'

Abbie, lying down, heard the excited sound of Oliver's voice calling to her, and opening her eyes she saw him running across the sand towards her. In the same moment she saw Louis and Maria walking a few yards behind.

'Look, Mama!' Oliver cried, 'I've got Daddy here! Daddy's come to see us.'

As Louis reached her side Abbie sat up, looked up at him and smiled. 'Yes,' she said, 'so I see.'

That evening after Oliver had been put to bed Louis went in to say goodnight. Sitting on a small stool beside the bed he leaned over, looking down into his sleepy eyes.

'You're a tired little chap, aren't you?' he murmured.

Oliver yawned. 'Just a little.'

As Louis adjusted the sheet about his chin, Oliver took hold of his hand. 'Daddy, did you know that I can swim?'

'Yes, your mama told me. What a clever boy you are.'

'Mama taught me. Now I swim every day. And every day I can swim a little further.'

'That's wonderful. I'm very proud of you.'

'Maria can't swim yet. Next year I shall teach her. Can you swim, Daddy?'

'Yes, I can swim. Not well, but a little.'

'Tomorrow we can go swimming together, can't we?'

'I'm sorry, Ollie, but I'm afraid I've got to get back.'

'But haven't you come to stay with us?'

'Not for long. I have to go back home tomorrow.'

'So soon?' Oliver gave a little groan.

'I don't want to go, but there's nothing for it. My patients have to be looked after.'

Oliver clicked his tongue. 'They always do. But you won't go without seeing me in the morning, will you?'

'Of course not.' Louis clapped a hand to his forehead in a melodramatic gesture. 'I'll forget my head next – I brought you a little present and forgot all about it.'

Oliver at once became more wakeful. 'Where is it?'

'In my case in my room. I haven't unpacked it yet.'

'Oh – can I have it, please?'

'It's too late now. You go to sleep and you shall have it tomorrow.'

'Oh, can't I have it now?'

'No, wait till tomorrow, there's a good boy.'

'What is it? Tell me what it is.'

'Wait and see.' Louis leaned down and kissed him. 'Goodnight now, my dear.'

When he had gone from the room Abbie went in to say her goodnights.

'Daddy brought me a present,' Oliver said as she bent to him.

'Did he now? And what did he bring you?'

'I don't know. I haven't seen it yet.'

'Oh, so you've a surprise waiting for you. I love surprises.'

'I do too.' A wide yawn. 'Daddy's going back home tomorrow, Mama. Did you know that?'

'Yes. He can't spare the time to stay longer.'

'Because of his patients.'

'Yes, because of his patients.'

A little pause. 'When are we going home, Mama – you and Maria and I?'

'Well,' Abbie shrugged, 'I haven't decided. Why?'

'I was thinking – can we go back tomorrow with Daddy?'

'Aren't you enjoying yourself here?'

'Yes, but – I want to go back home. Can we?'

Abbie paused for a moment before answering, 'Well – we'll see.'

With Maria sharing Oliver's room and watching over him, Abbie and Louis went downstairs to dine. Abbie was wearing a new gown, which she had bought in the town just the day before. It was of lavender cotton, decorated with bows and pleated frills. With it she wore a fine lace shawl draped over her shoulders.

When they had consulted the menu and Louis had given their orders Abbie said, 'I must say you gave us a surprise, appearing like that.'

Louis smiled. 'I guessed I would. But I got tired of being on my own, so I decided to come and see you both if I could find a locum. And I managed to, so here I am. Fortunately the hotel had a room for me.'

'How did you know where to find us this afternoon?'

'I learned at the hotel that you had gone off to the beach, so I just kept looking.'

'Oliver was so thrilled to see you.'

He smiled, pleased. 'Yes, I know.'

'What time are you leaving tomorrow?'

'There's a train just after ten thirty which I'd like to catch if I can.'

When dinner was over they moved into the lounge where they were served coffee.

Louis said, 'Well, you've told me all about Oliver – how he's been getting on. What about you? Have you been all right?'

She shrugged. 'Oh – I've been well.'

'Have you enjoyed yourself?'

'Very much.'

'Good. You look extremely well. The sea air suits you. Or perhaps it's a little more than the sea air.'

'What do you mean?'

'You're looking more – relaxed.'

When their coffee cups were empty Louis suggested they take a stroll and they went out into the balmy evening air. They walked along the promenade a little apart, and eventually came to a stop and stood at the rail looking over the beach. The waters of the Bristol Channel looked dark as ink, a darkness broken here and there by the twinkling lights of ships. The scene was very peaceful.

Into the silence Louis said, 'I've missed you both.'

'Have you?' She kept her eyes on the view before her.

'The house has seemed very empty. Not only without Ollie's presence, but without yours, too.'

She nodded and gave a little sigh. 'I've been doing some thinking while I've been here. About you and me.'

'Yes?' He waited for her to go on.

'Somehow – somehow in Frome I couldn't seem to think straight, but while I've been here things have made a little more sense to me.' She turned to him. He seemed very tall standing beside her. 'I'm sorry for what I've done.'

'Oh – Abbie . . .' His hand moved and rested on hers as she held the rail.

'You've been very good about – so much,' she said. 'And I think I understand why – why you – sought consolation elsewhere. I can't blame you for it.'

His hands moved to her shoulders, turning her to face him. His eyes were very steady upon her. 'Abbie,' he said, 'can't we put it all behind us – all that melancholy business? Can't we make another start – for all our sakes?'

She nodded. 'I'd like to. I'd like to try.'

'Do you mean it?'

'Yes.'

He let out a deep sigh and drew her towards him.

'Abbie, it's what I've wanted to hear. You can't imagine how much.'

She gave a nod. 'All I can promise is to try my very best to make it work between us.'

'That's all I ask. And I promise the same thing.'

A little silence, then she said, 'What about – what about your friend?'

'That's all finished,' he said. 'I've already been to see her, to tell her that it's over between us. She – she was most understanding.' He looked out over the water. 'We shall not speak of her again.'

'No.'

'And please, never again shall we speak of *him* – Mr Gilmore. Is that agreed also?'

'Yes.'

He gazed at her for a moment in silence, then leaned forward and very lightly touched his lips upon hers.

'Shall we all be going home tomorrow?' he said.

'Yes,' she said. 'We'll all go home together.'

They walked back to the hotel arm in arm. Upstairs they went into Abbie's suite where, stealing quietly into the connecting bedroom, Abbie looked closely at the silent figures in the beds and then crept out again. Softly she closed the door behind her and whispered to Louis, 'They're both sleeping very soundly.'

He came towards her as she stood beside the door, looked down at her for a second, then took her in his arms. He kissed her, his lips soft and warm and insistent upon her own. For a moment she felt a resistance building within her, so fast, so powerful, but she said to herself, *This is the path you have chosen. This is the only way.* And she forced herself to relax and she returned his kiss.

His hands reached to her lace shawl and slipped it from her shoulders. When he had laid it over a nearby chair he kissed her again, and this time she responded readily. His hands touched her breasts, then slid down her body and moved over her loins. At his touch she closed her eyes and gave a little gasp – surprised at the shiver of pleasure that ran through her. Aware of his touch leaving her, she opened her eyes in time to see him reach past her shoulder and slide home the bolt to lock the door between the two rooms. 'Just in case Ollie should wake,' he breathed, and then his hands were back upon her body and he was unbuttoning her dress.

Several minutes later, with the lights turned down low, Abbie lay naked on the bed, while before her Louis took off his own remaining clothing. In moments he, also naked, stood looking down at her. Gazing up at him, she thought how fine he looked – so tall and upright and handsome in his nakedness. He lay down beside her and smothered her face with kisses. She could feel the hot hardness of his sex against her thigh. After a little while he shifted and laid his long, firm body upon her own, and then his hands were moving down, parting her legs.

And suddenly that strange, elusive shadow was there straight out of her dream – and she froze, pressing her eyes tightly shut and gritting her teeth, while in her head a voice protested, no, no . . .

She became aware that Louis had stopped. She opened her eyes and saw his face above her as he leaned down, supporting himself on his hands. He was frowning, consternation on his face. She felt a sudden rush of guilt.

'Why – why do you stop?' she asked breathlessly.

He gazed at her for a moment without speaking, then said, 'What is it, Abbie? Tell me.'

'– I don't know what you mean.'

'What is it that gets in the way? Why can't you let yourself go?'

'I do,' she said. 'I do.'

'No.' He shook his head. 'Never fully. What is it that stops you? Are you afraid of something, is that it?'

'No, of course not.'

'Then what? Do you feel that it's somehow wrong?'

'It can't be wrong.'

'Of course it's not. It's right. It's right. And if you let it, then it can be beautiful.' He paused. 'Trust me, Abbie. Trust me.'

'Yes . . .' For some reason that she could not fathom, tears filled her eyes, spilled over and ran down the sides of her face onto the pillow.

'Oh, my dear . . . !' Louis touched at the tears. 'Don't cry. Don't cry.'

'I don't know why I'm crying,' she said. 'It's crazy, isn't it?'

He leaned down and kissed her tear-wet cheeks and temples. 'What is it? Tell me what it is.'

'I don't know. But it's all right. I'll be fine.' She was silent for a few seconds, then she said, 'I want to give you what you want, Louis. Believe me, I do. So much.'

He lay down beside her again, his arm across her body. They remained like that for several minutes, then Abbie spoke.

'Kiss me, Louis. Please, kiss me . . .'

He did so, and with a growing fervour that was at the same time very tender.

Feeling him pressed against her she felt the hardening of his sex once more. 'Tell me that you love me, Louis. Please . . .'

'I do love you, Abbie. God knows I do. I think I've loved you from the moment we met.'

He began to smother her with kisses, his lips moving down from her face to her breast, and then lower still. The feel of his lips and his tongue made her squirm and with an effort she held herself in check again. Sensing the sudden restraint he lifted his head and said, 'Give yourself to me, Abbie. Don't hold back. Take pleasure from me. Take it. Take it selfishly. Let me love you.'

Hearing his words, she felt momentarily freed, and she opened her mouth and gave a deep, deep sigh, with her breath letting go all the tension that was keeping her in check.

'Yes,' she breathed. 'Yes.'

And then, moments later, he was entering her, and she opened herself to him, suddenly wanting him inside her, wanting to keep him there. And she found herself revelling in the feel of him, in his nakedness, in her own nakedness, in their oneness. And, 'Yes, oh, yes!' she breathed again. 'Oh, Louis, yes, yes, yes.'

Chapter Thirty-Two

In all the rush to get everything packed and be off to catch the train Oliver still did not get his present from Louis.

'But Daddy, you promised,' he said as they sat in the cab on the way to the railway station.

'I know I did,' Louis said, 'but that was before you all decided to come back home with me. Then in all the hustle and bustle I'm afraid I forgot about it again.'

'You're very bad, Daddy,' Oliver said.

'I know I am. Can you forgive me?'

Oliver sighed. 'I don't know. It depends. You can at least tell me what it is.'

'Uh-uh.' Louis shook his head. 'It's going to be a surprise, I told you that.'

The boy turned to his mother. 'Mama, do you know what it is? You can tell me, can't you?'

Abbie shrugged 'I'm afraid I can't. Your papa hasn't told me.'

'Can't I have it now, then?'

Louis gestured with his thumb. 'It's still packed away.'

'Oh, Daddy, please.'

'But don't worry – he's quite safe. He won't come to any harm.'

'He?' Oliver said. 'He?'

Louis put both hands to his cheeks in an expression of mock horror. 'Oh, no! did I say "he"?'

Oliver laughed. 'Yes, you did! You did say "he"!'

'Oh, no!' Louis cried. 'I didn't say "he", did I?' He appealed to Abbie. 'I didn't say "he" did I, Mama? Please tell me I didn't!'

Abbie gave a nod. 'I rather think you did, you know.'

'Yes, you did, you did, you did!' Oliver was squealing with laughter. 'You did say "he". And now I know what it is! I think I can guess.'

Louis put his face close to the boy's. 'All right, then, so what do you think it is, Master Oliver Clever Clogs?'

'Well . . .' Oliver thrust his face pugnaciously towards his father's. 'I think it's . . .' He smiled broadly. 'It's the soldier I wanted. Is it? Is it, Daddy?'

Louis sighed, as if glad to be relieved of the burden of knowledge. 'It could be,' he said.

Later, on the train, with Oliver nestled in the crook of Abbie's arm, he was soon asleep. Abbie sat gazing out at the scenery. Beyond the smoke-begrimed window the fields and woodlands glided by. She was aware of feeling different on this homeward journey compared with how she had felt on the way out. When she and Oliver and Maria had left home for their stay at the coast she had, in spite of being hopeful, had many misgivings about the future. Now so much seemed to have changed – and in such a very short time. She was sure now, if only for Oliver's sake, that her place was with Louis. And perhaps not only for Oliver's sake, she said to herself; for last night things had happened that had somehow made it all different. Last night she and Louis had made love until the small hours. Afterwards, as she had lain there, drifting off to sleep in his embrace, she had been aware of feeling glad of all the pleasure she had known that night, the pleasure that she had found in Louis's body, and for what that unaccustomed pleasure had meant. For one thing it had made her aware of her own body's needs and desires. Needs and desires she had not known since the day of the fair.

Turning from the window, she looked at Louis as he sat opposite her reading a newspaper. With a little rush of pleasure she recalled again the touch of him as they had lain together, spent and sated, after they had made love. She could remember the feel of his breath upon her hair, the warmth of him, the strength of him. But most of all she could recall the feeling of safety she had known. It had been her final thought before she had fallen asleep.

It was quite late when at last they reached Frome. Oliver had slept on and off throughout the long journey, but nevertheless was still tired. Louis carried him into the house where, after a light supper, Abbie and Maria put him to bed. When Abbie had tucked him in and kissed him, Louis went in to say goodnight. He found him very tired, but not so tired that he had forgotten the present that had been promised him.

'But it's still packed up in our luggage,' Louis said when Oliver asked him for it.

'But you said I could have it,' Oliver protested.

'I know I did. But I tell you what: if you go to sleep now I promise – *I promise* – that it'll be unpacked tonight, and before I go to bed I'll bring it in and put it right here next to your bed. Then, in the morning when you wake, it will be the first thing you see. How about that?'

'You promise?'

'Cross my heart.'

'All right.'

'And you'll try to sleep?'

'Yes.'

Louis bent lower and kissed him on the cheek. 'There's a good boy.'

*

In the drawing room Abbie read a letter that had arrived the previous day from Iris inviting Abbie and Louis to her wedding. She and Alfred were to be married in London on 2 September. Iris wrote that he was still employed by the London Steamship Company, playing the cornet in one of the brass bands that entertained on the company's Thames pleasure steamers. It was only a temporary position, however, Iris added, for in the autumn he was to join the orchestra of a major London theatre.

'Oh, can we go to Iris's wedding, Louis?' Abbie asked as Louis finished reading the letter. 'Please say we can.'

'Of course we can,' he said. 'And even if I can't get away there's no reason why you shouldn't go.'

'I don't want to go on my own.'

'Perhaps Eddie and Violet will be going.'

'No, they won't go. Not with the girls and so much expense. Besides, how could Eddie get the time off?'

'I suppose not. But I should think I'll be able to get away. At least we've had plenty of notice.'

'I'm so glad everything is going well for Iris,' Abbie said. 'She sounds so happy.'

'Did you realize,' Louis said, 'that the pleasure steamers on which Alfred is playing are the ones that go down to Gravesend and Sheerness? Like the ones we've been on when we've been to see Father. That's an idea,' he added, '– while we're in London for the wedding we could go to Gravesend. It's been a good while since we visited my father, and it's high time he got to see his grandson again.'

While Abbie and Louis ate supper the maid unpacked their luggage. Later, in the main bedroom, Louis showed Abbie the present he had bought for Oliver. The wooden soldier was an upright, handsome fellow, with a shining helmet and gold braid on his shoulders and cuffs. He stood to attention, his right hand holding his rifle at his side.

'Oh, Ollie will love him,' Abbie said.

'Yes, I think he will.'

He put the soldier back in his wrapping of tissue paper in the box and carried it across the landing to the nursery. He silently eased open the door, found all quiet and peaceful, and crept in. The room was illuminated only by the flame of a little nightlight that burned beside Maria's bed, and in its glow he saw that she was sleeping soundly. Stealing to Oliver's bedside he saw that he too was asleep. In the faint glow he stood looking down at him for a moment, then placed the box containing the soldier on the little chest beside his bed. Then, as silently as he had entered, he left the room.

Back in the master bedroom he found Abbie already in bed. Without any mention of the subject it was now understood that their time of sleeping apart was over.

He undressed, climbed in beside her and took her in his arms. They made love and when at last they were sated Louis put his arms around her and drew her naked body to him. After a while, with his soft breath upon her hair, they fell asleep.

Oliver awoke to the silent room. He lay there for some seconds, then sat up in bed. He was thirsty and his throat felt dry. Turning to the bedside chest, he reached out for the beaker of water that was always there, and as he did so, he saw the box. His mouth opened in a little 'O' of pleasure and surprise. His desire for water forgotten, he swung his feet out onto the floor.

Taking the lid off the box he peered at the toy soldier lying in his bed of paper. Then, discarding the lid, he moved towards Maria's bed, beside which the nightlight burned. There, in the faintly stronger glow he took the soldier from the box, shook free his tissue paper wrappings and gazed at him in breathless adoration.

And then all at once the soldier was more brightly illuminated. For a second Oliver accepted it, but then he saw the bright, flaring light and felt sudden heat. A piece of the tissue paper had fallen onto the flame of the nightlight and drifted down onto the hem of his nightshirt. With sudden terror the boy saw that his nightshirt was on fire. Giving a shriek, he let fall the soldier and ran. There was no escaping from the flames, however, and in seconds they were rising up and enveloping him.

Across the landing Abbie and Louis were awakened by his screams, and they threw themselves out of bed and ran naked from the room. Flinging open the nursery door, they found the room full of smoke. On the floor Oliver was a small, writhing shape of flame, while Maria, shrieking in terror, was ineffectually trying to beat out the flames with a pillow.

Dashing forward, Louis snatched the counterpane from Maria's bed and threw it over Oliver's blazing body. Then, kneeling beside him, he wrapped it around him, suffocating the flames. As he did this Abbie smothered the flames that had taken hold of Maria's bed sheet.

In moments the fire was out, leaving behind the smoke and the smell of burning.

With Abbie kneeling beside him, Louis gently pulled aside the counterpane that covered Oliver's body. Seeing the extent of his burns he knew that he could not survive.

Within the hour their son was dead.

PART SIX

Chapter Thirty-Three

'We're in plenty of time for the train, aren't we?' Abbie asked as Louis handed her into the cab.

'Oh, yes. Why?'

'Could you ask the driver if we can go by way of the church? I want to stop for a moment or two. I shan't be long.'

'Of course.'

When they reached the church gate Abbie got down and went into the churchyard where she made her way between the graves to the one particular little grave that lay beneath a rowan tree.

As she bent over the earth the scent of the pink roses she had placed there two days earlier rose up sweet and fragrant in the early morning air. About her black mourning skirts white clover grew in the grass, while in the branches above a robin sang out, marking his territory. So often the robin sang while she was there – though she was rarely aware of his song.

Slowly, slowly the leaden days were passing. Today was the 1st of September. Six weeks had passed since Oliver's death and for most of that time Abbie had felt as if she were living in a nightmare. It could not be real; it could not be true; it could not have happened. It had to be a dream – yes, it must be a dream – and soon she would awaken and find that everything was as it should be. Waking, and realizing, she would sigh and laugh with sheer relief. And she would say, 'I had this dream, this awful dream,' and say no more for fear that she would tempt fate. But no, she knew that it was not a dream. This nightmare was reality and there was nothing to be done about it. That was one of the truly dreadful things about it all – that no matter what she did, no matter how she wept, no matter how loudly she railed at heaven, or how she pleaded, nothing could make any difference. Oliver was dead. Dead. Even the word, as dreadful as it was, could not summon up a fraction of the awfulness of the reality it signified.

Each day she had gone about her business, but it had never been with her full concentration; she remained continually preoccupied with the knowledge of what had happened. It was never far beneath the surface. She would be doing something, some mundane chore, when all of a sudden the reality would hit her, striking her with a force that almost took her breath away. Oliver was dead. And the terrible realization would stop her in her tracks. He is dead. It was like learning the dreadful news all over again, and all over again it had to be dealt with, and she knew that she would never, ever recover. She could never ever be the same again.

Other wives would have turned to their husbands for comfort, but Abbie found that she could not. The brief reunion she and Louis had known was over – as dead as if it had never been. She felt now that she was truly alone. It had been Oliver who had been the bond between Louis and herself, and with Oliver's passing there was nothing to keep them together except for their marriage vows – which had turned out to be so many hollow words and phrases. So what was to become of her? Of them as a pair? Only time would tell. For the moment she could only try to get through each day; and that took effort enough without attempting to look into the future.

Straightening, she wiped the tears from her eyes and brushed down her skirt. And remained standing there.

If getting through these present days weren't already hard enough, there was now the promise of added difficulties to cope with. With every day that had passed in recent weeks she had become more and more convinced that she was pregnant. Unable to deal with such a situation, she had prayed that it was not so, but she knew now that she could not be mistaken.

She bent her head to the grave and whispered one more tender goodbye, then turned and started back towards the churchyard gate where the cab was waiting.

The ride to the railway station was a short one, and they were soon on the platform, waiting for the train that would take them on the first stage of their journey to London.

Tomorrow, Monday, was to be Iris's wedding day. With the death of Oliver, Abbie had at first changed her mind about attending, but eventually, after some persuasion from Iris, she had agreed. Further, as Eddie was not able to be there, Louis had agreed to give Iris away.

On board the train Abbie sat with an open book before her. She had no inclination to read; it was merely a barrier against the difficulty of conversation. These days she and Louis talked so very little. They seemed to have nothing to say to one another any more. They had gone back to sleeping in separate rooms again, while for the rest they merely went through the motions of sharing their lives. And Abbie was sure now that it would never be different. Any chance they had had of happiness had gone with Oliver's death.

Louis had made reservations for them at a hotel in Paddington, which was not too far from where Alfred's family lived and where Iris would be staying overnight. On reaching the hotel, Abbie sent Iris a note to say that they had arrived in London and would see her the following day.

The next morning they drove in a cab to Queensway where Alfred's parents kept a tobacco and confectionery shop, living in a flat above it. After being warmly greeted by the couple, Abbie was taken to the bedroom where Iris was getting dressed for the ceremony, aided by Alfred's sisters, Julia and Eleanor. Alfred himself was not in evidence; he would be going to the church directly from the nearby home of the friend who was to be his best man, with whom he had stayed overnight.

Although Abbie and Iris had corresponded regularly, they had not met for several years. Now when Abbie entered the room they fell into one another's arms. As they did so Eleanor and Julia discreetly withdrew to leave them alone together.

Drawing back a little out of the embrace, Abbie looked at her younger sister. 'Oh, Iris,' she said, 'you look lovely – and it's so good to see you.'

'You too, Abbie.' Iris looked keenly at Abbie and then asked, pressing her hand, 'How are you now?'

At the oblique reference to Oliver's death, Abbie said quickly, 'I'm fine, I'm fine.' With a smile she added, 'No sad talk now, Iris. Particularly not on your wedding day.'

The marriage ceremony took place at a small church a short distance from the Timsons' home. Iris looked very sweet and almost pretty in her simple white wedding gown. As had been arranged, Louis gave her away. Afterwards the newlyweds and the dozen guests returned to the Timsons' flat for the wedding breakfast where, for the first time, Abbie had the opportunity to renew acquaintance with Iris's bridegroom.

As they talked, Alfred told her about his work with the London Steamship Company. As much as he liked it, he said, he was nevertheless eager to take up his position in the orchestra at Her Majesty's Theatre, which would happen in a little under a month. When Abbie told him that she and Louis were going to Gravesend the following day and might possibly return by one of the pleasure steamers he said, 'Well, try and get on the *Princess Alice*, why don't you?'

'That's the boat you're on, is it?' Abbie said.

'Yes, it is.' He added, not without a note of pride in his voice, 'She's the biggest of the fleet. Holds about nine hundred passengers. And I tell you, sometimes she gets pretty crowded. Still, I enjoy it so much when the weather's fine. And if you travel on her tomorrow you'll see Iris as well.'

'Iris will be on the boat?'

'She's got the day off work – because of the wedding – so she's coming down to Sheerness with me. It's just for the trip, that's all – so that we can be together. And listen, if I see you on the boat I'll try to arrange for the band to play a special tune for you.'

A little later Abbie moved to her sister's side. 'It's been a wonderful day, Iris,' she said, fondly putting an arm around her shoulders.

'Oh, it has. It has.'

'And when you leave here later on you'll be going to your own home.'

Iris nodded. 'That's right. It's only a couple of rooms at present, but it's a start – and we've been working to get them looking nice. We shall be getting a house of our own once we've got a little money together.'

She went on to say that later on during the week she and Alfred would be going away for a few days that Alfred would have free between his employment with the

Steamship Company and that with the theatre. For now, though, they had to keep on with their jobs. Looking across the crowded room to where Alfred sat at the piano, his mother bending to him in conversation, Iris added 'I'm just very, very lucky, Abbie. I love him so much. I'm not yet twenty-four years old and I've got everything I want.'

A little later, while Abbie was in conversation with Alfred's father, Iris went over to Louis where he stood near the window.

'Can I get you some more tea, Louis?' she asked him. 'Perhaps another sandwich?'

He thanked her but declined, saying he had eaten enough. 'And we shall have to be going soon,' he added. 'But it's been a grand afternoon, and I'm so pleased to have met you at last – and on such a happy day for you.'

She smiled and thanked him. 'What's made me even happier is that you and Abbie were able to come. It's meant so much to me.' A little wistfully she went on, 'So often when the parents are gone brothers and sisters tend to drift apart.'

'I've heard that's so,' Louis said. 'Unfortunately I have no siblings – to my great regret. I always wished I had. I could envy your brother Eddie, having three loving sisters to fuss over him.'

'Oh, I don't know about fussing over him.' Iris laughed. 'I don't think he'd have put up with much of that.' A little gravely she added, 'Mind you, if it had been our Beatie I dare say he'd have put up with it.'

'Ah,' Louis said, 'Beatie – yes. I met her once quite a few years ago. She seemed a very fine young lady.'

'Oh, she was. And Eddie was that fond of her. I don't think she could do much wrong where he was concerned.'

'It was two or three years after it – it happened that I

472

learned she had died,' Louis said. He knew nothing of the circumstances of Beatie's death beyond the most basic details. The sum of his meagre knowledge was made up of the fragments of gossip that had strayed his way some years before – the information that the eldest of the Morris girls had killed herself. There had been some talk about her young man throwing her over, he recalled. More than that he had never learned; nothing else had been volunteered and he had been loath to make enquiries. 'Abbie,' he added, 'will never speak of her.'

Iris gave a little sigh. 'Well – it doesn't surprise me that much. She was very much affected when Beatie died. We all were, of course, but with her it was . . . well, it was different.'

'Different how?'

'I don't really know. You say she'll never talk about it to you. Well, she would never speak of it with me or Lizzie – or Eddie either for that matter, so I believe. Of course, it was years ago when it happened. I wasn't at home at the time; I was away in service.' She gave a little shrug. 'I'm sure you can understand, though, it isn't something people like to dwell upon.'

Iris was called away a minute later and Louis stood there alone. A chord was struck on the piano and glancing across he saw that Alfred was about to accompany his sister Eleanor in a song. The chatter in the room died away and all heads turned towards them. Eleanor, a tall, slim girl of nineteen, began to sing 'Love's Golden Dream.'

I hear tonight the old bells chime, their sweetest softest strain;
They bring to me the olden time, in visions once again.
Once more across the meadow land, beside the flowing stream,

473

We wander, darling, hand in hand, and dream love's
  golden dream.

Louis was surprised at the sweetness of Eleanor's voice.
Although the song was sentimental it was affecting
nevertheless. There was something vaguely familiar
about its melody; he must have heard it before. He
listened more keenly. Eleanor began to sing the chorus in
a lilting waltz time:

 Love's golden dream is past, hidden by mists of pain,
 Yet shall we meet at last, never to part again . . .

She sang the second verse and the final chorus, and the
song was ended. As Louis joined in the applause he was
still trying to place the song in his memory. Then it came
to him – he had heard the melody played on the hurdy-
gurdy at the fair that day when he and Abbie had met.

As memory returned he could see Abbie as she had
been then, a girl of eighteen. How warm and passionate
she had been. It was upon her warmth and her giving
that he had based his hopes; the reason he had gone to
Flaxdown at the first opportunity to see her again. But
she had not been the same. When he had met her in
Flaxdown that day she had seemed distant, showing a
reserve that had taken him by surprise.

Now, looking at her, he realized that her air of bright
animation had quite gone. And as he watched her he saw
her put her hand to her mouth and close her eyes as if in
pain.

When the celebrations were over later that afternoon
Abbie and Louis got a cab and set off back to their hotel.
Away from the happy company of the wedding party
Abbie lapsed once more into near-silence. She and Louis

were polite to one another, but nothing more; beyond the words necessary for their surface interaction they had no real communication.

After dining at the hotel they went for a walk, strolling side by side in the cool evening air. When they returned to the hotel they got undressed, wished one another goodnight and climbed into their separate beds.

It had been a long day and Abbie was tired, yet it was some time before she was able to get to sleep. When she did eventually sleep the dream came back and there she was again, faced with the slowly moving shadow and having to support the weight in her arms.

The next morning they set off by train for Gravesend.

Louis had written to his father of their coming and when they got to the house just before noon they found him waiting eagerly for their arrival. They had a leisurely lunch and when it was over sat in the quiet drawing room where, against the solemn ticking of the clock, Abbie and Louis read newspapers and Louis's father dozed in his chair.

Tea was served just after four, after which Abbie, in order to leave Louis and his father some little time of privacy, excused herself, saying she wished to walk out in the air for a while.

The day had remained warm and pleasant. She walked the length of the garden and onto the lawn, where she sat on the bench as she had done on that first visit with Louis over four years before. Sitting there while the birds sang in the apple trees her thoughts went back over the previous day and Iris's wedding. How good it had been to see her so happy. Iris seemed to demand so little of life. She had Alfred and it was enough. If only it could be that simple for herself, she thought. But where she and Louis were concerned the situation had gone beyond saving.

And now, to add to her predicament, there was the likelihood of another child . . .

On the periphery of her vision she saw movement, and turning saw her father-in-law coming along the path towards her.

Coming to a stop before her, he said, 'Have you got to go back to London today, Abbie? Can't I persuade you to stay over for the night? Why not go back tomorrow? I've asked Louis; he says it's up to you.'

'No, we have to get back,' she said. 'I'm sorry. Besides, I told my sister and her husband that we'd try to see them on board one of the steamers this afternoon. Alfred is one of the bandsmen.'

He gave a little shrug of disappointment. 'Oh, well, that's a pity, but if you can't, you can't.'

He came and sat beside her on the bench. Without looking at her he said, 'Abbie, I know how you've suffered over Oliver. And how you must be suffering still. I know too that it can't help you if I say that I've known the same suffering. As have millions of others. It can make no difference; nothing can really ease your own pain, I know that much. I just want you to know that I understand.'

Abbie was silent, and his hand lifted and gently touched her shoulder. If he said much more she would weep. She could already feel the pricking of tears behind her eyelids, a tightening of her throat.

After a moment the old man withdrew his arm and said, 'But I can also tell you that the pain will ease in time. You think it won't, but it will. We think we shall never survive it but we do. We have to, for what is the alternative?'

She turned and looked at him, her eyes swimming with tears.

He gave a little shake of his head. 'We have no option

but to get through it, to get through that time – and it seems never-ending, I know, when there is pain in everything. We have to live, Abbie. We have to. It's in the way of nature. If we did not – if we could not survive such blows – then man could not survive. We have to carry on and we do. We get on with our lives. Our lives are different, of course, but that's to be expected. After such loss life can never be the same again. We can only make the best of things and hope that – that somehow it makes us better, stronger people.' He sighed. 'It would be comforting to think that something good came out of it.'

Never, Abbie said to herself, she would never recover. And all the wise words in the world would not help her to.

'But there is one thing,' the man said after a little while, '– you don't have to face it alone. At least you have that knowledge.'

'Oh,' she said quickly, 'I do have to face it alone. I *am* alone.'

'Oh – Abbie – don't say that.'

'It's true. I'm sorry to say it. You're the last person I should be saying it to, but it's the truth. And Louis – he is alone too.'

'No – I can't accept that.'

'It's the truth. Hasn't he told you? We have nothing, the two of us. Nothing at all.' She sighed. 'All we had was Oliver and now we have nothing.'

'Abbie, you say this because – because of what's happened. Your feelings of loss, of grief.'

'No,' she said, 'I'm stating facts. Louis and me – I don't know what's to become of us now.'

'No.' He shook his head. 'I can't believe that.' He paused. 'Don't turn away from him.'

Her fingers worked agitatedly in her lap. 'I'm sorry,'

she said, 'but I – I don't feel comfortable with this conversation . . .'

'Perhaps,' he said, 'I should mind my own business. Forgive me. I only want the two of you to find some happiness together.'

She nodded. 'I know you mean well. But it's too late for us now. It's just – too late.'

As he withdrew his hand there came the sound of footsteps on the gravel path. Turning, Abbie saw Louis coming towards them from the house. Mr Randolph got to his feet. As Louis drew near, his father said to him, 'I'm afraid I couldn't persuade Abbie to stay.'

'I'm very sorry,' Abbie said. Turning to Louis she added, 'Louis, the time's getting on. We should think about getting down to the pier soon, don't you think? Alfred's steamboat is due there at six o'clock.'

He looked at his watch. 'We've plenty of time. The boat probably hasn't even reached Sheerness yet.'

'Even so . . .'

'Anyway, do we have to go back on the steamer? We could stay on here a little longer and catch the train – and be in London no later.'

'But Iris and Alfred are on board the boat, and you know I said we'd try to see them.'

'Try is the word,' said Louis. 'Among all those hundreds of other people we'll be lucky to find them.'

Sensitive to the friction, Louis's father started away. 'If you're going on the steamer you might like to take some refreshment with you,' he said. 'I'll get Mrs Willett to make you some sandwiches.'

Abbie thanked him but said it was not necessary. He would have nothing of her protests, however, and went away to talk to the housekeeper. When he had gone Abbie got to her feet. 'I think we should get going.'

'Why are you so restless?' Louis said.

'Look – if you want to stay then do so. You must do as you please.'

'I would like to stay a little longer. After all, it's rarely I get to see my father.' He gave a weary shrug. 'Though perhaps it's as well we leave. It can't be that much fun for him having us here when we're barely on speaking terms with one another.' He eyed her, studying her. 'You're so restless – and even more uncommunicative than usual. God knows it's been hard enough to get three words together out of you since Oliver's death, but over the last few days you've been even more distant.'

She did not answer.

'What is it?' he said. 'What is it you want?'

'Oh, Louis, what does it matter?'

'Is that the way you feel – that nothing matters now?'

'Please.' She frowned, her lips set. 'I don't want to discuss it. This is neither the time nor the place.' She started to move past him, but he reached out and took her wrist.

'You can't always avoid the issue,' he said. 'Tell me what it is.' He let fall her hand. 'You still blame me, don't you? For Oliver's death.'

She turned away. 'Oh – Louis . . .'

'Tell me. I'm sure you do. You think that if I hadn't bought him the toy soldier he'd be alive today.' He nodded. 'Yes. And do you think I haven't told myself that same thing over and over?'

She did not speak. He went on, 'And shall we go on like this for the rest of our lives? It isn't something I look forward to.'

Still she was silent.

'Abbie,' he said, 'there is no harsh thought or word you can think up that I haven't already used about myself a thousand times. Do you think there's been a day when I haven't relived the events of that evening? When I

479

haven't wished that I had done things differently? When I haven't reproached myself for my part in what happened?'

'Oh, Louis.' Briefly she closed her eyes in despair. 'What are we doing? We shall end up destroying one another.'

He was silent for a few seconds, then he said sadly, 'I've come to realize that you're probably right: we should never have married. I suppose I just have to face up to it, finally, that our marriage was a colossal mistake. I must have closed my eyes to the truth. Thinking that in time I could make you love me, I didn't allow it to matter that you were marrying me for the wrong reasons. Perhaps if I'd given it all a little more thought I wouldn't have been so eager to wed.' He shook his head. 'Though I was so besotted with you I doubt that anything would have stopped me.'

Abbie avoided his gaze and said nothing.

'It's a great pity you didn't marry your Mr Gilmore,' he said. 'I used to think I was the lucky one. After all, I was the one who got you. But I've come to realize I was not. Yes, you should have had Gilmore, Abbie, because I know now – at long last – that you'll never be happy with me. You've made that abundantly clear.' He gave a shrug. 'Which means in a way that you're doomed to a life of unhappiness, doesn't it? Because you're never going to get him. He's got a wife already, so even if you were free it wouldn't do you any good.' He paused. 'God – I wish you could have loved me with just half the feeling you have for him.'

'Louis –'

Disregarding her interruption he went on, 'When I came to join you and Oliver at Weston-super-Mare I – I found a closeness with you that I had not thought possible. It didn't last, of course, but for that brief time it –'

'Please,' she protested. 'Please don't go on.'

He gave a bitter little smile. 'Does it embarrass you now? Nevertheless, that time in Weston – it somehow reminded me of when we first met – what you were like then. You were –'

'I don't want to talk about that time,' she said quickly. 'That's all in the past.'

'Indeed it is. And I soon discovered that I didn't marry the girl I met at the fair that day.'

She looked at him sharply. 'What are you talking about?'

He eyed her critically. 'You were different.'

'Different? I was younger, if that's what you mean.'

'No, there was a difference about you that had nothing to do with your age.'

'That – that's nonsense.'

'It's the truth. You've changed. I don't know how or when exactly, but you have, nevertheless. After our marriage I got to thinking that perhaps it was something in you – in your head, in your heart – that was stopping you from loving me. I didn't know what it was, but I felt there was something there. Something from your past perhaps, some unknown thing that just – just got in the way. And I thought that if I could find out what it was – that barrier – then I would tear it down.' He raised hands clenched into fists, then let them uncurl and fall back to his sides. 'No ... I see now that it was Gilmore all the time. And I can't fight that. I could fight him, but not what he means to you.'

He fell silent, then spreading his hands before her he gave a sigh and said, 'Which leaves us just where we were, doesn't it?'

She turned, gazing out beyond the end of the walled garden.

'I'd like to know what you want, Abbie,' he said, 'out of this – this charade we call a marriage. If there is something, tell me. It would be good if something could be salvaged from it.' He paused, then added, his voice sounding weary, 'Because I tell you now that I am sick to death of it all.'

She remained facing away from him, silent.

'If you like,' he went on after a few moments, 'we can live apart. If you would like a divorce you can have that too. I'll even give you legal reason for it if you want – to save your reputation.'

She turned to him now and said, 'It might not be quite as simple as that.'

'Simple? Oh, you think such a procedure is simple?'

'No, I don't. I mean –' she took a breath '– well – I think I'm going to have a baby.'

He took a step towards her, his face lighting up. 'A baby. Oh, God, Abbie – then it's true.'

'True?'

'I suspected it. I am a doctor, for God's sake. I am familiar with some of the signs.' He paused. 'No matter the lengths you might go to in order to hide them from me.'

'Yes – well . . . So – you asked me what's been on my mind over the past days. And now you know.'

The brief joy that had shone in his face had gone. He stared at her for a moment, as if trying to read her thoughts, then said, 'Forgive me. For a second I was pleased – mistakenly took it as good news. Quite obviously, though, that's not the way you feel about it.'

Stung, she retorted, 'They're your words, Louis, not mine.'

'Indeed they are. And close to the truth, I dare say.' He

paused, then added, 'Why are you giving me this news now? Is it your way of offering me congratulations?' His lip curled. 'Or are you saving them for Gilmore?'

She gasped, taking a step back, as if he had struck her. 'God almighty,' she said, 'how can you be so cruel?'

'Cruel?' he said. 'Cruel? This is you talking of being cruel?' His smile was like ice. 'If I can be cruel it's because I've been well taught.'

They stood facing one another for a second, then she stepped past him in the direction of the house. 'I'm going to say goodbye to your father,' she said, 'and then I'm going down to the pier. You do whatever you want. I don't care any more.'

Chapter Thirty-Four

Louis left the house and caught up with Abbie as she walked towards the pier.

'Abbie, why did you leave?' he said as he drew level with her. 'My father doesn't know what the hell's going on. Neither do I, come to that.'

'I told you,' she answered without breaking her stride, 'I want to catch the steamer. I intend to see Iris and Alfred, and go back to the hotel. Then I shall return home to Frome. What you do is up to you.'

'Abbie, wait. I'm sorry I said that. Please – we have to talk.'

'There's nothing to talk about. You've said enough.'

'But you're way too early, anyway. I told you, the boat isn't due for ages yet.'

'Then I'll wait for it.' She kept going. 'I really don't care.'

They walked on in silence towards the docks and on arrival saw that a number of people were standing on the pier.

'They must be waiting to go downriver,' Louis said.

Abbie didn't answer, but walked out onto the pier. Louis followed and, coming to a stop at her side a little distance from the waiting crowd, looked out into the estuary. A steamer was coming downriver towards them. When he turned to Abbie she did not return his glance – though she could not fail to be aware of it. Her face was as if set in stone. Lips compressed, she stood gazing out over the water at the approaching steamer.

Soon the pleasure boat was close enough to read the name painted on its bows. 'It's the *Princess Alice*,' Abbie said, and with her words turned and moved to join the waiting people.

'But it's going the wrong way.' Louis stepped along at her side. 'It's going down to Sheerness.'

'It's the *Princess Alice*. And it'll turn at Sheerness and come back, am I right?'

'Well, yes, but –'

'Then that's all that matters. Besides, it'll give me a longer time to spend with Iris.'

'But Abbie –'

'I'm getting on the boat. You don't have to come with me.'

The huge, iron-built steamboat came steadily closer, twin plumes of smoke rising from her funnels in the fine, clear air, her paddles churning in their side boxes, their sound set against the band's music as it drifted over the water. Slowly, smoothly, she came on until she was eventually lying beside the pier. When she was tied up and the gangplank was put down the little queue edged forward. Immediately behind Abbie and Louis came a loud-voiced mother and father and their five children, while in front was a boisterous, good-natured group of three young couples aged about twenty. Two of the young women – though not dressed alike; one was all in blue, the other in red tartan – were obviously twins.

Along with the others wanting to board, Abbie and Louis were forced to wait for a while to allow a number of passengers to disembark, and then they were moving forward again. Seconds later they had reached the ticket seller and there was no more time for debate; Louis was buying their tickets and moments after that the two of them were stepping up onto the gangplank and then onto the deck.

Recalling the seething throngs that she had experienced on some previous trips on the Thames steamers, Abbie was relieved to find that the boat appeared to be relatively uncrowded. As they crossed the lower deck she gestured up towards the source of the music. 'The band's on the upper deck,' she said, 'that's where I'll find Iris.'

Climbing a companionway, they stepped out onto the upper deck, and looking towards the sound of the music saw the seven-piece band raised up on a dais. Among them, playing his cornet, was Alfred, looking very smart in his blue bandsman's uniform.

'You go on and spend a little time with Iris,' Louis said. 'I'm sure you've still got plenty to talk about. I'll join you later. I'll probably go into the saloon and have a drink.'

'As you like.'

'Would you like me to bring you anything from the bar?'

'No.' She was so hurt she still found it difficult to look at him. 'No, thank you.' She turned and a moment later was stepping away from his side. He stood for a second watching her departure, then moved back to the companionway and started down.

As she made her way across the deck the band was giving out a lively tune – 'The Old Wooden Clock in the Hall' – and a few people were joining in, singing along. There appeared to be many whole families on board. There were numbers of children too – some sitting with parents and siblings, while others ran shrieking and laughing about the deck, getting in the way of the pedestrians. For a great many there, she surmised, the day's trip on the Thames would be the high point of the year. Also, many had no destination, but were there solely for the boat trip itself; they would not be disembarking at Sheerness, but would stay on board as it turned around and headed back upriver. As, indeed, so now would she and Louis.

As she neared the crowd around the bandstand Alfred caught sight of her and widened his eyes in greeting. She smiled at him and gave a little wave with her fingers. He responded by turning his head slightly to his left and giving a brief little nod. Following the direction of his glance, she saw Iris sitting on a bench near the rail. Reaching her side a moment later, Abbie laughed at the look of surprise on her face.

'What are you doing here so soon?' Iris said. 'We were expecting to see you on the way back.'

'A change of plan,' Abbie said. 'We decided to get on the boat as it went downriver.' She bent and gave Iris a hug. 'For one thing it will give us longer together.'

'Oh, indeed it will. It's grand.' Iris cast her eyes about her. 'Where's Louis?'

'He'll join us later. He said we should have a little time on our own. He's gone to the saloon for a drink.'

'Well, it's just as well he gets it now. The boat will be quite crowded on the way back.'

'Really? And I was just thinking how nice it was to have a little space – not to have all that seething mass of people around.'

'Oh, they'll be here, don't worry.'

'Well – nothing to be done about it.'

'Here – let's make room if we can,' Iris said. She pressed up on the bench, smiling encouragingly at an old woman beside her. The woman, who was just finishing taking some snuff, put away her snuffbox and moved up slightly, enabling Abbie to sit down.

Abbie thanked her, then turned back to Iris. 'Well, little

sister,' she said, 'you're looking very smart today – and very fashionable too.'

Iris inclined her head in self-conscious acknowledgement of the compliment. She wore a blue dress with a large ribbon bow at her throat and a number of smaller bows running down the front of the bodice. Her hat was a small blue Tyrolean affair trimmed with ribbons. Looking at Abbie, she saw something in her expression and immediately showed her concern. 'Abbie, are you all right?'

'Yes, I'm fine.' As Abbie spoke she felt the boat give a shudder and begin to move. 'We're off,' she said.

The boat was gliding away from the pier, out into the deep water. Near Abbie's back the paddle box thrummed and vibrated with the turning of the paddle, while higher up on the bridge she could see the captain standing at the wheel. As Abbie glanced at him Iris followed her eyes. 'That's Captain Grinstead,' she said. 'The crew say he's so nice. I believe he has his wife and two little daughters on board with him today.' She turned and looked through the rail at the swiftly receding bank. 'It won't be long now till we get to Sheerness.'

'You must have done this trip a good many times, have you?'

'Oh, yes, a good few – since Alfred joined the band. He likes it if I can be on board when he's working. I do too, of course.' Turning, she pointed back upriver at a steamboat that was heading for the pier just vacated by the *Princess Alice*. 'That's the *Duke of Teck*,' she went on. 'She's timed to sail ten minutes after the *Alice*. Alfred's played on board the *Teck* a few times as well.'

The tune that the band was playing came to an end and Abbie saw that the musicians were putting away their instruments. 'That's not the end of the music, is it?' she asked.

'Just for a little while,' Iris replied. 'They're dry and they need to wet their whistles. We can go with them if you like – down into one of the lower saloons.'

'Well – I'd rather not.'

'As you please. It'll get very crowded down there anyway, before long.'

Alfred joined them a few moments afterwards and he took Abbie's hand and gave her a self-conscious peck on the cheek. 'We didn't expect you yet,' he said. He enquired then after Louis, and Abbie replied that he was having a drink and would be joining them later.

Standing behind Iris, Alfred wrapped his arms round her, pressing his face to hers. Iris grinned at Abbie from the circle of his embrace. 'Abbie and Louis decided to catch the boat on the way down,' she said.

'Well,' Alfred said, 'lucky for us.'

Behind him his fellow musicians were heading for one of the companionways. Alfred asked the two sisters if they wanted to go with him for a drink, but Iris replied that for the time being they would remain on deck. 'But you go on and get your ale,' she said, 'otherwise you'll be too dry to play.'

'Yes, that's right.' He planted a kiss on Iris's cheek and straightened. 'Can't have that, can we.'

Alfred left them then to rejoin his colleagues and the steamer continued on downriver. 'Would you like to go for a little stroll around the deck?' Iris asked. 'It would be a good idea before it gets too crowded. Though we mustn't be too long, or Louis won't know where to look for you.'

'Oh, Louis, Louis!' Abbie said with a note of exasperation in her voice. 'Why is everyone so bothered about Louis?'

'Abbie . . .' Iris looked at her with concern. 'I didn't

mean anything by it. I just – wondered about him, that's all.' She paused. 'What's wrong, Abbie?'

'Wrong? Nothing.' Abbie waved the question away. 'Come – let's go for our walk.'

Together the sisters got to their feet and, linking arms, set off to stroll around the deck.

After they had walked a little distance, Iris said, 'Abbie, don't be cross with me, but – oh, it's none of my business, but it's clear that things aren't going so well with you and Louis. I could see that yesterday. You were both all right with other people, but with one another you seemed – oh, I don't know – constrained.'

'Well,' Abbie said, 'I have to admit that things are not as good as they might be.'

'Oh, dear. I'm so sorry.' Iris looked at her sympathetically. 'Is it – is it because of Oliver . . . ?'

Briefly Abbie closed her eyes. 'Well, Oliver's partly the reason, but – it's other things too.'

'I wish I knew what to say.' Iris's small face was a picture of concern. 'I hate to see you miserable. You deserve to be happy. I'll never forget how you looked after us when Mother went away. All that responsibility you had. We depended on you so. I didn't realize at the time, but later I came to be aware of all the things you had to do. And you were so young.'

Abbie waved a dismissive hand, but Iris went on, 'It's true. And when Mother came back you looked after her – and broke off your engagement in order to do so. But when you and Louis got married and had Oliver I thought . . . well, that everything was going to be so good for you – that all your troubles were over at last. And now . . .' She pressed Abbie's arm under her own. 'Oh, I wish I could help in some way.'

'It's all right,' Abbie said. 'We shall get things sorted out in the end. One way or another.'

'I hope so.' Iris gave a sigh. 'I'd just like everyone to be as happy as we are, Alfie and me.' She remained silent for a moment as if debating whether or not to speak further, then she said, 'Yesterday Louis and I talked about Beatie.'

'Oh?' Abbie's tone was suspicious. 'What about Beatie?'

'Well – nothing in particular. He said that you had never spoken of – of Beatie's death . . .'

'Well, of course not,' Abbie said, a little sharply. 'It isn't the kind of thing one wants to dwell upon. I don't want to talk about it now, either. And I don't particularly like the idea of being the subject of gossip.'

'Oh, Abbie, don't scold me,' Iris said. 'It wasn't like that at all. I'm not trying to interfere.'

Abbie groaned. 'I'm sorry, Iris. I know you only mean well. I shouldn't have snapped at you like that.' Briefly she touched a hand to Iris's cheek. 'I do love you, my little sister – you know that, don't you?'

Iris smiled. 'Yes, I do.'

The sisters continued on, their conversation moving onto safer ground, speaking of more mundane matters, of Eddie and Violet and their two little girls, of Lizzie and Adam and their small son, of various friends and neighbours in the vicinity of Flaxdown. When Iris spoke of Jane, and asked whether Abbie had seen her recently, Abbie replied in the negative and changed the subject. So their talk went on, with Abbie doing her best to keep it safe.

In a while Abbie noticed on the shore up ahead the buildings that marked out the little town of Sheerness situated on the Isle of Sheppey, and soon afterwards the boat was moving to pull up beside the pier. As it did so Abbie could at once see that Iris and Alfred were right with regard to an increase in the number of passengers on the journey back upriver. On that fine September day

Sheerness had been the destination for many day trippers from London and Kent, and now those holidaymakers were ready to start on their journeys back home. A great throng of people – several hundred, it appeared to Abbie – were waiting to get on board, and after a relatively small number of passengers had disembarked, the throng surged forward. A minute later they were pouring onto the decks, both upper and lower, taking every seat available and crowding at the rails so it seemed that soon there would be scarcely room to move. 'I can't believe it,' Abbie breathed, watching the new passengers swarming about. 'There's not enough space for them all.'

Over the voices and the laughter came the sound of the band striking up again. Iris turned towards it. 'They're back,' she said. 'Shall we go back too? We'll be leaving Sheerness any minute now.'

Side by side they made their way to the bandstand, both giving Alfred a wave as he sat playing his cornet. A couple vacated their seats as the two arrived and they sat down. No sooner had they done so, however, but Iris said, 'Abbie – I'm concerned about Louis. I wish he'd come and join us. It would be so nice if he were here too. You'll be going back to Frome tomorrow, the two of you, and there's no telling when I'll see you both again.'

Abbie sighed and smiled at her. 'All right.' She got up from the bench. 'I'll go and see if he's in one of the saloons. If it's possible to get down there in this crush.'

Moving to the nearest companionway, she started down. There were many other passengers milling about, ascending and descending the steps, but eventually she reached the foot of the stairs, pushed a way into the crowded saloon and made her way through, looking to right and left. She could see no sign of Louis, and after gazing about her for another minute she turned and retraced her steps. He could be in one of the other saloons, though finding him in such a crowd might not prove an easy task.

A moment later, reaching the foot of the companion-way again, she found herself face to face with Arthur.

The shock of seeing him before her brought her to an involuntary halt, so abruptly that a man following behind almost collided with her. Completely unaware, Abbie and Arthur remained standing there, looking at one another.

'Well – Arthur, hello,' Abbie gave him an awkward smile, while her heart pounded in her breast. 'I certainly didn't expect to see you here.'

'Nor I you,' he said. His smile was as uncertain as her own.

A continuous stream of people was moving past them on their way to and from the saloon, and more than one showed irritation at the obstruction caused by the couple. Now aware of the situation Abbie said, 'I rather think we're in the way here . . .'

'Yes, I rather think we are.'

'Perhaps we can find another spot.'

'Let's go up on deck, shall we?'

Arthur turned on the step and, with Abbie close behind him, started back up the companionway. Reaching the top, they emerged onto the upper deck and after a moment's hesitation turned towards the forepart. Together they found a relatively secluded spot at the rail beside a bulkhead. As they came to a stop, facing one another, the paddle wheels started to turn and the boat began to move away from the pier.

'Here we go,' Arthur said.

'Yes – here we go.' Abbie turned for a moment to look at the bank swinging away as the boat glided out into the river's deeper waters. Then, her eyes coming back to

493

Arthur, she said, 'Well, I can't get over this. Seeing you here.'

'Yes, it's quite a surprise.' After a moment's pause he added, 'I won't ask you how you've been, Abbie, as I can well imagine. I – I was so very, very sorry to hear about your little boy.'

She nodded, lips compressed. 'Yes – yes.' She didn't want to speak of Oliver and quickly changed the subject. 'What about you, Arthur, are you well?'

'Yes, thank you, quite well.'

'Good.' A pause. 'Are you here alone?'

'No.' He gestured with a wave of his hand. 'Jane and Emma are down on the lower deck. I was on my way to get them something to drink.'

'Oh – well, in that case I mustn't hold you up.'

'It's all right. I have a little time.'

Silence fell between them, then Arthur said, 'Is your husband here?'

'Yes. He's somewhere about. I was just looking for him. There's such a crowd, though. It's like looking for a needle in a haystack. I've never seen so many people on board.'

'They're making the most of the last of the fine weather, I imagine. How do you happen to be on the boat.'

'We've been visiting Louis's father at Gravesend. Then we got onto the *Princess Alice* so that I could spend a little time with my sister and her husband. He, Alfred, plays in the band. What about you?'

'We just got on at Sheerness. We went down yesterday. I had some business to take care of there. We sailed down on the *Cupid*. A smaller boat than the *Princess Alice* – and not nearly as crowded. I didn't realize the *Alice* would be so packed coming back, otherwise we might have taken a different boat.'

'She's obviously very popular.'

As they stood there other passengers continued to mill about, filling the air with their murmurs, their calls and their laughter. Up above their heads the smoke from the huge twin funnels drifted and spread in the air while below them the powerful paddles churned the fast-flowing water of the river. The band, which had started up again, was playing 'The Midshipmite.' As before, many of the passengers were joining in with the chorus, the voices of some of them, opened up by too many ales, now sounding rather more raucous than before.

'I can't get over it.' Abbie shook her head. 'Our meeting like this.'

'Yes,' Arthur said, 'it certainly is quite a coincidence.'

An awkward silence fell between them, and then suddenly, with a little intake of breath, Abbie was putting a hand to her face, fingers covering her right eye.

'What's the matter?' Arthur said.

'I think I've got something in my eye. A bit of cinder from the funnels, probably.' She lowered her hand, opened her eyes and immediately closed them again. 'Oh, it stings so . . .'

'Here – let me look.' He stepped closer, then, putting his hands on her upper arms, gently turned her so that her face came into the light. A hand under her chin, he tilted her head. 'Now – try to open your eyes.'

In spite of the discomfort Abbie, with an effort, forced herself to open her eyes. Arthur bent to peer closer.

Louis, sitting in the increasingly crowded saloon bar, had seen Abbie enter the room and stand looking around her. She must be looking for him, he thought, though clearly she had not seen him, almost hidden as he was behind a group of holidaymakers. Then in moments she was turning and going away again. For a few seconds he continued to sit there, then he finished the last of his ale, got to his feet and pushed his way through the crowd.

On leaving the saloon he climbed the companionway and reached the top just in time to see Abbie moving away. She was not alone, but with a man. A man whom he would recognize anywhere: Gilmore.

He took a few steps in their direction, came to a stop and watched. Now the two were standing together, almost hidden by a bulkhead. Not completely hidden, however. Abbie's back was towards him, but it was easy to see that they were talking. He continued to watch, and after a while he saw Gilmore place his hands on her shoulders and put a hand beneath her chin. Wrenching his gaze from the sight, he turned away.

'I can't see anything,' Arthur said. 'Does it hurt so badly.'

'Perhaps not so much now.' She blinked a few times. 'No, I think it feels a little better.'

Arthur let his hands fall; he and Abbie both aware of their close proximity. After a moment he said, 'Your husband – he's well, is he?' Then he added quickly, 'In the very sad circumstances, I mean.'

'Yes.' She nodded. 'In the circumstances.' Then she heard herself saying bluntly, 'Louis and I – we're talking of parting.'

He appeared momentarily taken aback. 'Oh, Abbie, I'm so sorry.'

'Well, things have got so – so bad between us lately. I can't see any hope of our mending them now.'

'I – I don't know what to say.'

She bent her head, picked at a thread on her glove. 'You must realize that it – it's partly to do with you.'

'What?' His tone, though soft, was incredulous.

'Why do you sound so surprised?'

'Oh, no, Abbie, don't say that.'

'Surely you must realize it.'

'I – I don't understand. I've never wanted to come between you, you know that.'

'But you already had. You always were . . . between us.'

'Abbie –' he protested, anguish in his voice now.

'Louis knows about us,' she said.

'Knows what? What do you mean?'

'He knows, of course, that we almost married – what we meant to one another.' She took a breath. 'And he knows also that we met that day back in the winter. When we sheltered in the barn.'

'But – but nothing happened.'

'Nothing?'

He leaned forward to speak softly. 'Abbie, we – we kissed. That's all.'

'Is that all it was?'

'It was nothing more.'

'Perhaps not to you.' She gave a deep sigh. 'But what does it matter? It's not that that's caused the rift. Not that alone; it goes far deeper. We've tried to make things work. But in the end you come to realize that things never will be better, that it was a mistake right from the start. Louis and I – we should never have married in the first place. Some people are wrong for each other, and when that's the case then all the talk and good intentions in the world aren't going to make it right.'

Arthur did not speak. In the silence between them she reached out and laid her hand upon his as he held the rail. 'It would have been different with us, Arthur,' she said.

'Abbie, please – don't.' He shifted his hand, went to move it from her own, but she grasped it, held on.

'I could have made you happy, Arthur. If you'd given me the chance.'

497

'Abbie – let's not talk of such things.'

'Why not? Are you afraid of the truth?'

He turned away from her gaze. 'That isn't the truth.'

'Arthur –'

'You have to know it, Abbie. You've got to realize, once and for all. No matter what might have happened in the past, I am married to Jane.'

'Yes, I know, but –'

'I'm committed to her. And I'll never leave her. Never.'

'Arthur, you don't –'

'Listen, Abbie. Listen to me.' His gaze was intense upon her own. 'God Almighty, I don't want to be cruel, but you've got to realize the truth. Jane is my wife. I love her.'

'You love her? But what about that letter you wrote when our engagement ended? Have you forgotten that? I haven't. I remember your exact words. "You may believe that it's all finished between us, but I know that it is not. One day we shall be together and I shall wait for that day." Do you remember writing those words?'

'Abbie, it's true – that's how I felt at the time, but that was years ago and –'

'I'm aware of that. But what about when we were together in the barn? That wasn't years ago. That was only this last winter. Or have you forgotten?'

'Of course I haven't forgotten. And I'd give anything if I could undo it.'

Tears sprang to her eyes. 'Don't say that.' She paused. 'You once told me you loved me. Do you remember?'

'Yes.'

'Didn't you mean it?'

When he remained silent, she said, 'I thought you meant it. Oh, Arthur, memories are all I've had to live on – and if you tell me now you didn't mean it – it makes the whole thing unreal.'

He leaned slightly towards her. 'It *is* unreal. The whole thing between you and me – it never was real. It never could have worked.'

She gazed at him as if she had never seen him before.

'It was Jane who made me realize it,' he said. 'What I have with her is . . . different. *That* is what is real.'

When Abbie spoke again her voice was small. 'So all along I've been bent on some fool's errand.' Tears spilled over and ran down her cheeks. 'Tell me,' she said. 'Let me hear you say it. That you never loved me.'

He did not speak, just briefly closed his eyes in anguish.

'Tell me,' Abbie said. 'Say it.'

'Abbie –'

'Say it.'

He sighed. 'Once I thought I did – love you. But I was wrong. I realized afterwards that I never had – not truly.'

'Oh, God . . .' She put her clenched hands up to her mouth. 'I can't believe I'm hearing these words.' And yet still she could not, would not give up. 'You did,' she said. 'You do. You do love me. I know you do.' But there was no conviction now in her voice.

'No, Abbie.' His own voice was soft. 'My future is with Jane. All my happiness is with her and Emma.'

She looked at him as he stood with bent head and lowered eyes. There was a strange coldness inside her. A feeling of numbness. She knew somehow, beyond question, that what he had spoken now was the truth.

'I believed in us,' she said.

'Well, if I ever encouraged such a belief I'm sorry. I never wanted to hurt you.'

'You've left me with nothing – except pain and humiliation.' She added dully, 'You love Jane.'

'Yes.'

'And – you never truly loved me.'

499

'I'm sorry – I realize it now.'

Into the silence between them drifted the sound of the band and its accompanying voices. Closer at hand to their left a young couple stood at the rail chuckling at some shared joke, their arms fast round one another. A little boy came skipping past, his laughter bubbling up like a spring, while his mother came laughing in pursuit. High at the top of the mast the boat's pennant fluttered in the evening breeze.

While everything around them seemed to be going on as normal Abbie felt lost, in limbo. And still the other people talked and shouted and laughed and sang, and the band played its sprightly tunes, and the paddle wheels kept churning.

She wiped at her cold, tear-wet cheeks and gazed at Arthur. 'It's strange – I don't know what I feel for you now, Arthur. For so long I somehow thought that, with other things being different, we could have a future together.' When he did not answer she turned her face away from him and looked out over the water.

After some moments his voice came: 'Abbie – there's something that has to be said.'

'Oh?' Her smile was humourless. 'I think I've had enough revelations for one day.'

'Abbie,' he said, 'I – I don't think you do love' me.'

Salvaging her pride, she said, 'Well, I don't know what I feel for you now.'

'I mean, I don't think you ever did – truly love me.'

'Oh, you know me so well, do you, Arthur?'

'Perhaps in some respects I know you better than you know yourself.'

She frowned. 'Go on.'

'I mean it. I don't think you ever really loved me. Not truly. You might have told yourself that you did, and it might have suited you to believe it. But in truth I don't think you cared that deeply.'

'Do I understand you?' she said. 'You're trying to say that I imagined it, what I felt for you? As if I'm one of those crazy spinsters who spend their lives in fantasies.'

'Abbie,' he burst out imploringly, 'for God's sake, give up this obsession.'

'Obsession?' Louis had used almost the same words to her. 'Is that what you think it is?'

'Yes, I do. I don't know what you'd do if you ever really got what you're asking for.'

'What do you mean by that?'

'Sometimes people should be careful of what they go hankering after – in case they get what they wish for.'

'You're not making sense,' she said.

He looked at her steadily for a moment then said: 'I wonder – what would you do if you had your wish? What would you do if I came to you and said, "I'm yours, Abbie – I love only you"? What would you do?'

'I don't know what you're saying . . .'

'I'll tell you what you'd do. If I said such a thing you'd panic – and run. Because, so help me, I don't think for a moment that it's truly what you want.'

She glared at him and said with a toss of her head, 'I can't stand here listening to this.' She took a step away, then turned back to face him. Her eyes were bright again with tears, tears of anger and disillusion. 'How much does Jane know about us?' she said.

'What . . .?'

'Does she know we – were together in the barn that day? That you held me and kissed me.'

'Of course not.' He frowned. 'Oh, Abbie, she must never know.'

'Why? Why must she never know? Are you afraid it might put your perfect marriage to the test? Surely if your

501

love for one another is so deep, so – so enduring it could withstand a little honesty.'

Turning away, she left him standing at the rail.

She wiped angrily at her tears as she made her way across the upper deck. Some of the passengers were dancing now to the music of the band. As she moved past them she avoided looking over towards the bandstand. She could not face Iris or anyone now; did not want to talk to anybody. She needed to find a place where she could get away from everyone and be alone for a while. But there was nowhere to escape to.

She came at last to the after end of the upper deck, where it looked out over the lower deck and the boat's stern. Moving to the rail, she held on to it while the tears ran down her cheeks and dried in the wind. She was aware of subtle, curious glances coming from a couple on her right, but she did not allow herself to care about them.

She had been so caught up in her preoccupations that she had been unaware that they were drawing near to Gravesend. And now, feeling a slight shudder of the deck beneath her feet, she realized with surprise that the boat had pulled in to the pier. Turning towards it, she could see a long queue of people waiting to get on and add to the vast numbers already on board. Had she and Louis not taken the boat on its way downriver they would have been among those waiting.

On the periphery of her vision she was vaguely aware of the young couple moving away from the rail, and someone else taking their place.

What was she to do now with her life? she asked herself. She had nothing. Her child was gone and her marriage was as good as over; and now she had made the discovery that the one on whom she had once set her hopes had never truly loved her at all.

'Abbie . . . ?'

The voice, a woman's voice, came from the figure to her right; a voice that she would know anywhere on earth.

Turning, she found herself face to face with Jane.

Chapter Thirty-Five

They stood facing one another, so close that their skirts touched.

Abbie did not speak for some moments, then quietly she said, 'Hello, Jane.'

It had been four and a half years since they had met, four and a half years since that day in London when they had walked together in St James's Park – the day Jane had told her that she and Arthur were to marry.

'How are you, Abbie?' Jane said.

'Oh – I'm well, I'm well.' Abbie smiled, her voice falsely bright. 'And you?'

'Yes, very well, thank you.'

Silence between them and, turning slightly, Abbie became aware of a young woman and a child standing nearby.

As she registered their presence Jane said to her, smiling, 'Abbie, this is our daughter Emma.'

Abbie looked down at the little girl. So this was the daughter of Jane and Arthur. She was a bright-looking little girl of almost four with a round, happy face, and a mass of honey-coloured curls falling to her shoulders from beneath the brim of her straw hat. She wore a blue cotton dress with an embroidered bodice. Looking shyly up at Abbie, she pressed back against the skirts of her nurse, a stocky girl of about twenty, with pink cheeks and reddish hair.

'Say "How do you do" to Mrs Randolph,' Jane said to the child.

Obediently Emma took a half-step forward and said carefully, 'How do you do.'

Looking down at the little girl, so close in age to Oliver, Abbie was for the briefest moment almost overwhelmed by a sudden, almost new, feeling of loss. Then, summoning a smile, she nodded and said, 'How do you do, Emma. Are you enjoying your boat trip?'

'Yes, ma'am. Thank you.'

'And this is Emma's nurse, Flora,' said Jane.

Abbie smiled at the girl. 'Hello, Flora.' The girl gave a little bob and muttered, 'Mum . . . '

'Do you like my horsey?' Emma said, moving a step closer to Abbie. In her hands she held up a little painted wooden horse, set on a wheeled platform.

'Oh, yes, he's a fine little animal,' Abbie said. 'Is he new?'

'Yes. Papa bought him for me in Sheerness.'

'That's where you've been today, is it?'

'Yes. We had a picnic.'

'We went down yesterday,' Jane said. 'Arthur had business there.' She turned, scanning the decks of the boat. 'He's about here somewhere. He went off to get some lemonade.'

'I know,' Abbie said. 'We already . . . ran into one another.'

'Oh, really? He's been so long, I thought we might go in search of him – but there are so many people on board I think we'd surely miss one another. I was just looking around for him when I glanced across and saw you standing here.' Jane paused for a moment then turned to the young nursemaid. 'Flora, Mrs Randolph and I would like to have a little talk. Will you take Emma for a stroll for ten minutes or so?'

'Of course, mum,' Flora nodded and took Emma by the hand. 'Come along, young lady.'

Hand in hand, the toy horse tucked securely under Emma's arm, the child and her nurse moved away towards the centre of the saloon deck. As they did so the boat shuddered and Abbie realized that it was moving away from the Gravesend pier.

'Here we go again.' Jane smiled. 'Next stop Woolwich.'

'Yes.'

Jane briefly watched her small daughter's progress, then turned back to Abbie. 'Well,' she said, a trifle awkwardly, 'what a surprise that we should meet like this. What are you doing on the steamboat?'

'We've been to Gravesend,' Abbie said, '– Louis and I – to see his father.' How stilted their conversation was. No one would ever believe that they had once been so close.

'Is your husband here now?' Jane said, glancing around her.

'Yes – though I don't know exactly where at this moment.' A pause. 'Iris is here on board as well.'

'Iris? She's here?'

Abbie looked across the deck. She could see Alfred, raised up on the bandstand, but with so many people moving across her field of vision it was impossible to catch a glimpse of her sister. 'She's sitting over there by the bandstand.' She briefly pointed to the group of musicians, adding, 'Alfred, her husband, is in the band – he's the one playing the cornet.'

Jane followed Abbie's direction, then smiled and shook her head in a little gesture of wonder. 'Iris – married.'

'Yesterday. She got married just yesterday. They're so happy.'

'She always was such a sweet girl,' Jane said. 'Though it's so many years since I saw her I wonder whether I'd recognize her now.'

'Oh, yes, you would. She doesn't change much.'

'I must go and see her later,' Jane said. 'And give her my congratulations. Obviously she's married a young man with taste.' Another brief silence and she added in a little burst, 'Oh, Abbie, you can't imagine how I've wanted to see you. Just now, when I saw you I – I couldn't believe it. There's so much I've wanted to say to you.'

Abbie could read the vulnerability in Jane's face and seeing it she became aware of the power she had – the knowledge that she held Jane's happiness in her hands, to protect or destroy as she wished; the choice was hers. She thought of Arthur's words to her in the barn that day of the snowstorm: *'Oh, Abbie, Jane must never know.'* And she realized that in the back of her mind she had held on to that knowledge, keeping it like a weapon, ready to use it should the time ever come. All she had to do was tell Jane about Arthur and herself, and Jane's peace of mind would be gone for ever. Into her mind came a sudden picture of Arthur and herself alone in the barn, while outside the snowstorm raged, and looking into Jane's eyes, she thought, *How fragile happiness is. And how easy it would be to shatter yours.*

But she knew that she could never do such a thing. And how, how in her wildest imaginings, could she ever have contemplated such an action? As she looked into Jane's concerned face a myriad thoughts and emotions were churning over.

'The last time we met,' Jane said, 'was in London when we walked together in the park near Buckingham Palace.'

'I remember.'

'And I told you that Arthur and I were to marry.'

'Oh – Jane, do we have to go into this?' Abbie wanted it all behind her now.

'Please,' Jane said. 'We must talk. I so want us to be

507

friends again. Real friends. Ever since that day I've lived with doubts and uncertainties. I've never been able to forget the way you looked when I told you of Arthur and me. You looked at me with – dislike. That coldness in your eyes – I never thought to see such a look. I thought you would hate me for ever.' She took in Abbie's silence for a second then went on, 'I never wanted to hurt you, Abbie. Good God, I wouldn't set out to do that for all the world. But when Arthur and I met again I believed that you no longer loved him, nor had any further plans or hopes where he was concerned. And we – well – we fell in love.'

She paused, took a deep breath then continued, 'I know what you thought, Abbie. I'm sure I do. You believed that Arthur married me because he had got himself trapped in a situation and was too honourable a man to withdraw from it – isn't that so?'

'Jane,' Abbie said, 'let's not speak of all that.'

'Please,' Jane countered, 'I need to say this. I'm quite sure you thought that notwithstanding his commitment to me, he would nevertheless always love you. And, furthermore that if he had his freedom he would – would choose you. And you know, once I had that thought – that belief in my head – I couldn't completely dispel it, no matter how often I told myself that it was not so. After all, you were such a beautiful girl, and you and he had been engaged to be married. So you see, there had to be the chance that it was the truth. Not that Arthur would ever have let me know, of course. Being the man he is, he would have kept it from me, never letting me guess by the slightest word or breath that he had any regrets.' She gave a rueful smile. 'It wasn't till I heard you'd married Louis that at last I began to feel secure.'

As Abbie tried to find words in reply she involuntarily blinked a couple of times. She could feel once more the sharp, stinging discomfort in her eye. 'What's wrong?' Jane said. 'Have you got something in your eye?'

'I think I must have. A bit of cinder or something. I thought it had gone, but it's still smarting.' From her bag she took a small glass and turning to the light of the sinking sun, examined her eye. Now she could see the tiny dark speck in the corner. 'I can see it,' she said.

Jane stepped towards her. 'Let me see.' She peered closely into Abbie's eye. 'The dratted light is going. Here – turn this way.' Under Jane's touch Abbie turned towards the fading light. 'Ah, yes,' Jane breathed, 'I can just see it.' She took her handkerchief, folded the linen to a point and gently, carefully removed a tiny speck of grit from the inner corner of Abbie's eye. 'There – it's done.'

Abbie blinked tentatively; the discomfort was gone. 'Yes!' she said with relief. 'Thank you.'

Jane smiled. 'It's what friends are for.'

'Oh, that feels so much better.' Abbie raised the small glass once more, held it up and examined her eye. It was slightly inflamed but the inflammation would soon go. Satisfied, she moved the glass further away, taking in the reflection of her whole face. She was just about to return the glass to her bag when in the dying light she caught a glimpse of herself at a certain angle – and for one brief, startling moment she saw her mother's face looking out at her.

Arrested by the sight, she stood staring at her reflection. And into her mind came her mother's voice: *Oh, my girl, you're more like me than you know.*

No, it is not so, a voice inside her head cried out. She was not like her mother. She could not be. Her mother had been everything that she, Abbie, abhorred. She had been mean-spirited, unloving, ungrateful and selfish. For the satisfaction of her own passing pleasures and needs she had turned her back on those who needed her – her husband and her children. She had been ready to disregard the happiness of anyone who stood in the way of her own capricious desires.

And then she heard other words in her head, another voice, that of her father: *Reality was never enough for your mother. Her desires were always for the unattainable, her dreams always for what was unreal. And they blinded her to everything that could have made her happy.*

Abbie dropped the glass back into her bag, held the rail and stood looking out unseeingly over the dark waters of the river.

Jane's voice came, with a little laugh of relief, 'Oh, Abbie, I don't know why I said those things just now.'

As Abbie turned to face her again, Jane went on, 'After all, it's all in the past, isn't it? I mean – you have Louis and – oh, but I so wanted to see you. So often I thought of writing to you, but I didn't know how you felt about me and I was so afraid that you would reject my approaches. But now – well, fate has rather taken the matter out of our hands, bringing us together again like this.' A little hesitation and she added, 'Are we friends again, Abbie? I want it so. I want it more than anything.'

Abbie didn't know what to say. From somewhere on her left she heard a man ask in a loud voice, 'Where are we now?' and then the voice of another in reply that they were approaching Galleon's Reach. 'In five or ten minutes you'll see the Beckton Gas Works pier,' the second one added. 'And over on the northern side the Talbot powder magazine.'

Having registered the men's words, Jane said, 'It won't be too long before we're at Woolwich.'

Abbie dimly realized that the musicians had stopped playing, and glancing over to the bandstand she saw that their places had been taken by two clergymen who now began to sing a hymn, their baritone voices ringing out in the air of the fine night: 'Onward Christian soldiers, marching as to war . . . ' The moon hung round and white in the clear sky. Against the noise of the boat and its passengers and the singing, Abbie seemed to hear again her mother's voice, the words appearing to come in rhythm with the churning of the paddle wheels: *You're more like me than you know . . .*

The steamer's lights had at some time been lit and, turning to Jane again, Abbie could see the warm glow of the red port lamp reflected in her cheek. Her mind was in turmoil. Carefully she said, choosing her words, 'I want to tell you how thankful I am that we've met again. That day in the park in London – I was angry and hurt, and I said things I should not have said. Things that were . . . not true.' Then, speaking from the heart, she went on, 'I have no doubt at all that it's you whom Arthur loves. It's you – only you. And always has been. Perhaps at an earlier time he was fond of me, but it was not *love*. It was never love. And then you came along – and for you his feelings were real. They *are* real.'

At Abbie's words there was a look of gratitude in Jane's eyes and Abbie could not bear it, for she had granted no favours. What she had said was nothing but the simple truth. And Arthur too had been speaking the truth: even if he had at one time felt deep affection for Abbie, those feelings had been as nothing compared with the love that he had come to feel for Jane. Abbie might have chosen to believe otherwise, but she had based her reasoning on pretence and now, at long last, the time of pretending was over. She had to deal with what was real. 'Jane – I caused you unhappiness,' she said. 'Can you forgive me?'

Jane reached out her hand and Abbie took it, clasped it. They stood like that for some seconds, then came the sound of Arthur's voice coming to them out of the general hubbub.

'Well – I finally got it.'

Drawing apart, they turned and saw him standing nearby holding a tray with glasses of lemonade while he glanced uncertainly from one to the other.

'Is everything all right?' he asked.

'Yes.' Jane smiled. 'We're fine.'

There was a look of relief on his face. As he handed Jane a glass, she turned to Abbie and said, 'Will you have some lemonade, Abbie? Take Emma's. We'll get her some more when she comes back.'

'No, really, thank you.' Abbie said. She felt suddenly preoccupied; she needed time to think. 'I must go and find Louis. Will you excuse me . . .?'

'Yes, go and find him,' Jane said. 'Bring him back. We'd love to meet him.'

Abbie started away. Over on the bandstand the two clergymen still stood, leading the singing. She could see no sign of Alfred and Iris. Perhaps they had gone down to the saloon for refreshment. In any case they were not her immediate concern. Turning, she looked back to where Jane and Arthur stood side by side at the rail. Seeing them there together, so happy, she wondered again how, even for a moment, she could have contemplated destroying their happiness. What object would it have served? None at all. And it would also have destroyed any chance she might have had of future peace of mind, for she would never have been able to forgive herself or live with her guilt.

She remained there, watching the happy couple, her view of them intermittently cut off by the people who moved back and forth before her. Arthur had said that people should be careful of what they hankered after, for they might get what they wished for. 'What would you do,' he had asked, 'if I came to you and said "I'm yours, Abbie – I love only you"? What would you do?'

Yes – what would she have done? If he had indeed come to her and said 'I am yours' – what would she have done? After all, it was what she had said she wanted. But she now knew that it was not. The knowledge came to her in a rush, like a blast of cold air – and as one fragment of understanding was formed so it led to the forming of another. She heard Arthur saying: *I don't think you ever did – truly love me.* And she knew, without question, that it was so. Of *course*. That was why she had rejected his offer of marriage – using her mother's return as an excuse to do so. But it had been a lie. The true reason was not her mother's return; it had been due to the fact that she did not love him.

Her mind was whirling, almost unable to keep up with the thoughts that crowded in. Now so much was making sense. Now she could see why she had pursued Arthur so obsessively. She had known all along that he loved only Jane, had known that he would never leave Jane for her – and yet she had continued to pursue him, while all the time aware in her heart that it was a lost cause. But why should she have done such a thing? Then the added realization came: it was precisely *because* she had felt safe in her pursuit of Arthur – for in her heart she had known that he would never be hers.

But why should she only dare to offer affection where it could not be returned?

Was she afraid of love?

And then all at once Louis was in her mind again. Louis – it had to do with him. But what? No matter how she wrestled with the question, it was as if there were some barrier in her brain, some part of her subconscious that refused to allow any profound delving. Yet it was there. A thought suddenly came to her: her pursuance of

Arthur – it had prevented her from committing herself to her marriage – stopped her from giving to Louis the love that he had so much wanted, so much needed. The love that had been rightfully his.

Louis . . . She had to find him.

She looked around, saw a companionway leading down to the lower deck and started towards it. As she did so she heard the sound of a man's voice, yelling out in the evening air, above the noise of the throng:

'Hi! Hi! Where are you going to?' And then again: 'Hi, there! Where are you going to?'

She came to a halt, glanced towards the sound and saw that it had come from the captain as he stood on the bridge, his voice amplified by the loud hailer he was holding. Along with all the other passengers who had heard, she looked over to see the object of his warning and in the dusk saw, about two hundred yards away off the starboard side, the dark shape of a tall screw steamer coming towards them.

The sight caused no fear in her; nor did it appear to among the other passengers; they were in good hands; no harm could come to them. Was not the London Steamship Company's safety record one of the finest? Did not the company's steamers sail the Thames day in and day out without mishap? And, as Alfred had so proudly said, the *Princess Alice* was the pride of the fleet. Built of iron, measuring two hundred and nineteen feet in length, and weighing a hundred and sixty tons, she was far too sturdy to be at risk. Turning from the sight, Abbie continued on her way. Louis, she must find him.

Like Abbie, after an initial glance in the direction of the steamer, most of the passengers began to resume their business, carrying on their conversations and their round-the-deck strolls, while the children got back to their games. At the same time the two clergymen who had been leading the hymn singing began the interrupted verse over again. But then, above all the other sounds came the captain's cry once again, and this time louder, and touched with a dark, contagious fear:

'Where are you going to? Can you hear me? Hi! Hi! For God's sake, you'll be down upon us –!'

At the captain's cry, Abbie again came to a stop. Then after a moment's hesitation she changed direction and moved back across the deck to where Jane and Arthur stood at the rail. When she reached them, Jane held out a hand to her. Abbie took it and the three of them moved a little closer to the bridge. As they did so, Abbie was aware that other passengers were doing the same.

Standing close to the starboard paddle box Abbie, along with Jane and Arthur, watched as the steam-screw collier drew closer. And as they did so she became aware that the carefree chatter, the singing and the games had ceased. A muttering passed through the crowd, the sound interjected with brief spates of nervous laughter and would-be witty comments from some of the young men who would brave out the threatened danger – for surely, even now, there could be no real peril.

But still the boat came on. And now, from many of the passengers there began to rise up little gasps and cries of fear. Abbie heard Jane give a murmured cry, while from a man on her left came the fearful, muttered words: 'God Almighty, it's comin' right into us.' Eyes wide with growing horror, Abbie stood transfixed, watching the vessel's inexorable approach.

Moving swiftly with the tide, the cargo boat came on. A hundred and fifty yards ... a hundred and forty ... Towering high above the low decks of the paddle steamer she came closer still – and now on her bows could be read her name: *Bywell Castle*.

The point of her prow was heading directly for the side

of the slow-moving *Princess Alice*. Sixty yards . . . fifty . . .
Cries of fear and shouts of warning to the oncoming
collier rose up from the throats of the steamboat passengers – hundreds of voices raised, shouting out for the
approaching boat to beware – while at the same time
there came warning cries from the high decks of the
collier herself.

Forty yards . . . thirty-five . . .

As the *Bywell Castle* drew nearer, those on the pleasure
boat shrank back, trying to move away from the threatening danger. But there could be no escape. It was too late.
Although by this time the engines of the *Bywell Castle* had
been switched to full astern there was neither time nor
space for the vessel to stop. Carried on by her momentum
on the swift-flowing tide and her own vast weight, she
ploughed on.

Seeing that a collision was now inevitable, the panic-
stricken passengers of the *Princess Alice* began to run.
Turning, crying out, they dashed away, heading for the
forward and after sections, while at the same time some
of those on the upper decks headed for the lower. In just
seconds the companionways were choked with desperate, terrified people.

'Emma!' cried Jane. 'Where is Emma!' In the next
moment Arthur was snatching at her hand and, along
with other passengers, was making a scrambling dash
towards the stern. As they ran, however, a man came
from behind and burst between them, breaking the link of
their clutching hands. Others followed immediately,
swiftly driving wider the wedge of their separation.
Seconds behind them, Abbie too reached the rail over-
looking the after part of the lower deck. Jane, she found,
was close by, though she saw that Arthur had become
separated from them, and with the crowd between

growing denser by the second, had no opportunity to rejoin them.

Turning back to look at the approaching danger, Abbie watched as the shrieking, yelling passengers continued to run in terror before the oncoming vessel, many of them falling over each other in their panic. And the coal steamer ploughed on.

Twenty yards ... fifteen ... ten ... five ...

The *Bywell Castle* struck the *Alice* amidships, her sharp cutwater smashing through the starboard paddle box and into the hull itself, the blow so violent that the pleasure steamer was pushed some distance before the *Castle*'s prow. Then the collier, still moving forward, struck her again.

Chapter Thirty-Six

The shock of the initial impact was so violent that many on board were thrown headlong to the deck. And even as they climbed to their feet, momentarily winded and stunned, there came the second shock as the *Alice* was struck once more.

At first there was hope in every heart that the pleasure steamer would withstand the impact and, although terribly maimed, would nevertheless stay afloat – at least long enough for the lifeboats to be manned and for help to come from other river craft. Such hopes were soon dashed, however. In spite of her iron hull, the *Alice* was as matchwood against the power and weight of the *Bywell Castle* and amid the deafening sounds of the smashing of glass, the tearing of iron and timber and the shrieking of her eight hundred passengers, the stricken vessel broke in two.

Standing at the rail, Abbie could see that the screw's head had smashed right through the paddle box and between the funnels, and seeing the extent of the damage she knew there was no chance that the pleasure boat could remain afloat. Turning, she saw that several men had run aft to lower one of the two lifeboats. She watched as they got the boat down, but as they lowered it to the water a crowd of people surged forward and began to scramble into it. To her horror she saw the lifeboat turn over, throwing its passengers into the dark waters of the river.

Pressing as far back from the broken centre of the steamboat as they could possibly get, people watched as the shattered ends of the doomed craft sank deeper into the water. The after part was the first to succumb, and as its broken centre section sank beneath the dark, flowing water, so its stern was lifted up. Feeling the decks rising up beneath their feet the terrified people let out great cries of fear. Abbie screamed out to Jane, 'Hold on!' As the stern and the prow rose higher there was a general scramble to gain handholds. There was not enough space at the rails, however, and those who had nothing to hold on to began to slip on the sloping deck and slide down its incline. Some of them came up against the funnels, and tried to cling on there. Others slid down into the water and the certain death that awaited them in the tangle of iron and timber at the broken centre part of the vessel.

Numbers of people on the upper deck were clambering over the rail and jumping down onto the deck below. A few others were attempting to climb a rope up towards the saloon deck in order to try to gain access to a ladder that hung down the side of the *Bywell Castle*. Had only one or two made the attempt it might have worked, but in seconds there were seven or eight clinging to the rope. Abbie watched as it broke and the men were pitched into the water, some of them being dashed against the side of the saloon as they fell. Others, seeing certain doom if they remained on board, began to leap into the river to get as far from the sinking boat as was possible.

In seconds the river's surface was teeming with people struggling to stay afloat. The screams of the women and children all around Abbie were unlike anything she had ever heard in her life before, a sound that she herself added to with her own cries of terror. Clinging to the rail on the high-tilting stern, she heard herself cry out 'Louis!' but it was a vain cry; not only did she not know where he was, but even had she known he would not have been able to help her.

With each passing second the stern of the broken vessel lurched higher above the surface of the water, bringing choruses of screams from the terrified passengers. And with each lurch dozens lost their footing on the steeply inclining decks and fell. Abbie watched as men, women and children, accompanied by a welter of umbrellas and baskets and bags, slid down the steeply slanting deck towards the broken centre that now lay beneath the water. It was a scene of utter terror and pandemonium. As people lost their footing they grabbed at others and dragged them down with them. In front of Abbie a man slipped on the sloping deck, and as he fell he reached out, clutching blindly, and his grasping hand snatched at the skirt of a young woman who, holding a child in her arms, was clinging to the rail at Abbie's side. The next moment the woman had lost her grip and her balance and, with her child rolling from her arms, was sliding screaming down the deck towards the deadly chasm below.

'Arthur! Arthur!'

Abbie realized that the cry came from Jane who was holding on to the rail at her side. Looking to her right, Abbie saw Arthur gripping the rail several yards away. Above the noise of the screams he had no chance of hearing Jane's voice, though it was clear he knew where she and Abbie were, for he looked over and mouthed some unintelligible words. He could not move towards them, however, for the moment he loosed his hold on the rail he would slide down the deck.

Two or three lucky men, Abbie saw, had grabbed at the anchor chain of the *Bywell Castle* and managed to climb up it to the safety of the collier's deck. It was terrifyingly clear to her, however, that she and the hundreds of others remaining on the *Alice* would have to take their chances in the water, for the outcome of the collision was inevitable. Already, scores were in the river, struggling, mouths open as they cried out, reaching up with their hands, snatching wildly at each other for salvation. Above Abbie's head the remaining lifeboat swung in the davits, useless without the time or expertise to get it into the water.

She did not know what to do. She only knew that death was certain if she remained where she was, for she was sure that at any moment the broken halves of the vessel would sink beneath the surface. Turning to Jane, she shrieked above the din, 'Jane – we must jump!'

Without waiting for a response she hitched up her skirt as high as she could and clambered over the rail. Holding on tightly with her right hand she pulled off her shawl and let it fall. She could do nothing about the weight of the rest of her clothing, and it did no good to curse the corsets and drapery that fashion demanded should be worn by the well-dressed woman.

She gripped the rail. She had never been so afraid in her life. Her heart thudding in her breast she looked out over the water, seeking a clear space; there were so many people floundering beneath her that it would be difficult to jump in without striking someone. But if she was to survive she had no choice but to make the attempt, and she could not afford to wait. Briefly turning her head to her left, she saw that many others, Jane among them, were also preparing to leap into the water. It was now or never. Taking a deep breath, she let go of the rail and jumped, propelling herself as far from the stricken vessel as she could.

As she struck the water the shock of its coldness took her breath away. She went under at once. Although the time she was beneath the surface lasted only seconds, it seemed to her an age and she thought she would never come up again. In moments, however, she had resurfaced, gulping at the air and spitting the vile-tasting river water from her mouth.

Although she was a relatively strong swimmer the present situation was far removed from those carefree times at the Flaxdown clay pit. Then she had swum free and unhampered. Now she found that the heavy weight of her water-sodden clothes was threatening to drag her under. Surrounded by other terror-stricken people, she turned just in time to see Jane fall and hit the water with a great splash about five or six yards to her left. At once, as fast as her leaden clothing would allow, she struggled towards her. As she did so, drowning people reached out, clutching at her. She evaded them, knowing that in spite of her wishes to see them saved they would only drag her down.

With great relief she saw Jane surface just in front of her, spluttering and gasping for breath. But as she reached her side Jane began to sink again. Desperately Abbie lunged forward. Jane's hat had come off and Abbie just managed to catch her by her hair. Quickly transferring her grip to hold her beneath the arms, Abbie turned in the water and, supporting her as best she could, began to swim with all her strength away from the boat.

Jane, Abbie knew, was not nearly as strong a swimmer as she herself. She also knew that unless help came soon they were both doomed. They could not stay afloat for long; not only were her own water-sodden clothes dragging her down, but Jane was very heavy in her grasp and seemed unable to do much to help.

Looking back towards the broken vessel, Abbie saw that it was sinking fast; the after section had settled back into the water and the lower deck was now only a few feet above the surface. She watched as the funnels were submerged and saw a great burst of steam come up. Then suddenly the whole of the after section began to turn in the water, rolling over completely. As it did so it pitched its remaining passengers screaming into the river. For some moments the keel of the hull was visible, but then that too vanished as the after part subsided and sank out of sight. Seconds later the fore section of the boat followed the same pattern, first toppling over and then vanishing beneath the surface. Not more than six minutes had passed since the collision, but now there was no longer any sign of the pleasure steamer except for the pieces of floating wreckage that strewed the river's surface and the shrieking people who struggled to stay afloat.

'Leave me . . .'

Abbie realized that the words had come from Jane.

'Leave you?' she gasped. 'No . . . no . . .'

'Leave me,' Jane cried again, choking as water filled her mouth. 'Save yourself!'

'Hush!' Abbie gasped. 'Don't talk. Save your breath.'

The exchange of words somehow seemed to give Abbie greater strength, and she forged on, swallowing water and gasping with the effort of supporting herself and Jane, but nevertheless making progress.

Abbie had already seen that both banks of the river were too far away to think of swimming to. Even without Jane she could not have managed it. Her only hope was to try to get help from the collier or some other river craft. Looking towards the *Bytwell Castle*, she saw that a number of ropes had been thrown over her sides, and that some lucky few were managing to cling to them. Renewing her grasp on Jane, she forced herself on through the water

The distance to the side of the collier was not more than forty yards and under different circumstances the swim would have presented Abbie with no difficulties. As it was, however, it seemed to take for ever and at times she felt that she would never get there. Not only was her way strewn with wreckage and desperate, struggling bodies, but she had Jane to support and drag along with her. To make her task even harder, the weight of her clothing seemed to grow greater by the second. Added to this, the narrow, sheath-like style of her skirt hampered the movement of her legs, so that it took all her strength and effort to make headway. And all through her struggles the evening air rang out with the piteous cries of dying people. Time and again she saw men, women and small children sink before her eyes; there was nothing she could do to help any of them.

She reached the side of the collier with what she felt was her last breath. There was a rope nearby with a man and a woman clinging to it. With a great effort she lunged towards it. But even as she did so, two men swam up, reached out for the rope and clung on, leaving no room for Jane and herself. But then, a moment later, just when she began to feel that they must surely die, there was a shout from the deck above and another rope came snaking down to hit the water with a splash only inches from her head.

Quickly she snatched at it with one hand, grasped it tightly and cried out to Jane, 'There's a rope here! Hold on to it. Help will be here soon.'

Next moment they were both holding fast to the rope, to be joined almost immediately by a man who swam up and grasped it above Abbie's clutching hands.

Hanging on to the rope, Abbie saw before her the continuing spectacle of people drowning. Wherever she looked she could see them floundering and thrashing in the water, their mouths opening wide as they screamed and shouted to the skies. A few feet away a woman appeared, struggling to reach the ropes that hung from the deck of the *Bywell Castle*. In one arm she held a child.

With a lurch forward she thrust the infant before her, at the same time crying out, 'Save my baby! Oh, save my baby!' Releasing one hand from the rope, Abbie snatched at the babe, managing to grasp it by its clothing. As she did so the child's mother lifted her head and blood spewed out of her mouth. The next moment she had gone down beneath the surface of the water. In Abbie's grasp the tiny child hung limp as a rag doll. She clutched it closer to her and looked down into its face, and saw its death-dulled little eyes turned unseeing up towards the darkening sky. With a groan she released her grip on the dead little burden and watched it sink out of sight.

Although the water still teemed with people, Abbie realized that the numbers were growing smaller with each passing second. So many had already drowned. She became aware too that the cries were fading, growing fainter as one by one the victims gave up their struggles and slipped beneath the waves. Only minutes ago they had been there in their hundreds. Now most had disappeared from sight, the only sign that they had ever existed in the vast number of hats, bonnets, umbrellas and bags that covered the river's surface.

Lit by the moon and by lanterns, boats began to appear – boats that had pushed off from the banks almost within seconds of the collision. Among them Abbie saw a barge, its crew pulling survivors on board. Then, as she and Jane hung on to the rope, waiting, there came a voice hailing them and they saw a dinghy approaching, one man at the oars and another leaning forward in the prow. Soon the little craft was beside them and the man in the prow was bending and hauling Jane into the boat. Abbie followed, and afterwards the man who had been holding on to the rope with them. Then, laden with its wet and shuddering burden, the little vessel set off for the southern bank.

Side by side in the centre of the dinghy, Abbie and Jane

sat huddled together, Abbie's arm round Jane's shoulders. As she turned, looking back over the dark water, the thought came to her of how swiftly things could change. Only a dozen short minutes ago there had been a pleasure boat there on the river, the *Princess Alice*, her decks swarming with more than eight hundred happy people – talking, laughing, singing and dancing. Now the *Princess Alice* lay in pieces at the bottom of the river, along with most of her passengers and crew.

Abbie tightened her hold around Jane and turned away, setting her face towards the nearing river bank. She felt Jane shudder in her arms and heard her murmur on a little choking sob, 'Arthur . . . Emma . . . Where are they?'

Abbie closed her eyes as the thoughts and the questions churned in her brain. Where indeed were they? And where was Louis? And where too were Iris and Alfred?

Chapter Thirty-Seven

As the dinghy reached the wharf on the southern side of the river, the smaller and younger of the two men leaped out and secured the painter. At the same time the older man turned to Abbie and asked whether she could walk unaided. Shivering uncontrollably, teeth chattering, she replied that she could. 'Though I'm not sure about my friend,' she added.

'Right.' He nodded and called to his companion, 'Let's get this young lady out first, shall we?'

While the smaller man steadied the boat, the other stooped and gathered Jane up into his arms. The vessel rocked as he did so, but he rode out the moments of pitching and carried her onto the wharf. He stood there then while the younger man first helped Abbie onto the shore and then the young male survivor.

Standing, so thankfully, once more on firm ground, Abbie turned and looked out over the moonlit waters of the river By the lamps that burned on her decks she could easily make out the tall shape of the *Bywell Castle* riding at anchor close to the scene of the collision. And there also was the *Duke of Teck*, the pleasure steamer that had followed the *Alice* upriver, now doing what she could to save survivors. Abbie could also see the dark shapes of smaller boats and barges moving about in continuing rescue efforts. How different now was the sound emanating from the scene. The screams of people thrashing about in the water had gone, and now only the distant voices of the rescuers could be heard.

Carrying Jane in his arms, the tall boatman led the way to a public house, the Steam Packet, which was situated on a corner a short distance away. There the two men left the three survivors in the care of the landlord and his wife and, hardly waiting long enough to receive thanks, disappeared again into the night.

The landlord, Plaister by name, was a tall, heavy-set man in his forties; his wife a short, plump little woman with greying hair tied back in a bun. They were kindness itself and set about doing all they could to make their unexpected guests comfortable. Their barmaid was left in charge of the saloon – though there were no customers present, all having hurried down to the river bank to witness what they could of the drama.

While the landlord took the young man into one room to get dry, the landlord's wife led Abbie and Jane into another.

In the little parlour leading from the kitchen Jane sank gratefully into a chair. She seemed to be in a state of stunned apathy, and it was only through the efforts of Abbie and Mrs Painter that she could be prevailed upon to get out of her wet clothes, to dry herself and wrap herself in the blankets the older woman provided.

As Abbie and Mrs Plaister helped Jane, it became clear that when leaping into the wreckage-strewn water she had sustained some injuries. Thankfully, however, it appeared that there was nothing really serious, though she had suffered a knock to her head, a grazed shin and, most painful of all, bruising of her ribs on the right side. Abbie herself had been very lucky; her only injuries were a slight bruise on her hip and another on her left elbow. She was aware of a feeling of discomfort in her lower abdomen, but as she had swallowed so much of the filthy, foul-tasting river water she was not in the least surprised by it.

When Mrs Plaister had cleaned and dressed the wound on Jane's leg she and Abbie helped her back into the kitchen and into a chair before the crackling fire. Abbie, also wrapped in a blanket, sat on a chair at Jane's side. On Abbie's right sat the male survivor, also enveloped in a blanket. Abbie knew nothing about him apart from what she had observed. He was of medium height with a lean build, a narrow face, dark hair and a small, neat moustache. There was a dark bruise on the left side of his face and the knuckles of his right hand were skinned raw. He had hardly spoken more than a dozen words since they had come together in the dinghy. Now, like Abbie and Jane, he sat hunched in his chair, staring dully into the flames of the fire.

While Mrs Plaister prepared food for the three her husband wrote down their names and addresses. That done, he hurried off to the local police station to give word of the survivors in his care and seek advice as to how they should be further aided. After he had gone Mrs Plaister poured mugs of hot lentil soup. Abbie and the young man – he gave his name as Henry McGibbon and an address in Pimlico – sat sipping the soup in a slow, mechanical way. Jane did not raise her mug to her mouth but stared into the fire, a look of dull incomprehension in her eyes. There were no tears shed by any of the three and, while no one wept, rarely did anyone speak. Each of them seemed to be stunned by what had happened. Like Jane and the young man, Abbie sat looking into the flames of the fire, while through her mind ran endless questions as to the fate of those she loved.

The landlord returned from Woolwich police station with the information that places of succour were being prepared at the Union Infirmary, the workhouse situated at nearby Plumstead, and that the survivors were to be taken there. So, a little later, dressed in fresh, dry clothing provided by the landlord and his wife, the three were taken by cab to Plumstead. Before they left they were assured by Mrs Plaister that their own clothes would be delivered to them as soon as they were dry.

It was gone midnight by the time they reached their destination. In the workhouse yard they descended from the cab to be met by the director of the house, Dr Rice, and the senior nurse, Miss Wilkinson. Entering the building, they were led to a comfortable room from which, one by one, they were taken into the doctor's consulting room a short distance along a corridor. Jane was seen first, and when she came out some minutes later Abbie was shown in.

She took a seat in a chair facing the doctor who sat behind a desk. He was a short man in his fifties with a rather dapper appearance that was added to by his neat, close-cropped white hair and beard. The nurse, Miss Wilkinson, sat nearby. She was a tall, stockily built woman in her forties who, in spite of her slightly forbidding no-nonsense air, looked at Abbie with an expression of kindness.

After taking down Abbie's name and address, the doctor said, 'This meeting has, of necessity, to be brief, Mrs Randolph – I'm sure you understand.'

'Of course.'

'Our priority for the moment,' he added, 'is to get you and the other lady and gentleman to bed to get some rest.' His manner was brisk but sympathetic. 'For the time being I just want to make sure you're not suffering from any injury that needs immediate treatment.'

She told him that all things considered she felt well and that she was not suffering from anything other than the odd bruise. For a moment she debated whether to mention her pregnancy, but she did not. She was more concerned about those who were missing, and in the knowledge that preparations were underway to receive relatively large numbers of survivors, she was in hope that there might be news of Louis and the others. When she gave the names to the doctor, however, he gave a slow, sad shake of his head.

'I'm very sorry,' he said. 'Your friend Mrs Gilmore asked me the same thing. But I'm afraid that so far only eleven survivors have been brought in – including you and Mrs Gilmore and the gentleman, Mr McGibbon.'

'Eleven? Only eleven?'

'So far, yes. But you mustn't give up hope. We're certainly expecting more to arrive. We understand from the police that survivors have been taken to various other houses and places in the vicinity – to be cared for for the time being. We expect them to come to us before long. Others, we're given to understand, have almost certainly managed to find their way home.'

Abbie dully nodded acknowledgement of his words, though she found no comfort in them.

The doctor went on, 'I understand that you and Mrs Gilmore are old friends.'

'Yes. We've known one another since we were children.'

'Right.' He glanced round at the nurse. 'We'll make sure that you have adjacent beds in the infirmary.'

Abbie thanked him. 'Jane – Mrs Gilmore –' she said, 'is she all right?'

'Do you have doubts about her?'

She gave a little shrug. 'Well, I don't think she came through it as well as I. I know that she's got a few aches and pains ... Her ribs and ... '

He gave a slow nod. 'I shouldn't worry about her. She's

suffering from shock, of course. Though she's also sustained some considerable contusions and a few other minor injuries. I don't think there's anything to be unduly worried about, but we shall keep an eye on her. Don't worry.'

Abbie left the doctor and returned to the room where Jane and the young man waited. When the nurse appeared a minute or two later she took the young man off to see the doctor, then came back to Abbie and Jane.

'Well,' she said, 'let's get you to bed, shall we? I'm sure you must be very tired. First of all, though, let me have the names of your husbands and other relatives and friends ... As the doctor said, we're expecting more survivors to be brought in tonight.'

Abbie and Jane gave her the required information, which she carefully wrote down. Then at her request they got up and followed her out of the room. Walking at Jane's side, half supporting her, Abbie went after the nurse down a long, narrow corridor of the women's wing. The place seemed vast and gloomy, and their echoing footsteps took them past door after door, each of which, Abbie imagined, was closed upon a little cell in which slept some destitute female.

Eventually they arrived at one of the newly prepared infirmary wards, a large, high-ceilinged room containing some thirty beds. The room next door, the nurse said, held a further twenty of the total of fifty beds set aside for surviving females, though so far only three were occupied. Looking into the dimly lit room Abbie could see the three occupied beds. In them their occupants lay still and covered up.

Abbie and Jane were shown to adjacent beds a little distance from those already taken. Speaking in a low voice so as not to disturb the other inmates, the nurse told Abbie and Jane where the WC was located and made sure they knew how to find their way to her office if she should be needed. 'I shall be up all night receiving more admissions,' she said, 'so don't hesitate to come for my help if you need it. Though in any case, one of my assistants will be making the rounds from time to time.'

After checking they had everything they needed for the time being, she said goodnight and left them.

The large, plain, spotlessly clean room was simply furnished with a locker and a chair beside each bed. Over Abbie's bed hung a cheap print depicting Christ surrounded by children of all nations. There was a screen there, and Abbie pulled it around the beds, and behind it helped Jane change into the coarse cotton nightgown that had been supplied. That done, she saw Jane into bed, where she lay silent and unmoving. She had spoken barely more than a word since being brought ashore in the dinghy.

Abbie put on the nightgown that had been left for her, then climbed into the bed next to Jane's and lay there looking up at the ceiling. She felt somehow unreal. It was as if she were living in a dream. There was a strange feeling of numbness about her – as if there were a shield that somehow kept much of the reality at bay. And not only she herself was affected in such a way; she thought of Jane lying beside her, silent and dry-eyed, and also of the young man, Henry McGibbon. On their arrival at the workhouse she had heard him making enquiries after his wife and two small daughters. There had been no tears in his eyes, no sound of hysteria or any kind of emotion in his voice. He had been strangely matter-of-fact, his words delivered in a dull monotone, as if he were slightly removed from it all. And perhaps he had been. Perhaps they all were – by that cocoon that protected them from the reality of the horror.

Perhaps it was nature's way of ensuring one's survival.

For how could one take in all that had happened, all the horror that had taken place? That day she had seen hundreds of people dying before her eyes – men, women, children – shouting and screaming as they had vainly struggled to stay afloat in the water. She had been one of the lucky ones, as had Jane. But what of the others – Louis, Iris and Alfred, Arthur, little Emma, and Emma's nurse Flora . . . ?

Now here she was, lying in a narrow bed in the workhouse infirmary of a south-east London suburb. In the next bed lay Jane, her old, much loved friend – her friend whom she had thought never to see, never to love again. She turned on her side to face Jane's back. She could hear her breathing. For the most part it was regular, though now and again it stuttered out of its rhythmical pattern as though she was disturbed by a bad dream or some physical discomfort.

As if in sympathy for Jane's physical hurts, a little stab of pain pierced Abbie's lower abdomen and lingered there with a small, burning intensity. Over the past couple of hours she had frequently experienced a similar pain – a kind of sharp, biting cramp – but it had never been this intense. Now she gritted her teeth, held her breath and waited for the discomfort to pass. It was due to the filthy river water, she told herself again; there was no telling what diseases one might not pick up from it. To her relief the cramps began to fade slightly after a few moments and she let out her breath on a sigh of relief.

Then, just as she felt the pain diminish to little more than an echo, it suddenly returned more sharply than ever, biting with a fierceness that made her catch her breath and sent her body into a spasmodic jerk. The pain lessened again, but did not go away. Instead, it lingered just below the threshold of unbearableness, all the while threatening at any moment to clutch at her again. Lying there, holding her breath and waiting for the next attack, she knew what she had tried not to face all along – that the pain had nothing whatsoever to do with having swallowed water from the river.

As she sat up the pain stabbed at her abdomen and she sucked in her breath. She swung her legs out of bed, took from the chair the towel that had been left for her, hitched up her nightdress and wrapped the towel about her loins. Then, holding it in place, she opened the locker and took out the shoes and the cape lent to her by Mrs Plaister. She put them on, gave one last look at Jane's still form beneath the bedclothes, and crept swiftly from the room.

The bleeding had started by the time she reached the WC. When, in the cold glow of the gaslight, she pulled up her nightgown and removed the towel she saw how bright – much, much too bright – was the blood.

How long she sat there, hunched over, forearms crossed over her belly, head hanging down, she did not know. Half an hour? An hour? When at last, wrapped in the towel again, she made her way along the corridor, her joints felt stiff.

Miss Wilkinson was still up and in her office. Standing at her desk, she looked round in surprise when Abbie appeared in the doorway.

'Mrs Randolph,' she said, frowning, 'is there something wrong?'

Abbie came into the room. 'I wonder . . . ' she said after a brief hesitation, 'I wonder whether I might take a bath.'

The nurse's frown deepened. 'Take a bath . . .? At this hour? It's almost three o'clock. Why don't you –' Becoming aware that Abbie was in some distress, she came to a stop. Then she saw the way Abbie was holding the towel around her beneath the nightgown; saw too the traces of blood on Abbie's hands.

'What's happened?' she asked, moving towards her.

Abbie steeled herself. 'I – I was pregnant. Getting on for eight weeks. And I've just . . . ' Unable to bring herself to speak the final words, she came to a stop and stood holding herself, hands gripping the towel through the coarse fabric of the nightgown. She knew that she had lost the baby. There could not have been so much blood without that loss. But she would not cry. She must not allow herself to cry. There would be another time for tears and perhaps others to weep for. 'Please,' she said, struggling to control herself, 'I must wash myself . . . '

'It will be difficult for me to arrange a bath for you right now,' the nurse said. 'But I'll get you some hot water, a bowl and clean towels.'

'Thank you.'

Later, when Abbie was clean and dry and wearing a fresh nightgown, the nurse gave her a sleeping draught of a little laudanum and accompanied her back to the ward. She followed her in and watched her safely into bed.

'Will you be all right now?' she whispered.

Abbie nodded and murmured her thanks.

'Is there anything else you need?' the nurse asked.

'No, thank you.'

'Right – you settle down. One of the other nurses will be in and out to keep an eye on all of you, and I'll try to call by in a little while to make sure you're all right.'

'Thank you.'

When the nurse had gone Abbie closed her eyes. She felt no pain now – only a dull ache. That, and a feeling of emptiness that was not just a physical sensation; it had to do with something else. Louis. She thought of how she had stood in the garden of her father-in-law's house and told Louis that she was pregnant. The thoughts, the memories began to pour into her mind, churning over and over, until she felt she would go mad. But then the sleeping draught began to take effect and sleep released her, for a time, from reality.

Towards morning she dreamed – a dream that was in many ways like the ones before. As in earlier instances she saw before her the shape, slowly swinging to and fro. But this time its movement was much less pronounced; it was hardly moving at all. Its shape was different, too. It no longer had the compact form that she expected to see. But had it ever had that? Now it appeared strangely amorphous, and still, try as she might, she could not make it out. Then suddenly the weight was in her arms – and too heavy for her. Much too heavy. How could she carry it? She had no choice but to set it down, let it go. But how could she? No, she could not, she dared not. She must never, never do that . . .

Suddenly she was awake and sitting up in bed, staring into the room. Dawn had broken and daylight was creeping in through the cracks between the curtains. For a few moments she could not get her bearings and she was on the point of panicking. But then the sight of the empty beds facing her brought recollection back and she realized where she was.

'Abbie . . . ' It was Jane's voice, deep concern in her whispered tone. 'Are you all right?'

She turned and saw Jane looking at her from the next pillow.

'You cried out,' Jane said. 'You sounded so – so frightened.'

'I'm all right. I – I had a bad dream, that's all. I'm sorry I woke you.'

'I wasn't asleep.' Jane's words were the most she had spoken since their rescue.

Abbie took in the rest of the room. All was quiet. After a moment she slipped out of bed, stepped across the intervening space and sat on the side of Jane's bed.

'How are you feeling?' she asked.

Jane gave a little shrug. 'I ache all over. Apart from that I don't know. I just don't know.'

'Poor thing.' Gently Abbie touched a hand to Jane's cheek.

After a few moments Jane said: 'Abbie . . .'

'Yes?'

'What is to happen now? What are we going to do?'

'I don't know,' Abbie replied. 'We'll decide when we get up. Go to sleep now, and try not to worry.'

A little later Abbie crept back to her own bed. As she lay there she thought with irony of her words. *Try not to worry*, she had said – while she herself was almost sick with fear.

Abbie woke again just before seven, looked around her at the cheerless room, and felt all the despair of the previous day come flooding back. And with it came the added, shocking, knowledge that she no longer carried the growing child in her body. Looking back on the miscarriage she had suffered in the night it was almost like remembering a dream, a part of the living nightmare that she was going through. As for her physical feeling, there was little to tell her that the miscarriage had even taken place. There was no pain now – nothing but a very slight, dull ache. Other than that she was aware only of feeling a strange kind of emptiness inside. Whether it was a physical sensation or one brought on by her mental condition she did not know.

In the next bed Jane lay with her eyes closed, breathing regularly. Further along were the other survivors. The furthest, a woman in her thirties, was sitting up in bed, staring dully ahead of her. Of the other, much nearer, only her grey hair was visible, giving an indication that she was not young. As Abbie passed by the woman's bed on the way to the washhouse she could hear her breathing, loud and rasping in her lungs.

When Abbie returned to the ward she found Jane awake and anxious to get up. Abbie tried to persuade her to remain in bed, but Jane would not, so Abbie helped her to wash and dress – a relatively slow procedure as the bruising to Jane's ribs and the wrenching of her shoulder made movement painful. Abbie put on her borrowed clothes without concern for her appearance. She made no attempt to dress her hair in anything resembling style but instead wove it into two braids which she then coiled about the crown of her head and fixed in place with pins donated by one of the nurses.

Breakfast was brought to them on trays, carried by two of the female inmates who regarded them curiously. There was oatmeal, eggs, bread and butter, and coffee. Abbie ate some of it – having to force it down, even though she was hungry. Jane ate nothing but sat looking off, her eyes fixed on some point far distant in time and space.

'Jane,' Abbie said, 'you must eat. You really must.'

As if coming back to the present, Jane turned to her and frowned while at the same time she gave an irritable little smile. 'What? Oh, yes – later on. Perhaps later on. I'm not hungry right now.' A moment's pause, then she said, 'I wonder whether there were any more admissions of survivors last night . . . ?'

'We gave the nurse the names,' Abbie said. 'If there had been any word she would have told us. But anyway, I'll go and check soon.'

'If there's no word I shall go and look for them,' Jane said. 'I must.'

'You're not fit yet to go anywhere.'

Jane made no response. Abbie did not know what to do; she felt helpless. Hearing a little moan, she turned and saw that the younger of the other two inmates was sitting on the side of her bed, head in hands, quietly weeping. One of the nursing assistants stood beside her.

After a while Jane set down her tray and lay on the bed. Abbie put aside her own tray and went to her. Jane lay on her side, her face towards Abbie, her eyes closed. 'It's this not knowing,' she said.

'I know.'

Jane opened her eyes. 'I shouldn't be speaking like this,' she said. 'After all, you're worrying about Louis and Iris and – oh, but this not knowing! This not knowing!' Her hand clutched at the pillow, fingers digging into the coarse cotton. 'I don't know what to do. I feel as if I – I'm not really alive. Just – just waiting. Arthur – Emma – shall I ever see them again?'

'Oh, Jane . . .' Abbie leaned closer to her, laying a gentle hand on her shoulder. But how could she give comfort? It was the blind leading the blind.

The doctor came to the ward not long afterwards. When he got to Jane and Abbie they at once enquired as to any survivors who might have been brought in during the night. As they feared, however, he could give them no good news. Five more male survivors had arrived at the infirmary, he said, but they were not those being sought by Abbie or Jane. When he was on the point of leaving he murmured to Abbie that he would like a word with her in private. She followed him out into the corridor.

'I couldn't mention it in the ward in front of the other patients,' he said when they were alone, 'but the nurse reported to me the matter of your miscarriage. What with that and the accident – you shouldn't be walking about.'

'What else can I do?' Abbie said. 'I can't stay in bed. For one thing I've got to try to find out what's happened to – to our families.'

Dr Rice nodded and gave a sigh. 'Well, I understand that, of course. But you must be careful not to overdo things. Otherwise – truly, I can't answer for the consequences.'

Abbie thanked him for his concern and then asked him about Jane. She was worried about her, she said.

'Well,' the doctor replied, 'she must rest for the present. Even if she just sits beside her bed. Certainly she mustn't try to get about.'

Abbie nodded then said, 'She's been talking about going out to try to find news of her husband and little girl.'

'That's out of the question,' he said. 'She's got to rest. She was very badly bruised in the accident – and that's apart from the shock she's sustained.'

Abbie nodded. After a moment she went on, 'You said that only five more male survivors had been brought in.'

'Yes. Four men and a little boy. We don't know the name of the child as I'm afraid he hasn't yet spoken a single word to anyone. He's a dark-haired little fellow of about five.'

'How many survivors are here now?'

'Sixteen including you and Mrs Gilmore.'

'Only sixteen? The nurse said you had beds prepared for a hundred.'

'That's right. But as I said, survivors are going to other places as well. There are certain to be more. We just don't know about them yet.'

'Who would know?'

He shrugged. 'The police are kept informed. And the people at the Steamship Company might also know. They've got offices in Woolwich. Near the wharf.' He frowned. 'You're not thinking of going out into the town today, are you?'

'What else can I do? I can't just stay here and wait for news.'

He shook his head in astonishment. 'Mrs Randolph, you had a miscarriage last night. You shouldn't even be out of bed – let alone thinking of going walking around the town.'

'I shall be all right, Doctor,' she said. 'But if I stay here I shall go mad.'

Back in the ward she found Jane sitting in a chair beside her bed. Abbie put on the cape that Mrs Plaister had lent her and said, 'I'm going out. I'm going to Woolwich to make some enquiries.'

At once Jane started up. 'I'm coming with you.'

'Oh, no. No, Jane, you stay here. Please. I'm just going to try to find out what's going on, and then I'll come straight back. Please – promise me you'll stay here and rest.'

'All right.'

'And will you try to eat something, too?'

'I'll try.'

There was a small, speckled looking-glass hanging beside her locker, and Abbie took a cursory glance at her reflection. What an awful sight, she thought. She had no hat and the grey cape had been mended on the shoulder. The plain brown dress lent to her by Mrs Plaister was not only a little too short but also slightly too large around the waist. At least the shoes, although old and worn, felt reasonably comfortable.

She moved back to Jane, kissed her on the cheek and assured her she would return as soon as possible. Going to the nurse, Miss Wilkinson, she borrowed enough money to pay for a cab to Woolwich and back, then went from the building.

To her relief she found there was a cab waiting near the

workhouse yard and she got in and set off for the Woolwich police station.

She had stopped off at Woolwich one day in the past with Louis, when returning from a visit to his father at Gravesend. It had struck her then as a quiet little town. Not so today. Now the streets were teeming with anxious people as crowds arrived by the early trains in the hope of finding news of loved ones. As Abbie was driven through the busy streets she saw that many of the shops had, out of respect for the dead, put up their shutters. The hired cab let her off at the police station and there she joined the many others who crowded into the building. Seeing a throng of people gathered around a board near the entrance, she joined it and eventually got near enough to be able to read a notice that was pinned there. It gave a list of survivors that had been reported to the police. Her heart thumping, she read down the columns of names. There were some ninety-odd listed. Among them she saw her own and Jane's, and also that of the man McGibbon who had been rescued with them. The particular names she sought, however, were not there. With a heavy heart, she turned from the notice board and pushed her way towards the entrance and into the crowded building.

There were a number of police officers on duty. Sitting at desks, they spoke in sympathetic tones to anxious searchers and carefully wrote down names and descriptions of missing friends and relatives. While Abbie waited to be seen her glance moved from one to the other of the careworn, desperate faces. Men and women of all ages were there, searching for news of lovers and friends, husbands and wives, fathers and mothers, sons and daughters, brothers and sisters. In spite of the mental anguish that was evident she was touched by the quiet dignity with which most of the people conducted themselves. Now and again she would hear a little cry and see perhaps a woman, near collapse, supported in someone's arms, but for the most part the people came and went quietly about their melancholy business.

Her glance moving on, she saw at the back of the room a sorrowful pile of personal belongings that had been gathered up from the river – a huge heap of bedraggled hats, bonnets, jackets, capes and bags. She could even see there a broken violin. Seeing the wrecked instrument she at once thought of Alfred and his fellow musicians.

Eventually it was her turn and she was beckoned forward by a middle-aged sergeant who sat behind a desk. She took a seat on a chair before him. He was a tall, lean man, with grey hair and a lined, weather-beaten face that bore an expression of kindness and concern. Abbie told him that she was a survivor of the riverboat disaster and that she was searching for her husband and other relatives and friends.

He nodded in sympathy then asked: 'Have we been officially informed that you are one of the survivors, ma'am?'

'Yes,' she said. 'My name is on the list at the front of the building – and that of my friend.'

'And you have relatives and friends who are missing, you say.'

'Yes, my husband and –' She came to a halt. The police sergeant waited for her to go on. 'And my sister and her husband,' she added. 'Also my friend's husband and little girl. And the child's nurse.'

The sergeant nodded. The situation, he said, was changing all the time. At that very moment divers were at work beneath the surface of the river, recovering bodies trapped in the wreckage. Every minute more bodies were being brought ashore. 'And not only here at Woolwich,'